PRAI... ...SERIES

'A first-rate police procedural by someone who evidently knows what he's talking about.'

Also by Peter Ritchie

Cause of Death
Shores of Death

Evidence of Death

PETER RITCHIE

BLACK & WHITE PUBLISHING

First published 2018
by Black & White Publishing Ltd
Nautical House, 104 Commercial Street
Edinburgh EH6 6NF

1 3 5 7 9 10 8 6 4 2   18 19 20 21

ISBN: 978 1 78530 145 2

A CIP catalogue record for this book is
available from the British Library.

Typeset by Iolaire, Newtonmore
Printed and bound by Nørhaven, Denmark

ACRONYMS & JARGON

Bampot	nutter
Bizzies	CID
Brown	heroin
Burd	Scottish spelling of slang 'bird' i.e. a young woman/girlfriend
Burning	surveillance being compromised by the target
Cludgie	toilet
Cough	an admission from a suspect
Coupon	face
DS	detective sergeant
Eyeball	the surveillance officer who can actually see the target
Fast black	taxi
Goldie	whisky
Hearts	Heart of Midlothian Football Club
Hee haw	another way of saying 'fuck all'
Hoops (the)	Celtic Football Club
Huns	Rangers supporters, or Protestants in general
Maze	the prison in Northern Ireland famous for its H-blocks containing legions of paramilitary prisoners from both sides of the conflict

Neds	non-educated delinquents (chavs)
Numpty	an idiot
OD	overdose
OP	observation post
Peelers	police (in Northern Ireland)
PIRA	Provisional Irish Republican Army
Plot	the name for an active surveillance operation
Pokey	prison
Possession with intent to supply	dope dealing
Prod	Protestant
PSNI	Police Service of Northern Ireland
Rubber heels (squad)	anti-corruption team
RUC	Royal Ulster Constabulary
SB	Special Branch
Scoobie	idea
Snash	insolence
SOCO	Scenes of Crime Officer
SP	information (taken from starting price in horse racing)
Squeaks	informants
Steamie	where there is widespread gossip; historically, the local wash houses where women would exchange gossip
Suits	CID
Tabs	tablets (illegal)
Taigs	derogatory term for Catholics
Tail-end Charlie	the last car in a surveillance convoy
Tanning	robbing

1

Patrick 'Bobo' McCartney was a horrible wee shite, and even his mother said that she should have strangled him at birth. His old man was a professional pisshead and in his cups he often claimed that he was ashamed of his one and only child. To be fair, he couldn't have worked out that Bobo was nothing to do with him, the boy having been given life against the back wall of a social club in the east end of Glasgow. Bobo's mother could barely remember anything about the man the next day, other than that he'd told her she was a doll and had bought her enough drink for her to say thank you in the only way she knew how. The 'accident' as his mother liked to call him was raised in Easterhouse, though his parents basically gave up on him when he was old enough to walk. His character was formed on the streets with all the other kids whose families had been numbed by a cocktail of deprivation, cheap booze, drugs and boredom. At least Bobo had been left something in his genes that made him a bit harder, a bit more aggressive and slightly less thick than the rest of his gang. The downside was that it gave him serious delusions of grandeur.

His team competed in their share of street battles with other gangs, became combat hardened and earned just enough to buy dope cut so much it wouldn't have put a bedbug under the influence. They got by running the odd packet of gear across the city for the next league up. That's how it was on the ladder – Bobo's level, the next level and the next, on up to the lazy bastards at the top who watched all those daft wee fuckers below them take the risks plus the time inside. There would be a form of stability for a time, and then one of the levels would get a bit of energy, decide it was time to move up. This tended to result in an 'outbreak of gang-related violence', as the constabulary liked to call it, and then it would all settle down again while the hospitals or the mortuary dealt with the wounded and the dead. Bobo's team were in their late teens now, restless and wanting to move up a division or two.

They were just back from Celtic Park, where they'd watched the Hoops stuff Motherwell 3–1. They'd screamed at the enemy all through the match, singing songs about Ireland and a history they knew nothing about besides the sectarian slogans they'd been force-fed since birth. They invaded a boozer and calmed themselves on Tennent's and analysing the game. Bobo wanted to talk some business but let them get a few pints in the blood first before discussing his master plan. It was a fucking beauty, and he was twitching with nerves and a couple of pills he'd slipped at the match with his Diet Coke. Bobo regarded himself as the brains in the team because he read every day, and that made him different. In fact he was obsessed with reading, but there was only one subject that interested him and that was crime and detection. He pored over everything he could get his hands on, and even when he watched the stolen telly in his bedroom it was all *CSI* or the spin-offs. He'd come to believe that he knew more than the bizzies did about detecting crime. To an extent he was right; where he got it wrong was that the police had to deal with the real world and people like him. Okay, he'd done his share of time in the Young Offenders', but he'd studied his subject and was confident that barring accidents he knew what the suits at the local pig farm got up to in their investigations. He was ready for anything, and the only way was up – at least in his own mind.

He looked round at the faces making up his team, all dressed in the same designer shite with matching baseball hats and pallid skin decorated with pimples in various stages of development. They were a testament to chain-smoking since primary school and a diet based on fast-food chains. Their chosen mastermind subjects rarely strayed beyond Celtic, hatred of the Rangers, 'burds' and the next gang fight – or the last one.

'Right, boys, I think it's time we stepped up our game a bit,' Bobo said. 'We've been fightin' the same people and shaggin' the same burds for the last few years, and it's time to make a move.' He nodded at his boys. They were interested – pissed but definitely interested. 'We're hardly earnin' enough to keep us in beer money while we take the risks runnin' messages for the local fuckin' mafia. Every man at this table is a violent headcase, am I right?'

His team agreed without a smile – he wasn't fucking joking. They looked at Bobo, careful not to give the wrong response, but he could have proposed mass suicide and they'd still have nodded in agreement.

The youngest and smallest of the team, Danny 'Danny Boy' Walker, spoke up. 'What's the plan, Bobo? I'm up for it an' tired o' gettin' fucked about for a few notes.'

Bobo smiled and punched the air. 'Then we're ready for some action! We need a big score, boys – something that'll get us up the ladder a bit quicker. If we're buying dope let's get a decent deal. We'll turn over a security van. Well, what I should say is that a van'll be turned over by half of us' – he paused for effect – 'but not by all of us. What I want you to do is find us a grass. Feed him the story that half the boys that are sitting round this table plus me are going to do the Royal Bank in Morningside in Edinburgh. We'll let the crime-squad guys follow us around for a few days, take a wee run to the capital city and while they're concentrating on us doing fuck all, the rest of the boys will be tanning the van on the other side of the town. We'll have a wee laugh at the polis, say fuck all and once it settles down we run down tae Liverpool and fill up on top-quality gear. What do you think, boys – brilliant or very fuckin' brilliant?'

The boys looked convinced, but then disagreement with Bobo usually meant a punch in the coupon. In fact Danny Boy was definitely unconvinced, but more importantly he was only out and about because he'd agreed to feed the local CID, who'd let him walk after he was found with half an ounce of brown in his filthy little mitt.

A week later Bobo drove his old man's car along the M8 and smiled as they passed the sign telling them they were in the city of Edinburgh. The car stank of the unwashed, but none of them noticed; they were keyed up for success. Bobo looked in his mirror, wondering which of the lines of traffic behind them were the surveillance team. He was pissed off that Danny Boy had called off with a bad gut.

'Fuckin' pussy, that Danny. When I see him he's gettin' a punch in the puss.' Bobo's answer to almost any problem was to punch it in the puss – man, woman, child, and on one occasion his dog: it didn't matter.

His mind drifted back to the daft bizzies who'd be lined up somewhere behind them in the heavy traffic. 'Wait tae ye see the look on their faces. They open the bags expecting some sawn-offs and what do they get, boys? Pork fuckin' sausages! Fuckin' lovely! Think they'll see the irony?'

They all stayed quiet – they hadn't a scoobie what he meant by irony. They'd fed the information through the biggest grass in the lawn and had made sure they were being followed. Bobo pulled the car up about two hundred yards from the Royal Bank doors and waited.

'Just keep calm, boys. They might come at us a bit heavy, but we can piss in their faces when they open the bags. A couple of minutes and the boys should hit the van. We'll get out the car at the same time, and remember to have the bags in your hands.' Bobo finally noticed the smell of sweat and felt the tension in the car. 'Steady, boys – it's a fuckin' walk in the park.'

Back in Glasgow, Danny Boy sat with his police handler wondering how the fuck he was going to explain the coincidence away. The detective couldn't give one for Danny's problem and gave him a half-hearted assurance. 'Look, it'll be a few years before the daft cunt sees the light of day again, and you never know – you might have won the lottery by then.' He laughed at his original line in humour. Danny Boy just sweated.

At the opposite end of Edinburgh the other half of Bobo's team were parked up in a side street in Portobello; they were tense but ready and knew Bobo had it covered. The security van should pull in to the supermarket dead on 3 p.m. and it would be a quick hit and away. The two sawn-offs should be enough to frighten the crap out of the guards – who wouldn't give a fuck about their wages – and they'd be on their way. The driver was Bobo's cousin, and he watched the van pull in slowly and stop.

5

'Here we go, boys.' He said it confidently to dampen the pre-match nerves.

But as they pulled on the balaclavas they realised something was blocking the light.

'Armed police!'

There was a small army of six footers with very large guns all pointed at the car or, more accurately, the half-wits in the car. The driver was the only one who spoke: 'Great plan, Bobo. Great fuckin' plan.'

Bobo looked at his watch and imagined he was in the army. 'That's it; let's give the boys in blue some tasty pork bangers.' They all snorted in support of their leader and about the same time noticed two people, a man and a woman, walking casually towards the car.

'They look like bizzies.' Bobo couldn't compute. He was waiting for, and expecting, the cavalry to rush them when they got out of the car. These two were bizzies, no doubt about it, but looked like they were going to stroll up to the car and put a fucking ticket on the windscreen.

Detective Inspector Jimmy McGovern tapped the window and made the international sign for 'roll down the glass, fucko!'

Bobo still couldn't work it out but at least knew the job was not going according to plan. He did as he was asked, put on his best supercilious grin, and spoke with that annoying nasal intonation perfected by Glasgow neds. 'Sorry, Constable, I hope we're not parked on a double yellow or something.' He sniggered and the boys joined in with him, but there was a lack of confidence in their synchronised attempt at sneering. Something was wrong – very fucking wrong as far as Bobo was concerned, and he knew these two strangers were about to let him in on their little secret.

McGovern put his face down towards Bobo and gave

him a smile that confirmed that somehow or other they were fucked.

'I'd like to introduce you to Superintendent Grace Macallan. You've probably never heard of her, but she's just about to arrest you and your wee pals. You see that big van pulling in, Bobo – you don't mind me calling you Bobo? Well there's six large policemen inside with violent tendencies and guns.' He waited for Bobo to reply but the boy was stuck for words. 'You see it?' Bobo nodded slowly. 'Well, we're going to put you in that van and take you to a very cold cell block where you can join the rest of your gang of criminal masterminds. That's the easy way, but if you decide to take the hard way then we'll collectively kick the shite out of you right here and now.'

Bobo finally worked it out. There'd been more than one grass, and he realised what had caused Danny Boy's bad gut. Macallan looked in the car and wrinkled her nose.

'Jesus, I think the first thing you boys need is a shower. Like the man said, you're all under arrest.'

She did the formalities and Bobo and his team looked like they'd been shot full of morphine, straight into the brain. The uniforms trooped them into the vans and Macallan slapped McGovern on the shoulder. 'Good job, Jimmy; no one hurt. They might not be the Kray twins, but it's a result and keeps the executive happy.'

McGovern shook his head and laughed. 'That lot are lower down the criminal league than the Rangers, and that's as bad as it gets. Total amateurs.'

'Don't knock it. It gets the troops a capture and an excuse for a piss-up. God knows they need it after the last few months; they've never stopped and the rate the marriages are breaking up we're going to have the social work on our case.'

They headed back to what had been the Lothian and Borders headquarters until the advent of the Police Service of Scotland, which had swallowed the eight forces of old. Macallan's major-crime team and the Special Branch had been subsumed into a new organised-crime and counter-terrorism unit, the logic being that in the modern world, organised crime and terrorism were merging in places and had to be tackled with new thinking. The team, however, had not been required to move offices, and the building itself continued to be known as Fettes, owing to its position in the shadow of one of Scotland's finest buildings – Fettes College. The police offices, however, could not have been more of a contrast to the college – square and brick built, it was a monument to the lack of imagination in publicly funded modern buildings.

Luckily Macallan was only on her first drink when she got the call from Bill Kelly's daughter. Bill, her friend and mentor in Northern Ireland, had passed away, peaceful and calm, just as he had been in life. She bought a round for the boys involved in the Bobo McCartney case before heading back to her flat to cry for her old friend and her own deep sense of loss. She got it all out then booked her flight for Belfast before deciding to go and see Mick Harkins. He'd been her DS on the major-crime team when she'd arrived from Northern Ireland, had helped her through a tough patch and became her friend when she needed one most, though he'd nearly died after being hit by a car driven by the serial killer Thomas Barclay.

She picked up the phone and dialled, knowing the call would be answered quickly. Where else would Mick be? 'Can I come round?'

Harkins knew Macallan better than she knew herself. 'I take it you're down, but that doesn't matter – just come and bring a bottle.'

She managed a smile; they did the same script every

8

time. 'What about your medication?' She waited for the reply she knew was coming.

'That is my fucking medication.'

Macallan hadn't seen Harkins for a few weeks, and though his recovery had been slow it was happening. One thing was for sure – Mick was a stubborn bastard and doing his best.

She pressed the buzzer on his door and the big surprise came when Harkins himself answered, walking on sticks. The initial prognosis had been bad, and he'd thought at one point that it might be a set of wheels for life.

'Jesus, look at you!' Macallan forgot about Bill Kelly for a moment and wrapped her arms round Harkins, who was always uncomfortable with this kind of close contact. She knew that and loved to wind him up. 'I never thought I'd see you on your feet again. It's brilliant, just brilliant.'

He disentangled himself and grabbed the bottle out of her hand. 'The only reason I'm happy to see you is in this bottle. Sit your arse down, and I'll do the honours. Don't think I'll ever be chasing the bad men again, but my target is to be able to get to the bookies under my own steam.'

The lines of strain cut in round his mouth and eyes. He should have died under the wheels of Barclay's car, and there had been many days when he'd wished that had been the outcome – until the day he became bored of feeling sorry for himself. The choice was clear: he either had to top himself or get the fuck on with it. He decided to give it a try and discovered for the first time in years that he liked himself. The old Mick Harkins could live on in the war stories that policemen love to spin; the new man didn't have to pretend any more, because there was no longer any need to act tough or cynical for effect

9

with those he'd pulled in for questioning – or with his colleagues for that matter. He slept at night, and when he woke he looked forward to the day. In Harkins' mind it was a minor miracle that his body was shattered but he was content at last.

'Say "when". It's evening, and I think you need a good shot.' He filled the glass halfway, and she screwed up her face in mock annoyance.

'Are you trying to kill me?'

He did his own glass and she filled him in on the Glasgow robbers. It was a requirement that she always had to give him a full debrief on the latest operations. He was out of the job but loved to hear what was happening at the front end. He laughed loudly when Macallan described the arrests and the reactions of Bobo McCartney and his team of outlaws.

'It's funny, Grace, they never show it on the TV detective shows, but the reality is that for every professional villain we have to sweep up, there's twenty numpties in-between. It doesn't half make life entertaining though. Cheers! Sounds like it's going well with the team. Tell them I said well done.'

Macallan sipped the warm malt and felt the tension ease out of the knot between her shoulder blades. 'The best of it is that if the lot we captured at the bank had kept quiet, we might have toiled proving a case, but two of them coughed up the whole story, so they're well and truly done.' She laughed and felt her mood lightening with the drink.

Harkins looked down into his glass, his mind shifting from the antics of Bobo McCartney and his team of desperados. 'I'm sorry to hear about your friend Bill – I know from the way you spoke about him that he was a special man.'

Bill Kelly. Where should she start? Images and fragments of conversations crowded into her mind. She began by describing the small things, the things that made him the man he was and why he'd been her friend and mentor. Harkins had heard some of this before, when she'd first confided in him about the fallout from the Jackie Crawford incident, which was what had ultimately brought her to Edinburgh. But story after story fell from her lips as other, half-forgotten memories rushed back. Harkins didn't interrupt. This was why she'd come to see him – she trusted him to listen while she poured her heart out.

She finished her story and stared down into her empty glass through the blur of tears.

'Are you going to the funeral?'

She looked up, and he watched the little girl exposed. He was always surprised when he saw this look – vulnerable, unsure and not the image of the cast-iron detective the papers had created for her.

'Yes, I'm flying over to Belfast the day after tomorrow. I'm going to take a couple of days off, as I'm pretty well knackered. We've hardly had a day off in the last few weeks.'

He smiled. That was the job – that's what it did: gave you the adrenalin rush and the constant question 'Why do we do this?' Harkins knew better than anyone what the job was like – a parasite that invades the body, pumps it full of feel-good highs while it eats you from the inside.

He put his glass on the table. 'Can I tell you something?'

She took a deep breath, anticipating a dose of Mick Harkins truth. 'No, you can't.' She knew it would make no difference – it had never stopped him in the past, even when she outranked him by two rungs on the ladder.

'You need to get someone into your life again. Someone you can come home to at night and share this stuff with. Or maybe a short meaningless relationship –

but someone. Man or woman, just someone to share the moments with.'

She knew he was right and nodded weakly.

'Can I make another suggestion?'

She nodded again.

'If you can't get a man, get a fucking budgie; you can train it to talk and all that shite.'

Macallan choked back a laugh. 'What are you like? There was me thinking you'd become all touchy-feely!'

He poured another drink for himself and told her to go home. She kissed the top of his head on her way out.

2

Bill Kelly had wanted to be buried in the grounds of the church he'd loved since moving to the area – when he'd first joined the RUC from the Met – and where he had worshipped even in the darkest days of the Troubles when his faith had been tested to the limit. His family had made sure that it was all arranged properly, and he would lie in the grounds of Drumbo Holy Trinity Church, a few miles south of Belfast in the rolling green hills of County Down.

Grace Macallan walked slowly up the short, sloping path towards the church, lost in the stream of men and women making their way to say goodbye to a good man. She passed under the ancient yews lovingly sculptured into arches, admiring the vision of the people who'd cared enough to make the effort. They were long gone and forgotten, but the yews had endured longer than much of the carving on the stone monuments that decorated the grounds.

Some of the mourners were in the uniform of the PSNI, and she recognised many of the faces. There were a few nods towards her, and a couple of old colleagues even said hello. She wondered if time was healing and whether at least some of them were leaving the past behind them. Two of the mourners were in wheelchairs, and she knew both of them as damaged survivors of PIRA gun attacks.

There had been an unseasonal Arctic blast the day before, and now a glowing autumn sun was struggling to keep the afternoon air above freezing, but it cast an almost golden light on the church tower, and the grass that decorated the old churchyard was sparkling for Bill's funeral. Macallan stopped outside the church and smiled, knowing that he would have been pleased that such a beautiful day had been laid on for him. She closed her eyes and spoke to her friend. 'You must have done something right to get a day like this, Bill; the rest of the year it's pissing rain.'

She shook her head slowly, trying to accept that he was gone. It still didn't seem possible.

She looked again at the churchyard and the dozens of spider webs exposed by strings of water pearls that hung like fairy lights among all those names on stone. So many stories in the ground there – and most of them forgotten, save for the odd grainy photograph in the back of a drawer, their names and lineage a mystery to their puzzled descendants. They'd lived though, just like Bill. She wouldn't forget him, and she'd carry a piece of the man right through her own journey.

Macallan hadn't been in a church for a few years, and although she was a contented atheist, she loved the feel of them, with their connection to communities and what had gone before. She barely heard the words of the sermon but scanned the gathering, watching the faces that were there that day. She saw some hard men squeezing their eyes shut as they struggled to hold back their emotions. Bill was loved, and the proof was there for all to see.

It was cold at the graveside, and thankfully the ceremony was kept short for the sake of the older men and women who'd made the effort to come.

'Daddy.'

One word, spoken very quietly by Bill's daughter as the coffin was lowered into the ground, but hearing it was enough to make Macallan bow her head and push the back of her hand into her eyes. She hardly noticed the other mourners as they started to drift away.

As they wandered back towards their own lives, she moved closer to the grave to have her own last moment with her friend and mentor. She stared down and promised him again that she'd do her best and be what he'd hoped for her.

'Grace.' The voice startled her out of her moment of reflection. She turned to find Jack Fraser standing behind her. 'How are you?' He said it gently.

She hadn't any idea what to say to the man who'd ended their relationship at the moment she'd needed him most. No explanation, no fond farewells when she was forced to leave Northern Ireland after giving evidence against a colleague. She'd loved him – and he'd almost driven her over the edge. As a barrister and her lover, he'd known better than anyone the months of anguish and isolation from her colleagues she'd suffered.

'What do you want me to say? "Nice to see you" or something like that? I'm here to have a moment with a fine man, so perhaps you could let it be.'

He looked older but still good on the eye. She didn't even try to hide the anger, although somewhere deep inside there was a flicker of pleasure just from seeing him. She felt it and buried the emotion before he saw the signs. He didn't deserve that compliment.

'I know what Bill meant to you, and I'm sorry – he was the best, and I had the utmost respect for the man. Look,

I have my car if you want a lift back into the city; I'll wait outside for you.'

He looked at her expectantly, but Macallan didn't answer and turned back to the grave as Fraser walked back to his car.

'Jesus Christ,' she murmured, 'am I cursed for a past life?' She tried to let her thoughts find Bill again – but the sight and sound of Jack Fraser had put an end to that.

'Goodbye, my friend. I'll see you in a bar that needs no coin one day,' she told him as she turned from the grave, promising herself that she would come back again some day.

As she walked towards the parked cars Macallan still had no idea whether to accept a lift or tell Fraser to go back to whatever his life was now. But the moment she saw him sitting in the 4x4 she knew. What was it about women that allowed them to take men's worst and come back for more? Yet a man could turn his head away from a relationship and walk off as if it had never happened. She'd seen it in her early days in the uniform of the Royal Ulster Constabulary, attending domestics, watching women take abuse over and over again from the same men they forgave every time. There would probably be a rational evolutionary explanation why, but even as a confirmed non-believer she thought it had to be some ancient curse on the female gender. She pulled open the door.

'I'll take that lift on one condition. You take me back to the city and buy me a coffee – not a drink, because I only do that with trusted friends – and then tell me what happened when you walked out of my life without an explanation. No prevarication. I'm doing well and not about to let you fuck it up, but I'm human and always wondered why.'

Macallan had booked into the Radisson Hotel on the Ormeau Road. The red-brick building in the grounds of

16

the old Belfast gasworks towered over the area and was a reminder of the confidence in the city after the Troubles. She would fly back to Edinburgh the following morning and had expected a quiet night in her room staring at the TV, but life was never that simple. They'd hardly exchanged a word on the drive back to the hotel, and she had ordered Fraser to wait in the bar while she changed and cleaned up. When she came back downstairs he was looking uncomfortable, holding a newspaper that she guessed he wasn't reading. She ordered coffee for both of them and didn't ask if that's what he wanted. She felt hard, in control and wasn't about to give him any room to avoid her earlier question.

'Talk to me then.' She said it tight-lipped and waited.

'You look good. I've heard how well you've been doing – quite the celebrity detective now. How's Edinburgh?'

She saw he was trying and there was no act. 'Edinburgh's good, and yes, I'm doing well but I seem to be working harder than ever. I'm settled though and have a life.' She knew that was part lie or Harkins wouldn't have suggested buying a budgie. 'And how's it going with you?'

'Work is fine and, like you, too much of it. A few of the boys who won't give up the war and the rest are into drugs and organised crime now. Still, keeps me in balance with my maintenance payments.'

She tried not to look surprised that his marriage had finally broken up. Since he'd left her she'd made up her mind that he'd used her downfall as an excuse to rebuild his relationship with his wife. She waved to the waiter for alcohol and gave up pretending that she was enjoying or needed the coffee. Fraser told her he'd moved to the city centre since his divorce so he would leave his car and join Macallan over a glass of average house white. It spilled out – all of it. He told her about the call from the

17

Commander and the blackmail over his occasional use of cocaine – the demand that he had to give up Macallan, who'd betrayed the force by giving evidence against her own. There had been a struggle with depression and then a walk along the edge with booze. Eventually his marriage had decayed naturally and they'd parted on good terms, although she'd made him pay financially for his sins. But he'd pulled himself together, submerged himself in work and got his life into some sort of balance.

'It was hard, Grace, and every day I wanted to call or make some explanation or apology. There's no defence for the way I handled it; I was away in the head, as we say back home. But when I saw you at the funeral I thought I'd try. By the way do you know the Commander had a massive stroke a few months ago?' He sat back in the chair, looking drawn.

'I'm not sure what to say. You look knackered. I want to be really angry, hurt you, but you just took the sting out of that one.' She considered for a moment. 'I have to say I'm glad you've had a bad time though – you deserved that. It's still a fraction of what I went through. I have no idea what I would have done without Bill to support me. As for the Commander … well, the funny thing is I feel sorry that he's so ill. He did what he did because he thought it was the right thing – he was trying to defend the force, and God knows he fought PIRA harder than any of us.'

She watched sadness dip the edges of Jack's slate-grey eyes and gave him a warm smile. He looked pained, and for a skilful advocate he was short of a good line. Macallan thought the wear and tear that had occurred since she'd last seen him just made him more attractive. The extra lines were in the right place, and the additional grey hair gave him that air of importance that distinguished a certain kind of man. Women spent their time and fortune

18

trying to hide these signs, but she guessed that when he was in his golden years, women would still be slavering over Jack Fraser.

'I guess I better head off,' he said. 'Big day in court tomorrow and trying to be Mr Sensible these days. Boring but keeps me sane.'

He'd surprised her; she'd expected some play to her emotions and had intended to hit him hard if it came. She'd decided she wouldn't hesitate to wound him, get some revenge in, but it hadn't happened, and Macallan surprised herself by feeling sorry for her former lover. She'd always imagined that he'd been living the charmed life, the stuff of glossy magazines, when all the time he'd been suffering in much the same way she had in the aftermath of that night on the Ormeau Road.

'If you are back in Belfast anytime and want to meet up for a drink, just say the word. That would be good for me. I don't expect anything from you but would hate never seeing you again.'

He looked beaten, and she decided enough was enough. *What the fuck?* she thought, picturing the rest of her life with Harkins' budgie. 'I've no plans to come here in the near future, and meeting you hasn't changed that. But if you want to meet for a drink you can come to Edinburgh. No strings; and if you're there on business, pleasure or to have that drink with me just let me know. You can't have my number, but you can get me at my office.'

He lifted his gaze and nodded. Macallan wondered if she'd overacted and fucked it up.

'Okay. I'm over at the Faculty of Advocates from time to time and will give you a call.' He rose awkwardly, wondering how to leave, and Macallan saw the problem.

'Don't try to give me a peck, and don't try to shake my hand. I'll see you in Edinburgh.'

She watched him walk away towards the city, shook

her head and smiled. And there was a thought: *I might not need that budgie after all, Mick.*

Macallan went back to her room and stared over the rooftops to the Markets, remembering how it had been during the Troubles. Sometimes it all felt like a dream – that none of it had actually happened.

She switched on the television and groaned when she found it was *EastEnders*. 'No way.' She flicked the channel and saw the coalition being wound up by Ed Balls in a parliamentary bun fight. 'Jesus, give me peace!' she said. 'One last go and I'm off to the bar.' Third time lucky proved to be the latest report on the Jimmy Savile saga and breaking news on the umpteenth celeb. She escaped to the bathroom, sloshed some warm water on her face and patted it dry, deciding there was no other option but a proper drink.

Back down at the bar, Macallan pretended to read a book but spent most of her time watching the various characters coming and going in the lounge. All those lives squeezed into the hotel – business people making the most of their expenses, married couples ignoring each other and the inevitable pair of fools in the middle of a very passionate affair. She wondered what their partners were doing at home. The star act was a couple of very confident transvestites who hadn't quite got the hang of the clothes and make-up yet, but they looked pleased. *Good luck to you; you're probably a lot happier than I am*, she thought. Her mind inevitably drifted back to Jack, and she couldn't decide whether she'd handled it well or completely misjudged the situation.

She looked back at the couple having the extramarital. They were lost in each other's company and appeared to be about to spontaneously combust unless something was done about it. They were fools, but she felt a pang of loneliness and headed back to the room.

Hotels could be the most intimate or the most isolated of places – it just depended on which straw you'd pulled on the day. She undressed, wrapped the hotel dressing gown round her shoulders and stood at the window, looking at the orange glow from the street lights round the Markets and Ormeau Road. It looked quiet, the days of the Troubles far away now. A couple of teenagers walked away from the hotel hand in hand, making for the city centre, and they seemed at ease with the world.

Macallan climbed into bed, tired but knowing that there was little chance of sleep – the first night in a strange bed was always a problem, and she had Jack Fraser on her mind. Once again she flicked the TV from station to station in the vain hope that there would be something to grab her attention. Finally she gave up, switched the lamp off and lay staring towards the windows and the glow of the street lights over the city.

The only sleep she could find was fitful, and being in Belfast again filled her mind with old memories. At some point she dreamed that she rose from her bed, hearing the sound of a heavy, regular beat. She stood at the long window and realised there was no glass, the night breeze cooling her skin. The heavy rhythmic beat drew closer and then in the orange glow of the street lights she saw lines of men, lucent as if they were ghosts, marching proudly up the Ormeau Road. Endless lines of men, who gradually dissolved until there was only the orange light, but the heavy beat of the drum continued into the distance before fading into nothingness.

3

By the time Macallan had fallen into a deeper sleep, leaving her dream behind, two young Asian men were heading home through the cold drizzly streets of Belfast. The gift of youth meant that they hardly noticed the weather. They were keyed up after a good night and still had the buzz that only the under twenty-fives experience. They needed to be home before their families started to panic and walked quickly, the sound of their pounding feet echoing off the damp brick walls of the street.

When the peace process began to calm the conflict in Northern Ireland, their parents, who'd been friends with each other, had seen an opportunity. They'd wanted to escape the overcrowded community that was their home on the south side of London. The incentive of a developing economy with money being pumped in to aid peace, and open spaces outside a much smaller city had been too much to ignore. Nearly a quarter of a century earlier they'd travelled across half the world to live in a strange country where they might make a good life away from their harsh existence in Pakistan, so the short journey from London and across the Irish Sea should have held less risk for the family.

The boys had been in the gay quarter of Belfast and both knew the shame it would cause their families if they were discovered, but they were what they were. Their parents belonged to a generation caught between the traditions of the subcontinent and the freedoms – or excesses as they saw it – of modern Britain. The boys had made friends in the gay community, both white and black, and now felt part of something positive in the relaxed atmosphere of the pubs and clubs just a few minutes from the city centre.

They trotted past St Patrick's Church in Donegall Street and were so busy laughing at the night's events that they didn't hear the four sets of footsteps trailing them from the club they'd left only minutes before. Their mistake was to cut through Stephen Street and then Union Street, where it was just too quiet. The men behind knew the right time to attack. Three of them had trained in the Ulster Volunteer Force and the fourth man, Billy Nelson, had served in the British Army, with two tours in Iraq and two in Afghanistan.

Nelson and his friends were formed in the Loyalist stronghold on the Shankill Road, which runs a mile and a half from the centre of the city through West Belfast. He was brought up in the Hammer district of the Shankill and as a boy saw too much evidence of man's inhumanity to man. It still visited him now, the memory of the 1993 bombing, when an IRA device had exploded prematurely in Frizzell's fish shop, killing nine people. One of the bombers had died along with the locals. Nelson had been close enough to feel the heatwave from the blast wash over him, and from that day he and his mates had just ached to get in on the fight. They wanted to get into the

UVF as soon as they were shaving, and Nelson had been identified by the local men as a hard bastard of the first order, but they had other plans for him. He'd been taken into a safe Loyalist pub, and the man who'd spoken to him was someone that had to be listened to – you did not fuck with him.

'We don't need you to hit Taigs, son. You've a head on your shoulders, unlike those fuckin' eejits you hang around with. They'll do fine when it comes to violence, but we need to plan for the future. You're going to join the Queen's army, son, be the best and come back to us with something better than the ability to break bones.'

That had been it and Nelson had lived up to his task. The Parachute Regiment became his home, he took to the military and they took to him. He was good even among the best, and fighting Catholic boys seemed to become something he'd left behind with his youth. But what changed Nelson started in the Iraq War in 2003 and then Afghanistan. He saw too many friends maimed and killed by an enemy who fired from the shadows or planted a bomb that at best took a leg and at worst your face. Muslims replaced Catholics as the enemy in Nelson's mind, and his control went after his closest mate in the regiment lost everything, including his balls. After that, he just wanted to hurt someone – and so that's what he did. A young Afghani suspect had been detained, and Nelson had decided to do it there and then. The miracle was that the boy hadn't died, but it was enough to see Nelson take a sentence and a discharge from the Army. The only place he could go was back to Belfast, where the Troubles were over and his hatred needed a new cause.

On his return, Nelson couldn't believe the modern face of the province, especially Belfast and what had been the front line when he'd left Northern Ireland. But Nelson had changed as well – during combat, Catholic soldiers had saved his skin in more than one firefight in the deserts of the Middle East, and they were no longer the enemy. No, the new problem was the influx of immigrants and foreign workers with new ideas that were washing away the Northern Ireland of the twentieth century. Nelson had discovered a different cause, and there were others in the Loyalist movement who thought the same. He'd found his old team of friends were bored and had drifted into small-time drug dealing and a bit of extortion, but the problem was that they didn't have a brain between them. To them, Nelson's homecoming had been a big occasion.

'A gay quarter? You have to be fuckin' kiddin' me on, Andy.'

The youngest of his old team, Andy Clark, couldn't wait to fuel what was burning in Nelson's gut. Nelson was prepared to forgive the Catholics, but there was still plenty to hate.

'I'm telling you, Billy, these fuckin' gay boys are all over the place. Doing it in the open they are – can't fuckin' stand them. Ain't that right, boys?'

Dougie Fisher and Rob McLean made up the rest of the team. They just wanted Nelson to lead the way and knew that their days of selling a few tabs of ecstasy for beer money were over.

Nelson had looked at his old team and decided it was time to get involved.

Fisher was the oldest and slightly less rash than the other two. 'What about the top boys though, Billy?' he'd said. 'The war's over, but they still control most of what's what. Shouldn't you try and get the okay from them? Christ, with what you can do they'll be eating out of your hand so they will!' he'd added, knowing that upsetting the former paramilitary leaders made no sense.

Nelson had known he was right and that would need

to be taken care of. 'No need to go aggravating people before we even get started,' he'd agreed. 'Look, I've already reached out to the top men – they know I'm back, but they aren't exactly rushing to shake my fuckin' hand. I can wait, though that doesn't mean we can't see who's fuckin' around the queers' patch.'

Fisher had looked pleased and excited; he'd always liked dishing out some pain. 'There's been warnings from the Loyalist side to the queers that they wouldn't be tolerated so we're doing nothing wrong.'

It was way too late when the older boy realised they were in trouble – in the wrong place at the wrong time. The first blow hit him from behind, below the ribs, where it would hurt like a bastard. He gasped out all the air from his lungs and fell to his knees retching. Nelson and Fisher were all over him, but they were experts and each blow was calculated to achieve maximum effect. The second boy tried to run, but his legs were clipped, and when he hit the pavement he'd already fractured his arm. He wondered why the two men attacking him were laughing.

Nelson and his team took about a minute and a half to beat their victims. By the time they walked away, the boys were both unconscious, and the damage done would stay with them the rest of their lives. Nelson slapped his friends on the back.

'Job well done, boys, and good to be back. Paki queers, that's a result and a half. Let's get some beers in.' Nelson laughed, on a high from dishing out a beating.

He'd miscalculated badly though. His mindset was still in the old Belfast – in the time of the Troubles – so he thought bashing the Asian boys would earn him some credibility where it mattered, and at one time it might have done. The new Belfast, however, was not the place he imagined; for all the sins of the past, the peace process showed there was a remarkable ability for tolerance even among the bitterest foes of old. There had been some Loyalist picketing in the gay area round the Cathedral Quarter of the city at one time, but the sensational revelations that a number of Loyalist paramilitary killers had been in the same closet had caused the movement to re-examine its own attitudes towards the subject.

The Loyalist organisations set up at the start of the Troubles to defend what they saw as a Dublin-backed policy through the arm of PIRA and Sinn Féin had changed following the peace process. Some of the men of violence had gone on to become leaders in the political developments, and the same was true for both sides of the conflict. Others had lacked the conviction to follow and support peace, realising instead that they had a talent for organised crime, and once they saw the profit margins their career paths were set. Nelson thought that his talent for violence would catch the eye of a few people and they'd welcome him with open arms, but that was his first mistake.

4

Over the next month Nelson and his gang attacked another gay couple, and an Asian boy on his way home from work. They were all hospital cases, and the media went on fire, claiming the attacks would bring a return of violence not seen in the city for years as the victims' communities fought back. The PSNI had taken a beating in the press and from community leaders, so they reacted the way they always did – which was to use it as an excuse to target the men and women involved in the drugs trade and prostitution, knowing it might not get the culprits but would placate the average taxpayer. The men who ran the rackets were pissed off and business was suffering.

Jackie Martin had been a UVF leader in Belfast when the movement needed men like him. Short but muscled like a pit bull, he'd hardly changed in looks, mostly down to good genes but partly due to the hours he spent pushing weights every day. There wasn't a spare inch on his arms for another tattoo pledging his allegiance to God, the Queen and Glasgow Rangers. His head was permanently shaven, his eyes clear blue and deceivingly friendly – though his close allies knew this was just a trick on the senses, as his ability to move from friendly banter to headcase was legendary. He'd built his reputation defending Ulster, and like all good legends had done his time in the Maze prison before coming out an even more violent bastard than before. He'd fought his way through the Loyalist internal feuds, and at the same time taken out enough innocent Catholics to get him to the top of his section in West Belfast.

The peace process had come as a shock to Martin. Once the guns had been silenced and most of them handed back, he'd sat at home with a wife who hated but feared him, wondering what the fuck he was going to do next. He knew a lot of the boys had their sidelines in drugs but hadn't needed that himself. As a top boy, he paid for fuck all, and no door was closed to him in his particular empire. Once he decided that the politics of peace bored him, the move into the rackets was remarkably easy. He already knew how to run illegal operations, was even more violent than the other violent bastards and knew how to smuggle contraband and guns into the province. The money had flowed in. His wife had seen the results and decided she didn't hate him quite so much, and the flash car plus shop-till-she-dropped money helped her to ignore her husband's addictive use of the prostitutes he managed and abused on a daily basis. She thought he was a beast of the first order, but he left her alone, and when she needed to she presented the front of the good Loyalist wife.

Martin loved watching *The Sopranos*, over and over again, and having the added gift of looking a bit like a short-arsed James Gandolfini, he'd even taken to mimicking Tony Soprano's mannerisms. His wife sneered carefully behind his back and thought his only similarity to the mob boss was that he was a fat bastard. He'd been devastated by the actor's death, and it had just made his wife loathe him all the more. What he did have in common with his hero was that he never hesitated to use extreme violence where it was necessary. He never lost a moment's sleep for the poor bastards he'd either sent to their maker himself or ordered others to take care of.

As far as Martin was concerned life was good – very good – and he just sat at the head of his criminal, almost criminal and legal businesses and watched the profits roll across his desk. His biggest problem was laundering the cash, and he needed to pay top whack to the best but most corrupt accountants to keep the PSNI off his back.

Today, as Martin sat back in his leather seat and sucked deeply on a fat, expensive cigar, he was angry – furious in fact. Things had been stable apart from the occasional so-called Real IRA tosspot who still thought there was a war on, or the fucking idiots on his own side who thought the Union Jack was worth a riot, while the rest of the world just looked on and shook their heads in disbelief. They were the past and could stay there as far as he was concerned. He'd toyed with the idea of topping a few of them, but they were a useful distraction for the Peelers while he was getting on with both business and his latest plan – to build a home just like Tony Soprano.

Now though, Billy Nelson had marched back from killing the Taliban and had set all the fire alarms off, and the newspapers were having a collective orgasm and pointing fingers at the Loyalist paramilitaries who'd dirtied their fingers on occasions with some serious right-wing nutjobs. The chief constable – or chief cunt as Martin liked to call him – had been all over the television looking a bit too serious and promising to crack down on those responsible. That was a coded message for 'grass these fuckers or we'll be all over the wrongdoers in this city'.

'Perfect, fuckin' perfect,' he said out loud, prompting his minder and comrade from the Troubles to look up from his football magazine.

'Did ye say something, Jackie?'

Martin looked round at him, annoyed. 'Aye, I fuckin' did, but I was speaking to someone intelligent ... Me! So go back to your fuckin' comic or eat a banana or something.' He leaned back in his chair again.

The Peelers had been as good as their word and were all over his and everyone else's business. This was how it always was; there was peace then some pain in the arse would come along and screw it all up, and how it was presented to the citizens all depended on what action was taken. As far as Martin was concerned, Nelson and his team would have to fuck off out of Belfast or they'd get a big fat fire escape for the worms in their thick fucking heads. 'Cunts!'

His minder looked up again from his magazine, saw Martin give him the look that said 'shut the fuck up' and went back to reading about his beloved Glasgow Rangers.

Martin knew what had to be done – it was simple and just like the old days when there was a bit of tension in the ranks. Nelson would be pulled in, told that he was on a red card and he'd have to leave Belfast or take what came next. That order would apply equally to his team, who could be buried in the same grave if they wanted to take it on. The word would be quietly passed along to PSNI HQ that the problem had been sorted, then eventually it would all settle down again. They could live happily ever after. The world would soon forget a few shirtlifters and immigrants, and they could all get on with the rest of their lives till the next daft bastard came along and gave everyone a headache in the arse. He turned to the minder and told him to find Nelson and haul him in. Conscious or unconscious – it didn't really matter.

Billy Nelson sipped the cold Guinness, looking round the pub for faces – friendly or otherwise. His experience of the Troubles plus the Middle East had made him instinctively sniff the air for warning signs everywhere he went. The run-down old boozer near the city centre was on its last legs, only attracting the odd loyal pensioner who remembered it in its heyday and the punters who liked the fact it was next door to the bookies. Nelson's head hurt after a night and a half with the boys that had dehydrated his brain to a raw thumping engine trying to beat its way out of his skull. He doubted the rest of the team would be up and about before it was dark again, but the army had taught him to take the pain and just get on with it. They'd had a good score with a bit of dope, and he'd managed to pull his first woman since getting kicked out of the regiment.

The regiment – every time he thought about it he wanted to break something. He gulped the second half of the Guinness in one go then signalled the barman to fill her up.

'You got a thirst there, son?' the barman said routinely.

Nelson looked up at the man on the other side of the bar. About five stone overweight and the wrong side of the half-century. He guessed the fat bastard had never been beyond the edges of Belfast in his life. 'Why you asking?' Nelson issued the question through tight lips. There was no smile to go with the reply, and his look dared the barman to make a smart-arsed return of serve. The older man had seen his share of headcases over the years and knew by heart all the warning signs in the man opposite.

'No reason. I'll just get your beer.' He shrugged and got on with it.

Nelson nodded, disappointed that there was no challenge from the man. His head started to ease halfway through the second pint, and he ordered one of the sandwiches that looked like it had been dried under a sunlamp for a few hours. After two bites he decided to stick to the beer.

He saw the two apes come in and scan the bar. There was no way they were looking for any of the undead reading their racing sections, and it took him about two seconds to work out they were either there to settle something with the barman or him. He could see their tattoos in the mirror and knew what kind of men they were – big, thick and violent. He had a good view and decided not to bother with any sudden movements till he was sure he knew what it was about.

The apes spotted him and moved towards the bar with that strange waddle exhibited by weightlifters with overdeveloped thighs. They stood behind him and gave him the look via the bar mirror. He nodded but didn't bother turning round.

'You alright there, boys? You look like you might know me, but I certainly don't know you. Now state your business and let me get on enjoying this beer or go and stare at someone else.'

He knew enough to work out that if they'd come to hurt him, it would have started already. Someone was delivering a message, so he could afford to take the piss. In any case they were big but wouldn't be that dainty on their feet, and Billy Nelson was very fucking fast when it was needed.

'Jackie wants to see you, young man,' mumbled the larger of the two primates.

Nelson relaxed at the name and hoped this was the call

he'd been waiting for. All those years ago it had been Jackie Martin who'd told him he was heading for the Army and not a Loyalist paramilitary unit. He was the man who'd seen the young Nelson's potential and what he might achieve for the cause in the future.

'That's fine with me, boys. Just let me finish this beer and I'll be right with you.'

He took his time and let them wait, knowing they were pissed that he had the balls to sit there and sip his beer when a man like Jackie Martin was waiting. They thought he was a smart-arse and hoped Jackie would give them the nod to soften him up a bit.

Nelson paid for his beer and they walked outside to a two-year-old Beamer. One of them climbed in behind the wheel and the other squeezed in the back. Nelson decided to keep winding them up; he pulled out his cigarettes and took as much time as he could with the ceremony of lighting one up before jumping in. Their faces were set in seriously fucked-off expressions, but that was a result as far as he was concerned.

They made the short drive up the Shankill and stopped outside the pub that Martin used as an unofficial office. Nelson knew the place well – it held its share of secrets from the Troubles, and the rumours were that one or two suspect touts had walked in the front only to be carried out the back.

Martin was in the small back room that stank of old beer and a general lack of hygiene. He had his feet up on the battered old table that served as his desk. Nelson thought he looked in good shape – he was clearly still lifting some serious iron, and he'd never been shy about steroids in the past, though the last thing a violent psycho like Jackie Martin needed was a dose of steroids making him even more unstable. The story went that he could have been in the *Guinness Book of Records* for the number

34

of road-rage incidents he'd kicked off without any help from the other driver.

'Billy boy, it's been a long time, and you look a right fuckin' handful now. All that hard graft in the regiment did you no harm.'

Martin nodded at the only other seat in the room. Nelson sat down, felt it sway and wondered if it would collapse under his weight, but he decided it wasn't the time to complain about the furniture. The escorts were behind him, one each side of the door.

'How's it going, Jackie? You look like you're still hitting the weights and not changed a bit. How's business now we're all at peace here?'

Martin studied the younger man and realised that he'd been right all those years ago. This boy was hard core, but more than that he was sharp – most men sweated their guts out when they sat in that chair, wondering whether Martin was happy or pissed off with them. But Nelson never turned a hair and just sat there with a cocky half-smile on his face, as if everything in the garden smelt of fucking roses. He'd only been in the place two minutes and he was getting under Martin's skin. The older man wondered whether the boy was a complete nutjob or just hadn't worked out that he was up a very large creek with no sign of a paddle. He decided to dispense with the sweet talk and get straight to the point before he lost it and did Nelson there and then.

'Billy, you've not been back that long but sad to say you've caused waves – big bad bastard waves. I thought you'd have been smart enough to stay low, get acquainted with the city again and in time you'd get on a payroll then earn a bit.'

Martin's face darkened as he went on, and Nelson realised this was not what he wanted to hear. *Too bad*, he thought, but he still didn't give a fuck, though he regretted pissing off Pinky and Perky, who were hovering somewhere behind him; that might have been a mistake as Martin was definitely not about to make him vice-chairman of the board.

'What's the problem, Jackie?' he asked. 'I've not interfered with any of your business – at least not to my knowledge.'

Martin pushed himself up from the table and leaned over it, his face tightening and unable to control it – but then he never could. Nelson didn't move a muscle and kept eye contact, which sent Martin's soaring blood pressure up another ten points. He looked at his minders, who stared into negative space in case he lost it with them as well. 'Do you hear that, boys?' he said. They continued staring into space. 'Billy here doesn't know what the fuckin' problem is.'

A small white fleck of saliva bubbled from the corner of his mouth as he walked round the table, and he just became angrier when Nelson kept his cool as if they were discussing the best place to get a Chinese. He sat on the edge of the table and tried not to wade into the smart-arse and crack his skull – he had enough problems without a body to get rid of.

'I'll tell you what the problem is, Billy,' he said. 'Everything was going fine: business excellent, problems zero – or close to fuckin' zero. Then you decided to hand out a yellow card to a member of Osama Bin Laden's fan club. Correct?'

Nelson kept eye contact. 'Not quite, Jackie.'

Martin had had enough. He grabbed the younger man's jaw with his right hand and pushed his face as close in as he could; he'd seen Tony Soprano do this a couple of times and liked it as a move.

'You've come back to this city and started a war against the outsiders. The Peelers are all over us – not just me

36

but a lot of serious people. Where the fuck do you think you are?' He stepped back, cooling down and controlling his breathing again. He sat back behind the table – saw Nelson straighten his jacket. At least he'd dropped the smirk. 'Well?'

Nelson rubbed the marks on his cheeks but kept eye contact. 'I'm sorry. I hate these fuckers and didn't realise I was causing a problem for anyone's business. No one got in touch with me; that would have helped. I thought the plan was that I'd come back and be of use to someone, but nothing seemed to happen.' He felt a dull pain in his gut and wondered again if he was landing an ulcer. During his time in Helmand he'd had constant discomfort in his stomach, but that wasn't unusual in combat zones. Drinking Guinness in the morning was probably off the menu for him.

Martin had calmed down and told the shorter of the apes – Robby – to go and fetch a couple of beers.

'The world's changed a wee bit, Billy, and Belfast has changed a big fuckin' bit. You've seen it. You left here when it was a war zone and that's gone, apart from a few nutters who've nothing else to do but throw bricks at the Peelers because someone took the Union Jack down. The truth is that to the good people on the mainland, that fuckin' flag pish represents a wish that Northern Ireland would drift away into the Atlantic and sink.'

The drinks arrived and Robby the ape pushed one in front of Nelson then took up his position at the door again. Martin gulped down half the beer in one.

'I'll tell you what's going to happen,' he said. 'There's a red card out on you if you stay here, and that's a done deal. You're a hard fucker no doubt, and you might try and fight it, but eventually you'll go down. You know that?' He waited for a response.

'I know that. Just trying to think where I'll go though.'

Nelson had given up the smart-alec pose. Martin nodded, pleased that he had control of the situation. 'Look, I pointed you at the Army, and with your talents it would be a waste just to leave you at the side of the road or see the back of you.'

Nelson saw a door opening – what could have been the day he died turning round again.

'The business we run is expanding, and we do a lot of trade with the mainland in working girls and dope. We've got good links into Glasgow but there's a demand now from the east, but no one from our side's in Edinburgh. As far as the others here are concerned you've been kicked out, but that doesn't stop you earning once you settle down. How does that sound?'

Nelson was smart enough to know that not being killed was a reasonable deal, and he was pissed off with the new Belfast anyway. 'Sounds fine to me, and I appreciate it.' He was lying, but so what?

Martin looked pleased with himself. 'Take that daft fuckin' team of yours with you, because there's a bullet in the nut for them as well if they hang around. It has to be this way, and then we can pass a message to the Peelers to go back to harassing the poor fuckin' motorists.'

He sat back and spread his arms like Tony Soprano. Nelson smiled and thought what a tosser Martin was – but if it put some money on the table he'd settle for it.

He leaned over and shook the man's hand then got up to leave, noticing the look of disappointment on the faces of Robby and his pal. He winked at them and watched their expressions twitch just a bit as he walked to the door.

'One more thing ...' Martin dropped the tone of his voice to very fucking serious. 'When you're over there you'll eventually get noticed by the law – that's just part of the game. Don't be a fuckin' cowboy. You're one of us, so act like it. Phone me tomorrow and I'll get you set up with a bit of cash to get started. All you need to do after that is use your specialist skills to cut us out a business over there. I'm counting on you.'

A few minutes later Nelson was walking down the Shankill towards the city and pulling on a cigarette. He shook his head at what had just been said: *you're one of us, so act like it.* 'Jesus, he thinks he's an example to other men!' Nelson murmured to himself. He pulled up his collar and started thinking about an exit strategy before someone changed their mind and gave him permanent rest, then he called his team and told them where to meet and that he wasn't taking any excuses.

They sat trying to take it in and there was a bit of panic that Nelson had to calm. 'We're not getting nutted,' he told them. 'It was on the cards, but the man has given us a chance. The trouble is that you boys don't think there's life outside Belfast.' He looked round the faces of the young men who saw Nelson as the only one that could think for them. On their own they were daft enough to stay in the city and take a long nap in a landfill site.

'We'll set up on the mainland; the man has even said he'll give us a leg-up with money so we don't need to sell the *Big Issue* to survive.' The boys nodded and looked to him as their saviour, even though he'd been the mad fuck who'd put them where they were in the first place.

'So that's it. We're on our way, we've to set up a market over the east side and make a good bit of a life for ourselves. There's one thing though; the man thinks we're finished with the fuckin' Muslims, queers and the like – well he can go and take a fuck on that one. As far as I'm concerned if we want to hand out a bit of a lesson, well that's fine by me. You okay with that?'

The boys were with him.

5

Nelson crawled out of bed, shivering in the cold morning air. He pulled on a woollen sweater and walked over to the window, cursing the sight of the streaming rain blurring his outlook.

'Some view,' he muttered. There wasn't much to see apart from the identikit concrete building opposite.

He tiptoed over the freezing tiles to what passed for a kitchen, opened a fresh pack of untipped cigarettes, fired one up and promised himself again that he'd stop – but not just yet. His cough compounded his throbbing headache, and he spat into the kitchen sink, not bothering to rinse out the foamy stain. His face twisted at the feel of the sticky coating of dirt on the floor, unwashed since they had moved in, as he switched on the heating and kettle. He smiled as the memories of the previous night's antics came back to him in fragments, like partial images on shards of glass that gradually coalesced into a hazy image. The main thing was that he was pretty sure he hadn't made an arse of himself and that the rest of the boys had behaved as far as they could.

They'd gone into Edinburgh city centre and spent the

night trawling the George Street bars trying to pull some 'decent office females' as Nelson liked to label them, but their crude Belfast patter had only worked on one woman. The problem was that she was on her own, severely pissed, and looked like she'd escaped from a chuckle wagon and was still on the run. They'd decided to give her a miss and went on to lose a few notes at the casino. The bouncers had looked less than happy at the four drunks arriving at the door, and under normal circumstances they would have turned them around and given them a boot in the arse to help them on their way. If anything, though, the doormen were realists, and the Belfast accents and something in Nelson's eyes had told them it might not be a battle worth fighting, so they had let them in.

The four men had had a laugh and could afford the loss at the tables. The main thing Nelson was sure of was that there had been no trouble, which was vital, as he was trying to stay under the radar of the local police. He knew it couldn't last forever, but the longer they could build the business without hassle the better. He wanted, and planned to get, into a position where he could step back then let the mugs take the risks on his behalf. *Just like that fat fucker Jackie Martin*, he thought.

In his quieter moments he imagined putting Martin on his arse and burying his boots into his teeth. *One day, Billy, one day*, he kept promising himself.

His first impression was that Edinburgh was a city with too many Asians and weirdos, which meant he'd have to take some action, but all in good time – that would have to wait till he was established.

He pulled on the cigarette, sipped his scalding tea and as he felt the heating kick up, the shivers eased off and he relaxed. *Christ I'm getting soft*, he thought; when he was in the army he'd spent days out in the open on patrols in Afghanistan and never turned a hair.

He stood up and looked at his reflection in the mirror – the abs were still there but maybe the definition was starting to blur. *Not bad*, he thought, *not bad at all, but I think we'll need to get you a gym membership or you'll lose it.*

Nelson had inherited via his father's genes a body that was tall and heavily built, which gave him a powerful shape that was all in proportion. His strenuous training in the regiment had hardened it all up into slabs of deep muscle, a physique he was proud of. His dense, coal-black hair was kept cropped short and the large oval eyes he'd inherited from his mother looked almost dark blue, with a hangdog drop round the outside edges. In addition, he seemed to carry an almost permanent grin, which was no reflection on his mood, just a fixture from the way he was formed in his mother's womb. In the right circumstances, or with the opposite sex, it gave him a boyish charm, but in his business it could piss people off when they were trying to be serious and Billy looked like he was on the receiving end of a good joke.

It seemed like an age since they'd left Belfast and settled in Scotland's capital city. Jackie Martin had been as good as his word and made sure they'd money enough to get somewhere to live and a start in the business. This hadn't been done out of a generosity of spirit – it was purely a business loan that he wanted back at a high rate of interest once they were earning. The rents in the centre of town were out of their league for the time being so they'd settled for a flat in Wester Hailes on the south-west edge of the city, a huge concrete overflow built with the best of intentions in the seventies and recognised as an eyesore ever since. The concrete tower blocks and purpose-built flats had eased the congestion in the city, but it had a sizeable population with not much in the way of prospects and a crime problem that mushroomed round the drugs trade. The city fathers had given redevelopment a go in the nineties and had courageously pulled down some of the worst of the architectural offences. The problems remained though, and an increasing influx of immigrants added to an area that was a million miles away from the opportunities and wealth enjoyed round the centre of the old city and Georgian New Town.

The Ulstermen managed to rent a couple of flats near to each other, Nelson sharing with Andy Clark, who was the youngest and probably the least bother for him. Clark was still in awe of Nelson and hung on every word he said, and if he was told to fuck off to bed because Nelson needed peace, he fucked off to bed without being told a second time.

They'd played it low-key at the start, just showing up in the local boozers and using the tale that they were on a labouring job outside the city, acting the daft Belfast boys for the benefit of the Wester Hailes punters. There was always a bit of shyness from the locals when they mentioned Belfast as their hometown – the legacy of the Troubles still meant something even to people who'd never read a newspaper in their lives.

Once their faces were known and they'd bought a few rounds for people, they'd steadily built up a picture of who was doing what in the realm of low-level dope dealing and criminality. They'd eventually started buying a bit themselves for personal use, and the dealers saw them as good payers who never asked for tick – that always went down well because half their normal clientele were living from uncertain day to uncertain day. The local cowboys started taking an interest in the boys and felt it gave them a bit of 'cred' being seen leaning against the bars with men who hinted at Loyalist connections. They hadn't realised till it was far too late just how wrong they were; they thought they were streetwise yet went sleepwalking into a fuck-load of problems courtesy of Billy Nelson and those nice Belfast boys.

Nelson had been patient, and it had worked a treat. They were becoming mates with most of the local lowlifes, and that would do for now. He knew there would be harder problems and men to deal with in time, but he'd planned his moves, and at the end of the day it would come down to willpower and the willingness to use force. He knew he had all that and more.

He noticed small white lumps floating about on the surface of his tea and screwed up his nose as though he'd never had anything like it. The curdled milk annoyed him, but given the shit he'd endured in the past, it was more a symptom of his erratic mood swings than of taste.

'Andy, what the fuck is this?' he bawled, even though Clark was still under the blankets, sleeping off the previous night. 'Andy, I'm going to come through there and haul you on your arse!'

Nelson's voice pierced the sleeping brain of the younger man and stabbed down into his subconscious, setting off an alarm – that same sense that catches the attention in a crowded room when someone mentions your name, like radar locking onto a hazard. He swam up to the surface of consciousness, knowing he had to react to the alert that had dragged him away from a dream that was already fading into oblivion.

He sat up too fast and worked the heels of his hands across his eyes.

'Andy, one last time – will you get your lazy carcass through here?'

'I'm coming, just give me a minute,' he croaked through the closed bedroom door, his mouth feeling like a Brillo pad had been stapled to his tongue. He felt the quick stab of apprehension that hit him every time Nelson turned his attention towards him. He was a tough young man, only

44

four years younger than his flatmate, and he could dish out violence with the best of them, including Nelson. His problem, however, was that his mother and father were just too closely related, and he was the product of a gene pool that had needed freshening for at least a couple of generations before he was born.

Nevertheless, he was a good-looking boy, his blonde hair and blue eyes suggesting some Nordic blood had seeped into his Scottish ancestors. In common with Nelson, his looks gave the impression of a gentle soul, but as his mother had whispered many times to her sisters and mother, 'The boy isn't quite right.' He struggled to think for himself or make any rational decisions, especially under pressure. He would follow the pack, and why they were doing what they did wasn't something he worried about.

He couldn't feel afraid in the same way the other boys did either – and certainly not where violence was concerned. He really wasn't quite sure what fear meant when he heard the other boys speaking about it and only understood it in relation to rejection from those he cared about.

Clark tended to channel his energy through other people, but they were few and far between. He had no siblings, and through his lonely childhood the focus of his attention had been his mother – certainly not the bastard of a father who'd nearly killed her on one occasion through his love of the bottle. His father's fists had put an end to the chance of his mother ever giving him a brother or sister, and with nothing to admire or aspire to in his family it was the hard men who drew his attention. They were his role models – the tough bastards in the paramilitaries who tended to spot his strengths and weaknesses, exploiting them both at the same time.

Women on the other hand were a mystery to Andy

Clark, and all he'd experienced was the occasional drunken fumbling when the boys had managed to pick a team of females as pissed and daft as they were. More than a few Belfast girls had tried to build bridges with the nice-looking boy belonging to Mrs Clark, but they'd soon realised they were talking to themselves and that his mother's assessment of his mental state hadn't been far off the mark.

Nelson was something else though, and Clark had looked up to him when they were boys – but when he came back from the fighting in Afghanistan it was as if a movie star had walked into his life. Clark didn't know much, but he knew his films, and any night he was on his own he made for the stalls in the local cinemas to watch his idols. Sylvester Stallone was a standout, and Bruce Willis and big Arnie weren't that far behind for him when it came to pure acting talent. He was a slow reader but loved to pore over his cinema magazines the way most of his friends tended to study their well-worn editions of *Razzle*. His mother used to watch him at night as he silently mouthed the words in the magazine as he read and had bitten her lip frequently at the shame of bearing such a good-looking but idiotic son.

As far as Clark was concerned, Billy Nelson was the centre of his universe, and whatever Billy wanted Billy would get. When Nelson had picked him for a flatmate, Clark had believed it was Nelson's vote of confidence and confirmed him as his trusted lieutenant. The truth was that Nelson thought Clark was a useful and potentially violent fucker with less than three brain cells that actually worked on their own. He knew the angelic looks could fool people and, as a bonus, living with Clark meant he had a stooge and manservant who allowed Nelson to sit on his arse and click his fingers when he needed anything done.

Despite what the young man thought, Nelson didn't give a fuck about him and described him to the rest of the team as his own personal Baldrick. Dougie Fisher had listened to it one day after a few beers and whispered in Rob McLean's ear, 'If Andy ever hears that he'll go over the edge and put Billy in Accident and Emergency – and that's only if he fuckin' survives.'

Clark padded through to find Nelson sitting with his feet up watching *Jeremy Kyle* with the sound down. 'What's up, Billy?' he asked.

'What's up? The milk's fuckin' rancid and that's your job.'

Clark looked upset but he knew that when Nelson was dealing with a hangover it was always better just to let him be. 'I'll go and get some, Billy. It's no problem.'

'Hurry it up and pay attention to your job in future. If you can't get the fuckin' milk right, how are you going to manage anything else? Fuckin' twat.'

That hurt him. Hurt him in a way that only happened with someone close. He walked out onto the street with his face set, determined to try and do better for his friend.

6

The time came for Nelson to make his first move. They were all up for it and getting bored with acting as straight pegs – they wanted to make their mark and earn a bit of respect. They'd identified a number of local dealers in the Wester Hailes area who would be given a couple of options. Nelson looked round the team and grinned. 'The first option is cooperate with us, buy our gear and pay tax on it, and the second option is there is no fuckin' option.'

The boys nodded and felt the trembling rush of adrenalin working up their systems, the thought of a bit of violence going down a treat.

Dougie Fisher smiled. 'I haven't laid my hands on anyone in weeks. I was afraid I might be turning into a nice person.'

Nelson slapped him on the back and they belly laughed at the thought of bringing down some pain on the local dealers. Then Nelson opened a cupboard in the hallway that seemed to be jammed up with crap. He struggled to take out an ironing board and a hoover that had rarely been used before pulling out the rest of the dross and unscrewing a wooden panel at the back of the cupboard.

'Jackie Martin sent over some tools for us if there's any heavy action in future,' he told them. 'We shouldn't need them at the moment, but they're available if required, boys.' He pulled out the worn holdall and opened it up. 'You all know how to use these and there's ammo enough if we need it.'

The bag held two dull grey Uzi machine pistols – a gun that had become an icon around the world and a fashionable 'must have' for upmarket drugs gangs. In the world of fiction the word Uzi had a special resonance. Even Arnie's Terminator had favoured the weapon, and his order for an 'Uzi 9 millimetre' had made the weapon immortal. The Loyalist ranks were full of men trained in the heavy-engineering workshops of Belfast, and replicating the weapon had been a major success for them. In fact, to the surprise of observers and their enemies, they'd produced a weapon that was at least as good as – and in many cases better than – the original.

'If we need to use these fuckers it'll be pressed up against the man's skull. We don't need them for a gunfight at the O.K. Corral.' He smiled and nodded at his team, who looked ecstatic – they were in business at last. 'I think Jackie had too many anyway. The greedy bastard kept back more than his share when they were supposed to be decommissioned in the peace deal.'

He closed the bag and stashed it back behind the false wall.

'Okay, boys, let's go and spread some good old-fashioned Belfast sunshine on our new pals here.'

Banjo Rodgers came out of his near coma with a start that jarred his pulse up to 175 beats a minute. He wasn't drunk or hungover, but it took him a couple of minutes to make sense of being awake. It came back like Post-it notes being fed through a letter box. The gradual realisation of who and what he was drip-fed into his brain.

'For fuck's sake,' he mumbled as his vision cleared enough to see that he was still in the same shithole he'd been in when he'd stuck the needle in his arm. He looked across the room and saw his lady still knocked out and half hanging over the edge of her chair. Her mouth was open, her eyes not quite closed and a line of saliva was being drawn down onto the manky carpet by the force of gravity. Banjo loved her though, and she was all he had to love.

He pushed himself up and waited a few seconds until he was sure his balance had clicked back into place before leaning over her and running his hand through her hair.

'Maggie, you alright there, honey?' He pulled her up into a sitting position and felt her move. It calmed him, as it did every time they went through the same script where he was convinced this would be the day she would be stone cold and booked into the exit lounge at the crematorium. She'd overdosed a couple of times already, and both of them knew it was only a matter of time before shit happened. To be fair they'd cut down on the gear and only hit a bit extra at the weekends. This was their weekend and their idea of time off from dealing.

Banjo had inherited his moniker from his father, who just couldn't avoid a fight and won about seventy-five per cent of his duels. In his own often-repeated words he 'just loved to "banjo" some bastard after a few beers'. The twenty-five per cent he lost eventually reduced him to a wreck and the humiliation of shadow-boxing non-existent opponents after the pubs shut. He ended up barred from them all, including the dives where the landlords got pissed off with someone who had one drink then talked to the wall for the rest of the evening.

Young Banjo had eventually buried his unmourned

father when he was still only seventeen years old and, given his mother had run out well before his death, was then all on his own. He'd failed at everything he'd tried after that. In an early career move he'd had a go at breaking into shops, but he was such a clumsy bastard he invariably made so much noise that the residents buried in the local cemetery would have heard him. After some prison time he'd decided to step up his game and joined a gang of incompetents who'd tried to rob a post office, then ran out of fuel during the escape. He did four years for that then wisely took the decision that he needed another line of work. That was how he'd become a very low-level drug dealer. Prison had taught him everything he needed to know about the trade, and although he'd developed a habit of his own, he controlled it as best he could. Despite his efforts, however, the years had still taken their toll on his physical state, and in his early thirties he looked like he'd lived another fifteen years but not worn well even then.

Banjo's big plus was that he was somewhat of a rarity: he got on with just about everyone, never ripped anyone off, and paid his suppliers on time and in full. That was probably just as well given that he was supplied by the Flemings from Leith, and Danny Fleming was his linkman. Cut young Danny in half and the word bastard was printed the length of his body.

The Flemings were one hundred per cent mental, and they made enough in profits to be delighted when someone ripped the piss and gave them the excuse to hand out a bit of physical education, as Danny liked to call low-level torture. Banjo always kept the right side of them and dealt just enough to keep him in the essentials of life plus a bit of clean gear for himself – and Maggie when she came into his life.

Maggie Smith was somewhere in the same age group

as Banjo, and despite her lifestyle looked nearer her years. She'd been working the streets at Leith when she started buying her supply from Banjo, who'd taken a shine to her, and given that he could pay his bills and was rarely in a fit state to bother her physically, it seemed like the best deal she could get in this life. He'd been kind to her and she'd started to like him as the first man who'd never taken from her – and that included her father.

She still worked the street, but only when Banjo could come down with her. She'd been badly shaken up when the serial killer Thomas Barclay had attacked some of the other girls at the same time she'd been working punters. She knew a couple of the victims and in fact had been friendly with Pauline Johansson, who'd barely survived one of the attacks and had looked after Maggie a couple of times when she was down on her luck. What had happened to Pauline had spooked her, and she still saw Barclay in her dreams.

Banjo didn't mind going down to Leith with her – he quite enjoyed getting out occasionally if it helped her keep safe. As shit lives went, Maggie and Banjo got by as long as they had each other.

The knock at the door was just a bit too loud – not loud enough for the bizzies, but if it had been a raid they wouldn't bother knocking anyway.

'Who the fuck is that?' Maggie muttered as she started to get herself together again. 'They know we don't deal on a Saturday night.' She pushed a cigarette into her mouth and raked among the crap on the coffee table for something to light it with.

Banjo didn't like it, and years of keeping his arse out of the grinder gave him a sixth sense of when things were right and when things were definitely wrong. The knock at the door was wrong.

He pulled on the slippers Maggie had shoplifted

out of Marks and Spencer's for his Christmas and then tried to shuffle as quietly as he could to the door. It had been reinforced after the bizzies had caved it in twice looking for a result, and it would take a rocket-propelled grenade to get through the thing now. Banjo pressed his eye against the peephole and nearly pissed himself with fright at the giant eye on the other side. He stepped back. 'What the fuck?' Unfortunately he said it loudly enough for the men outside to hear.

Maggie came up behind him, put her hand on his shoulder and sucked on her cigarette.

'Banjo, it's Billy Nelson. Will you open the fuckin' door? It's not the police for God's sake.'

Banjo exhaled and nodded to Maggie, pointing back towards the lounge. 'Go and sit back through there, doll; it's only the Belfast boys. I'll tell them to fuck off.'

He kept the door closed and told them it was Saturday night, lied that he was out of gear till Monday and could they come back then.

He pressed his eye back to the peephole and saw that Nelson was with Dougie Fisher. He liked Fisher; he was the quiet one but always bought a round of drinks and spoke to Maggie as if she was a lady. They weren't welcome on his night off, but they were good guys as far as Banjo was concerned so he opened the door.

'Look, boys, I'm having a quiet night in with Maggie if you know what I mean.' He winked, hoping they'd believe that because he was in his vest and pants there was something else going on apart from him injecting heroin into his veins.

Nelson didn't wait to be asked and pushed past Banjo, Fisher following him. Banjo shrugged, deciding it was better to sort it out so he could get back to the rest of the powder he'd put aside for later.

He went to the bathroom first, did what he had to do to

relieve the aching pressure on his bladder and splashed cold water on his face. He looked in the mirror and wondered who the fuck the wreck looking back at him was before heading back through to his guests.

But when he pushed the door to the lounge open he stopped dead. Because what he expected to see was not what he was seeing. In a normal human being this could stop a man in his tracks for a few seconds while the brain reconfigured and tried to answer its own questions. It took Banjo a bit longer, as it had been a while since his brain had been normal. Maggie was back in her chair, slumped again and nothing unusual in that. What Banjo couldn't work out was why her nose was quite clearly broken, blood trailing down the front of her old dressing gown. Nelson and Fisher were sitting smoking as if everything was as it should be, but Maggie moaned quietly, only half-conscious.

'What the fuck?' He hesitated for a moment and could think of nothing to add. 'I mean, what the fuck?'

'Sit down, Banjo, and I'll explain everything to you – but could you make us a nice cup of tea first? Had fish and chips earlier and I'm parched.'

Nelson drew on his cigarette, pointed the remote control at the TV and clicked onto a programme about crocodiles.

Banjo's earlier instincts had been on the money, and he knew that for the moment the best thing he could do was make the tea and hope he'd survive. He was a born survivor; his instinct was to take Maggie in his arms, but he knew that everything he'd previously thought about Nelson and his boys was wrong. Until he worked out what they were going to say, he would do whatever it was they wanted. They'd torn up the script, and whoever they were and whatever they really wanted was about to be revealed. He knew drug dealing carried risks but this felt a bit fucking ridiculous – Maggie was badly hurt and the blood was bubbling at her nose.

He sat down beside her but he couldn't take his eyes off Nelson, wondering what had just walked into his flat and wrecked Maggie's face.

Nelson leaned forward and stubbed out his cigarette on the wooden surface of the coffee table, ignoring the ashtray about six inches away. 'I'm going to make this simple for you, and I really hope you understand everything I tell you. We're going into business, and when I say "we" I certainly don't mean a dirty little fuck like you. I mean you're going to work for us.'

Nelson looked straight at Banjo, just to make sure he was getting the message. He definitely got it, nodded and reached for a cigarette, managing to put one in his mouth despite the worst case of the shakes he'd had in a while.

Fisher leaned over, lit him up and winked as if that would make him feel better.

'It's this way: the boys and I've decided that the market round here needs a bit of freshening up – so we're taking over. As of the moment Dougie belted Maggie, you work for us, will be supplied by us and pay your dues to us. It's that simple. No need for any fuss, and I'm sure we're going to make a happy team.'

He nodded as if that was it and seemed to be waiting for Banjo to say how pleased he was. Banjo was incapable of forming the words.

'By the way,' Nelson continued, 'you'll be pleased to know that we're signing up most of the other dealers round here so you're not alone.'

As if that made him feel like he was part of a greater good. Banjo tried to think before opening his mouth and drew on his cigarette. And that's when he noticed it. Standing on top of the ironing board, which always sat in the same position by the kitchen door, was the iron. What was strange was that it had been switched on. Neither Banjo nor Maggie ever used the iron, and it took no more than a moment for him to work it out. He stared at a tiny mote that was bouncing around in front of him and realised that whatever he was about to say was going to mean less to Nelson than that tiny speck of dust. All he could do was give it a try. He was annoyed at himself as the shakes had taken hold of his voice and he knew that the Billy Nelsons of this world savoured fear like ticks on blood.

'Look, I'll do whatever you say, but I get my gear from the Flemings, and I don't know if you've met them yet but they'll cut my fuckin' throat if they think I'm pissin' them about.' He lit up another cigarette and glanced at Maggie, who seemed to be sleeping – she was breathing steadily and the blood seemed to be drying round her nose. He knew they weren't there for excuses and would know all about the Flemings.

He looked at the iron again and heard a slight hiss as the remaining water boiled. They were there to send out a message: a very loud and clear message.

Nelson smiled, nodding to Fisher, who stood up and walked over to the ironing board. 'I'm sorry, but that's not what I wanted to hear. Now go sit in the fuckin' corner or I'll kick you there myself.'

Banjo did as he was told and froze in that paralysing combination of fear and helplessness as he watched Nelson rip open the dressing gown covering what was left of Maggie's dignity. Fisher laughed as he pushed the hot iron hard onto her left then her right breast, holding it in place to make sure the flesh was burning properly.

In the flat next door the elderly neighbours heard the screams and looked at each other, shaking their heads in synchronised irritation that there was a disturbance during *The X Factor*. The screams they heard were coming from Banjo. The old couple turned up the volume to drown out the noise.

Half a mile away Andy Clark and Rob McLean were handing out a severe beating to another dealer who'd made the mistake of believing the Ulster boys were dreaming and worse than mad if they thought they were making a move to take over. They were pleased when he told them to 'fuck right off' because then they didn't have to pretend they'd come with an option. That's how it all kicked off.

7

Grace Macallan sat behind her desk and stared at the chaos that was her in tray. She tried to think of an excuse to put it off to another day, but the more she stared at it the more it refused to move. 'No excuses left,' she murmured.

There was no one else in her room, and she liked to talk out loud as a kind of stress relief. She knew that hidden in the basket were overdue requests from the assistant chief's office asking for updates on progress and figures so they could keep the politicians happy for another month. It was a pain in the arse, so she decided she was going to pull rank and delegate.

She picked up the phone and asked DI Jimmy McGovern to come through, knowing that it was an excuse to drink a coffee and speak to him as an alternative to taking on her correspondence.

McGovern stepped through the door and smiled. 'In-tray problems? Don't worry, I've ordered the coffee.'

McGovern always had a smile – he was the man who reminded her almost every other day that it was only paperwork and they'd get it done. He knew where the real problems lay, and they were not in the requests for stats from the vast bureaucratic swamp that sucked in figures, projected trends, spending, staff movements and all the other trivia that was created then disappeared over the heads of those that demanded it. So much of their lives seemed to be a constant battle to shape the figures in a way that kept everyone happy; the doers cooked the figures, and the bean counters knew they were cooked, but as long as they looked good and had something positive to say then they could all sleep happily in their beds.

After the chaos that had followed the arrest of Jonathon Barclay, McGovern had been drafted into the team at the worst of times. He was pure gold for Macallan and just what the team had needed. Harkins had been pensioned out with his injuries, the former head of the squad, John O'Connor, had been packed off to lead the professional standards team and counter-corruption unit for his perceived failings, and Macallan had been promoted into his place. In another couple of years that might have been the right move for her, but it was probably too quick, and O'Connor, who'd been her lover for too short a time, blamed her for his downfall. Now he was head of counter corruption, which could make her life difficult.

Counter corruption was proactive and had its own intelligence unit that looked for exploitable gaps in the system and bent officers. Professional standards took care of all the rest of the barrage of complaints levelled at officers both good and bad. The problems didn't have to be real – there just had to be someone with an axe to grind.

Unusual for a detective because he had a stable private life, McGovern was steady, which made him worth his weight, and he could kick arse without the tables being turned on him. Royal Navy as a young

59

man, he'd married his first girlfriend and had two kids who did him proud. He didn't suck up to anyone, which meant some investigators just didn't get him and always suspected there had to be a flaw somewhere, but McGovern was just one of those guys who took it as it came and was happy with his lot. He watched the rest of the pack as they scrambled for position, back-stabbing each other as if it were a requirement of the job, shook his head and went home to his wife and kids. What was not in dispute was that the man was hard – it was in the shape of the face, the walk, the way he was in control at the worst of times and, best of all, he had a lifelong passion for amateur boxing. Five foot ten but seeming taller, he was a middleweight and everything was in proportion. McGovern verged on good-looking, and if anything the scar tissue around the eyes and the twice-broken nose added to his attractiveness. He still trained whenever he could, and good health showed in his eyes and skin.

The coffee arrived and McGovern poured out the steaming brew, watching Macallan's shoulders relax as he handed her the cup. She'd been running the team for months without a chief inspector and was trying to do both jobs, which was next to impossible. He liked her though, as much as anyone he'd ever worked for or with, and there was a good reason for it. When McGovern looked at Macallan he saw someone who actually cared about the job and the people she worked with, yet she seemed to have very little regard for her own well-being. It seemed to be work and then more work.

He knew her story – how she'd left Northern Ireland under a cloud and how badly her relationship with John O'Connor had ended. O'Connor had become a bitter man and a pest for the team – rumour had it that he'd been the one keeping them short of a DCI. In addition to all that, the fact that Macallan had lost her friend Harkins meant she needed all the help she could get.

She looked weary and those green eyes that could sparkle in a darkened room were tired and dull. The type of man he was meant that he could never be another Harkins for her, but he'd be there when she needed him.

'Can we get one of the overambitious ones to take care of some of this crap I've got?' she asked him. 'I can't face it and think I'll take a bit of time off. Haven't had a day away from the office for weeks, and we seem to be having a quiet spell so I might as well use it. You can look after the shop, and it'll look good on your appraisal.' She smiled. 'As if that would matter to you.'

'Consider it done. I've got the perfect sycophant out there who'll be delighted to clear the mess. He wants to be chief constable before he's thirty so dealing with the dross in your tray should be good practice. You get yourself away before we have to carry you out. I'll take care of anything he can't deal with and pretend I'm you.'

'That obvious I'm knackered?' She said this with a frown as it made her feel even worse.

'That obvious and no wonder. When the balloon goes up again you'll need to be sharp and get it right. You're exhausted, and that's when mistakes get made. You don't need mistakes when Mr O'Connor is waiting on his perch to swoop down and devour you.'

She sipped the coffee and decided he was on the money. 'Okay, I know you're right. I'll book off for a week, but if anything happens I'll be straight back. I've never been to the far north of Scotland so maybe I'll drive up there, find a place with a bar, walk and read a book.'

'That sounds about right, and don't you worry – I'll keep in touch.'

She nodded and felt herself give in to the thoughts of

time away from the job. '*Is* everything quiet out there or is there anything I need to know?'

'The jobs we have are all in the early stages of development or we're preparing the evidence for the ones we've finished. There's a bit of research going on for future jobs, but you know about them.'

She nodded and drained the last of the coffee. 'Jesus help me, I'm knackered,' she said and stretched her arms above her head.

'There is one thing worth mentioning, but I'm not sure what it means yet. There were a couple of dealers found messed up in Wester Hailes over the weekend. One of them is in a pretty bad way but will make it. I should say the other is the female partner of a dealer rather than the dealer himself. She's in a bad way too but will also survive. Strange one – her nose is smashed and she has an iron burn on each breast. The docs thought it was domestic violence and called the cavalry. Apparently the boyfriend was there but, for whatever reason, the boys don't think it was him, and he seemed to be scared shitless.' He shrugged and shook his head. 'Maybe just coincidence but you never know.'

'How bad is she?' Macallan asked, but her mind was already on the north of Scotland and the thought of escaping for a few days.

'She'll be in hospital a few days and then it depends whether she'll agree to further treatment. She's a sex worker down Leith – so she's saying nothing and not making a complaint.' McGovern waited for Macallan to respond, but she was still thinking about walking on long empty beaches. 'Maybe someone's taxing the small dealers or taking over. Who knows, but there's a couple of intelligence reports from human sources that a team's moved in from Northern Ireland and getting a bit heavy. Nothing to connect the two things, but we'll keep an eye on it.'

Macallan felt a tremor in her stomach and forgot about the beaches. Northern Ireland – two punters messed up and one of them tortured. McGovern wouldn't realise it but somewhere deep inside her, tiny electrical impulses started to fire up and search.

She looked out of the window across the green playing fields and knew whoever these boys from Northern Ireland were, they were only a few short miles from her office. She felt them. 'Keep me informed,' she told him. 'Anything at all.'

McGovern saw the look in her eye and wondered what it was that she was seeing. 'Don't worry, nothing will start without you,' he replied.

As he left the office he told her not to answer the phone or speak to anyone on the way out. 'Just go and relax.'

Macallan decided to walk back to her new flat in Inverleith (which was, as always, an impulse buy) and wondered again how she was going to pay the mortgage. She loved it though, and when she walked in the door it was like an old friend wrapping their arms round her. She was in the process of throwing whatever came to hand into a small holdall and rucksack, with the intention of quickly getting as far away from crime and horror stories as she could, when she saw her phone shimmy across the dresser. There was no caller ID so she told the phone to fuck off, but the phone rules the user and finally she caved in and put it to her ear. 'Hello?'

'Hi, Grace, how are you? It's Jack.'

She had missed a call from him at the office earlier and, without even thinking, she'd texted him her mobile number. She closed her eyes and tried to think of the right thing to say. *Don't make an arse of yourself, Grace*, she mouthed without a sound.

'Jack, didn't think I'd hear from you. Long time now since the funeral.' She thought that wasn't too bad, then closed her eyes in a mini panic, unsure where the feeling was coming from.

'Hadn't forgotten. I've been tied up with a difficult case involving some UDA boys from Carrickfergus who won't move into the twenty-first century.'

Macallan knew all about the case and that Fraser had been prosecuting counsel, by all accounts doing a brilliant job – but then he always did. She decided to keep up the pretence that she wasn't interested in him. He carried on, and she squeezed her eyes shut, trying to figure out exactly what she wanted or hoped he would say. Mick Harkins' imaginary budgie flew past her face.

'I've got a conference on European legal assistance to attend in Edinburgh in a couple of weeks and wondered if I could buy you coffee, dinner or a drink when I'm there?'

She tried to keep it calm and slightly disinterested, but later in the evening she would finally admit to herself that the invitation was exactly what she'd wanted.

'I'm going away for a few days, Jack, but should be back then. When things take off in this job it tends to be intense to say the least, but I'll do my best.' She thought that sounded just about the right tone, then realised that the reflection in her hall mirror was punching the air.

'I'll call you before I arrive to let you know what the arrangements are and see what we can fix up.'

She said goodbye and put the phone down, excited and pleased. He was someone who'd torn her up and left her struggling against a tide of recriminations before she left Northern Ireland. But she'd learned to forgive, and if her life had taught her anything, it was that all men carried flaws – and the greater the man the greater the flaws.

She went back to packing her case, felt that warm sense of anticipation and decided to enjoy it. An hour later she closed the door behind her, climbed into the wreck with wheels that was all she could afford with her mortgage, and headed north.

Macallan's jaw dropped at the endless stretch of wild country she was discovering in the north west of Scotland. The sun shone through the chill air, and the light sparkled off Sutherland's damp hills and lochs. Every few miles she stopped the car to look at some new marvel, and the effect seemed to charge energy through her veins and make her feel young again. The quiet in the ancient landscape was proof that there was something apart from the worst parts of the human condition – that there existed a place in which peace could be found. This was a different country – a different world. She'd been to the Highlands, but this wild place had its own character, and she was overwhelmed by it. This was what she needed more than anything – the chance to escape from the city and the masses of people crowding each other's space; away from the memories shaped by deviant human behaviour; reaffirmation that life didn't have to be like that.

She drove the last couple of miles down into the small, busy fishing town of Kinlochbervie and felt her spirits lift. The tension melted from her shoulders, and she turned up the radio thumping out an old Stones classic and started to sing along like a teenager. That was all she wanted to do for the next week – just stare at the horizon and let her mind drift. A break from the pretence that she was above it all, the archetypal hard-bitten detective so admired in fiction, the reality being that she rarely had the opportunity to be what she was – a woman with needs and dreams. She couldn't remember the last time she'd danced or bought a dress for something or someone special. Too long.

She'd booked a small stone cottage near the sea and the owner, who lacked company herself, seemed to want to spend the rest of the day talking, but Macallan managed to ease her out of the door so she could be alone. She'd spent so many days and nights longing for human company, but that wasn't what she wanted here. She was tired, so tired it hurt, and her muscles felt like they'd been through a marathon.

After she'd piled wood onto the fire and watched it blaze, she poured a glass of wine and settled down to let the flames entertain her.

She woke up with a start a while later and took a few seconds to settle the panic in her breast. The fire had calmed down, but she realised she'd only drifted off for a few minutes and that it was her mobile, alerting her to an incoming text message, that had woken her up. The text was from Fraser telling her to enjoy her break and that he'd see her soon. The message ended with an 'x'. She smiled to herself, dropped another couple of logs onto the fire and sipped her wine. The cottage was warm now, and she just wanted to stay in the moment for as long as possible. In the end it was 2 a.m. before she eventually sank into bed.

Macallan hardly moved from the cottage for the next two days. She was exhausted, ached and needed to do nothing but forget the job.

8

Maggie Smith stared out of her window as the darkness fell over Edinburgh. The sky was a deep cobalt blue and cloudless, and the air blown down from the Arctic on freezing northerly winds had coated the world in a hard, glinting frost. It hadn't lifted all day, and the ancient heating system in the flats was barely coping with the temperature change. She had a cardigan pulled closed over a jersey she'd taken from Banjo's limited supply of warm clothes.

The windowpanes turned black as the sun disappeared for another day, and she could see the dark silhouette of her head looking back at her in her reflection. She couldn't see her eyes, but when she turned her head to the side she could see the altered shape of her shattered nose.

She dipped her face and looked down to avoid what she knew was there. Every time she looked away she would be back at a mirror ten minutes later, as if the damage would be gone and it might all have been a bad dream. She wasn't a vain person – couldn't be, given the life she led – but she was human, and the image she'd always known mattered to her, till those animals from Belfast had decided to use her to get to Banjo.

She looked round at him snoring in his chair, the telly blaring out some crap music channel. She wasn't naive – in fact she was probably a bit smarter than Banjo when it came to real life – so she understood they'd hurt her to send a message to the local dealers and the Flemings that a change was taking place. It happened every so often, but she knew that this was going to be messier than normal. She'd seen the look in Nelson's eyes and what had terrified her was that he wasn't the least bit angry – just cold and in control.

Dougie Fisher had laughed when he'd pushed the iron to the soft flesh of her breasts. She'd hardly been conscious, but Banjo had, and she'd never seen him as distressed as he was when he told her what had happened.

When she'd arrived at the hospital the pain had been unbearable till they put her under. Later, the doctor had told her that she could get surgery and everything would be fine.

'Fine.' She'd mouthed the word quietly. Then she'd lain there, wondering about what he had said. Why did they always say 'fine'? 'That'll be fuckin' shinin' bright,' she murmured as she remembered. How could she be fine when she was a part-time hooker, living with a league-division-four dealer who'd been reduced to a nervous wreck, caught in the crossfire between the maniacs from Belfast and the Flemings who were still to come? Her face and body had been defiled, she was still in shock, and yet she did something she tended to avoid: she thought about the future. That frightened her almost as much as Billy Nelson.

She remembered how she used to dream all day about what might lie ahead when she was a girl. She'd dreamed of children, a home of her own and a good man to hold her in the dark. Now the future was shapeless, and her imagination could not overcome the reality of what she was.

She pushed a soiled hankie gingerly under her nose to dry the constant streaming. She'd thought carefully about suicide but wasn't sure that life frightened her enough yet; she remembered someone telling her that when you really wanted to do it, the fear was of living rather than of death itself. Death was the goal.

She sat down opposite Banjo and felt tired in the marrow of her bones as she dozed off.

Banjo's phone chirped 'The Birdie Song' and he took time to realise where he was and what had woken him. He'd gulped down a few cans of extra-strong lager, and his brain felt like mush with the combination of anxiety, exhaustion and a variety of abused substances. Maggie was out for the count as he shoved the phone against his ear.

'We're just pulling up outside, Banjo, be up there in a minute.'

The sound of Danny Fleming's voice snapped him to full alert, and he reached for the cigarettes. Leaning over towards the sleeping woman, he pleaded, 'Maggie, wake up for fuck's sake. Danny's here, and he's got company.'

He grabbed her shoulders, shook her awake and her eyes widened when she took in what he was saying. They hadn't seen the Flemings in the time since their visit from the Belfast boys and had been dreading trying to explain what had happened. Banjo had decided to tell them everything and hope that their inevitable retaliation would take place well away from his arse. There would be a winner, and he'd already made up his mind who he was backing.

He snapped his head up when he heard the tap at the door. He always thought it was strange that a violent fucker like Danny Fleming was so light on the door.

A quick look through the peephole made Banjo groan inwardly; Danny was with his father, Joe, who was even more unstable than his bampot son and just couldn't do diplomacy. These were big, hard men, who were definitely not used to being on the losing side.

When Banjo opened the door, they walked in without waiting for the nicety of an invitation. Maggie looked at the floor, trying to hide her face and her shame, but Danny took her roughly by the chin and pulled her face up to examine it.

'What in the name of fuck happened here?' he asked, as if he cared – conveniently forgetting that he'd dished out some of the same to other women.

Banjo started shaking again as Joe Fleming took him by the throat and pushed him against the kitchen door, his face close enough for both of them to realise that they shared a problem with bad breath. He knew this was all part of the script; he had to get the story over to them and focus their attention on the real enemy.

'What the fuck you blamin' me for?' he asked. 'Come on, look at the lassie's face – that's what they did, and I fuckin' told them I worked for you and Danny.'

He would have licked their shoes if it would've calmed them down. His main issue was making sure they understood he was still in their camp and not working for the other team. In their world there were no contracts or loyalty pledges, it was just eat whoever was in front of you – even if they'd been your best friend for life.

The father and son sat down, pulled cigarettes out of Banjo's packet and waited for the story. He told them every detail as it happened, and knowing he had to get their anger channelled towards Nelson and his crew, he threw in the embellishment that they'd laughed when he told them he worked for the Flemings.

'They just pissed themselves, Joe, and said they'd enjoy seeing you in the Water o' Leith.' He kept his face as neutral as possible and relaxed as he saw their anger rise again, but not at him.

'Don't you worry – we'll sort the bastards for what they've done to Maggie,' said Danny.

On hearing this, Maggie had to bite her lip, thinking about what he'd done to other women, including Pauline Johansson. It was a relief to see Banjo was in control, and she had to admire his acting abilities.

The Flemings left without closing the door and told them the Belfast boys would be in Accident and Emergency in a couple of hours if they were lucky.

Banjo closed the door and lit another cigarette before picking up the phone and calling Nelson. 'That's the father and son on their way, and I guess they'll have baseball bats or something with them.' He looked at Maggie as he made the call, and she nodded in agreement, hating herself and her life but seeing no alternative.

What Banjo had left out in his account to the Flemings was that he was backing the other side; he wanted to live and knew the winners when he saw them. He put his arms round Maggie and prayed that he'd made the right move. He felt her body shake uncontrollably.

'God help us.'

The Flemings had already made their first and worst mistake. For years no one had taken them on to any real extent, and like any good fighter it was match practice that kept you at the top of the game. They'd gone soft and forgotten that in the criminal world you needed to keep your senses sharp and remember that in the city no one is more than a few yards from a rat. As they'd done so often in the past, the Flemings thought that all they needed to do was call on Nelson, give him a good seeing to and everything would go back to normal. They failed to remember they'd hit the top themselves by taking out the opposition who'd made the same mistake.

Danny Fleming was angry and drove the BMW the half-mile to the block where the Belfast man was waiting for them and parked up outside. They stared up at the fourth floor where Nelson lived and saw the lights on. Joe Fleming pulled out his phone and called Banjo. He'd ordered him to check that Nelson was in, using the excuse that he needed to make arrangements to pick up gear from them.

'Are they in?'

'Just called and Billy's there on his own. The other boys are out on the piss.' Banjo tried to keep his voice steady to cover the lie.

Joe was pleased. 'Excellent, we'll take care of them later.'

They walked round to the boot, pulled out a pickaxe handle and Danny took charge of a twelve-pound mash hammer. They already had their knives stowed inside their jackets.

They walked into the flats then took the stairs to avoid any noise, but by the third flight Joe was blowing too hard. He'd made another mistake – he was just too fucking old for going toe to toe with younger men. Certainly not men who'd served in the UVF or the Army. Danny shook his head, realising that his father was human, and his reputation had been gained in a time that was long gone now.

'Jesus, are you up for this?' Danny mocked his father.

'Shut the fuck up. I'll show you in a minute whether I'm up for it,' Joe gasped and stopped to catch his wheezing breath.

When they got to the fourth floor they stood at the door, settling themselves down, and listened for any movement inside. The stair lighting was out so the landing was in near darkness when Joe nodded to his son to do the door.

Danny smiled, excited at the thought of handing out a double dose to Nelson or maybe even killing the arrogant bastard. As he always told people – and particularly his victims – 'No one fucks with the Flemings.'

Danny had the hammer on full backswing when he felt the hard end of the Uzi pressed against the back of his head. Joe managed to get out, 'What the fuck?' when he felt the other machine gun being stabbed into his ribcage. The sound of harsh Belfast tones told father and son just about all they needed to know, and Dougie Fisher gave them their next instructions.

'Now put down the hammer, Danny boy, and just knock at the door. No need to break the fucker open. Billy's expecting you.' Fisher laughed quietly.

Andy Clark took the heel of the gun and whacked it against the back of Joe's ear, opening up a three-inch cut that bled onto his jacket. The older man gasped with the shock, but it had the desired effect and his son did exactly as he was told. He knocked at the door in that same quiet tap that had puzzled Banjo.

Nelson opened the door and looked pleased. 'Come in, boys. It's nice to see you. We've heard a lot about you, and so far you're living up to all the descriptions. A couple of useless fuckers living on their reputations. Tape them up.' He spat the last three words.

Clark, Fisher and Rob McLean got to work on them and by the time they'd finished the Flemings could barely breathe with the amount of duct tape wrapped round the lower half of their faces. Their hands were secured behind them and swelling from the pressure. Joe was scared in a way that he hadn't known since the days his father used to come in drunk and visit him in his room. He'd already worked out that Banjo had fucked them over and that he would only have done that if he was more frightened of Nelson than him. Banjo had seen what Joe and his idiot son had missed – these boys were playing to win and they weren't about to give quarter to someone who'd arrived at their door with a mash hammer and a pickaxe handle.

Sweat poured down his face even though the flat was cold, his ulcer springing to life and aching like a hot stone in his gut. He looked at his son, whose eyes were filled with confusion, and he realised they were done for. A few people would pretend that they'd had some redeeming qualities, but the truth was that in a month they'd be forgotten. The drugs and crime trades have to move on, and the competition means there's no time to look back. He closed his eyes and prayed, even though he'd never considered a god other than himself for decades.

Nelson sat and smoked quietly as the boys did their work. When they were done he looked satisfied and smiled at old man Fleming.

'There's no need to tell you what happens now I suppose, and I'm not great on speeches, but you two are finished. If I was a gentler man then maybe I could mess you up a bit, but we all know that you or the rest of that Catholic family you belong to would come back at us. I'm guessing that you're Catholics given the boy's name. Is that right, Danny?'

Danny nodded like a child trying to please his elders, as if it would make any difference, and Nelson continued: 'You know what we Loyalist boys are like about Catholics trying to kill us. Doesn't get you a lot of brownie points where we come from, does it, boys?'

His team smiled and muttered in agreement, and Joe saw the bloodlust in their faces, the primeval need to do unto their enemies what had been intended for them.

'Take the old man first.' Nelson lit another cigarette as Joe was helped up then guided out of the lounge and walked through the hall into what was no more than a box room. When they opened the door there was only the hall light behind him and the room was empty, but he saw enough to try screaming though nothing escaped from his throat beyond a dull moaning sound. The walls and the floor had been covered with plastic sheeting stapled tight and sealed so no blood, bone or bodily fluids would stain the room for some nosey fucker from the scenes-of-crime department to find.

He fell to his knees and prayed again as the pickaxe handle he'd brought with him collided with the base of his skull. It was only part of what was inflicted on him, but thankfully he knew nothing after the first blow.

Nelson sat quietly staring at the television with the volume up loud. He didn't hear a sound, and after about twenty minutes Clark came into the room wearing only underpants.

What struck Danny when he saw Clark was that his face was spattered with blood, and he managed to work out that Clark had removed a boiler suit or protective clothing before he came back into the room to get him. He passed out cold, which meant that when he was carried through to the box room he wasn't able to see his father's mortal remains. Danny did come round but only for a very short time before the blows to his head and body dropped him into a dark pool of oblivion.

Human beings possess a remarkable capacity to survive the most horrific of injuries, though there are times when mind and body get it wrong and it would be far better to die, and while the boys had been thorough with Danny, they would soon discover they hadn't quite achieved their goal.

Nelson stayed in the flat and watched the football

highlights as if nothing of interest had taken place that night. He'd known men both in the military and the paramilitaries back home who reached a high state of sexual excitement when there was a killing. But Billy felt almost nothing and sometimes had to act out a form of anger to look what he thought was normal. He felt dead inside. The only things that troubled him were his dreams, when his thoughts turned to the bombing he'd witnessed at Frizzell's fish shop as a boy, or the carnage in Helmand province. That really did disturb him, and he felt his chest tighten whenever he thought about what had been done to his own people.

As Nelson watched a repeat of Wayne Rooney scoring a classic goal for Manchester United, the rest of his team were driving the Flemings out into the country to their final resting place. They'd already scouted the area to make sure they could pull off the road without attracting attention, and the spot they'd chosen was close to the Borders and perfect for the job. Casual walkers were unlikely to stray off road and find it by chance.

They lifted Joe out first and in half an hour he was in the ground with space beside him for Danny. They swallowed a beer then got Danny out of the car. And that's when he chose to moan and startled his pall-bearers so much they dropped him.

He groaned again.

Fisher saw the funny side of it and laughed nervously. 'Can you fuckin' believe it? The bastard's still breathing after what we did to him. Come on – let's put him to bed.'

They heaved Danny up again and threw him in the hole. He was nearer death than life, but he opened his eyes, and the last thing he saw was two of his tormentors urinating into his grave. Clark picked up the spade and threw a load of soil onto his face, and Danny felt some of it fall into his nostrils as he suffocated to death and joined his father.

Around midnight Banjo took a call from Nelson, who never mentioned anything about the Flemings – and Banjo wasn't stupid enough to ask. Nelson told him to order what gear he needed every Monday and it would be supplied to him by the Wednesday.

Later on he took another call from Danny's partner asking if he knew where Danny and old Joe were, so Banjo said that he'd seen Joe and Danny but didn't know where they'd gone after that. They were gone; in one short, violent act the Flemings had been gutted by their own stupidity, and the criminal hierarchy in Edinburgh changed until the next contender arrived on the scene.

Banjo was asleep and knackered when the phone dragged him awake again later. He looked at the clock and saw it was 2.30 a.m. It took him a moment to work out that it was still night-time.

'Fuck me, who's this now?' he said as he picked up the phone, ready to blast the arse of whoever it was. Unfortunately it was Nelson again. He did his best to sound pleased but failed miserably. Not that Nelson gave a fuck.

'The boys have been busy and need a bit of rest and relaxation, if you know what I mean. I've got drink in, but they're young men and need a bit more than a drink tonight. It's been busy what with one thing and another.'

Banjo sensed where this was going, closed his eyes and said no – but only to himself.

'It's a bit late for them to go wandering round the town at this time of night looking for females, so why don't you send Maggie over here pronto. Her nose is a fuckin' sight, but beggars can't be choosers. Make sure she has a good wash first.'

Banjo couldn't make the words to reply.

'Banjo, did you hear me, or do we have to come round there?'

'I'll get her, Billy. No problem.'

He put the phone down and walked through into the darkness of their bedroom and woke the woman he loved.

9

When Macallan opened her eyes it was well after dawn, and the first thing she saw was a clear blue sky. *Okay, Grace*, she thought, *let's do this – let's get going.*

She smiled at the order, got ready quickly and after a light breakfast set off in the car along the single-track road to Blairmore. There were few other cars in the parking area as she pulled on her walking boots and headed off over the moorland for Sandwood Bay. All the bumf claimed it was one of the best beaches in Europe, and the bonus was that it was over four miles of walking to get there so the only visitors were the determined ones.

The track took her across fairly unspectacular moorland, but the sun shone, and the light glittered in a way she'd never seen before. There were lochs everywhere, and the reflected sunshine formed on thousands of tiny wavelets that almost dazzled her. Despite the cool December air, the sweat trickled down her back, but eventually her breathing eased, and her skin began to glow with the exertion.

She met a couple wearing his and her adventure gear who appeared to have enough equipment to conquer

Mount Everest. Macallan had already decided that the beach probably wouldn't live up to its billing, but they assured her that it would be worth the effort. She didn't really believe them. The legends said that the bay was haunted, that the waters round Cape Wrath were littered with the bones of ancient ships and sailors, and she could feel the intense isolation of the place.

She looked to her right to Sandwood Loch and the ruins of an old house. Macallan had read her guidebooks and liked the story that the ghost of a long-dead mariner would come to the house on stormy nights and tap on the window.

When she walked over the last rise, she wasn't prepared for the sight of Sandwood Bay, which opened up before her like a cinema screen. There was nothing in front of her but the horizon, stretching up to the cold northern waters, and a mile and half of almost pink sand. Even though it was near calm, heavy rollers roared towards the beach, leaving a hissing trail as they crashed and melted into the sand. It was as if the sea was taking a deep breath as the depleted waves ran back to the deep, crackling over the endless small hard stones.

Macallan sat on a flat rock, poured some hot coffee from her flask and let the sights and sounds wash over her. She wanted to spend a few minutes there before she walked downhill onto the beach to take it all in, because she would never have this feeling of wonder about the view again. It was marvellous – a daylight dream – the power of the northern waters and the remoteness of a place that deserved to be seen and appreciated.

At the southern end of the bay she saw the huge sea stack Am Buachaille – the Herdsman – fully deserving of its Gaelic name. It seemed to stand guard over the bay, powerful and forbidding.

After a time, Macallan headed down to the beach,

running the last few yards down the smooth side of one of the grass-topped dunes. She took her shoes off and felt the clean sand smother her feet and work her leg muscles.

Feeling the warmth in the sun, but only just, she stripped off to her shorts and decided to try the water. She sprinted the last few yards and fell into the foaming spume.

Jesus Christ! She would have shouted it but the cold had literally taken her breath away. Belatedly she realised that the waters were a long way from the Med, which was the last place she'd dipped her toes in the sea. It might be sunny, but this was Scotland, and it was winter. She felt as if someone had shoved her in a freeze dryer.

As the upper half of her body came clear of the water, she gasped and wondered for a moment whether her lungs were too cold to ever draw in another breath. It was a struggle, but she waded as fast as her legs could manage back to the beach, still gasping with the shock of the cold water.

Grabbing her rucksack, she pulled out the small hand towel she'd brought and rubbed heat back into her skin. Soon she felt the prickling rush of blood and a wonderful feeling of heat spread through her, as if she was glowing inside. Macallan laughed at her own naivety in forgetting that the waters there could stop the heart – she'd imagined crawling gracefully through the waves with the dolphins diving round her and a romantic picture to remember, and she was thankful that no one witnessed her unladylike exit from the waves.

After walking back to the sand dunes, Macallan lay down away from the cool breeze and let her mind drift away till she slept. It was over an hour before the sound of gulls calling above gradually brought her back up from a dream. She spent the day on the beach and by habit periodically checked her phone, but there was still no signal. No one could reach her.

The fresh air and exercise helped Macallan get yet another good night's sleep, and she was beginning to feel more her old self again when she awoke the next day. After a late breakfast spent perusing one of her guidebooks, she packed an overnight bag and set off, in no hurry at all, along the single-track A road that led to the north coast via the beautiful Kyle of Durness. She stopped every now and then to enjoy the views, glad she wasn't being controlled by any kind of timetable.

It was almost dark when she arrived in Tongue, where she stopped for a drink in a small hotel. The locals were chatty, and to avoid unwelcome discussion of her real job she told them she was a civil servant on a walking holiday. A room was available so she booked in, had a quick shower and went back down to the bar, where she was invited to join in playing pool. Later on, when the live music started, she knew she'd made the right decision to stay. The music was wild and the drinkers joined in dancing, including Macallan, who soaked up the night.

Two hundred and forty miles south of the hotel in Tongue, Billy Nelson tried to sleep. He sweated; he turned; he drifted in and out of dreams. His nights were often haunted by images of the past – the young boy feeling the heatwave from the bomb blast on the Shankill, turning his face to the source of the explosion and watching frightened people running towards him, crying for help. The strange calm after the blast interrupted by moaning and the sounds of building confusion and anger. He was only a boy – what could he do?

He woke, drank a glass of water and lay down again on the damp sheets, only to drift halfway towards sleep again. This time he was walking along a rock-strewn road in Afghanistan; there was only Billy and his best mate, a poor working-class boy like him who'd joined the Army to see the world. Billy couldn't understand why they were on their own, and he was frightened. Somehow he realised he was in a dream and tried to find a way back to the conscious world, because something he couldn't see was trying to hurt him.

He heard his friend call his name and looked round to see a small IED take his leg clean off from the knee. He'd just walked where his friend had walked and survived.

He tried to pick his injured friend up, but he was too heavy and insurgents were closing in to kill them both. He sucked in a lungful of air and it woke him as if he'd been punched in the chest.

Billy was soaked. He pulled his legs over the side of the bed and reached for his cigarettes. His nights were following a familiar script where sleep was a struggle; he was beginning to hate the dark, with these visits from his demons; all the uncertainty about what he was and what he was doing. He wondered whether one single person actually cared about him. Why would they? He was a killer – a sadistic bastard struggling to find something to give him satisfaction or excitement or just purpose. He felt dead with women, and it was only in the brief moments he saw terror in another person's eyes that he felt something that might have been pleasure. That was all that was left to him: power had become his drug, and like most drugs the shame gnawed at his thoughts.

The clock showed 3.30 a.m. and he remembered someone saying the only people working at this time of night were policemen and prostitutes. He walked through to the kitchen, made some black tea and dumped four laden spoonfuls of sugar into the swirling brew. He'd learned to take it sweet in the Army and wished he was back there – back with the men who'd been his family; who felt like him and understood. He thought again about the blood rage that had made him pulp the Afghan boy half to death. That bastard had cost him his career. 'Fuck him. Hope the cunt never walks again,' he whispered into the darkness.

He'd seen it in Iraq and Afghanistan – the look in their eyes; the hate when all they were trying to do was get rid of those mad bastard insurgents. He hated them, having seen so many of his mates wounded and killed. Some of the injuries were the stuff of horror films and rarely reported in the press. It made him angry, and he felt his chest tighten thinking about the politicians who'd ordered them into war zones without a plan. The dead were reported and the closed coffins were driven past respectful crowds throwing flowers. The television didn't show the faces blown off, the screaming wrecks trying to stuff their guts back into their bodies.

'I'll pay these fuckers back,' he murmured. 'They'll never forget Billy Nelson.'

He lay back down on the bed and stared at the ceiling, praying for untroubled sleep. The gnawing pain that he guessed must be stress started up again in his stomach. It was happening more and more now.

10

Only eight miles from Nelson's bedroom, Maggie Smith walked along the cobbled streets of The Shore by the Water of Leith. She wasn't working, and she definitely didn't need the company of some frustrated punter whose wife didn't understand him. She was still sore when she walked and cursed those bastards from Belfast for the way they'd treated her, using her like an animal and then kicking her out onto the street. Nelson was a puzzle though – he'd just watched with that stupid grin as they'd hurt her over and over again. Whatever drug they'd taken that night had made them burn with energy.

'I wonder if he's a bender?' She nodded at her own whispered question. 'That must be it, the bastard.' She was sure of one thing though – they were a sick bunch, and she'd seen her share of sickos in her time.

What had really hurt was seeing the look in Banjo's eyes when she got home. He was helpless – useless – and he knew it. She never spoke a word to him – what was there to say? She'd slept on the settee since then. That was the night she'd lost her fear of dying. She'd finally discovered that there were far worse things in life than death.

She touched the fresh bump above her eye where Fisher had whacked her for good measure, as if she'd needed any more after the mess they'd made of her nose.

'Bastards, bastards, bastards,' she sobbed quietly.

A police car pulled up, and the old beat man rolled down the window. He was alright; she'd known him for years, and he'd once saved her skin from a half-mad drunk who'd tried to rob her after she'd left a generous punter.

'You okay there? Want a lift home before you freeze to death?'

'I'm okay, Charlie, just need a walk, that's all. The punters are all wrapped up next to their good ladies so I'll be away shortly.'

'Take care then, Maggie.' He rolled the window back up and went off to find a warm cup of something.

She walked on and noticed that she was down to her last cigarette. *Might as well have that*, she thought, a wry smile crossing her face – smoking wasn't going to kill her anyway.

She dragged on the cigarette and walked on into the semi-dark lane that was Timber Bush, the site of the old timber market when Leith was a great port, welcoming ships from all over Europe. At the corner where the lane turns sharp left towards Tower Street, she walked into a small private car park, then squatted down against the wooden fence, leaned back and decided to get it done while the fag was still burning.

She was sick, tired and weary, and she cursed Nelson and most of the other men she'd known. Not Banjo – he'd done his best, but he was as big a failure as she was. No way was her future going to end up with her sitting on a bench with him, drinking Special Brew at 9 a.m. like the winos she used to watch, talking to each other without listening, graduates from smack to cheap cider and oblivion.

She wasn't afraid any more; she just wanted to be on her way and leave the life she'd lost interest in. She wished she had time to say goodbye to her friend Pauline Johansson, but this was her time – it couldn't wait.

She sat down and was thankful that the ground was dry. *Can't end up with a wet arse tonight,* she thought. *Had too many of them in my time.*

She managed to smile at her own joke, but it held a certain truth. She'd brought Banjo's gear as well as her own; left him knocked out in his favourite seat, the telly blaring away as always to no one in particular.

She rolled up her sleeve and cooked up the hit as she sucked greedily on the cigarette. A mongrel dog trotted up to her, staring at her for a while before it seemed to decide it wasn't welcome and moved away into the darkness again.

She pushed the needle into her arm as someone in the area, who obviously had their windows wide open, put on The Proclaimers full blast.

'Jesus, what a thoughtless bastard,' she whispered, thinking it kind of summed up the world she lived in. All those thoughtless bastards who'd come her way.

She took the massive hit, hardly moving a muscle till she died, and the last sounds she heard were the stirring words of 'Sunshine on Leith'. It had been one of her favourite songs.

At 5.30 a.m. the patrol car sat quietly, the two occupants getting themselves ready to head back to the station and sign off for the night. Then bed. Nothing like slipping between the sheets after a night shift – two seconds and you were out. It had been one of the quietest turns of the year, and the two policemen had yawned half the night away. Apart from bumping into Maggie Smith earlier in the evening, there had been nothing to lift the boredom.

87

Charlie, the older of the two men, had only a few years to go till retirement and dreamed about never having to do another night shift. He'd worked in Leith most of his days and had just about seen and done it all as he'd watched the place transform itself from a down-at-heel but proud corner of the city with its own identity to a trendy village by the docks. The truth was that he missed the old Leith but guessed it was because he was getting past it all.

'I'm too old for this shite,' he said needlessly to the younger man, Tony, who'd heard it a hundred times already in his short career but wasn't big enough, brave enough or daft enough to tell Charlie so.

Tony was still in his probation, after training as a teacher then deciding he'd rather face the street than the nutters in class every day. He loved being a cop, as most do in the early years – didn't even want to take days off or complain about night shifts – and despite Charlie's moaning, he looked up to the older man, who was a bit of a legend in his own way.

'You'll soon be retired. Then no more nights.' He couldn't think of anything else to say.

'I used to be like you, but you'll change,' Charlie said needlessly again.

The young man had started the engine and put her in gear to head back to the old station at Leith when the call came across.

'Woman lying unconscious in Timber Bush on The Shore – can you attend?'

Tony was happy that they had something to do, but Charlie was pissed off. 'Fuck it!' he muttered before telling his partner to, 'Get a fuckin' move on, Stirling.'

Tony had no idea who Stirling was but was sure it was yet another sign of the age gap between them.

It was still dark, the December night air was cold and a light drizzle made the cobbled streets around the Water of Leith shine like black glass. The patrol car pulled up near to Timber Bush then crawled along the lane to the corner at Tower Place. In the small car park they could see the figure of a woman, sitting, back against the fence with her knees bent. He hoped silently that she was just a pisshead sleeping it off, but Charlie had been doing it for so long he knew otherwise. The wiring in his head had already made the connection between the woman in the close and their short encounter with Maggie Smith. The old man who'd found her stood with his dog at the entrance, eager to tell the beat men what had happened.

Charlie wasn't really listening and gave Tony his orders. 'Get a brief statement and personal details from this gentleman and I'll check what we have here.'

He walked softly towards Maggie as if it was possible to disturb her. He knelt down beside her, shone his pocket torch at her face then noticed the needle and works lying next to her legs. Her sleeve was still rolled up.

'You've done it this time, Maggie. I should have known something was up,' he said quietly. Nevertheless, Tony and the old man heard him, and they looked towards the two figures in the car park and wondered what exactly he'd said to the woman.

Charlie was annoyed at himself – he'd always had sharp instincts, he'd known Maggie was out too late and he'd seen the state of her face. They'd had a fuck-all-happening night and he'd missed it completely – or maybe he just couldn't be bothered any more.

Tony had let the old man and his dog go on their way and came up to stand behind his partner.

'I'm too old for this shite,' he said again, and Tony knew he meant it this time.

'Guess that'll be the end of her career then,' Tony said, trying a bit of the black humour hard-nosed cops in films used all the time. He realised he'd got it wrong when

Charlie stood up and gave him a look that told him just how badly he'd fucked up.

'Why don't you shut the fuck up till you have something useful to say? Get onto the station and call this in,' he snapped.

'Sorry.' He was hurt by the older man's words and would have done anything to take the joke back.

'Listen.' Charlie said it tight-mouthed. 'This still-young woman didn't get a break her whole life. I knew the family – the mother and father were just shite, and she was out on the streets from no age. Shite life, only knew shite people and ended up selling what she had to shite punters. Have a hard look at her, son.'

Charlie switched on the torch again and shone it on the woman at their feet. 'She'd have been lucky if she had one really happy moment in all her life. Just remember that, and show her some respect.'

They called it in, and a couple of bored CID officers came and took over the paperwork side because she'd been found in the open and there'd have to be a post-mortem. Once the scene had been examined and photographs taken, the two beat men took the body to the mortuary and then processed the eternally despised paperwork.

Their next job was always the hard one – at least that's how Charlie felt – and he'd just done it too many times. Telling the nearest and dearest. He remembered the first one: a seventeen-year-old boy who'd been the pillion passenger on a motorbike doing eighty when they'd hit the back of a parked car. By some miracle the rider had survived, but the boy had come off and skidded along the road face down. One of the old cynics described it as something out of a *Tom and Jerry* fight scene. Charlie had the job of telling his parents that they'd lost their only son. It had been a Friday night, so the old man had been out for a few beers and was more pissed than sober. They'd had to get him out of bed, and while it had hit his wife like a shockwave, the old man hadn't been able to get it through his drink-addled brain. Charlie had never forgotten the expression on the man's face as it had gradually sunk in that his namesake was lying in a mortuary fridge.

Banjo was up and about, still wondering what had happened to his gear, when he heard Tony knock on the door. He was seriously pissed at Maggie for taking off in the middle of the night without letting him know, but he couldn't get too angry, as he knew she was in a bad place after what Nelson's team had done to her. Banjo was still struggling with his own sense of futility, and he couldn't stand the way Maggie had looked at him since she'd been beaten in front of his eyes.

He opened the door, and the sight of two uniforms told him things had just reached an even lower point than he'd thought possible.

He recognised Charlie as a Leith cop from the times he'd been down there when Maggie was working the street. Maggie always said he was alright and didn't hassle the girls unless he had to.

'It's Maggie, isn't it?' he said.

'Can we come in?'

They told him as much as they could and what he'd have to do. Banjo sat quietly with his face in his hands, occasionally taking a drag on his cigarette and shaking his head. He asked a couple of questions, and Tony wrote down the details needed for the form filling when they got back to base.

'Fuckin' bastards. Fuckin' Irish bastards,' he muttered.

Charlie heard Banjo say it twice. 'What was that, Banjo?' he asked.

Banjo just shook his head and said almost nothing

more, but Charlie knew it could mean something so he'd pass it on to the suits.

When he'd seen them out, Banjo ran a hand over his face and sat down heavily in his chair. Maggie was gone, and there was nothing he could do to bring her back – he couldn't rewind the clock to before those bastards had knocked on the door, or even to when they'd phoned up telling him to send her over like she was something off a room-service menu. He tried to think if there was anyone he needed to tell and realised that no one gave a fuck except him. There was Pauline Johansson, but she'd been the only one, probably because her life had been just about as shite as Maggie's.

It was after 11 a.m. and both policemen felt the aching weariness in their joints as they changed in the locker room. Charlie had hardly spoken to Tony since his words in the close. The young man was down and hurt like a dog. He'd thought himself a man when he joined the force and had felt like a kid ever since. He just wanted to get back to his flat and hide under the sheets.

He was pulling on his jacket when he felt his partner's hand on his shoulder.

'Come on, son. We're going for a beer and then I'll tell you a story,' Charlie said quietly, a tired smile on his face. He liked Tony, liked him a lot, and knew that in a few years he'd be the business while Charlie was off tending his tomatoes or whatever the fuck.

'A beer at this time of the morning?' Tony realised again that he should have just kept his mouth zipped. He tried to pull it back. 'Only if I'm paying.'

'That was always going to be the way. You must have heard from the other guys that I never buy. I just tell stories and entertain. Everyone else pays for the pleasure of my company – except that torn-faced wife I've got indoors.'

His smile widened, and Tony felt relief wash through him.

The local watering hole had been the station haunt forever and at least longer than Charlie had been in the job. It had gone from extra basic in the old Leith days to candles on the table and ridiculous prices for the privilege of the warm glow. Charlie cursed the fact that he couldn't get a decent pie to go with his beer now, but it was just another reminder that the clock only went forward. Pies were not fashionable pub grub any more.

Tony got them in and sat down opposite the older man, who was looking all his years – the bags under his eyes seemed to be even heavier than normal. The term hangdog came to mind, although Charlie tended to describe his looks as etched by the pain of public service and always finished off by saying 'the ungrateful bastards'. He gulped half the beer in one go and smacked his lips; Charlie loved his beer.

'When I was your age I was just like you. Trying to play a part, trying to be what I thought I was supposed to be or copying some TV detective who'd never seen a real angry man in his puff.' He took another sip, and it was clear that Tony was just to listen, not speak.

'I want to tell you a story. I was on nights, only had a couple of years in the job and thought I was God's gift to the service. I watched the experienced guys and tried to learn from them. What I didn't realise was that sometimes what looks like a good line or action just covers the fact that the man's an arse. The sharp talkers, the cynics, the ones that hate everyone in the job usually turn out to be about as much good as the smoking ban, which I regard as an affront as it's ruined my pub time.'

He nodded, holding up the empty glass. Tony hadn't taken his first sip yet but took the prompt and had Charlie refilled.

'Anyway, one night I had this call to a sudden death, and it was routine – guy with a bad ticker had died in his chair. The guy I worked with at the time hated dealing with bodies – said he'd go back to the station and do the paperwork if I took the man to the mortuary. That was a good deal for me so I got a driver and the van and off we went. The mortuary wasn't manned at night, and we always lodged the bodies ourselves. That place used to spook some people out, down in the darkest corner of the old Cowgate. I sometimes wonder if they were having a laugh when they built it there. Anyway, it wasn't unusual to find other policemen there with bodies, and on that night, when I arrived at the door, there was a light on. I went in and found one of the fridges was open, and there was a priest giving the last rites, or whatever the fuck they do to one of the guests. I had a blether with him. He was the old Irish priest from St Patrick's just up the road. Turns out the body he was with was an old wino who'd been found dead in the street by a couple of beat men – there were a lot of winos round that area at the time. It struck me that no one would have known if that priest had just stayed in his bed. He got the call in the middle of the night and went down to the mortuary on his own to carry out his religious obligations. This was for a wino – not a friend in the world, absolutely filthy – and yet that old priest believed that he should get the same respect as anyone else. He did his duty and thought nothing of it. The man who died wasn't a wino to him; he was a human being and deserved respect. I never forgot him. I'm not a religious man, but I used to call in and see him from time to time. He thought he was a simple man and deserved nothing apart from doing what he did. He believed it made a difference and you know what? It did.'

Charlie sat back and looked at his young friend. 'Just remember that story. Now it's time for bed, son, so off you go – we're back out there tonight.'

11

Macallan opened her eyes and looked at the clock – 9.30 a.m. She couldn't believe how well she'd slept again. The night came back to her and she smiled, despite the desert that was the inside of her mouth. It had been more fun than she'd had in a long time but innocent enough. Lots of music in the hotel bar, singing songs she didn't know the words to and laughing at some very politically incorrect stories.

She ran a hand over her face. She needed breakfast, and the hotel owner had promised her a full, artery-clogging plate when she was ready.

The shower brought her back to life, and she promised herself a return when she had the time. The fact that she'd not checked in with the office for days chewed at her guilt centres, even though McGovern had told her that he'd call her if necessary. She had a feeling he might not be making that call because he was trying to be kind to her.

'Eat first and then call him, 'cause there's bound to be a problem,' she said into the mirror as she tried to waken up her face.

The breakfast lived up to the owner's description and though she enjoyed it she felt guilty as soon as she'd finished the last scrap of bacon. She sipped her tea, surprised she had almost no trace of a hangover and realised the combination of fresh air, open spaces and no office was doing her good. She wished she had a month. But that would have to come later, and Macallan forced herself to make the call from her room. She got McGovern almost straightaway, and it was good to hear his voice – it was always calm around him.

'Sorry, Jimmy, the phones are almost useless up here, been in a hotel for the night so I'm on a landline. How's it going?'

'Nothing we can't handle at the moment. There is stuff developing, but it's in bits at the moment.

'Joe and Danny Fleming have gone missing, and according to a couple of informants they're probably dead rather than off to Magaluf for an impromptu weekend on the piss. Divisional CID have it, but the Fleming clan won't even answer the door to the police. It's got a bad smell, and if the Flemings really are toast it has to be a heavy team that have taken the chance. More is coming in about the Belfast boys cutting into the drug business and leaving a few casualties about the place. Too early to say that there's a connection, but we're working various confidential sources, and no one's making an official complaint against these boys.

'Other than that, there's a lot of routine stuff – might be something, might be nothing. One of Pauline Johansson's buddies from the street, Maggie Smith, overdosed last night and was found dead at The Shore.'

Macallan knew Maggie's name but hadn't met her. 'I have to go and see Pauline,' she said. 'I haven't been for a few weeks.'

'The last thing is probably not going to make your day,

but they've placed a new DCI with us to fill the vacancy and I'm guessing they didn't tell you before you left?'

Macallan tried not to sound annoyed but not consulting her meant internal politics – it never ended.

'Who is it? Go on.'

He heard the tension in her voice. 'Lesley Thompson.'

'Isn't she one of O'Connor's protégées?'

'The very same. I'm talking out of school and she's senior in rank, but she's a career shooting star – father was a chief constable south of the border and she's been carefully prepared for stardom. My concern is she's never been anywhere near an investigation – we just have her so she can get a tick in the box.'

'Okay, I'll see the chief super when I get back but no doubt there'll be some story that it's a great idea. I'll get stuck into him, and it'll go in one ear then straight out the other. I see the hand of Mr O'Connor in this one.'

'One of my spies reckons O'Connor went easy on the chief super's nephew who's a PC on the south side. Apparently he got into a bit of bother, pissed and ended up rolling about with some punter in a bus shelter. He's still in his probation and should have been emptied, but O'Connor saw mileage in it and it was all smoothed over off record. One law for some, and I guess you know the rest.'

'Christ, that's all we need – a plant from professional standards. I'll pick up my stuff back at the cottage then I'll come down the road in the morning and be in the office first thing Monday. Holiday's over.'

Macallan settled up at the hotel and felt heavy as she dumped her overnight bag in the back of the car. She felt the problems in Edinburgh drawing her back like a magnet. The short break had been a relief, but now she was going back to pressure and dealing with the worst side of humanity. Most of the time it was the nutters committing crime, but now she had to deal with nutters inside the job making her life even more difficult than it was already.

As she drove the lovely coastal route back to Kinlochbervie, she promised that her next break would be a longer one and she'd come with someone. She'd show them Sandwood Bay in all its glory. *That's if it's not pissing rain*, she thought, grinning at her own joke – she knew she'd been incredibly lucky with the weather.

'If you have to invite Mick Harkins along as a drinking buddy, well that's how it'll be, Grace, my girl,' she said to her reflection in the rear-view mirror. She put on Mumford & Sons just as loud as she could stand it and enjoyed the trip back round the coast to Kinlochbervie.

12

Billy Nelson knew his military tactics and had learned the hard way from Basra to Helmand province. Press home the advantage. He'd made his first move – now it was time to nail down what he'd started, and in his world there were always other predators looking for signs of weakness. He'd recognised it in Joe Fleming and spotted the soft underbelly of his arrogance. The rest of the Flemings were badly wounded, not completely out of it but the message had been sent to the other players that things were about to change. Nelson or his team couldn't shout it too loudly, but it was handy if that's what people thought.

The issue was that without bodies, other theories were spinning out of control among the bad men out there – not just in Edinburgh but in Glasgow, where the Flemings had sourced their gear. Nelson was the clear favourite – all the evidence pointed to him – but the Flemings weren't the most popular people in town so maybe, just maybe, some other team had taken their shot at the title. Nelson needed to send out another message and make it clear – without a public declaration of who was doing what.

They had to keep quiet about what had happened to the Flemings because at some stage the local constabulary would come sniffing round and any evidence of a double murder could land them some serious prison time. As it stood there was little or nothing that could stick to them – they'd taken care to burn everything they'd worn that night and had torched the wheels that had been used to move the father and son to their final resting place. What was left to do was handle a few more dealers who needed to be forced over to the Belfast team, and there were still plenty who would work for what was left of the Flemings till someone told them different.

Most of the locals didn't give a fuck who they worked for as long as they made their cut. It didn't make a difference. As far as they were concerned, whoever was running the show would likely be a horrible bastard anyway, or how else would they have got in that position? But they were wrong. Edinburgh had been pretty stable for a long time, but outside the city a new breed of horrible bastard was taking shape, and Nelson ticked all the boxes in the curriculum vitae for the modern, violent criminal.

He sat in his rented BMW and blew a lungful of smoke out into the damp night air. The four Belfast boys were watching the front door of a block of flats that looked like all the other blocks in the area. On the fourth floor they could see the kitchen light on in the flat where Andy 'Cue Ball' Ross spent pretty much all of his existence – except for when he was picking up his gear from the Flemings (or at least from the Flemings that were still alive).

Cue Ball had earned his handle while he was doing his second stretch for possession with intent to supply. For no particular reason, a warder had decided he enjoyed giving Cue Ball a hard time, but he should have realised like everyone else had that the man was a psycho. His mother and father had known it soon after the pet cat they'd bought for their infant boy had died mysteriously. Cue Ball had strangled it, but they didn't know that at the time, although they had wondered why he wasn't in the least bit concerned. When the replacement cat went the same way, they'd known there was a problem, especially as he'd taken the time to cut its throat so he could watch it bleed.

The mistake that most people made with Cue Ball, as did this particular prison screw, was that he looked like the original eight-stone weakling, so he got picked on till his wiser contemporaries realised that his tormentors all seemed to end up in the hospital. The screw thought plain Andy Ross as he was at that time wasn't up to it, but Cue Ball had set him up perfectly, creating a diversion so that he could get the screw where he wanted and attack him with a sock filled with three snooker balls – including the cue ball that would give him his name. The screw never worked again and ate all of his meals through a straw after that. No one saw a thing and no one was convicted, though everyone knew what had happened; the screw had been despised by his colleagues as well as the guests, so it all worked in Cue Ball's favour.

Cue Ball was another local dealer on the same level as Banjo, and as far as Nelson was aware was still onside with what was left of the Fleming business, which according to his information was being run by Joe Fleming's wife. She'd put it about that what had happened was down to Billy Nelson and that it wasn't over.

'That fuckin' Fleming woman is next on the list,' Nelson said quietly, breaking the silence. No one replied; they didn't need to because when Billy spoke it was a done deal. 'But first of all we need to take care of this cunt.'

They watched another junkie press the bell to get up to Cue Ball's flat.

'We sort this boy and then everyone knows who's running the show.' Billy looked round at Fisher and Clark, who were in the back seat. 'Okay, boys, when the next junkie fuck comes to the door, we go in with them.'

They pulled on their balaclavas and waited.

They could tell the figure heading towards the flats was a junkie from his nervous walk – he twitched like there was a cattle prod being shoved in his arse every few seconds – and the way he kept scanning the street to see if anyone was watching. He was right on that one, but he was wrecked and didn't notice the four Ulstermen weighing him up. They all came to the same conclusion, which Clark voiced for them.

'Well I don't think we'll need to struggle much with that wee fucker.'

'Dead right on that one,' Nelson replied. 'Think we just need to give him a hard stare and he'll run a fuckin' mile.'

The junkie wiped his streaming nose with the back of his sleeve and couldn't believe how bad he felt. He was desperate and prayed that Cue Ball had some gear. He'd just screwed a couple of flats and flogged the goods for a fraction of their price, but he was desperate to get some relief into his veins.

He looked around again to make sure there weren't any bizzies with nothing better to do and still he missed the car with Nelson and his pals, even though it was no more than twenty yards from the door.

The junkie felt a wave of relief when Cue Ball responded to his pressing the bell.

'It's me, Andy – need a bag or two.'

Cue Ball looked at the hazy black and white face on the entry service but could still make out the sweat running down the boy's face.

'What a fuckin' state you're in, boy. Come up,' Cue Ball said, as if he gave a fuck about his customer's health.

He walked back to the living room and waited for the junkie to make it up to his floor and thump on the door.

Nelson and his boys were close enough when the junkie walked through the main door to let it just about shut before making a move, which Nelson thought would give the dealer time to put down his phone and walk away from the small screen. He was dead right. At the last possible moment Nelson caught the door with the end of his fingers and waited, knowing there was no way the wreck they'd seen at the door would run up the stairs. Right again. The junkie was trying to take the lift, and they heard him pushing the buttons repeatedly and muttering to himself.

Nelson looked round and nodded, pushed the door open again and walked up behind the junkie, who was still cursing the speed of the lifts.

He knew before he turned that more than one person had walked up behind him – and too quietly to be innocent citizens. He decided not to face whomever it was and stared at the lift doors, listening to the winding gear finally lower the carriage down to the ground floor.

'Got a light, pal?' Nelson asked without a note of tension in his voice.

The boy had to look round then and took in the four balaclavas and baseball bats. He was coming apart already and needed a shot more than anything. He was afraid but knew he had fuck all but the price of a couple of bags; if this team robbed him there was no way Cue Ball would give him anything on tick. His addiction was greater than his fear of the violence that might be dropped on him if things went up the swanny. The young man had lost all self-respect a long time ago and pleading was all he had left.

'For fuck's sake, boys, just a wee break please. I'm a fuckin' junkie; I need fixed up – please.'

Nelson smiled. This was it; this was what got him going – the fear in those eyes, weakness that could be exploited. He was as much of a junkie as the shaking remains of the human being he was tormenting, and he stared at the boy, who was pleading to keep the price of his drug of choice. This was all he had left. Some people looked forward to their next drink, sexual encounter or football match, but for Nelson all of that had been burned out of him in Afghanistan. It frightened him in his quieter moments, but for now he felt alive.

He felt the stab of pain in his gut again, winced, and fat beads of sweat popped out of his forehead. He did his best not to show it – weakness was not an option, and any such signs would be like blood in the water when sharks were around.

He pulled himself straight, trying to ignore the knot that seemed to pulse currents of pain deep in his midriff. But Clark saw the milky pallor in the exposed part of Nelson's face and wondered. He'd spotted it a couple of times before, and he'd started to try and guess what the problem was.

Nelson concentrated on the junkie. 'We're here for your pal up the stairs; wouldn't dirty my fuckin' hands on you, sunshine.'

The junkie realised that the accents were Irish. His education hadn't got him as far as recognising that there was the north and the republic, so for him they were just Irish.

His throat tightened when he remembered there was a story going the rounds that there were some mad Irish fuckers who didn't seem to take any prisoners. It was at that point in his thoughts that Nelson headbutted him so hard the back of his skull rattled off the concrete wall at the side of the lift. The lights went out for the junkie as the four men walked past him and entered the lift.

'At least he gets to keep his fuckin' money,' Fisher sneered and gobbed on the half-conscious addict whose shit life had just taken a turn for the worse.

Cue Ball was a careful man, and he had to be, given the trouble he'd had in his life. Everyone taking a shot at him because he was a short-arse, the police sticking him inside twice just for selling the punters what they wanted. He was human though, and like everyone else he made the occasional slip. The junkie was a regular and although he'd let him into the stair, he should have double-checked with a look through the spyhole in the door, because you never knew when some demented bastard would try and rip off your stash. Cue Ball had presumed this one was far too much of a fuckwit to try anything so macho. The result of this carelessness was that when he opened the door, McLean hit him square on the end of his bearded chin. As he crashed down, Nelson and his crew rushed in and closed the door behind them.

McLean grabbed Cue Ball by the collar of his shirt, dragged him through to the living room and dropped him in front of the TV. Clark turned the sound up on Ray Winstone growling on about what a great deal it was to bet on some match.

'Don't you think that's a mercenary fuck-and-a-half trying to get the punters to part with their money on gambling? It pisses me off that – all that money and he's working for a fuckin' bookie.'

Most men would have stayed where they were after the haymaker McLean had landed on him, but Cue Ball was mental. The sight of four balaclavas and baseball bats should have been enough to give him pause, but for someone like Cue Ball it was just another challenge to add to a long list in his life. He came off the carpet like a scorched wildcat, and at least for a moment he surprised the visitors.

On the way up he grabbed an empty wine bottle and without losing momentum he whacked it across the bridge of McLean's nose. The bottle smashed and McLean groaned, sinking to his knees as blood seeped out through the woollen balaclava. Cue Ball was left with the neck of the bottle and enough of a jagged edge to make the Belfast men think twice.

He backed into a corner and rubbed his chin with one hand as he waved the remains of the bottle about to keep his guests focused. Clark and Fisher kept him trapped in the corner as Nelson pulled the injured man onto the settee. He lifted up the balaclava, and although there was enough blood to keep a vampire happy, it was no more than a broken nose, and McLean had suffered worse in his days in the paramilitaries.

He patted McLean on the back, looked up at Cue Ball and admitted to himself that the stories about the short-arsed little runt in the corner had been all too true. He couldn't believe what he was seeing. Cue Ball was smiling at him. That took balls – or was he just completely off his fucking trolley?

Cue Ball nodded towards McLean. 'How'd you like that, petal? Anytime you want some more just give me a call 'cause I'm always in, and I get a bit fuckin' bored at times.' His smile broadened, and he started to bob up and down on his toes like a boxer.

'You really take the fuckin' biscuit, my friend,' Nelson said, in part expressing some admiration for the nutcase who clearly believed he could win. And that's when he had an idea. The original plan had been to make pâté out of Cue Ball's head, but Nelson was smart enough to know that although they could get the job done, it would be messy. He remembered his old army mentor's words: 'If there's an easy way and a hard way to do a job, only a fuckin' idiot does it the hard way.'

'Put the glass down, take a seat and let's talk.' Nelson said it as calmly as he could muster. His gut hurt like hell and he wondered again if he had an ulcer.

He pulled off the balaclava, lit up a cigarette and offered the packet to Cue Ball, who'd stopped dancing around like Muhammad Ali. Cue Ball shrugged, took the packet and dropped the remains of the wine bottle on the carpet.

'Fancy a cuppa, boys?' he asked. 'You must be fuckin' knackered after all that.' He said it as if his best friends in the world had just dropped in to watch the big match then turned the TV volume back to normal, went into the kitchen and flicked on the kettle to make a brew.

Nelson shook his head; before entering the flat he thought he'd seen them all, but this fuckin' midget was something else. 'Three sugars in mine,' he called through the kitchen door and shrugged at the other three men in the room.

'Sit down, boys. I'll be through in a minute, and I'll bring some cotton wool for the girl's nose.'

Fisher and Clark pulled off their balaclavas and shook their heads in wonder at the man making their tea.

'Do you believe this guy, Andy?' Fisher said, still trying to make sense of it.

'They always say the wee men are the fuckin' ones to watch . . . well there's the proof getting us a brew.'

'I'm going through there to keep an eye on the bastard. He'll probably piss in it or something.'

Cue Ball came back through and had opened a packet of shortbread, which he usually kept for special guests. He reckoned these Irish cowboys could be classed as special. 'I'll be fuckin' mum if that's alright with you?' He poured the tea and sat down, slurping the brew wetly.

'Come on then, tell me what the deal is. Old man Fleming and his favourite miscarriage of a son are missing in action.' He looked for a reaction but Clark and Fisher didn't even twitch. McLean was still nursing his nose so he definitely wasn't going to act as spokesman. He'd worked out that Nelson was the pack leader and could see why. He was in a different league from the other three, who'd struggle to find the door without the hard man he'd decided to address. 'My guess is your plan was that I'd be begging for mercy and then all the other dealers would just fall into line. Good plan.' He nodded at Nelson and waited.

'That was the plan right enough. But a wise man should always have the sense to change it if needs be.' Nelson fired up another cigarette to go with the fresh brew and had the sensation of heat in the throbbing knot that was his stomach. 'One way or the other we're taking over the business. I guess putting you in the hospital would send the right message, but now we've met, just getting you on board would be good enough. What do you think, Rocky?'

Cue Ball liked the Rocky bit. It was respectful, and whatever they wanted to do, they now knew Cue Ball Ross was no pushover.

'I think that we could either take lumps out of each other or do some business. To tell the truth I was fuckin' sick of the Flemings. They were greedy bastards, and all I need to know is that they can't come back from whatever holiday camp they're in.' He bit down on another piece of shortbread, offered the plate round and continued. 'All they have left are Joe's youngest, the twins; they're not long out of their teens and not ready to take on the world. The mother is a fuckin' mouth, but that's your problem. You supply me and don't take the piss on prices and we can do business.'

He finished the last biscuit, feeling slightly guilty about his greed. 'If I come on board then all the other dealers will fall into place. I'll expect a discount of course for my cooperation.' He sat back and waited.

Nelson felt sick and wanted to get back to the flat so he could swallow some gut tablets. 'That's okay with me. One of the boys will be round tomorrow to make the arrangements. Welcome aboard.' He felt the pain subside and the relief eased the knotted muscles in his stomach.

Nelson started up the car, revved the engine and turned the heaters on full. 'Well I didn't expect that, but the result's the thing.'

'I'll pay that fuckin' boy scout back. We should have burned him,' McLean said through gritted teeth, and he meant it. He was also questioning Nelson's judgement without coming right out with it. No one had dared to do that before.

Nelson felt a trickle of sweat. Had they sensed his struggle with the pain in his gut? It was always the same, the fighting for power like rats in a sewer, ready to kill each other over a scrap of rotten food.

He stopped the car and looked at McLean, who was next to him in the front passenger seat.

McLean stared ahead and wished he'd shut the fuck up, especially when he was punched hard just below the ear.

Nelson watched McLean suck in air with the shock of the blow and looked round at the men in the back seat. 'Anything else?'

No one spoke; no one needed to, but Clark realised that Nelson was human after all.

13

Macallan sat on the edge of the bed and wished she could find an excuse not to go into the office. She had period pain that was squeezing the energy out of her; it was just part of life, but it felt like the perfect reason to disappear under the duvet. If only they lived in a more sensible world.

She wondered what the reaction would be if she phoned in and said to the chief super that she had what was the most common pain in the world? 'They'd find it unacceptable,' she said out loud, as if it would help, and pulled the hot-water bottle against her abdomen. She just wished that all the criminals, all the murderers, all the fucking terrorists and every male who'd ever pissed her off could feel what she was feeling right now.

Dragging herself into the shower, via the bathroom cabinet for some strong analgesics, Macallan felt like her holiday had been a dream and she was just destined to have problems rather than the life promised in glossy magazines.

The water splashed on her back, and she rubbed the

soap functionally, just to get the job done. When she stepped out of the shower she peered into the steamed-up mirror, rubbed the surface and saw her image again. Her face was looking older, noticeably older than just a couple of years ago. She thought she looked like shit but that maybe there was a man or even a woman out there who would tell her otherwise, and she ached to be loved. During the working days the squad saw her as the tough, glam detective who made headlines, never suspecting that when she went home and stripped off she might stare at the image of herself in the mirror, trying to find what was left of her youth. She remembered, years before, a nineteen-year-old friend being surprised when Grace had told her she was twenty-one and feeling for the first time that something had passed – twenty-one had suddenly seemed old.

'Twenty-one. I wish.' She turned from the mirror and decided she would just have to get on with the day.

She dressed and sorted her face. It was going to be a tough return, but she would deal with it; that was who she was – someone who dealt with the fuck-flood that pounded the force every day while most of the good citizens went about their business in blissful ignorance.

McGovern had given her enough of a briefing over the phone for her to know there was a problem developing in the city and that the Belfast boys were involved. She knew, however, that it wasn't enough, and it would be wrong to gamble on just getting through the day without more information. This was a bad start, because the people who didn't know how to deal with it would want answers. Once again the rather average shoulders of Grace Macallan would have to square up. No one was sure to what extent these Belfast men were implicated, but she'd known they'd be up to their Protestant arses in it since she'd first heard mention of them. Poisoned by the Troubles, they would make most of the locals seem like cartoon characters.

An hour and a half later Macallan walked in through the back door of the square, uninspiring old HQ building. It was strange but, even after all her years in the job and the many difficulties she'd faced, she always felt slightly nervous when she came back after a break. She'd had an inferiority complex as a child and thought it must have been a legacy of that condition.

She smiled, remembering one of the many pains she thought she had as a child being reported to her very old-fashioned GP one day. After hearing him telling her mother quietly that she had an inferiority complex, she had spent the next few weeks fretting that it was an incurable disease. This went on till her mother explained as diplomatically as she could what it really meant.

As always, she'd worried when she was away in Sutherland – that the job would discover that it could do well without her, that someone would fill her role and do it better than she could. Once she was back it would be okay and as if nothing had changed. It was just another of those burdens she would carry from childhood to the grave.

The briefing was in the chief super's office, which probably meant he was pissed off, and Macallan guessed that the press must have started to give him grief. She only had time to throw her bag into her office and have a quick catch-up with McGovern beforehand. He introduced her to Lesley Thompson, who seemed to have been parachuted in almost as soon as Macallan had left the building the previous week. She'd seen her around, usually walking in John O'Connor's shadow, but this was the first time they'd spoken. Thompson looked businesslike, though perhaps a bit too stiff, her short, jet-black hair contrasting with a complexion that was pale and flawless. Painfully thin, she cut a nervous figure, and Macallan wondered how she'd cope with a team of hairy-arsed detectives. Her voice was strong enough though, definitely honed by money and a very decent education.

'Welcome to the team,' Macallan said to her when they were introduced. 'Sorry we don't have much time to get to know each other, but we'll do it after this meeting with the chief super.' The painkillers were just about beginning to take effect so her smile wasn't quite as forced as it might have been earlier.

'Thank you. I'm looking forward to working with the team. I've heard so much about you.' Thompson didn't bother with a smile when she said it.

Macallan saw McGovern's eyebrows twitch upwards, and like him she wondered what exactly that meant. She had a bad feeling about Chief Inspector Thompson, and she needed a problem with her new deputy like she needed Mick Harkins' proverbial budgie.

'Okay, let's get to this meeting; don't want to be late on my first day back. Jimmy and Lesley, I'd like you both along with me. I'm not up to speed with everything that's gone on during my break and don't want to get caught out by his lordship.'

The chief super's office was a world away from most of the cramped boxes that passed for working accommodation in the rest of the building. Like all police plans it had been adequate for about a month after it was built then completely inadequate for the rest of its existence; such was the lot of publicly funded offices. But here there was light and air and space to work, and Macallan would have sold her beloved collection of books for this luxury.

The chief super was new in the job and trying to deal with the aftermath of the unification of the Scottish forces. There were still a few wars raging, with some of the old top dogs skirmishing for positions close to the leader of the pack. He'd transferred from the Met three years before and had walked straight into high office in Strathclyde. The unification had completely fucked up his carefully laid plans, and he was pissed at the whole world – and particularly at those who worked under him.

He was average build, with average looks and without the decoration of his uniform would have passed for a rather uninspiring clerk. What he did have was an almost fanatical drive to succeed in his chosen career, which had just edged out his original plan to work in insurance. He'd managed to climb the ranks with a minimum of fuss, and no one had really noticed him till he was promoted to chief superintendent, when there was a widespread corporate intake of breath and general chorus of 'how the fuck did that happen?' He detested the front-end troopers, regarded them as a pain in the arse and was convinced that they believed they were God's gift to the service.

Macallan nodded to him, but he stayed behind his desk and pretended to write something, like a politician doing a ten o'clock news film shot. He barely acknowledged her presence and looked at McGovern and Thompson as if they were coming to infect his place of work. His secretary directed the three of them to the large oval desk next to the windows looking out onto the rugby pitch at the back of Fettes.

Macallan smiled broadly; she knew well enough that she was working for a total wanker but she did her best to treat everyone in the force like human beings. She'd been there for fifteen years and had seen them all – some good, some bad and most somewhere in the middle. This one came fairly low in the 'some bad' category, and she reassured herself that at least he wouldn't last long. Too far from the chief, he'd soon find a sewer to crawl along to be nearer the man at the top and the radiation of power.

The other senior officers trooped in and a nerve in Macallan's neck twitched uncontrollably when John O'Connor arrived, all businesslike as always and looking like he'd just stepped out of the window of Austin Reed. He gave the chief super a broad smile and got back a 'Good morning, John' with lashings of mutual admiration. She'd been near to loving this man and asked herself again how she could have felt so good with him when it had been so wrong?

She looked to her side and saw that McGovern was thinking at least some of the same things she was. O'Connor thought he had the chief super where he wanted him, and that couldn't be good for Macallan or anyone on her team.

O'Connor sat opposite them, gave the pair of them a professional smile and then a real one to Thompson.

'How's life as a detective then, Lesley?' O'Connor asked, as always brimming with self-confidence.

'So far so good, sir. Can't wait to get started.'

Macallan wanted to do the two-fingers-down-the-throat act, but she kept still. She played with her papers to divert her mind, though she hadn't actually read what was in the folder. McGovern meanwhile was asking himself where this would end up, knowing for certain that something would definitely go wrong.

The seats filled up till the chief super felt he'd kept them waiting long enough to annoy them, at which point he looked up, frowning. His non-verbals and lowered brow showed he was not a happy man – and they were about to share his pain.

'I've had the press office beating on my door all morning wanting a statement about what seems to be happening in the drugs trade here.'

He paused, checking the blank faces for signs, but there

115

was nothing but neutral expressions. His gaze hovered on O'Connor for a moment. O'Connor was his kind of man, and he'd become close to the head of professional standards – anyone who spent his time trying to root out the rotten core of the force that he knew existed was his kind of officer.

'I've had Jacquie Bell on the phone telling me that there's a gang war going on and that two of the Flemings are missing, presumed dead. I've no idea who they are but presumably drug-trafficking scum.'

He paused again for effect but the faces were still neutral, although O'Connor gave him a slight nod of encouragement.

Macallan suppressed a smile, knowing that her undeclared friend would be on top of the case and wondered why she hadn't been hassling her for an inside lead. Bell, who was widely regarded as the best and most ruthless crime reporter in the game, had become a friend to Macallan, and not long after they had met for the first time they'd slept together. This still puzzled Macallan; it was the only time she'd ever been with a woman, and she really couldn't make sense of it though she'd enjoyed it at the time. Bell treated it as a good night with no strings and occasionally liked to tease her about it.

Macallan liked Bell because she knew exactly where she stood with her, and the journalist had published a flattering profile that had made her something of a minor celebrity in the media, although a very reluctant one.

'Superintendent Macallan, can you please tell us what's going on and whether we're on top of these people? You worked in Belfast so presumably you'll have some expert advice for us.'

He had barely concealed the sarcasm in his voice and she wondered what crap O'Connor had been feeding into his general dislike of the whole criminal-investigation arm of the force. She tried not to panic, but she knew she should have got herself up to speed before she came to the meeting. She'd fucked up, left her flanks exposed and unless she could bullshit for Scotland, she was going to look like she wasn't wearing a skirt in public. She shuffled her papers then remembered attending training on non-verbals, where she'd been told that anyone spotted paper shuffling was just buying time when they hadn't a fucking clue what to say.

'These men are skilled in terror tactics, police methods and, most importantly, they will use levels of violence that our criminals here are not prepared for. They've been moulded by conflict, and I have a number of proposals.'

Macallan hadn't known what she was going to say when she'd started speaking, but she'd dug up a nice line there from somewhere in her survival reserves, though the truth was that her years of experience in Ulster meant certain courses of action seemed blindingly obvious to her. Nevertheless, she was surprised and pleased at how well she'd rescued herself and decided to get onto the front foot.

She could hear Bill Kelly again in her mind's voice: 'Even if you don't know what you're doing, look like you do know. Very rarely does the game go according to plan. Deal with it, and if you get to high rank your job is to stop the troops panicking.' It was as if he was by her side. Bill had always believed that she was special; convincing Macallan had been his task.

'We need to form a dedicated team, and I can tell you that the PSNI will hold intelligence on every one of the Belfast suspects. I believe we need to get them to come across, share what they've got and promise them that we'll reciprocate. We also need to skip a couple of steps and treat these men as if they were in Northern Ireland.'

She paused for effect, just like the chief super, but the

difference was that everyone was listening – she was talking about something only she knew about. The room was full of people who wondered what it was like to face a gun, and they were aware that they were in the presence of someone who did have that experience.

Energy pulsed through her as she took command, and they all recognised her authority.

The chief super wished he was back in his office in Scotland Yard, well away from these demented Celts. He was fenced in, knowing he would probably have to back whatever she proposed, because if he didn't and it went wrong, the minutes of this meeting would expose his weakness in the face of a real problem. That would keep him trapped just outside higher office till the day the troops cheered his departure. When that day came no one was going to volunteer to buy him a gold watch.

'If the intelligence backs it up we need authorities for full surveillance and electronic monitoring – there will be informants in place in Northern Ireland who can help. I believe we should involve the security services, who may have information on this team ... but we'll figure out what we need after the initial analysis of the information has been made by my senior analyst.'

The chief super had turned pale. He'd been imagining Macallan naked during her briefing and suddenly felt ashamed, knowing that it could only ever be a fantasy. The thought had come to him when he'd realised just how capable she was – that the stories were true. He had presumed she'd fold – O'Connor had told him that she hadn't been briefed properly and that she needed to be shown up in front of the others in the meeting. It had gone badly wrong, and he stared at O'Connor, who looked as calm as always but would be seething. He needed to make some gesture to show that he was king of the castle.

'You can have whatever toys you need, Superintendent, but I want a cast-iron case before applying for an authority. I'm not going to be responsible for a disproportionate response.' He experienced the smallest tremor in his hands and did his best to conceal his rising anger.

Macallan saw the opening and knew she should have ignored it, but it had to be said. 'I'm just back from leave, sir, but as far as I understand it we have two of the Flemings likely to be lying dead somewhere. On top of that there's a trail of serious assaults on low-level dealers and a possible takeover of the trade by a gang of Belfast men who are likely to have been involved in paramilitary activity – that's something we need to find out from the PSNI. There must be a serious possibility of gang war here, and I think that definitely needs a proportionate response.'

Everyone in the room saw the challenge and they were glad it was Macallan and not them who'd decided to wind up a man with a notoriously thin skin. McGovern was loving it and decided that sexual equality worked – Macallan had just run rings round the boys. For someone who delivered all her lines in the most understated tone, she was a force of nature. Men didn't get Grace Macallan – at least the men who saw her as just another woman – but for McGovern she was the dog's bollocks, Sir Alex Ferguson in a skirt and Jock Stein all wrapped up in an average-sized, very female body. She scared her opponents but had become sacred to her team. They didn't know why she inspired them, just that she did, but it was that thing – that glowing warmth, when you stare at another human being and decide that you can give them it all because they led for all – that ultimately made them follow her.

The chief super knew he had to cut and run but he wouldn't forget this meeting. He wrapped things up as diplomatically as possible and dismissed them, but to his annoyance, Macallan hung back as they left and asked if she could have a private word. He stared at her. He could have refused, but he wanted to know what she was after. He always believed that everyone was acting primarily out of self-interest, because that was what he did himself.

'Sit down and close the door first,' he replied. 'I have ten minutes before a teleconference meeting with the chief.'

Macallan sat down, trying to get the words right and wished she'd rehearsed something before the meeting. She'd pissed off the man opposite and knew she might have picked the wrong time.

What the fuck, girl, you've never been good at diplomacy, Macallan thought, trying to look calm and in control, before she said, 'I know you have other things to deal with, sir, but I think the investigation we have in front of us is going to be as tough as it gets. These are serious people we're dealing with.'

'Get to the point, Superintendent.' He hissed it out through tight lips.

She wanted to recoil but kept still and maintained eye contact. She was stronger than the man opposite and only his rank protected him. Still, she had to play it smart – proving she had a pair of balls might just backfire, and his face was telling her that she might regret this conversation.

'The thing is, sir, that I'm not sure Lesley Thompson is ready to run the operation. As chief inspector she would be directly involved as my deputy. She'd be on the ground, making difficult decisions in real time. She has no experience of this type of situation. As far as I know she's had little operational experience. I just worry that she'll be thrown into a situation she's had no training for.'

She thought that was enough and that at least she'd

said it, making sure it sounded like she was concerned for Thompson. What she couldn't say was that they couldn't afford to have someone making a critical decision that would basically clusterfuck the job and leave the Belfast criminals undamaged.

The chief super saw it all now. It was as he suspected – and as O'Connor had told him. Macallan would not like an equally talented female officer grabbing success in front of her eyes. The old excuse that detectives knew best. He gripped his pen so tight his knuckles turned white.

'First of all the decision to move staff around is not yours, Superintendent.' He couldn't meet her eyes but carried on, and she caught the strain in his voice. 'Lesley Thompson is a highly qualified officer and quite likely to reach executive rank. She's managed staff, and according to Superintendent O'Connor, she is someone who can take charge wherever she goes.'

That was it, and Macallan should have seen it coming. O'Connor must have played mind games with Thompson, seeing her as a weakling, before managing to dump a potential disaster right into her lap. He'd manipulated Thompson as much as the chief super. He was an experienced detective and was fully aware that filling the deputy's post with Thompson would under- mine the confidence of every detective on the team.

The chief super decided to stick the boot in where it hurt most. 'I hope this has nothing to do with your personal feelings and your previous failed relationship with him. I know my predecessor took the view that he had been at fault for the Barclay case, but I have my own views.'

Macallan couldn't see it but she felt a scarlet flush spreading up from her chest to neck. She was angry and wanted to walk round the table and squeeze his undoubtedly tiny balls till he squeaked an apology. Their conversation was going nowhere, and she conceded that she'd made the wrong call.

'Okay, sir. There's nothing more to say, and I'll do everything to help Lesley.' She turned to go.

'Just a second, Superintendent.'

The chief super had turned the tables, at least in his own mind. 'I hope you *will* support her. I don't want to hear any reports to the contrary. You may be popular with your admirers in the media, but I can assure you that makes no difference to me. Are we clear?'

She nodded, and as she closed the door behind her she squeezed her eyes shut and lifted her face to the ceiling. Under her breath she squeezed out the word 'tosser', not noticing that his secretary was watching her through the open door of an adjacent office.

When she opened her eyes she stiffened at the sight of the smiling woman sipping tea before nodding back and heading to her office, trying to dampen down her rage. It was always the same – people seeing motives that didn't exist. The man was just an inadequate little fuck.

When Macallan summoned McGovern, Thompson and Felicity Young into the office she was tight, pale and pissed off. They all knew she'd spoken to the chief super in private and whatever had happened obviously hadn't made her day.

She gave them orders to get the research going on Billy Nelson and a conventional surveillance running on his life. 'Let's see what picture we can build up in the next week but hopefully we'll be able to go for the technicals. I also want you to urge the source unit to get their handlers rumbling up their informants to see what they can find out for us. Anything they can get on the dealers who've been attacked. It all helps.'

After she'd answered their questions they left the

room, and Macallan closed the door of her office and did not emerge till she decided to go home.

McGovern was sure he could work out what the problem was as he looked over to where Thompson was sitting, trying her best to look like a working detective. *Good luck, Grace – you're going to need it*, he thought. He wondered again where men like the chief super came from. Who the fuck decided they deserved high rank?

He saw Macallan leave the office about five, which proved she was upset – even on a good day she normally had to be surgically removed at seven or eight.

On the bad days she hardly went home at all.

Macallan had been struggling with her door key for weeks; there'd been a problem with the door that she'd simply ignored as something that would go away. She wondered why she just didn't get someone to fix it and imagined being trapped inside with her phone out of juice. She managed a smile at the thought that she'd be found dead and alone, which would be followed by the inevitable propagation of numerous conspiracy theories. When she finally got inside, she made some decaf tea, fighting against the urge to have a shot of the Talisker she kept in case of emergencies. Experience of living alone had made her very aware that the bottle just stood there, waiting for her moments of weakness. She tried to divert her need for a proper drink and stuck Bob Dylan on, skipping tracks until she got to 'Watching the River Flow'. The twanging guitar and lyrics always soothed her, sucking her into words that were all about escape.

Macallan bounced around the room and wondered why she'd never been able to dance. It was as if her body was being charged with intermittent shocks. Even at the booziest function she only did the slow dances, or the 'walk round the floor' as she called them.

Dylan worked his magic on her, and after another couple of tracks she felt the need to climb under the sheets and shut out the world.

She had only been asleep long enough to feel exhausted when her mobile rang.

'Grace? Sorry it's so late but I've just finished. You okay there?'

Jack Fraser's voice brought her back to life.

She buried deeper under the covers and found herself chatting to him, just as she had before their enforced break-up. And as they talked, they forgot the past and returned to what had made them good together in the first place.

The clock moved but they lost all sense of time. One of them had to end the conversation at some point, but neither seemed to be inclined to be the instigator. Eventually Fraser caved in: 'I'll be across later next week, so book me in for dinner. Looking forward to it.'

Reluctantly she put the phone down and tried to settle again, her mind full of Fraser and wondering what was coming. It wasn't until about 4 a.m. that she finally dropped into sleep.

She dreamed and saw Fraser playing his last game of rugby. She was there and tried to put on her sympathetic face as he came off the field, secretly glad that he'd retired before one of those younger sixteen-stone hooligans left him damaged for the rest of his life.

The dream changed to faceless men who whispered to each other in the shadows, and all she could hear was the harsh edge of their Belfast accents. She didn't recognise the street they were on. It was snowing, and when she looked behind her she could see her footprints.

The men came out of the shadows towards her, but she couldn't see them, just the marks they made in the snow, coming at her from all sides. Her throat started to close in panic and the snow had the consistency of mud, sucking her downwards until it reached her waist. She called for Bill Kelly, but he didn't come.

The footprints were all around her now, and the whispering grew louder and louder as the snow covered her mouth and her lungs froze as she tried to draw breath but only sucked in the suffocating white substance…

Her eyes sprang open; she looked round and thought for just a moment that Fraser was beside her again. Then the dream was gone and she knew who those voices in the dream belonged to – and that she'd meet them in the flesh.

Billy Nelson was awake as Macallan drifted back into sleep. The cruel, dead light from the street lamps half-lit his room, and the pain in his gut was like a rat slowly gnawing his insides and causing all the pain he could take in one go. He had next to no education but was intelligent enough to know that whatever was wrong, it was bad. When he'd shaved the previous morning he'd noticed the loss of flesh round his cheeks. There was a vein near his left eye that had been barely visible all his life, but now it shone clear and blue through his tight skin, and he'd stared at it for what seemed like an age.

He'd asked himself a dozen times whether it could be his imagination but the rat in his gut was nothing to do with imagination. He was angry, and a shiver of fear sparked through his body. It had never occurred to him that he could be suffering from an illness – that was for other people, not Billy Nelson the paratrooper and all-round hard bastard.

The air was cool in the room, but there was a film of foul-smelling sweat covering his body. He curled up into a ball and accepted that he needed help, but he couldn't tell the rest of the team – any form of weakness would attract the wolves, and they were always close, smelling the air, and savage when they attacked. There was no friendly handshake at the handover of power. Look what he'd done to the Flemings: buried while life still flickered inside at least one of their ravaged bodies.

'Fuck it, fuck it, fuck it!' He squeezed his eyes shut and prayed that it was no more than an ulcer; given the number of combat missions he'd taken, an ulcer wouldn't be such a surprise. He could recover and be as good as new. He decided that whatever it took, he would visit Joe Fleming's widow and straighten her out. She was still running her mouth off around the city, telling anyone who would listen that she was going to take Nelson out.

He managed a smile at the thought. 'No fuckin' way, Billy boy. No fuckin' way.'

14

Macallan was trying to wade her way through the deluge of paper that crossed her desk every day. She shook her head and wondered what half of it had to do with her, although such questions didn't get the replies completed. Luckily the phone rang to tell her that the PSNI officer was at the front counter. She'd sent a request to the Belfast HQ asking if they could provide intelligence on Nelson and his associates, knowing they would have it and that the intelligence-gathering machine that was still in place could hold some answers for them. Paramilitary attacks still took place, and there were enough dissident Republicans to keep the security services on guard. Up until then all Macallan had was names from informants in the drugs trade. The intelligence was patchy but it was clear that people were terrified to cross the men from Belfast, which came as no surprise to her.

The PSNI officer was Detective Inspector Barry Wallace, who she knew from her Special Branch days in Belfast, although she'd never worked with him. He had a good reputation, which had been enough for a PIRA active service unit to try to kill him when he was out jogging during the bad days of the Troubles.

McGovern showed him into the room and he greeted Macallan warmly, which was a relief, as she was never sure how her past in the service would affect people. He was a tall, thin man and looked more like an old-fashioned preacher than a Branch officer. Of course, she reminded herself, there was no Branch now, the name having been buried as part of the move to the new Northern Ireland. It had been anathema to the Republicans, who saw it as the murderous arm of an oppressive state that had spent decades persecuting and exploiting the Catholic community. What had been the Branch had been rechristened with the rather anodyne label of C3.

She took to Wallace immediately; he was an engaging man with the typical Ulster sense of humour that could find a way to laugh at almost anything in life – an antidote to the tragedies that had taken so many men and women from the old RUC force.

Senior analyst Felicity Young joined them for the meeting and Macallan knew that she would be needed. Young was known affectionately as 'the brain' with good reason – she was capable of seeing and making links in intelligence even where the information lay buried in the mountains of reports that flowed into the ravenous systems of law-enforcement agencies across the UK. It was a gift, and she could take leaps of imagination, landing squarely on the smallest detail that would complete a hypothesis or a possible line of investigation. She'd had a relationship with Harkins before he'd been so badly injured, and she still regretted losing him. Macallan knew that Harkins felt exactly the same but would never want Young taking care of him; in his view he was only half the man she'd found so appealing at the time.

Wallace was blunt with his – or rather the PSNI's – position. 'I'm sure you understand we still have more than enough problems keeping our eyes and electronic ears locked onto those men whose sole aim in life is to kill soldiers or police officers. We will provide intelligence but only under strict assurances of how it's used. You know as well as I do that much of it comes from human sources, and we're not prepared to risk agents' lives just because your team don't understand the concept of "sensitive sources".'

That was how Macallan wanted it – straight and to the point.

'There's probably no one who understands more than I do about what's at risk,' she replied. 'You'll know I had my own experience of the consequences when it's not understood.'

They'd both served in the RUC and its successor, the PSNI, and in that closed community everyone knew everyone else's story, so Macallan's downfall and ruined personal life had been hung out for all to see. It had kept the canteen gossips going for months, and Wallace would know every detail of that particular tragedy.

After a pause Wallace nodded, confident that she meant every word she said. She had to, and he couldn't believe she would want another disaster involving her old force.

They agreed the protocol that any intelligence would be passed through secure systems and heavily sanitised to protect the sources, meaning the relevant information would be passed, but any references that could expose the source would be removed or disguised. They agreed that Young would liaise with her counterpart in PSNI HQ and completed the agreements on information exchange before the coffee was brought in and they could get down to business.

Wallace asked Macallan for a briefing on what exactly their problem was and she asked Young to take the floor, knowing the analyst would take up more of their time than necessary but that she would miss nothing. There would be diagrams and some language that could only be understood by someone of an equivalent intellect – but by the close they would be clear about what they had and, more importantly, what they were missing. The man from Belfast would be left with no doubt about where the holes were, and he might be able to provide the information they were missing.

Young treated intelligence and information like a recreational drug and was pleased to have something big to sink her teeth into. She needed intelligence to get to her solutions, and this was where she found her highs now that Harkins was no longer in her bed at night.

Wallace watched Young perform, realised that his hosts had a problem and that they had no idea of its scale. He could tell that Macallan sensed it was worse than her colleagues suspected and that it needed to be hit hard and early. Her intuition told her what he knew as fact – that if these ex-UVF gangsters took a grip on the drugs trade in the east of Scotland, it would be the razor-sharp edge of an extremely toxic wedge. There was a struggle going on for control of the organised-crime market in Northern Ireland, which was overpopulated with para-military veterans of the Troubles. These men had all the skills learned in the conflict, and there was a demand for their expertise, but now they were all looking for other opportunities outside Belfast. There had been headlines for years about the Loyalist fallings-out and banish-ments to the mainland. The tabloid readers had seen the pictures and horror stories about shaven-headed steroid junkies taking up residence among reluctant taxpayers on the west side of the country. If Nelson managed to establish a solid base, there would be other Loyalists happy to come in and enjoy life in the capital city. The police would be blamed – and careers fell for less.

'I think I can help you,' Wallace said. 'First of all you have a number of problems – and you're only seeing one side of it. Let me introduce you to some people; they're all good Loyalist boys from the Shankill.' His sarcasm came from bitter experience and the memories of innocent Catholics picked up by the Loyalist gangs and killed for being in the wrong part of the city. 'They're all hard men, and if they're planning to operate here that's bad news.'

Wallace pulled two photographs from his briefcase and laid them out on the table. One was of Jackie Martin, a custody picture taken after a serious assault in an East Belfast pub. The victim had been happy to help the police until his wife had taken a phone call explaining who had been arrested and what the price would be for pointing his finger at Jackie Martin. Her husband had developed a delayed case of amnesia and Mr Martin had been home for dinner the following day. The second photograph was of Billy Nelson and was obviously a surveillance shot taken on the day he was summoned to see Martin. Next to the surveillance photograph was an army-identification photograph of Nelson in uniform.

Macallan had seen so many like Nelson – handsome and hard, ready for trouble whenever it came. His blood would be orange; his mind indoctrinated since birth.

Wallace outlined what Jackie Martin had been and what he was now. 'He's a bastard of the first order, and we know he killed a number of innocent Catholics during the Troubles. Like some of his more well-known colleagues, he was one of those who enjoyed pulling the trigger himself. An animal. He only cares about the Loyalist cause now when it suits him and has made a complete move over to organised crime. He's involved in drugs, money laundering, runs a number of prostitutes and enjoys using them as much as his other customers.'

Wallace went on to explain what else was known about Jackie Martin, and Macallan understood from what he said that they took him seriously – and that he was clearly a main target for the PSNI. Macallan guessed that they were receiving both human and electronic intelligence and hoped that would help with whatever was to come with this Billy Nelson character.

Wallace paused and it was obvious that he was choosing his next words carefully.

'Although he took the decision to kick Nelson out of Belfast, he was using him. He wanted to open up on the east side of Scotland, and Nelson's misjudgement suited him perfectly. He's using him to feel out things in Edinburgh, and if it goes wrong he can just wash his hands of him.'

Wallace changed tack and described what they knew about Nelson. It wasn't much, but they had intel on his early days in Belfast, along with his army record and the details of his dismissal from the service.

'Apparently the young Afghan should have died after the beating Billy boy gave him. He was lucky to get off relatively lightly, but Nelson was a bit of a hero in his regiment and the Army don't like lynching heroes – it's bad for morale. We know that Nelson attacked the two Asian kids in Belfast and left them in much the same mess as the Afghan boy. The military shrink believed that Nelson was seriously damaged goods and had just had too much combat; however he also discovered that memories of the Shankill bombing had damaged him even before the Army. Apparently he was close to the scene and saw some things a kid of that age could have done without.'

He sipped his coffee then leaned forward, wanting to

make sure they understood. 'This is a dangerous man, and his behaviour can't be predicted using normal profiling. He's chewed up with hatred, and although he has a team round him, it's unlikely he'll have any loyalty to them. If necessary he'll drop them if it suits whatever plan he has. The shrink thinks all that makes him function now is inflicting pain. We have information that even where he's tried to have a sexual relationship, he's impotent and rages at the failure. He is, not to put too fine a point on it, a time bomb.'

Wallace pulled out other documents and photographs of the rest of Nelson's team, gave Macallan as much as he could and looked at his watch. He had to fly back to Belfast to cover an operation that would take out some dissidents in South Down.

'One last thing: I don't know if it's connected but Jackie Martin still has access to a large stash of arms that weren't declared during the decommissioning process. We know that quite recently he sent two Uzis to Scotland, but we don't know who to. It might have been Nelson, but there's nothing to substantiate that. If they do turn up, please keep us in the loop.'

Macallan had a lot to think about but was as pleased with Wallace's attitude as she was with what he'd provided. If they could keep the PSNI onside it was a good start. She knew that their top targets would be monitored, and if Martin mentioned Nelson she wanted to get the message.

'Thanks, Barry, and as soon as we start intelligence gathering, you'll have what we have.'

15

On the first night that Lena Fleming had been out since her husband and son had gone missing, she walked the short distance from her flat at Ocean Terminal to meet a couple of friends and watch a film at the multiplex. She'd been distraught about her son but she'd had to put on the best act she could for her husband. Joe had bored her to tears, and the fact that he lived his life on past glories had pissed her off a long time before he walked out of her door for the last time. There had been many a night where she'd lain next to him, the thought of what her life could be if he died in an accident running on a loop in her head.

It was different for Danny. He'd been trouble since the day he was born, but he was her boy, and she'd spent days moaning in painful sorrow or raging against the men who'd taken him. Unfortunately father and son had tended to keep their business from her, and they hadn't said where they were going the night they'd left her house together. All she knew was that they'd been seriously pissed at some Irish fuckers living in Wester Hailes. She'd heard more through Joe's friends, who'd told her a bit but not enough.

She'd been hitting the bottle pretty hard and mouthing off threats whenever someone shared the latest rumour with her. She'd tried to call on the loyalty of Joe's team, but hey presto they didn't want to get involved. Her children had become weary listening to the same lines over and over again about the threats that she couldn't really carry out. At least not as long as none of Joe's team gave a fuck. Without muscle it was just so much noise.

'Typical.' When she'd swallowed too much brandy she always started her latest rant with that word. 'All those big fuckin' men Joe paid too well for years. Where the fuck are they when they're needed? My boy's probably lying in the ground somewhere, and no one gives a fuck. If it's the Irish bastards, I'll knife them on my own.'

Her daughters were about as concerned as Joe's former team of hooligans. The sisters couldn't stand their old man, and they were well aware of what their loving brother Danny had done to the women in his life. He'd even tried it on with his sisters over the years, and they were terrified of him. Danny Fleming on permanent holiday was no problem to them.

Lena met her friends, who only chose to see her so they could tell everyone else what a state she was in. They wanted to get close enough to gloat, because Lena had been a cow when Joe had ruled the streets. She'd loved to shove it in everyone's faces, and now they wanted to suck in the sweet smell of distress on Lena fucking Fleming. They had a drink, and after the third round decided on a curry rather than watching a film, which would require concentration. An hour and a half later the manager of the curry house asked Lena to leave after she announced to the paying customers that she was looking for whoever had taken her man and boy. Her friends loved it – couldn't wait to get the story out and enjoy what remained of the Flemings' downfall. Joe's friends saw the vacuum as a business opportunity and believed they'd be foolish not to try and pick up some pieces, although they were wary of the stories about the Belfast boys, and the name Billy Nelson was definitely getting mentioned in criminal dispatches.

The problem for Lena was that her ranting could be heard across town and Nelson had enough creeps in his pocket to hear what was being said. Cue Ball had put him onto a bent detective, DC Donnie Monk, whose coke habit was bad enough for him to sell his soul to the Belfast man.

'That bitch is bad-mouthing you all over town.' Monk whispered it down the line and decided to embellish it a bit, in case it got him some extra coke vouchers. 'She says she's got a team together and she's going to cut your balls off. Think you need to do something about her, son.'

Nelson smiled at the thought that she might even try. 'Never mind that fuckin' woman, I'll take care of her today. Is there anyone looking at us? That's all I need from you.'

'No, you're sweet. I've got my ears open, and if any of the squads take an interest I'll hear about it. They will at some stage, but no worries. I'll be right on it, and I'll let you know who's pulling the strings.' He hesitated, trying to cover the self-loathing in his voice. 'Usual arrangement for the envelope?'

'Yes, of course. I'll get one of the boys to drop it at the usual place and you can stuff that big fat fuckin' hooter of yours.' Billy didn't try to hide the contempt in his voice; he didn't need to when he was paying the man's poison-of-choice bills.

He dropped the phone into the cradle without any niceties. 'Doped-up pig. I fuckin' hate these guys,' he said, loud enough for Andy Clark to hear him in the next room.

Clark wondered at the man he'd admired so much. Nelson looked changed, but when he'd told him that the previous day, Nelson had threatened to cut his face. He'd had him by the throat and shoved his face close enough for Clark to see the change in the eyes, the dullness above the grey shadows below. Still handsome, and after all he'd put a few pounds on when they'd first arrived in Edinburgh, so maybe he was just making an effort? Still, Clark was confused – and he didn't like confusion.

Eventually Lena was abandoned by her friends, and she walked unsteadily back to her flat a few hundred yards away. By the time she got to the front of the building she was cursing the heels of her shoes and missing the point that it was the half-bottle of brandy she'd just consumed that was the problem. She fumbled for her keys, swearing loudly to no one but herself.

The arm that nearly choked off her breath was hard and strong, and even though she was under the influence she managed to feel the panic that sent her heart into overdrive. Rob McLean held her tight, lifting her just enough to leave her on her toes and in extreme discomfort, her eyes bulging with the combination of fear and confusion.

'Please. I've got money in my bag. Just take it for fuck's sake,' she said, struggling to get the words out with the compression on her throat.

McLean didn't answer; he looked round and was smiling as if it was a kid's game. He was enjoying himself and was disappointed with the look he saw on Nelson's face. He tried some humour. 'Jesus, she stinks. I wouldn't do her with yours, Billy.'

Nelson's face was set, and he continued to stare at Lena, ignoring McLean's feeble attempt at comedy. McLean wondered what the fuck was wrong with the man. There'd been a time where this would have just been a bit of a laugh – easy work.

'Get her in the van.'

The hired blue transit that Lena was bundled into the back of was dark and stank of tobacco smoke, and she could see two men waiting for her. Andy Clark and Dougie Fisher stared at her as she gulped in air, trying to steady her breathing and sense of dread. The accents told her that the men who'd probably taken Joe and Danny were dragging her away from her home in the night. She thought the worst and threw up on Fisher's brand-new trainers.

'For fuck's sake. The dirty cow's just wasted the new Nikes.'

Nelson swung round, anger drawing his lips back into a snarl. 'Shut the fuck up and put the bag on her head.'

Fisher did as he was told but Lena didn't really need it. She'd already passed out cold.

She came round slowly and for a brief moment thought it was just another hangover day, then her mind down-loaded reality and she started to shake through the length of her body. The van was moving very slowly and covering very rough ground, so she knew they weren't in Edinburgh any more. Her mouth was paper dry and had the rank taste of the night's drink, but her hands and feet were free, though when she tried to move to relieve her cramping muscles, she felt a foot stuck into her back. The worst part was that she'd wet herself.

'Stay the fuck down, darlin'; we're nearly there. Your man'll be happy to see you.'

She tried to make sense of the words 'her man'. Joe – how could that be? Had it been a kidnap after all? Was there still a chance that Danny was alive? They could keep Joe as long as Danny had survived. Hope started to beat in her chest. The smell of drying vomit on her dress, plus an overdose of stress, made her gag, and she tried to salivate to relieve her mouth and throat. She asked a question in as quiet a voice as possible. 'Are Joe and Danny okay?'

'He's first class, darlin', and never looked better – can't wait to see you,' Fisher sneered.

Her hope raised another level – all she wanted was to live and bring Danny home. Whatever the fuck these lunatics wanted they could have.

Nelson knew what Lena would be thinking and that was the point. It would have been easy enough to snuff her, but he knew his tactics. They didn't want to raise another red alert for the police – her disappearance would start to bring serious heat their way. He was a product of the Troubles and had learned enough about the use of terror in Basra and Helmand province to last him the rest of his life.

The men from Belfast were taking over the trade in the east of Scotland and there would always be the predators just out of sight in the dark shadows. He knew they had to send a message that would keep them where they were. Fear would make them think of the consequences of an attack. Let them imagine themselves with mouths frozen in a last attempt to gasp in air, their heart and soul torn out in agony, nightmares...

Lena had set herself up perfectly – she was about to face a terror that she could never even imagine. After this night she would never have another day in her life when she wouldn't remember what Nelson was going to show her. He was going to take her where he'd been, time and time again. She'd realise that his will was stronger than anything she'd seen in Joe or Danny – or the pretend criminals who'd inhabited her previous life.

The van stopped, leaning to one side, and she knew that

wherever they were it was well off-road. Nelson opened the doors but left her there in the van. She knew that the two men were still in the back with her and they sat quietly. The driver and passenger doors had opened then closed, and more than one man had walked off some distance, though they were still audible. It was deathly quiet, no traffic noise, but there was a soft crunching sound, and she guessed rightly that the men were walking through cold, dead leaves. She waited a few moments then heard a faint, almost repetitive sound; she was sure she knew what it was but couldn't tie it down. It was the sound of something smooth cutting through a yielding substance. What was it? The left hemisphere of her brain lit up with energy trying desperately to identify what the right side was telling her was important to survival. The ancient mechanisms struggled inside Lena, sensing danger and trying to find answers.

A picture of her father appeared in her mind's eye – she was a kid again, those happy days when she'd played in the garden, the sun beating down on her back. She'd loved those summers, and her father, whose passion had been working in his garden or vegetable patch. She'd looked up from the dolls to see he was sweating, his face red from effort and too much sun on his white Scottish hide. He'd dug the soil rhythmically, the turned earth black and clean, with only the occasional earthworm thrashing in annoyance at the disturbance.

'Oh no – please, God, no!' It was the sound of someone digging.

Fisher snorted a laugh at her distress. 'What's the matter? Nice evening drive out in the country, bit of fresh air. Ungrateful cow.'

Clark looked across the darkness of the van and wondered at the sadistic pleasure Fisher was enjoying. He'd started to doubt himself and what they were up to, was struggling to sleep at night after seeing the pain they were handing out to whoever was in their road. They'd driven Maggie Smith into her grave, and now they were about to show Lena a place that would haunt her for the rest of her life. Clark had dished it out to anyone who'd needed it in the past, but now they were doing women. He felt the corner of his eye twitch and he balled his hands into fists to stop the shakes. What they were about to do was bad, worse than that, but he was trapped, and he knew what Nelson would do with any protest.

Lena struggled to control her breathing, and it sounded as if it was being relayed through a loudspeaker. The sound of footsteps and laboured breathing made her twitch her head upwards. She didn't need anyone to tell her that the men were coming for her.

'Please let me go. I promise I won't tell anyone what happened. I'm no one,' she pleaded in the tones of the condemned who know they can't change a thing on the way to the scaffold.

Nelson was at the back of the van. He dropped the shovel, leaned in and ripped the bag from her head. He grabbed her at cheek level and squeezed as hard as he could. She felt an expensive crown give way and slip into the back of her throat, making her gag. She couldn't spit it out as Nelson held her face like a vice. She managed to swallow it.

'Apparently you're the bitch who's going to take care of me and the boys. Well, here's your chance, missus.'

She caught the smell of damp earth and leaves on his hands, but there was something else, rancid, that caught the back of her throat. Nausea almost overwhelmed her. She made a long groaning noise, low and without words – an expression of horror. Were these her last minutes? She was in dread of the pain they could inflict. These strangers had done enough to show her that the violence she'd seen dished out by her husband over the years was nothing compared to what they were capable of.

She tried again, looking for pity from a man who had none. 'Please don't kill me.'

Nelson held onto her face and with his other hand grabbed a full handful of the hair at the back of her head, then, letting go of her damaged cheeks, he twisted till her face drew tight with the pain. He walked her towards a small copse surrounded by birch trees growing in an almost perfect circle. They looked like black drawings against the dark blue of the night sky.

Lena arched her back, trying to ease the agony in her neck and scalp. A bright three-quarter moon cast deep inky shadows, but the sky was cloudless, and where there was light the night was sharp and clear. Her thoughts were a churning mess; her mind was shattering, unable to confront the horror in the darkness of those woods. The other men were behind her but no one spoke, and she was sure they'd already worked out what would be done. Although her head was pulled back she kept her eyes looking downwards at whatever was in front of her. In the middle of the circle of birch trees she saw it. It wasn't the professional job she'd seen so often when she'd gone to the cemetery to see friends or family on their way. In the contrasting moonlight and darkness it was no more than a black oblong shadow and the depth couldn't be seen – but it was a grave.

Her legs gave way despite the pain at the back of her head, and she pleaded quietly for her life as Nelson dragged her the last few feet and let go of her hair. Her face dropped into the mixture of fresh earth and leaf mould. She squeezed her eyes closed, trying to make the night leave her; all she wanted was to be home and safe again. Her chest heaved as she hyperventilated and waited for the end, praying for it to be over.

It didn't happen. Instead there was a pause, and the men stood quietly round her for a moment. Then her hair was pulled violently again, forcing her neck back till she thought it would snap from her spine, and she pushed up onto her hands and knees. Nelson forced her forward to the edge of the pit and she looked into the blackness until, at his nod, Fisher switched on the powerful hand lamp.

Lena couldn't recognise what she was seeing for several seconds because of the sudden illumination and her subconscious refusal to take it in. Then her mind separated the shapes below her. There was little difference between the colour of her husband and son's faces and that of the reeking earth around them. There were only shades of grey in the harsh mixture of moonlight and the beam from the halogen lamp. It was them though – Joe and Danny. Only their faces were exposed, but what else did she need to see? Joe's lips were stretched back in what looked like a snarling last look at the world. At the opposite end of their grave Danny's face stared back at his mother. She tried to make a sound but nothing came.

Nelson let go of her hair and knelt beside her. She didn't try to crawl away; she was unable to move, nothing in her motor system was working. Lena was in a kind of agony that in the days and years that followed she would not be able to recall at will – it would come back to her in the night or unannounced, replayed in exactly the same form, over and over and over again.

Nelson gave her a few moments to be with her family. Unlike the boys with him, Nelson had been educated in warfare by the British Army, so he knew the benefit of tactics, unlike the blunt instruments that made up his team. He always remembered one of his instructors who loved to quote the words of the ancient Chinese general Sun Tzu: 'The supreme art of war is to subdue the enemy without fighting.' And he had decided that in letting the late Joe Fleming's wife live, he could subdue other enemies.

'Now, Lena, the good news is that I'm going to let you go. I could dig another hole so you could have a "his and hers" plot but I'm sure you'd rather go back and get a good drink in you. You open that big fat fuckin' gob and we'll come back and bring you here forever. You just stay out of our business now. How does that sound?'

She turned her head and stared at Nelson like a whipped dog. Then it sank in that he was going to let her live and nothing else mattered as long as she didn't go in the ground beside Joe. She tried to kiss Nelson's hand, but he recoiled.

Fisher laughed. Nelson stared at him without speaking and the look stopped Fisher in his tracks.

Nelson stood up. 'Say goodbye to your husband and boy, Lena, and hopefully you'll not be seeing them again.'

He threw a shovel over to Fisher, told him to cover up the Flemings and then dragged Lena back to the van, where she lay shaking, imagining the grave all the way back to Edinburgh.

Two hours later the two beat officers who'd found Maggie Smith were back on nights and responding to a call that a drunk woman was staggering around behind the restaurants and shops that fronted Commercial Street in Leith. It was 4 a.m. and Charlie hated these late calls that came in when they should have been sitting quietly, maybe taking forty winks till it was time to go home and get the bacon rolls. He turned to Tony.

'Four in the morning and some twat is pissed. Can you believe it?'

Tony was happy to get the call, being at the opposite end of the cynic scale and still loving the job. Any time, any day as far as he was concerned; but he also knew that although Charlie had done it all before – and despite him acting the tired old cop – the cynicism was seventy per cent acting.

They drove slowly behind the old bonded warehouses that now housed the trendy shops and restaurants in sight of the dominant Scottish Government complex. They couldn't see anything and got out of the car, lighting up their hand lamps to check the edges of the car-park area.

'She probably made it home,' Charlie said hopefully, lighting up a cigarette to annoy Tony, who hated the smell and was a confirmed gym addict. He leaned against the car as his partner scuffled around the edges of the car park.

'How far do you think I should look? She could be anywhere.' He flashed his torch around a little more, recoiling as a refuse-fattened rat scuttled towards the back of a top restaurant to see what the fine diners had left for him.

'Just let me finish this in peace, son, and I'll be right with you.' Charlie saw his role as a constant process of teaching his young friend about reality. Patience, street skills, seeing it all for the farce that it was – and above all keeping his head straight. Later, when he eventually married, the task would be making it work and realising that one day the job would be over and he'd just be another old cop with a bagful of war stories.

Tony was about eighty yards from his mentor and getting ready to throw in the towel when he heard it – a low rumbling growl. He felt the muscles in his back and neck almost lock up with tension. He was sure it was a dog. He had a fear of large, aggressive dogs, a legacy of his childhood and an incident with one of those sad bastards who parade their devil dogs round the area because they couldn't afford a proper penis extension like an expensive car. The dog had been off its lead and ten-year-old Tony had been kicking a ball about on his own, dreaming about the day he'd line up for Manchester United. The dog had cornered him and stood about two paces from his face, dribbling saliva and half-frightening the life out of him. He'd never endured fear like it and all he'd been able to hear was the dog's owner laughing in the background. He hadn't been able to take his eyes from the animal's, realising how vulnerable and weak he was and that the world was a dangerous place.

He fought against his instincts and shone the torch towards the noise. 'Charlie, over here!'

'What the fuck is it now?' Charlie stubbed out his cigarette and knew that it was going to be another late finish. 'Fuck it.'

He ambled across and crouched down, taking in the figure trying to squeeze into the space behind a parked car and a low stone wall. It was Lena Fleming, but not the Lena that he'd known since they were both a lot younger. She'd always liked the company of criminals and had the looks that Joe Fleming as a rising star had wanted on his arm, and that had been good enough for her. Charlie had developed quite a thing for her, and when Joe was doing his first stretch for a post-office robbery, it was he who had put a smile on her face on the occasional night shift. Lena had enjoyed the affair – especially with the added spice that Joe would have gone mental if he'd known it was a copper on his side of the bed.

'Jesus, Lena, what's happened to you?' Charlie hardly recognised the woman, her knees pulled up tight, recoiling from the two policemen.

'Get that fuckin' light off her face; she's terrified!' he barked at his partner, and he was right. Lena was terrified and would be for the rest of her life.

The policeman took in the bruising, dirt and vomit,

146

the eyes bulging as if her lids had been stapled back. He knew that she'd been hurt – more than hurt – and that the damage went beyond what he could see.

She was shivering with cold and shock. Charlie took hold of her gently, talking to her as if she was a child and managed to lift her up, forgetting about his chronic back problem.

'Get a blanket from the car, Tony, and an ambulance. Pronto.'

Tony ran to the patrol car while the older man lifted Lena up and carried her like a child. His back objected violently and would make him pay for several weeks to come, but he didn't even notice it at the time.

The ambulance was there in minutes and the paramedics thought Lena had been in an accident. As it drove away with the blue light swirling, Charlie shook his head and saw the threads of a problem. He didn't know what they meant but could sense it was bad and there would be a price to pay. Joe Fleming and his son were missing and now this.

'She looks like she's just seen her own grave, son.'

Tony nodded in agreement, but he was still remembering the dog's snarling face.

16

Macallan shifted nervously from one foot to the other. That didn't work, so she walked to the counter and scanned the board, trying to make sense of an endless list of coffees topped with enough calories to sink a small ship. She'd never been able to make sense of it and just wanted an ordinary coffee, but she sometimes wondered whether that product existed any more.

'Just a coffee with milk, please.' She looked pleadingly at the waitress, hoping she wouldn't offer her a dozen alternatives. The girl, whose name tag said Anna, took pity on her and got Macallan exactly what she'd asked for.

She wondered why she even bothered with coffee – every time she finished a cup she told herself that she hated the taste and that it corrupted the breath for about two hours. It was the drug of course – caffeine, the most popular legal high.

'Jesus.' She thought about her breath and decided to leave the coffee alone once she'd bought it. Jack Fraser was about to arrive, and she didn't want to put him off before they'd even said hello again.

The airport was choked; some delays in London had knocked on and caused inevitable jams everywhere else. At least his plane was on time, she thought as she scanned the arrivals board for the tenth time. She asked herself again why she was so nervous, but of course she already knew the answer.

Macallan could pretend that Jack's visit was just him attending a conference, that it was old friends getting together for a catch-up and drinks, but that was nonsense – and she knew it. It was as clear as the blue skies above the airport that Fraser wanted to rebuild what he'd shattered in Belfast.

It seemed a lifetime ago, but Macallan would never forget her feelings of despair about what she'd gone through in Northern Ireland, especially those associated with him. Everything else that had happened she could have dealt with if he'd been there for her. She'd thought she'd never trust anyone again after he'd walked out of her life, and what had made it harder to bear was that, at the time, he hadn't even attempted to tell her why. Since she'd met him again and he'd explained, she could see the dilemma for him, but no matter what, he'd acted selfishly and must have seen how isolated and alone she was. The contrast had been Bill Kelly, who'd ignored his own position in the force and stood by her, right until she'd stepped onto the ferry, swearing never to touch the soil of Ulster again.

Macallan had learned a lot about herself since leaving Northern Ireland and starting her new life in Edinburgh. It had given her distance, time to see it all in context, and Harkins had taught her to accept the flaws in other people as well as her own. The failed relationship with John O'Connor should have been enough to turn her off relationships for life, but she knew that would be foolish. Fraser had wanted to avoid simply walking out on his family and, in truth, if he had done that, Macallan would have thought less of him. The commander had caught him in a hard place, and he'd folded in the face of a man who was simply in a stronger position than he was.

She'd seen the change in Jack, the sorrow for all the things that had happened. He'd probably had as many sleepless nights as she'd had herself. She accepted that in a way they were both new people, and they both still cared deeply for each other – and now he was free.

She thought about Harkins' budgie again.

'No contest then,' she said, loud enough for a new arrival to swivel round and look at the woman who seemed to be talking to her.

Macallan smiled and turned her eyes back to the arrivals board again.

Jack Fraser walked through the gates, scanning the waiting friends and families for Macallan, and he saw her walking towards him with a broadening smile. As always she was dressed simply: jeans, a roll-neck sweater and a long dark coat. Her hair was cut short, and he could see the light from her green eyes across the concourse. It was all simple, but the effect was stunning. Had someone asked him, he would have been hard-pressed to say there was any feature that was outstanding, but that was it – Macallan was always understated, yet when she walked into a room she projected energy, intelligence and a complete lack of vanity. That was her trick on the world. A more physically attractive woman would seem to lose definition in her company.

He felt a trembling in his stomach and realised he just felt glad to be where he was for the first time in an age.

Macallan had already run through the scenario where they met at the airport and had decided on a hug and kiss on the cheek. She wanted to play it carefully as there was too much at stake for both of them. She'd thought they might become friends and that, perhaps, would be the wisest course. But when she walked the last few feet towards Fraser and saw what his eyes were telling her, the plan, like most plans, was filed in the 'no-further-action' box. Fraser dropped the briefcase from one hand and the suitcase from the other. They kissed each other and then embraced till most of the other arrivals had gone.

'Let's go; we've a lot of catching up to do.' Macallan let him go and saw his eyes were full. 'Come on, that's my job,' she said, smiling as she took him by the hand and led him to the car.

As she drove through the darkening streets of Edinburgh, she realised that all she wanted was to be alone with him. He'd booked into a hotel, but she told him that he'd have to take a loss because he was staying at her place. 'It's huge and I can't afford it, but it's lovely. There's a really nice spare room and you'll be comfortable in there.'

Fraser kept quiet. The spare room was good for him. He was just happy to be with her, and she was right to take it easy. He knew he wouldn't sleep being in the same house, albeit in a different bedroom, but that was fine. What he couldn't see in the semi-darkness was the mischievous sparkle in her eyes.

'Just kidding! You've pulled.' She smiled and suppressed her laugh, knowing how he'd have been struggling with the idea of the spare room.

'Oh, I don't know. Let's just take it easy and see where it goes. I think the spare room is best.' His face was serious, but Macallan had forgotten that Fraser was an advocate, a good one, and some said great. He let her struggle till he thought they had a draw. 'Just kidding! You've pulled.'

'God, look at us, Jack. Two of the most serious people I know teasing each other.'

The night was all that Macallan and Fraser could have wanted. They talked, ate and drank till the early hours but never once looked at the clock. Without saying it they'd both decided to be as open and honest as possible, filling in the spaces that had opened up between their lives. He told her about his struggle with the divorce, the heartbreak of leaving his children and his attempts to build a new life. Macallan told him about Edinburgh, the people she'd met and some of the cases she'd managed. He'd followed the news reports and knew parts of the stories. She also told him about John O'Connor.

'I am impressed, you know. To come here the way you did and build a new career is quite something. All that press coverage has made you quite a star.'

Macallan looked into the dregs of the wine in her glass. 'Well we have this unified force in Scotland now, but it'll take years to settle down so I think I'm stuck here for the time being. That suits though – I love Edinburgh. It has all these sides, and it's not a big city so everything's close. A bit like Belfast without the guns and bombs.'

She told him about the problem that was developing with Billy Nelson and he felt a knot of worry. 'Watch what you do there. You were always involved with the Republican side. I prosecuted a few cases against the Loyalists and believe me they're a whole new game.'

They changed the subject and talked about rugby, Fraser admitting that he still played the odd game despite his supposed retirement and had been picking up new injuries every time. She shook her head but wasn't in the least surprised.

Around 3 a.m. Macallan stood up, took Fraser by the hand and put the lights out on their way to bed.

17

Eddie Fleming was the older twin by two minutes and had taken the call from Leith police station that his mother had been hurt and was on her way to hospital. Eddie presumed that she'd been pissed again, fallen and managed to break something this time. He was in his own flat and rang his sibling Pat, named after his father's all-time favourite Hibs player.

Pat was lying beside a girl he'd only met the night before and would probably never see again. It had been the result of too much drink, and he'd already decided that she was a dog. He wasn't too upset by the call from his brother – he just couldn't see the urgency.

'What's the rush? They're probably pumpin' her gut or somethin'. You know what she's been like about Danny and the old man.'

Eddie was the smarter of the two, knew what was what and was a reincarnation of his father at the same age. Pat had his brother Danny's nature, hard and vicious, but no business sense.

'Get your arse into gear and I'll pick you up in fifteen minutes,' Eddie said. 'Things are bad enough already.

We're what's left, and how does it look if we can't be fucked to go and see the old lady.' He snarled it down the line so his brother wouldn't miss the point.

He put the phone down without waiting for a reply; he knew his brother wouldn't dare ignore the order. Pat was hard, but Eddie was all that with a brain to match. He'd even excelled at school, which was a rarity for a Fleming, and university should have been the next step, but Eddie had known where his career path lay. It was the age of the gangster, the films glamorised the life and it seemed a better option to Eddie than sitting in an office staring at a computer for half the day, which seemed to be what three-quarters of the working population were doing for a job.

Eddie stood just over six foot and a daily routine of weights and cardio had developed a hard body to match his even good looks. His hair was cropped short and a flawless complexion gave him an almost male-model look, but that was far from what Eddie Fleming was. He would have been difficult to tell apart from Pat, except that the younger man had a six-inch scar on his left cheek after he'd been slashed in a bar fight with some Hearts fans after a heated derby match.

The twins had barely finished celebrating their twenty-first birthday and had been kept in the background of their father's criminal business. Old Joe had always said he was like a top football coach and would bring the boys along slowly till they were ready for the big league. They were eager enough themselves, but Danny didn't want them cutting into the profits. He'd preferred to keep them running the odd message – low profile and nothing that would get them mentioned in dispatches. Like their sisters, the twins despised Danny for what he was, and the trouble was that Danny had known it. But as far as he'd been concerned, when old Joe popped his clogs, he would take over, and the rest of the family could either work for him or fuck off and get proper jobs.

It was the early-morning rush hour by the time they headed to the hospital, and on the way they stopped for some flowers.

'Appearances, Pat – that's what matters. Got to do the right thing so all those other fuckers out there know that we're the real business.' Eddie spoke like an older man, and in a way that's what he was. 'We've sat back long enough. The old man's business is getting cut up under our noses while we fuck about the pubs in Leith. After we've seen what's up at the hospital we need to get serious – find out what's going on.'

Pat was less confident but knew that Eddie was smart enough for the both of them. They were isolated; Joe's team seemed to have disappeared, and he wasn't sure what the two of them could do in the world of men. He didn't mind getting involved, but there were some dangerous fuckers out there who'd been doing it for years, and it was only now becoming apparent to the young brothers that they'd relied too much on Joe. Without him they were rudderless. Their father had been the one with all the contacts and he'd made the deals; he'd been reluctant to delegate responsibility because he mistrusted Danny, knowing his firstborn was as much of a danger to him as the other scumbags waiting for a turn.

The twins walked along the corridors on the lookout for their mother waving at them and apologising for the amount of sauce she'd taken the night before, but there was no sign of her, and when they arrived at the ward and asked the staff nurse for directions, she said the doctor needed to talk to them first. It was only then they began to realise the situation might be more serious than they had presumed.

The doctor arrived shortly afterwards and explained

that their mother had experienced a significant mental trauma and was in a state of shock. There was no doubt that Lena had suffered an assault, and though her injuries would heal, there would have to be an assessment of her psychological condition.

Eddie was the one who asked the question, through tight lips, that had first come to mind for both of the brothers. 'Has someone interfered with her?'

The doctor's briefing had hit them like a good right hook. They hadn't been ready for it, and now they realised they were facing yet another problem – as if they needed any more. Father and brother missing and now it sounded as if their mother had turned into a candidate for the chuckle wagon.

The doctor patiently explained to them that as far as they could see there were no indications that she had been sexually assaulted.

They walked into a side room, which was quiet apart from the low buzz of the machines hooked up to their mother. A uniformed policewoman was standing outside the room; she recognised the twins and nodded, but they ignored the gesture. Lena's eyes were closed and she seemed to have aged by about twenty years. Her face was pale and covered with small marks and bruises. Nothing too bad on their own, but they knew those marks hadn't come on their own.

'What the fuck is this?' Eddie hissed. His fist balled then unclenched as he tried to suppress a growing sense of rage and confusion. His brother didn't really feel much for any other human being, but this cut him somewhere deep in his instincts. It was their mother; someone had done this to Lena, so it had been done to them. Whatever had happened would never have happened in the past. There was no one in the east side of the central belt who would have dared.

'We've gone soft – fuckin' soft as shite,' said Eddie, running his hands over his head, and he made a silent promise that there would be a reply.

He leaned over and his nose twitched at the foul odour of his mother's breath. She half-opened her eyes and seemed to recoil in fear at the sight of her son. Eddie took her hand, which seemed weak and frail, but she tried to pull away. Whatever she was seeing, it wasn't her two boys.

'It's Eddie and Pat, Ma. You're okay; we're here with you and everythin's goin' to be okay.' Eddie felt the lump grow in his throat and it threw him. He didn't want to show emotion – he was a Fleming for fuck's sake. But although he was a Fleming, he was still not much more than a boy in years.

Whatever the Fleming family was, Lena was his mother, and for all her faults she loved her sons and had always taken care of them – even Danny. She stared at him for what seemed like an age, and her lips trembled like an old woman's. She stared wide-eyed at her son and gradually he felt her grip tighten as she tried to mouth something.

'What happened, Ma? Did someone hurt you?' He tried to keep his voice strong, but there was a tremor of mixed anger and fear.

Pat stood behind his brother and felt the same emotions washing through him. He took a step forward to his brother's side, trying to make sense of what he was seeing and hearing.

Lena looked towards Pat and then back to Eddie.

'Don't let them hurt me again,' she pleaded. 'Please don't let them hurt me again.'

'Who hurt you, Ma?' Eddie was trying to deal with too much frustration, and he was short of patience. He took his mother's hand out of his own and told Pat to stay with her, went outside and against his instincts spoke to the female police officer.

'What the fuck happened to my mother?'

The officer had worked out of Leith for nearly ten years, knew the Flemings, and Eddie recognised her. As far as she was concerned they were the dregs. She was going through a break-up, having caught her bastard of a boyfriend giving it to her best friend, and she couldn't care less about Lena Fleming or any of her offspring. She'd heard the story that old Joe and Danny might be in heaven with the angels, and as far as she was concerned that was a result.

'I'm sorry, sir. I don't have any information. I was told that if any of the family arrived I was to ask you to contact DS Baxter at Leith CID. I think they'd like to take a statement.' She barely concealed the contempt and boredom in her voice.

Eddie knew he was wasting his time, but he decided that on this occasion he might just give the filth a visit.

'Thanks, officer. It's good to know that you're giving it your best.' He tried to give an equal measure of contempt back.

'Anytime, sir; we always like to help.' Her face was expressionless.

Eddie decided that the exchange was getting nowhere and took solace from the fact that the officer was an ugly bitch and looked like she was incapable of being happy, so that was something.

He went back to his mother's bedside and put his hand on his brother's shoulder. 'She said anything, Pat?'

His brother looked round at him and Eddie saw his eyes were red and filled up. He was shaking. 'She said she saw Danny and the old man. She's said it over and over again.'

Eddie looked down at his mother, who was indeed

whispering it over and over. 'I saw them in the ground. Danny and Joe. I saw them in the ground. Danny and Joe.'

Eddie took his mother's hand and put his other hand on her brow. 'Listen to me, Ma. Please listen. You have to help us.'

He stroked her brow until she stopped and seemed to be calm again.

'Eddie.' She said his name quietly, but at least it meant she was in the room with them.

He kept stroking her gently. 'You're okay. You're safe, and no one's going to hurt you now. We'll take you home soon. Now try and tell us what happened.'

Lena could only remember fragments of the horror she'd endured in the wooded area outside the city. Her memories were moments of terror exploding in her mind's eye. She would see an image of trees, then it was gone; remember the smell of earth and corruption, before it too disappeared; and then, worst of all, she would see her husband's near-black face snarling at eternity.

What Eddie and Pat knew was that their mother had been lifted, taken somewhere and shown a nightmare. It was beyond anything they'd experienced and, as Eddie raged, Pat was frightened of whoever could go to the lengths his mother's tormentors had.

Lena had told them enough to be sure that someone had taken her – that she'd seen the dead faces of her husband and son. She'd become incoherent after that, and a doctor, who didn't look any older than the twins, intervened and told them enough was enough, so they decided to give up for the time being. There was a possibility that this was simply her imagination, but Eddie knew that whatever had happened to his mother had shocked her into a terrifying place, and he wondered if she would ever be able to escape the experience. If she had seen the dead faces of his brother and father, what did it mean and how should they move on it? No one from Edinburgh would have had reason to do it this way. He knew there were plenty out there happy to see them fall, but not like this. It could have been nutters from the west, because Joe Fleming had sourced his gear from the same Glasgow crew for years. They were hard core, but as far as Eddie knew there had never been a problem, and Joe had always paid on time. The Weegies were mental, no doubt about it, but they didn't do subtle, and there would have been more warnings that something was wrong.

It was more likely to be the Belfast team, who were already the top suspects. But if this was what they were capable of, what could the twins do in response?

Eddie realised that for the first time in their lives they needed to use the police and get them onside. The obvious place to start was with what had happened on the night Lena had met her friends and then try to fill in the black hole that followed. It could mean going round the doors where his mother lived, and the truth was that the only people that might have a chance were the police.

He had the sense to admit to himself that he wasn't ready to get into a battle when they still didn't know for sure that their mother's ramblings were real. And if it was the Belfast team then Pat and Eddie Fleming would need some serious fucking backup – and a plan.

'Let's go,' Eddie said.

'Go where?' Pat scratched his arse, thinking his older brother was declaring it opening time.

'Leith police station to see DS Grant Baxter, git that he is.'

'Are you having a fuckin' laugh?' Pat stopped mid step and looked at Eddie as if he'd just come out of the closet as a secret Hearts supporter.

'Look, Pat, we're in no man's fuckin' land at the moment. The old man and Danny are probably potted; you've seen her ladyship and the so-called Fleming gang seem to have taken a holiday.' Eddie faced his brother and tried to talk the blindingly obvious into his one-track brain. He'd always been convinced that in the womb they'd split everything fifty-fifty till it came to brain cells. Pat had definitely lost out there, but Eddie had always been protective of him, and whatever happened they'd share what destiny brought, or, just as likely, dumped on their heads.

'We need answers, and I don't think we can get them at the moment. The cops probably can, and we need to buy time. Whoever's doing this to the family might not be finished. There's only you and me left, Pat. Think about it – these fuckers might be on our tail right now, just waitin' for their chance.'

Eddie watched his brother's face gradually take in then accept what he'd just been told. Pat would have taken on a small army on a normal day, but the unknown frightened him.

Eddie carried on. 'If it's the Irish then as it stands we're fucked if we try to take them on face to face. That's just how it is, but they fuckin' bleed just like us, and if we can get organised then maybe, just maybe, we can level the scores.'

The twins jumped into their 4x4 and headed for Leith, calling DS Baxter on the way.

Baxter thought he must have been hallucinating if a Fleming was volunteering to walk into the beautiful old police building without a battle. Like everyone else, Baxter had heard that Joe and Danny were AWOL, but so far no one had reported them missing.

He checked the rota and found that the beat cops who'd found Lena were on duty. He walked into the mess room just as the two uniforms were ripping into some black-pudding rolls, which obviously the DS was interrupting.

Baxter explained who was coming in and asked if they would speak to them then take them up to the CID office. Charlie forgave the interruption because he was interested in seeing the youngest fruit of Old Joe's loins. No one knew about his link to the Flemings, and he wanted it to stay that way, but he'd seen with his own eyes that something terrible had happened to Lena, and she hadn't deserved that.

He realised that he was actually feeling sorry for the Flemings, which prompted him once more to work out how long it was till his retirement date. He was definitely getting old.

The twins arrived on time and Charlie told them what he'd seen when Lena had been found in the car park. He offered them some tea and the older boy's initial hostility seemed to calm, but Pat had been told from birth that the police were the enemy and that's how it would stay.

He remembered as an infant in arms the drugs squad crashing the door in and basically wrecking the place, looking for the heroin that Joe was dealing in increasing quantities. Joe had been on an upward track and the squad were getting the message from their 'squeaks'.

They'd found fuck all but as compensation they'd torn the place to shreds. Joe had steel balls in those days and had taken young Pat from his mother's arms as she'd sobbed and wasted her time asking them to stop. Joe had just smiled, knowing that two kilos of brown had been moved from the flat just an hour before they'd arrived. He'd pointed to a detective sergeant who was built like a small truck and the boy had followed his words.

'See them, son. They're what you call bastards, scum,

shite. They hate us, and we fuckin' hate them. What are they, son?'

As any boy does, he'd taken his lead from his father. 'Bastas, shite, shite, shite, shite.' The infant Pat had laughed and had at least pronounced the word 'shite' correctly. He'd pointed at the DS, who'd shaken his head and carried on ripping the fireplace out.

Joe had loved it. 'That's my boy. Someday you'll give that big fat cunt some Elastoplasts to cover that big fat ugly fuckin'—'

Joe hadn't got the word 'mug' out; the big DS had moved at surprising speed and held Joe's face as if he'd been in the grip of a pneumatic shovel. Although he'd played rugby like some unleashed demon, the DS had essentially been a quiet, gentle man, but Joe had waved the red rag just a bit too much. The hand that gripped his father's face had been only inches from the boy's. His father's eyes had popped in fright at the grip, and his mouth had definitely been shut.

As far as young Pat had been concerned, his father's enemy was his enemy, and he'd bitten down as hard as his small teeth could manage. The DS had yelped in surprise rather than pain, but he'd backed off, knowing he could hardly left hook a preschool-age Fleming. Old Joe had recovered from his shock and nearly pissed himself laughing. 'That's my boy. That's my fuckin' boy,' he'd crowed.

Charlie finished telling them what he could, but it was obvious to Eddie that the old uniform didn't have much else to add.

Charlie took them to the CID interview room after that, and the twins felt the nerves that all career criminals suffer within the four walls of a station even when they're not under arrest. Horror stories had been passed down the generations of criminal families about what had

163

happened inside the confines of the old Leith station. In the days when discipline had a greater margin of error, and no one had a mobile phone with a camera, summary justice would take place for special customers. Unfortunately everyone who'd been locked up then felt they had to claim a beating after they were released. It was a badge of honour, and you weren't worth much unless ten hairy cops had allegedly beaten all the colours out of you.

Baxter was old school, six months from his pension and still working his arse off every day because he loved it. He was one of the greatest bastards and cynics in the job, but at least he was consistent. He just didn't like anyone, including his wife, and especially his gay son, who he believed had brought disgrace on his house. His redeeming feature was that he lived and breathed his job, and was always there when it counted. He just didn't do friendships or political correctness. Fortunately, he wasn't bright enough to take the jump to inspector, but it had never bothered him.

Baxter sat the twins down opposite him and wanted to shake his head at the old question of where had all that time gone? As a young officer he'd locked up their grandfather, who wasn't a criminal, other than the fact that he'd fight his shadow on a Friday night after a hard week in the docks. He'd burst Baxter's nose on their first encounter, so the cop always made sure to get his retaliation in first after that. The funny thing was that the old man had liked the police, and never had any hard feelings, invariably blaming himself and the drink.

Their father Joe, on the other hand, had been a pain in the arse all his life, and though Baxter had tussled with him down the years, he'd never managed to put him away for any length of time, which bugged him. Now it looked like someone had stamped old Joe's ticket, and he waited to hear what the twins had to say. He sighed at the thought that he was dealing with the third generation, and every day that passed emphasised that his world was disappearing, and fast. The boys sitting opposite would be pissing off the constabulary when Baxter was dribbling into his soup.

The old force had been sucked into the new Police Service of Scotland, his hero Maggie Thatcher had taken over in heaven and his beloved Heart of Midlothian were shite and skint. His world was changing, and all he could do was push on, but he locked down the negative thoughts till later.

'How can I help you?' He thought for a moment then remembered he was only months away from the winning post and realised that he could say whatever he liked.

Eddie was about to answer but Baxter gave him a talk-to-the-hand movement. 'Look, I don't know why you're here. I'm busy chasing fucking criminals. Now I've heard your old man and brother are – how do we put it? – not answering their phones. No one's reported it to us, so if it's serious we're miles behind the ball. Your old ma looks like she's been abducted by aliens and then dropped back to earth.'

Pat didn't like his attitude and tried to get out of his seat, but Eddie whipped an arm across his chest and eased him back into his chair.

Baxter was unimpressed, sniffed and continued. 'Now something fucking awful is going on in this city, and I think for the time being we should declare a truce. Tell us what we need to know and let us get on with it. I know it's not in your interest to tell us everything, just enough. Otherwise fuck off out of my station.'

Pat shook with temper, but Eddie read the situation better than his brother.

'He's windin' you up, Pat boy – keep calm.' He smiled at Baxter, who smiled back, satisfied with his delivery, which had been honed by years of taking the piss out of criminals.

Eddie leaned forward and put his arms on the table. 'Get some tea, Sergeant, and I'll tell you what I know, which isn't much, but I want to make an official report that my father and brother are missin', plus my mother has been abducted and assaulted. Not by aliens I might add. I believe my brother and father have been murdered.'

Baxter hadn't expected what he'd just been told and leaned back in his chair, trying to assess the young man opposite. He was good, no doubt about it. He'd have to be if someone had taken out Joe and Danny then scared Lena half to death.

Baxter smiled again, knowing that he wasn't going to bed that night and the alarm bells were going to start going off all over the shop. He fucking loved it.

'Okay, gents, let's get some statements from you. It'll take a bit of time.'

Across the city Nelson looked out of the window of his new home. The money was rolling in, and his terraced villa was straight out of a glossy magazine. It made no difference; he felt empty, and though his gut had been okay for a couple of days, he didn't feel right – life didn't feel right. He should have felt like sipping a nice glass of something, enjoying the smell of new furnishings and the welcoming comfort of a very expensive home. He should have had a woman by his side, but there was no excitement. Just hollow emptiness and growing anger.

No more than a couple of hundred yards away McGovern was setting up an observation post in an empty flat. They'd been lucky getting it; it had clear sight to Nelson's front door and would be ideal for controlling the surveillance teams when he moved.

When the chance came they would covertly enter his place and bug it up.

McGovern slapped the two young officers he was with on the shoulders. 'Over to you, boys. I'm off to bed. The privilege of rank and all that shite.'

In Wester Hailes, Banjo Rodgers sat in his favourite chair. He hadn't bothered to put the lights on when darkness fell on the city. The TV was on but the sound was turned down. He rocked back and forward with a steady rhythm, trying not to think about Maggie and his failure.

Macallan watched Fraser disappear beyond the departure gate as he looked back for the last time before disappearing airside. She turned away, smiling to herself. It had been good – better than good – and forgiving him had been the right thing to do. It had only been a short visit, but they'd talked easily and confessed their sins. They'd been careful not to make too many promises, but when Macallan could get time she'd go to Northern Ireland and spend a weekend with him. No big commitments – they'd just take it as it came.

She walked back to the car and shivered at the biting cold before driving over to Portobello, the faded, once-busy holiday spot where for decades thousands of stressed-out blue-collar workers had enjoyed a day by the seaside. It was quiet now, but the long promenade was ideal for a blow in the sea air.

She walked along from the King's Road end, looked over the wide estuary towards the sparkling lights on the Fife shoreline. The sky was cloudless, and she guessed that Fraser's flight would be up there somewhere in the darkness on the short hop to Belfast City.

She walked as fast as she could to counteract the freezing easterly breeze, and her skin tingled with cold and energy. She thought that perhaps, with a double slice of luck, things might work out with Fraser after all.

A couple of snowflakes nipped her face, and she looked back up at the sky, but it was still clear. She walked further on and her eyes scanned east along the darkness that was the place where the Firth of Forth became the North Sea. She couldn't make out the horizon in the darkness but saw a grey line of cloud heading her way and realised the forecasters must have got it right. There was a snowstorm coming, and it would envelop the city in a few hours.

She walked on and ignored the cold.

18

The surveillance team had waited patiently, charting what routine there was in Nelson's life, photographing him from every angle, noting the way he walked and dressed, his habits and who he met. Even the information from an ordinary day where he was just living his life started to build up a picture. The records from his phone calls had started to come in, and the senior analyst, Felicity Young, researched the lists, plus all that was known from his previous history in Belfast and the Army. His family, friends, comrades in the regiment – all were studied, and deep in the electronic systems of law enforcement a target profile was created for Billy Nelson. When it was opened, his picture flashed up on the front page with the routine benchmarks of his existence: age, date and place of birth, description, marks or scars and previous convictions. Everything that was known from the shell scarring on his thigh to the Red Hand of Ulster tattooed on his right arm, it was all there in the blossoming files. He'd become the main target in Operation Ranger. The name had been created randomly, so any bent officer couldn't guess at potential sources – which had happened in the past – but it could be regarded as appropriate given Nelson's history. Once the bugs were in his home and authority had been granted to tap his phone, the surveillance assets would all be in place. What it would need then was focus, patience and, like almost everything else in life, a portion of luck.

Macallan knew that without that luck it could all go wrong. Surveillance was a manpower-intensive discipline that tied up dozens of skilled officers in covering the target 24/7. The reality was that they could take on Nelson 24/7 but not the rest of the Belfast boys, because the force was running dozens of other operations against organised crime and terrorists. If the other members of his team were seen with him it would be recorded and they'd be photographed, but unless the situation became more serious, they could target only him for the time being.

Macallan knew that as Nelson became settled in, he might follow the familiar pattern where the top man becomes hands-off and lets the workers take the risks. If that happened they might switch to whoever was next down the line. A greater and recurring issue was when some other serious incident cropped up for the force and resources were redirected towards the new problem. Their finances seemed to be getting squeezed all the time, and the fact was that the uniformed oligarchs, whose problems came at them day to day and needed answering promptly, didn't quite get long-term surveillance and investigation. It was understandable – if the head honchos didn't sort something immediately they got it tight from politicians trying to keep the restless masses happy, but it didn't help those at the coalface.

As it was, reports of the 'gang war' that seemed to be escalating in the city had reached the press, and they were pushing their own sources for a story. Jacquie Bell had her own criminal contacts and was picking up the sound of the beating war drums, so she'd left a couple of messages asking Macallan to contact her. Despite always being suspicious of the press, Macallan owed Bell and knew that she might be able to pick up useful information herself if they talked. Ultimately it was better to try and keep control of the story before the media poured fuel on the fire; the last thing she wanted was Nelson to be spooked then take cover. Already she had been summoned to attend a meeting with the chief super, who was bursting blood vessels about the Fleming twins' report to DS Baxter.

She decided to squeeze in a call to Bell before she had to endure another meeting with the insufferable bastard who could play the cards that would make her job a misery. She closed her office door and took her pay-as-you-go phone from her bag. She kept it for contacting Bell, just to be sure that her name couldn't be traced back to the reporter through her phone records.

She tapped the only number in the phone memory and it was picked up after two rings.

'Hi, gorgeous. Don't tell me – you're feeling a bit frisky and thought about me?'

Bell said a variation on the same theme every time she spoke to Macallan, knowing that it still wound her up. Macallan, however, smiled patiently and took it with a shrug – it was best just to let the reporter do her thing. In fact, she decided it was time to start batting back across the net to Bell, who loved any form of verbal sparring.

'Jacquie, good to hear you, but just for your information I might be involved with someone.'

Bell was impressed and tried a lob: 'Get you, Macallan! Hope he's an improvement on the previous failures.'

'Believe it or not, he *is* one of the previous failures, but

I'll fill you in the next time I see you.' Not exactly game, set and match but that ball was now out of play.

They got up to date on the trivialities but knew what the call was really about. Bell got to the point before Macallan.

'What's going on? All my little weasels are telling me that we have a situation and it might just get worse. What I hear is that Joe and Danny Fleming aren't renewing their Hibs season tickets next year. Correct or what?'

'Without the bodies we just don't know, but I'll be amazed if they're still with us. Look, this is bad and if you want we can meet up. The press could cause us a major headache on this, Jacquie, so let's get the heads together.'

'Heads together – sounds good to me if you know what I mean.'

Macallan laughed; she definitely felt she needed that lighter kind of moment before she saw the chief super. 'You're sounding more like Julian Clary every day!'

They arranged to meet at Macallan's flat because Bell lived in a bomb site that never had food or drink of any description. Bell claimed she only went there to change her clothes.

Macallan put the phone down and smiled broadly; it was strange to her that a reporter like Bell was one of the people she trusted most.

The smile dropped when she remembered the meeting she had a few minutes ahead of her. She called in Thompson, who, being the DCI, was the officer in charge of Operation Ranger. Macallan was less than happy about it, but she had no choice in the matter. She just hoped that Thompson would have the sense to defer where necessary – to McGovern when they were out on the ground and to her at other times. They'd rushed her through a surveillance training course and she'd scraped

172

through, probably because of her rank, but the feedback had been borderline. There had been a footnote saying that she seemed to struggle under pressure.

Macallan and Thompson bumped into the chief super's secretary on the way to his office. Macallan smiled warmly at her. 'What mood is he in?'

The chief super's right hand looked from Macallan to Thompson and there was a slight hesitation. Macallan saw it, read the non-verbal, and had no doubt she was taking care with her choice of words in front of the DCI. It had been apparent from the previous meeting that the secretary was no admirer of the man polishing the top seat in the city with his fat arse. She obviously knew something that put her on guard and Macallan made a mental note to see if she could get it out of her later on.

'He's fine, Grace, just very busy and a lot to deal with.'

Thompson must have picked up that she was the problem.

When they walked into the chief super's office he was staring out of the window with his hands behind his back. There was no pretence at good manners as they waited for a few moments till he turned and nodded to the seats opposite his desk.

Macallan tried a 'Good morning, sir', but all he managed in response was a grunt and a shuffle at his papers. He stuck his glasses on the end of his nose and drummed the desk with his fingers.

Thompson shifted uncomfortably, but Macallan knew this was just his childish attempt to prove that he was king of the castle. She never moved a muscle, knowing that would piss him off, and her eye contact was full on when he finally flicked his gaze in her direction.

'I'm not happy, Superintendent – not happy at all. The press are wound up about this gang-war stuff, and it seems like someone is running riot in the city. A father and son missing, presumed murdered, a wife and mother abducted. How many arrests have we made?'

'None so far, sir. In investigation and surveillance terms we've hardly started, but so far it's going well. And we haven't even deployed the listening devices in Nelson's home address yet.' She decided to keep her answers to a minimum because the man clearly wanted to lay blame and she was going to give him as little room as possible.

'The chief has been on to me this morning and he's not happy either. I want results on this and soon – am I clear? Who's running the operation on the ground?'

'Under my command, Lesley is the operational commander and Jimmy McGovern is her deputy.'

He looked at Thompson and his expression softened. If Macallan had been in any doubt that she was fighting on more than one front, she'd just had it confirmed. She would need her eyes both back and front.

'Good stuff, Lesley, and I have every faith in you. Please feel free to come directly to me anytime if you feel there's something worth briefing.'

Macallan had to fight her own instincts at the snub to her rank. He'd basically declared that Macallan didn't count in his particular loop. She managed to sit tight but it was hard, and she saw how much he'd enjoyed delivering the kick in the ribs. She reminded herself that he was an over-promoted lightweight and not really much of a man when it came to it. She knew men, had loved and served with the best, and the chief super didn't deserve to be mentioned in the same breath.

The tension eased off as she knew she had nothing to prove, and she gave him the lover's smile. 'Will there be anything else, sir?'

He walked back to the window and turned his back on her, imagining being with her again. He squeezed his eyes shut and tried to dismiss the thoughts. He knew the smile was false and that's what she'd meant it to be. It was disrespect without a word being said and he ground his teeth in frustration. 'That's all. Keep in touch, Lesley.'

'I will, sir – and thank you.'

Macallan looked round at her deputy and wondered if Thompson knew what game she was in. She was naive and being manipulated by people with agendas that didn't take too much account of her position. She was playing in a tough game and oblivious to the traps.

They walked through the corridors without a word, both knowing that they were on opposite sides despite there having been no formal declaration of war.

When they arrived back in the office, the surveillance team who'd been out since the early hours were back in, having been replaced by a fresh shift. Thompson was due to go out and join them and Macallan kept it sweet as she bid her goodbye. She wasn't going to risk the operation with a cat fight in front of the team; that would be fatal.

McGovern had led the early-shift operation and Macallan could see how knackered he was the moment she spotted him.

'Any chance of a quick brief on what happened before you hit the hay?' she asked.

'No problem. Let me mix up some caffeine and I'll get Felicity in as well.'

Macallan wanted some reassurance from McGovern that the job was moving along. She wished she could be out there with them, but she had to let her deputies have their place. The surveillance and investigation would be debriefed during the day, and all the new records would be examined for information and intelligence, which would be extracted and fed into the guts of the system. Young and her team would analyse every scrap of information and Nelson's life would start to open like a book. They just had to identify the mistakes, the oppor-

175

tunities or the human weak links who might be turned into informants and deliver the fatal blow to Nelson and his team.

Macallan felt the buzz that every hard case brought her. Like all detectives she would curse it during the sleepless nights, the reports of new casualties and unforeseen fuck-ups, but that didn't stop the kick, the feeling that they were testing their strengths to the limit, or the thrill if they came out on top. They were dealing with men who had killed and would kill whenever or wherever it was necessary, and Macallan knew that those same men would see the police as just another problem to be knocked over. If they were UVF, they'd proved time and again in Northern Ireland that politicians, the police or the press would be taken on if necessary.

The thought brought Jacquie Bell to mind and she was concerned the reporter might press too hard, not realising what they were capable of doing. If Bell had a weakness it was that she thought she was fireproof. That was the difference between Macallan's working life and Bell's: Macallan knew through bitter experience what people were capable of, and in her early days in the RUC had scraped up some of the bodies that proved it. Bell would probably laugh it off, but Macallan decided that she would pass a warning to her friend anyway.

'Anything interesting, Jimmy?' she asked.

McGovern rubbed the back of his neck. He was exhausted, but that's what fourteen hours on a surveillance operation did to you. It was hard going, but for most of the team it was like being paid to play cops and robbers – big adrenalin rushes and highs, watching people who didn't know you were there. So many little secrets leaked out from their unsuspecting targets, and the fear of having their other life exposed was often enough to turn someone into an informant.

He remembered his early days in surveillance and a request from the Met to follow an animal-liberation foot soldier who was on his way to Edinburgh on a scouting mission. The man had been an avowed vegan and friend of the animal kingdom, an enemy of all carnivores who was responsible for attacks on research establishments all over the UK.

McGovern smiled at the memory of watching Dr Doolittle get off the train at Waverley Station and head straight for Scotland's favourite bakers, where he'd bought two sausage rolls. He still kept one of the surveillance photographs of the sanctimonious bastard munching his way through the remains of one of his porky friends. Sometime later the man had been pulled in and gave them nothing but snash – until his guilty pleasure had been slapped in front of him. At that point he had decided, quite wisely in the circumstances, to become an informant rather than risk the humiliation that would undoubtedly come from a leak to the press.

'So far so good,' said McGovern, sipping coffee that gave him an enjoyable caffeine kick, even though it was the usual office muck. That's what tiredness could do for the palate. 'He tends to get up late, and he kindly leaves his curtains open so we can get sightings of him from the OP in the flat opposite.' He laid out some photographs from the previous day. 'That's him leaving the house and getting into his car. He looks quite like the surveillance photographs the PSNI gave us, but I'd say he's maybe a bit thinner now.'

Macallan looked at the shots of Nelson – he was good-looking and everything she'd expected. He'd met up with the rest of his team during the day, and they'd managed to get pictures of them all. Apart from their meeting they'd done nothing unusual, but that was just how it went. Most of the time surveillance targets just lived ordinary lives and did what Joe Public did, aside from the fact that they were better off than Joe Public and didn't pay tax.

So far the police were only drawing the outlines of the picture. Patience was the key – and moving against them at the right time. It could take weeks or months, and reputations could be destroyed in the time it took to give the wrong order – the targets spooked, hundreds of man hours down the swanny and the racket of sneering from professional enemies.

'Okay, good work – now go and get some sleep. See you back here tonight before you go out again. Felicity, anything for Jimmy before he departs?' Macallan nodded towards the senior analyst.

'It's fine so far. We've a pile of historic information on the various characters involved, so early days. The main thing is that the team need to report everything – even the smallest deviation from the norm might be crucial. They will be surveillance conscious so until we get the electronic devices in place we can't be sure that they don't know that we're there. They must expect it at some stage.' She pulled her glasses off the end of her nose, a habit that always made her look even more like a teacher talking to her students.

McGovern was putting his own glasses away. 'The only unusual thing we saw was that he stopped on the Southside in Nicolson Street and went on a walkabout for ten minutes. We didn't want to get too close, but he was clearly looking for something. He didn't go in anywhere so maybe he couldn't find what he was looking for.'

Young pushed her glasses back onto the bridge of her nose and said she'd keep it in mind, scribbling the observation into her ever-present notepad.

Macallan stood and put her hand on McGovern's shoulder. 'Enough – your family await you.'

He smiled wearily and headed for the exit, wishing that he could just be transported by magic into his bed, preferably with his wife beside him, but there was no chance of that in the middle of the day. No matter – he knew he'd be asleep almost before his head hit the duck feathers.

Halfway out the door he remembered something else and turned back. 'By the way, I had a call from the Crown Office. Bobo McCartney is going to trial and we've been cited as witnesses. All the rest of his intrepid gang of robbers are pleading guilty but unfortunately not our Bobo.'

'Oh God, you're joking! We need standing about at the High Court like a hole in the head.'

'True. But we're guaranteed a laugh – he's alleging that he was fitted up and all his friends are informants. The other piece of news that'll probably bring a tear to your eye is that the Drews are up for their appeal the same day. The word on the street, as they say in the gangster movies, is that they have a fighting chance with the appeal.'

'Is there any good news?'

McGovern shook his head and failed to stifle a yawn. 'Afraid not – such is the lot of the poor detective. See you later.'

Macallan let the news sink in. The trial was nonsense, but the appeal by the Drew clan was something else. They were a team of home-invasion gangsters who'd killed an ethnic Chinese couple in Glasgow. When Macallan had been the DCI in Major Crime for Lothian and Borders they'd tracked the Drews down and arrested them. It had been a solid case until the discovery that their lawyer was an informant for Mick Harkins. They'd claimed the case was tainted because Harkins was on the investigation team, and if they were released there would be a shitload of problems to deal with. Not least of which was that Drew would be looking for revenge on a number of people, including his idiot brother, who'd left evidence he was supposed to have destroyed and then cracked when he was being interviewed.

There was also the problem of his lawyer, Jonathon Barclay, who'd been exposed as an informant. If Drew was released, there was no doubt that he'd be on the hunt for Barclay, although the lawyer was keeping his head down and no one was quite sure where he was.

Macallan wondered if someone else had got to him first and he was already enriching the soil somewhere. Worst of all there was the question of whether Drew would see Harkins as culpable in his downfall, Harkins being in no position to defend himself.

Macallan decided she needed to shelve the questions for the time being but that she'd have to speak to Harkins in case Drew did walk from the appeal hearing.

'All I need,' she sighed, deciding she was going to have a long drink when she got back to the flat – and make a call to Jack Fraser to arrange a weekend as soon as.

Young gave her a sympathetic smile and followed McGovern out, leaving Macallan to stare out of her window at the rain-filled skies that had been on the edge of drenching Edinburgh all day. So far the clouds had just teased them, but it was coming – the air felt heavy and damp – and it only added to her apprehension.

Too many things had the potential to go wrong this time. The targets were hard men, she had problems trusting her deputy and for some reason the chief super was right on her case. O'Connor was keeping his powder dry, but she was smart enough to know that there was an unofficial communication channel running between him and Thompson.

'Jesus, you seem to piss off an awful lot of people,' she said quietly to her reflection in the window.

Christmas was coming, and she wondered what that would bring. Alone and staring at the rubbish on the box with a glass of something? If all went well on her next trip to Belfast maybe she would be with Jack … but then again, he might have an arrangement with his family.

By 9 p.m. she was pretty well shattered and had seen McGovern back out on the plot, as surveillance operations were known by the troops.

She opened the back door to head home and the rain beat down on her like some religious punishment. She punched a number into her phone and waited on a fast black to take her home. All Macallan wanted at that moment was to be dry, warm and in bed.

19

Eddie Fleming sat down beside his mother's bed, searing emotions churning his gut with a toxic mixture that he fought to control. She looked more peaceful than on his previous visit, and the doctor told him that she'd had a good night, whatever that meant. It didn't impress him anyway.

'It couldn't be fuckin' worse than the previous one, doc.' He pushed his face close to the consultant's as he said it, just to make sure he recognised that Eddie was pissed off – seriously pissed off.

The doctor, who'd come from the Middle East over a decade before to make a better life, shook in the face of an aggression he didn't understand. He turned and walked away.

'How's it goin', Ma?' Eddie asked her.

Lena opened her eyes at the sound of his voice and there was a hint of a smile on her face. She put her hand on his forearm and squeezed lightly. Then the fragments of memory started to bombard her awakening mind. 'Oh no, Eddie, please make it stop, make it stop.' She squeezed her eyes closed, trying to push her thoughts back into the dark recesses of her memory.

'It's okay, Ma; I'm here. Can you remember any more about what happened?'

His mother seemed to overcome her instincts; whatever her faults, Lena possessed a tough streak – she had to as part of the Fleming clan, where gender equality hadn't quite been taken on board. Billy Nelson had almost broken her spirit, but her fear was being interrupted by a growing sense of anger at how she'd been driven to the edge of madness and barely survived. She'd faced something that no one deserved to confront, and the rotting face of her firstborn was burned into her memory – but so much else from that night was gone. Her mind couldn't cope with what had happened and to remember it all would have driven her completely mad. So she focused on the image of Danny and let her rage at his killers flood every vein in her body, until strength slowly began to seep back into her bones. Eddie was the one man in the family who cared about his mother and sisters, who saw women as something other than sexual objects, and he would look after her. She just had to tell him what she could.

'Get me a drink of water, son.' Lena felt exhausted but realised that at least she was feeling something and her will to survive had taken part control. She was damaged, had wounds that were deep and sore, and they would visit her for the rest of her life, but this wasn't the end. 'Where's Pat? He's alright, isn't he?'

Eddie held the back of her head and helped her sip the water. 'Pat's fine – just out on a job. He's trying to get the team back together. They seem to have run for cover since the old man and Danny went missing.'

The words brought it back to her and a single tear rolled across the deep lines under her eyes, but she refused to weep openly. 'It wasn't my imagination you know. They're dead; I saw them in their grave.'

Eddie clenched his hands into fists. He'd hoped that his mother had imagined it all, but instinct told him there was a terrible truth here and it had to be faced.

'Who picked you up, Ma? Who was it?' He lost it and stood up, his face stretched into a furious darkening mask. 'Who the fuck did this? I'll kill them all!' He wanted to hurt someone, but it wasn't the right time, and he saw his mother dissolve again in the face of his rage.

Lena had already lost a son and a husband, so she would do everything in her power to make sure the twins survived. She had to try and keep control or they would run into the same trap that had taken Joe and Danny.

'Please, Eddie – please let me explain,' she said. 'I can only remember parts of it. I'd had a lot to drink. Most of it's blacked out. Please sit and let me explain.'

Eddie looked through the window into the hallways and noticed the policeman guarding his mother was doing his best to hear what was going on. He sucked in a deep breath and realised he needed to think straight or his own life might just come to a sudden and very premature end.

He sat down, nodded at the uniform outside to signal that everything was hunky-dory and took his mother's hand again. She told him what she could, but all that was clear was the grave and the sight of the dead faces of her son and husband. She couldn't remember being taken and had only vague flashes of being in a van. Almost everything else had been wiped from her hard drive – but not the image of dark skeletal trees against a moonlit sky.

What Eddie and Lena Fleming couldn't know was that Billy Nelson had failed in his plan. He'd wanted to use abject terror to frighten Lena into submission and force her to back off with what was left of her family. If she'd had complete recall, in particular of the inflexible will of the men who'd taken her, she would have been wise enough to run. But Nelson had taken her too far into the darkness and hadn't factored in this loss of memory. All he'd done was raise the stakes, and instead of subduing his enemies, he'd simply set out a challenge, meaning he was unprepared for a response.

'Is there anything about the men? Anything at all?'

Her eyes that had seemed almost lifeless sparked, and hatred stretched her lips across her teeth. 'I remember someone laughing at me. I was so frightened ... What kind of men are they, Eddie?' She pulled him close. 'You can't take them head-on. Not without help. Promise me.'

He was calm. Calmer than he'd been for a long time. His brother Pat would do exactly what Joe and Danny would have done and he'd end up taken out. Eddie had to think for both of them and keep his brother on a tight lead. If it was the Nelson team again they were in trouble because that lot weren't stupid. He could back off till another day, but a better idea was slowly taking form. *Use that brain that God gave you*, he thought.

His mother watched as his face twitched with the swarming impulses he was dealing with.

'You've got it, Ma. Nothing mental, and I'll keep a hold of Pat.' The rage had passed; Eddie was in control. He smiled and kissed her forehead. 'Just get well, Ma. I'll be in later. By the way, I've told the bizzies, so they'll want to talk to you.'

'The polis?' That took her by surprise, and although the Flemings didn't normally do police cooperation, she could see that they needed all the help they could get. Lena thought briefly of her one-time police lover, Charlie, and wondered if he was still in the job before she drifted off into sleep again, praying for what was left of her family.

Eddie walked away from the hospital, deep in thought.

A light fall of snow had already melted on the streets of Edinburgh, but winter was gripping the city ever tighter and the east wind cut through his light clothing as he shivered in the chill. He walked as fast as he could to make his blood flow and forgot about the cold as he struggled with the options he had available. He knew what his first move was, so there wasn't any point in hanging around.

The call was picked up and transferred straight to Baxter, who was just about to call it a day.

'It's Eddie Fleming. Any chance we can talk?'

Baxter was in a foul mood, which wasn't unusual; this time it was because his wife had invited friends over and he couldn't stand them. The truth was that he didn't like anyone connected with his wife, and to boot, there was a European game on the box. So he didn't feel he had to be nice to anyone.

'Well I actually have a life and wanted to go home,' he lied. 'Is it going to be in my interest?'

'I can guarantee it, Mr Baxter, but if you don't want what I've got, I'll call someone else who gives a shit.'

Baxter liked straight talking. 'Okay, I'll meet you at Leith cop shop as soon as you can make it.'

'I'm on my way.' Eddie smiled to himself; he knew he was on a hard road but what other choice did he have? It ran against the grain for him to cooperate with the police, but he wanted to press Nelson from as many sides as possible. There was no way that the Belfast team would admit anything to CID, but it was all hassle, and when he saw Baxter he'd put the other pieces of his gamble into place. If he survived he would move into his old man's shoes. Joe had been a kingpin in his twenties, and there was no reason Eddie and Pat couldn't do the same. It just needed balls and brains – and he had both.

20

Eddie sat opposite Baxter again and smiled at the detective on the other side of the desk. Baxter clearly wasn't happy to see him.

'If you're here to see how the investigation's going, we're doing all we can but we're still treating it as a missing-persons enquiry. All we have at the moment is your suspicion that they've been toasted. It'll probably change in time to a full-blown murder investigation, but I'll let you know. What about your old lady?'

'I'm not sure she'll really get over this, and the doctors aren't sure she'll make a full recovery. Apparently her mind can't cope with what happened.'

Baxter looked like he wanted to be somewhere else, so Eddie decided it was time to get his full attention. 'She can't remember a lot but what she does remember is Danny and the old man in an uncovered grave.' He let that sink in and watched Baxter's face change colour.

'What?'

'You heard me.'

Baxter saw the implications and the headlines if it leaked to the press; it would create a shit storm for the force. He knew he had to get his finger out his arse because if there was a sniff that he'd dragged his heels on the case, his reputation would be lucky to stay above city-banker level.

'I'll try and get a statement from your mother, if she's able, and then speak to someone up the line to see where we go with it. You'll get action, but first of all have you any fucking ideas? Your family pump dope into the blood of half the junkies in the city so who's favourite?'

The young man smiled again, knowing that he had just taken control and he liked that. Making the bastard jump appealed to him. He'd read Baxter's mind and knew what the press would do with what he knew. He decided to give the screw another half turn.

'I don't know what happened to the old lady. Something – but her head's mince at the moment, so who knows? As for Danny and the old man, there's a Belfast crew moved into Wester Hailes that seem to be taking over some of the business. Hard bunch apparently, and old Joe had some problem with them. That's all I can tell you at the moment.'

Baxter shifted in his seat as he realised the Flemings might just be trying to fuck an opponent for their own purposes. He leaned forward and stabbed his finger at Eddie. 'You'd better not be fucking me around, boy. If this is a stroke then I'll make it my business to turn your life into a shitload of misery.'

Fleming smiled again and felt relaxed at the threat, knowing that he was holding the cards. He leaned forward and locked stares with the detective. 'My old man and brother might be in a fuckin' hole in the ground. God knows where, so we can't even give them a proper Catholic send-off. My old lady gets lifted in the night, and she thinks some fucker dug them up to show her the result. If you think I'm fuckin' around then you need to get that big, thick pig head examined.' He sat back and let Baxter digest that for a minute. 'The other thing is that if you play this right then I'll come on board with you.'

'What do you mean?' Baxter looked confused, and Fleming started to play him. The detective wasn't used to being played, and he didn't like it one little bit.

'I mean you do things for me and I'll throw you the occasional skull. You make the arrests, and I feel like a good citizen doing his duty.'

'A Fleming informing.' Baxter shook his head; he'd never thought he'd see the day. He paused for a moment, but he knew a good deal when he saw it.

What Baxter couldn't know was that Eddie knew his old man had been an informer for years. When he was in his teens he'd come back to the house early one day and heard Joe speaking on the phone – basically sending a competitor straight into the welcoming arms of the law. He'd never told anyone and had never mentioned it to his dad, which was probably just as well. He'd thought about it a lot though and realised that to get to the top you either had to have a bent one in your pocket or a friendly one who you could do business with when it was required. As far as Eddie saw it, the police were just like them – trying to be successful in a difficult world. He didn't know which pig had handled his old man and didn't really care. If he could work with DS Baxter that would do for the time being. He was an out-and-out bastard, so seemed to tick all the right boxes, and he would have no problem with an attack of the old scruples.

'Okay, son. I'm up for that.' Baxter smiled across the table, knowing he was facing someone who was just as much of a bastard as he was himself, despite his youth. That took some doing in his book. He shook Eddie's hand and the arrangement was sealed.

Shortly afterward, Eddie left the station and walked

across the road to the pub where he'd arranged to meet his brother. The place was nearly deserted, and his twin was chatting up an old barmaid who looked like she was enjoying the attention. He nodded to a table as far from the bar as he could get and sat down while Pat ordered a half of lager for him and a date with the pensioner for himself.

Eddie shook his head when his brother sat down and pushed the drink over to his side of the table. 'You have to be fuckin' jokin'? That barmaid is older than our mother and looks in worse condition when it comes to it. Perv!'

'Variety, my brother, is what the doctor orders every time.' Pat waved to the barmaid, who was staring over at him as if he was her first love.

Eddie told his brother what had been said in the station but left out the part where he'd signed up as an informant with 'Bastard' Baxter, as the policeman was known by most of the criminal fraternity in Leith. Pat had been pulling Joe's team back together; most of them were on board again and had just been waiting for Joe to make a miraculous reappearance. Joe had always been the boss and hadn't delegated to his sons, perhaps because he'd realised that handing things over to Danny would have been the end of them.

'There's something else, and I definitely think you'll be interested,' Pat said with a broad grin.

Eddie looked up from his drink. 'What?'

Pat explained to him that he'd been stamping the card of one of the escort girls who worked for Joe. She was a Lithuanian and the best-looking of the bunch by a mile. Apparently she'd been old Joe's favourite when he was in the mood and was game for anything, so Pat had been filling his boots with the girl and they'd formed a kind of relationship.

'Think I've got feelings for the lassie. She's a pro but...'

Eddie put the palm of his hand six inches from his brother's face. He just couldn't be arsed to listen to the romantic delusions of his twin – and certainly not after he'd pulled the granny at the bar. Given that she was still beaming an enormous set of false gnashers across the room at them, Eddie could only wonder at what Pat had suggested to her.

'Get to the fuckin' point and spare me the details,' he snapped before slugging back the beer and holding the glass up to the barmaid, who gave him the thumbs-up. He gave her a weak and insincere smile in return.

'The thing is that one of the Belfast team pays her as an escort and it looks like he's eating out of her hand. Phones her all the time, wants to go out every night and all that shite.'

Eddie had to ask, and interrupted Pat in full flow. 'Wait a minute. This is the woman you're in love with?'

'It's different with me – the others are for money. Okay, I'm still paying, but she says she likes me and wants us to have a regular thing. The point is this – Belfast boy Andy Clark hasn't done the business with her yet. He just wants to talk to her and he's all loved-up. He's got to be some kind of fuckin' pervert if you ask me.'

Eddie dragged his hand over his face and then caught the funny side of it. He broke into a smile and slapped his brother's arm. 'I'm fuckin' delighted for you and think you'll be really happy. Now give me the details before I burst into tears.'

Pat seemed encouraged. 'Thing is this: Clark is there for the asking if we need to take action on him. The girl is giving us the wire anytime he phones, and he normally goes round to her flat. There's plenty of cover there if we need it.'

Eddie nodded and saw the possibilities. He'd already considered some kind of an attack, but his plan was to make a move but stay quiet about it – confuse them and not lay down a direct challenge. The twins weren't strong enough to take them on directly, but they could nip away at Nelson, and hopefully Baxter and the CID would stick the boot in at the same time. There was one more move he needed to put into place though, so he tossed a twenty down on the table and stood up.

'I need to make a call to that mad cunt in Glasgow. Stay here and I'll get in touch once that's done. Get yourself a drink and you can chat up the creature from the black lagoon till I get back to you.'

He headed for the door and his brother headed for the bar and the barmaid.

21

Eddie Fleming put the call in to the man who'd supplied his old man with dope for years. It had always worked well because Joe paid on time and never took the piss. There was a very good reason for that, and his name was Magic McGinty.

Magic's first name was actually Dominic, though few people knew his first name. Even his mother used his sobriquet rather than the good Christian name he'd inherited from his grandfather. He was called Magic simply because he used the word all the time. Everything was magic to Dominic McGinty. Sometimes it would be shortened to plain M and he quite liked that, imagining it made him sound like the head of a spy organisation.

He was no giant – even stretching to his full height and with two pairs of socks on he barely touched five foot nine – but he was built like a pit bull, and every inch was nail hard. Brought up in the east end of Glasgow, he'd fought his way through the gang system and, like so many from the city, had used violence as a way to the top of his trade. Heavy scar tissue bulged above both his eyes, and his nose had been flattened to a state where his greatest frustration was the ever-present problem with his nasal passages.

His eyes were almost black and looked like two bullet holes; they never wavered, and he had a way of stressing friends and enemies alike just by staring at them. What made him different from so many other Glasgow hard men was that he always seemed to be in a good mood, smiling his way through the craziest situations, even when his own life had been at risk. The legend went that even when he was torturing someone who'd crossed him, he'd crack jokes with the condemned man or woman. One story was that as the victim passed into eternity the last thing he witnessed this side of heaven was McGinty running round the room, punching the air in front of him and shouting, 'Fuckin' magic!' He'd even resigned himself to a violent end, and that was okay by him. He hated the thought of growing old, and as a lover of old gangster movies, he really quite liked the idea of going down in a hail of bullets. There was no doubt about it – Dominic 'Magic' McGinty was clinically insane.

He'd sold dope to Joe Fleming for years. The Edinburgh man had put a lot of money his way, and there had never been a problem. Magic didn't like problems; he thought the world was a bad place and if people just played by the rules he wouldn't need to maim or kill them.

'Life's far too fuckin' short for aggravation' was one of his favourite mantras, and all part of the paradoxical image he'd built up around himself. Even some of the most violent men in Glasgow would break into a sweat if they thought McGinty was on their case, but Magic had met Eddie a couple of times when he'd come through with his old man and had quickly come to the view that the boy had the eye and in time would be a mover on the Edinburgh side. He had no reason to worry about dealing with Magic.

'Eddie. Good to speak to you, son,' Magic said when he picked up the phone. 'Hearing stories that there's a problem with Joe. What's up?'

'Hi there, Magic, need to talk offline. Would it be okay if I came through to see you?'

Magic rarely left his home anyway and was fed up trying to make conversation with the brainless bastards who worked for him. 'Can you come now?' It wasn't really a question – what he really meant was 'you're coming now whether you like it or not'.

This suited Eddie, and after he'd called Pat (who, much to his disgust, was becoming even more involved with the elderly barmaid in a back room of the pub) he jumped in a taxi and told the driver to head for Glasgow. He also promised him a nice bonus if he could wait for the return journey. The driver knew the Flemings, and even though this was the younger version, he wasn't about to argue.

Magic had told Eddie to come to his home and that made the Edinburgh boy just a bit nervous. When he'd met him before with his old man it had always been in neutral venues or one of McGinty's pubs. Eddie was about to deliver some news that was going to piss off his host big time, and he worried that Magic might make an executive decision to take it out on him. He tried to put it to the back of his mind; he'd elected to play a dangerous game and he had to live with it or go under. 'What the fuck.'

The taxi driver's head jerked up. 'What's that, chief?'

Eddie looked at the driver's eyes in the mirror. 'Just thinking aloud, pal, just thinking aloud.'

When the taxi drew up in front of Magic's home address an hour later, both driver and passenger were impressed. 'Who's the friend, chief?' the driver asked.

'You really don't want to know, pal.' That was enough

of a warning for the driver to shut it, and he got the message.

Anyone looking at the front of the house would have taken it for the home of a banker or city lawyer – definitely someone with class. How wrong they would be. Magic had been born in the worst kind of slum and had made it to a six-bedroom Victorian pile with a security system that would have done justice to the Pentagon. The first giveaway was the sign on the gates telling visitors (or the interfering detectives with a warrant) that there were several large, savage dogs waiting for them – and he wasn't talking Standard Poodles.

Eddie pressed the bell next to the six-foot wrought-iron gates and watched one of the CCTV units swing round and clock him. He could hear the dogs snarling somewhere at the side of the building but thankfully kept back from him.

The gates opened and something resembling a human being answered the door. The guy must have been six five, but God had forgotten to issue him with a neck, and there was hardly a clue that he had eyes under two tight slits beneath his brow. The strange thing was that he smiled, and it was a good one for such a fearsome-looking man. 'How you doin', son?' he asked. 'Come on in. The boss is in his office.' He had a high-pitched voice, which in a different specimen might have drawn a bit of piss-taking, but Eddie thought the man probably didn't have many problems in that area of his life.

Eddie walked inside and took it all in. The place had that smell of money – everything was the best and the carpets felt lush. He guessed that Magic had brought in an interior designer. He couldn't imagine that he'd acquired this level of taste in the Easterhouse gangs.

'Would you mind taking off the shoes? Magic gets a wee bit annoyed if people drag crap in off the streets.'

Eddie wasn't about to argue and felt his heart rate jump as he was drawn deeper into the man's lair. He tried to imagine Magic McGinty getting 'a wee bit annoyed'. It didn't sound right somehow. He was in a strange environment and had no idea how it would pan out. It was a house full of contradictions: owned by an Easterhouse boy but decked out like something from *Homes & Gardens*, the door answered by an ogre with a squeaky voice. He thanked God that his brother wasn't with him. He would definitely have said the wrong thing, which would probably have resulted in a series of unpleasant injuries.

Eddie walked into the office … and there he was. He wanted to say 'Fuck me' at the bizarre scene he was confronted with but kept his mouth closed. Wee Magic McGinty was sitting behind a Victorian mahogany desk that seemed to dwarf him, but that was the least of it. Behind him was a six-foot painting of Celtic's greatest player, Billy McNeill, in full flow in the famous green hoops. The captain of the Lisbon Lions, the first British team to win the European Cup. It was a shrine, and a Celtic scarf and jersey had been hung each side of the picture.

Magic caught Eddie's look and seemed pleased. 'That's the man, son: King Billy, the Big Man, Caesar and just fuckin' magic. Like it, Eddie?'

He knew that it would probably be the right side of politeness not to offend. 'It's lovely. Did you ever see him play?'

Magic got up from the seat, walked round to stand beside Eddie and stared up at the picture of the great man. He was about a head shorter than Eddie but radiated energy, and Magic had no hang-ups about being slightly short-arsed – in fact it had made him what he was. He'd realised at an early age that all he had to do to compensate for being two inches shorter than the average man was to fight harder and dirtier. He put his hand on Eddie's shoulder and said, 'I never saw him play, but my old man talked about it all the time, and of course he became the manager so I saw him from that point of view. I expect you'll be like your old man and support that fuckin' pile o' dross at Easter Road?' He walked back round to his seat and told Eddie to sit down.

Eddie, relieved, did as he was told. He'd felt as if a venomous creature had touched him and was uncertain as to whether it would bite or leave him alone. He relaxed back into the chair. As far as he could, he'd run through what he wanted to say in his head on the way over; every word had to count and, more importantly, not turn Magic into the screaming psychopath of legend.

'What's up then, Eddie? Tell me all about it.' Magic pinned those black bullet-hole eyes on him and Eddie realised the stories about him had not been exaggerated. His natural instinct was to turn away, but it was clear that the man opposite would sense a lie before it had passed his lips – would see it in his eyes.

He felt sweat bubble out of the pores on his back, and he shivered with cold even though the room was overheated. His body was taking instinctive action – his blood moved to his core and his skin turned pale in the 'flight' response. He fought it and had to sit tight, tell the truth as far as he could and spin it his way.

'Relax, Eddie – we're all pals here, and if I can help then it'll be done.'

'The thing is, Magic … I think the old man and Danny have been taken out, but we don't know where they've been dumped. I know you made a big delivery just before they went missing, but I don't know where they stashed it, and worse still …' he hesitated before the real bad news, 'I don't know where the old man hides his money and I guess you haven't been paid.'

The sweat poured down the small of his back. He felt the Glasgow man's eyes sear through his pupils and there was no defence. He looked towards Squeaky Voice, who stood about six feet to the side of Magic, and wondered what they talked about in their quieter moments.

Time seemed to hang still. It was as if they'd been freeze-framed as Magic digested the words, then analysed it according to all his experience dealing with the horrible creatures that inhabited his underworld. He was a great believer in not rushing to judgement; the wrong move in his world could bring down hard-won empires.

He walked round the desk again without speaking and put the palms of his hands on each side of Eddie's face. His mug was no more than a foot away, and Eddie wanted to retch. In that moment he felt like a frightened child.

He tried to close his eyes, but he couldn't. All he could see were those black holes, and he thought about all the stories that said they were the last thing Magic's enemies saw before he dispatched them.

'You're freezing, son; you know what that is? Fear. You're right to feel it, and it's a healthy sign. Controlling that fear – that shows me you've got balls, coming here to tell me that I'm down a hundred grand. Not many people would have dared, so you're either very stupid, which I know isn't the case, or you're trying a scam – and as I said already you're not stupid. So I'll discount that. Let's just put it down to the fact that you're young, ambitious and hard, but with a bit to learn. I like you and don't think I can say that about many people – but most importantly you weren't lying. If I thought that, you'd already be with Joe and Danny.' Magic looked satisfied with this assessment, patted the right-hand side of Eddie's face and walked back to his chair, winking at Squeaky Voice on the way.

Magic pulled a cigar from a walnut box and Squeaky Voice whipped out a lighter and did the needful for him. Magic blew three perfect smoke rings and smiled at Eddie, who was still cold but had stopped shaking. 'Now I suspect you didn't come here to see me because I'm an entertaining fucker. I guess you want help, so talk, Eddie, and just tell me what you want and what's in it for me?'

Eddie did as he was told, recounting as much as he could and let him know that the problem was Billy Nelson. As soon as he mentioned the words Loyalist and UVF, Magic McGinty's flint-hard eyes glinted with interest. He was brought up in a dirt-poor, but devout, Catholic home and was the product of starving Irish immigrants who'd come to the Scottish shores because there was nowhere else to go. He still had relations in West Belfast and they'd been the victims of both Loyalist paramilitaries and, as they saw it, the British Army. When Magic thought of Loyalists, his mind automatically conjured up a picture of the screaming Hun hoards that made up the support of Glasgow Rangers. He hated the Rangers right to the depths of his corrupted soul, and their collapse into the lower region of Scottish football had been like a blessing from heaven.

'Stop there, son. Did you say Belfast Loyalists in Edinburgh did for old Joe?'

Fleming was aware of Magic's pathological hatred for all things on the blue – or sometimes orange – side of the religious divide, so he had intentionally played the card with as much emphasis as he could. He finished the rest of the story and added his last bit of intelligence – that as far as he knew they were being supplied from Belfast. It couldn't be from anywhere else or they would have heard.

'Belfast Loyalists on your (or should I say our?) turf, and the gear likely coming from Belfast.' Magic shook his head at the thought then sucked hard on the cigar, closing his eyes and leaning back in his chair to think it through.

Eddie was starting to speak again when Magic's free hand shot up, palm outwards before he'd finished the first word of the first sentence. The room was freeze-framed again and he waited as if there was no such thing as time.

Somewhere in another room there was the sound of a clock signalling that the world was still moving forward. Then Magic opened his eyes and sat forward, those black bullet holes still glinting; he looked like he had a plan and that he was enjoying the thought.

'Okay, Eddie, let me look into this and I'll get back to you. I'm going to have a word with Mr Billy fuckin' Nelson and see what the man has to say. I don't want to start a war, but I'll make him an offer he can't refuse, just like the mafia…eh, Eddie?' He sucked on the cigar again and blew another three perfect smoke rings. 'Fuckin' magic!'

Ten minutes later, Squeaky Voice let Eddie out of the front door and waved goodbye like a good housewife seeing her man off to the office. The young man stepped back into the taxi, closed his eyes and sank into the back seat, exhaling with relief.

'You look pale, chief – everything okay?' said the driver, making eye contact via the rear-view mirror.

Eddie opened one eye and met the man's stare. 'Once again, pal, you really don't want to know, but let's just say it was fuckin' magic and leave it at that. Just get me back through Edinburgh way.'

He closed his eyes and said a quiet prayer of thanks as the driver pulled out into the traffic.

Halfway along the M8 he was startled by his phone trembling in his pocket. He opened his eyes and found they were sticky with exhaustion. The meeting with Magic had drained every ounce of energy out of him; he just wanted to get back to his flat and curl up in a ball.

It was his brother Pat. 'Just had a call from the wee female who's got the line on Andy Clark.'

'And?' He hoped it was simple; he didn't have the will to deal with complications after his meeting with Magic.

'Up to you, but Clark's called her, and he wants to come round to her place tomorrow night. Don't know what you think but that's the story. I said we'd give her a nice wee wage for it, and she's as happy as fuck.'

Eddie was weary but he had the advantage of youth, and the thought of action fizzed up his blood like a hit of good-quality amphetamine. He pulled himself up in the seat and his eyes cleared. He'd started the ball rolling with Bastard Baxter and then Magic so what was the point of fucking around till something happened?

'Let's go for it and see if he bleeds.'

The taxi driver was a nosey fucker who earwigged Eddie's call. His eyes shot up instinctively and were reflected in the mirror again.

Eddie put the phone down and met his gaze. 'For the third and final time, pal, you do not want to fuckin' know.'

The man's eyes went back to the road, and he kept them there all the way back to Eddie's front door, where he was handed a pile of money that was more than he normally earned in a week, but he still hoped he didn't have to pick the boy up again. His instincts told him he'd been on a journey where business had been done in a world inhabited by an alien race, who might walk the same streets as he did but lived with an ever-present and terrifying uncertainty about the future. It was accepted as their way of life, but the driver couldn't understand it – he just wanted to get home and be with his wife.

But what frightened him most was that there was still a part of him – somewhere deep inside – that wished he could be more like them.

Eddie Fleming felt the hot stream of water from the shower wash away the stinking sweat that had leaked from him in fear when he'd looked into the eyes of Magic McGinty. He towelled himself dry, sat down in front of the television and watched the latest bad news from the Middle East without actually taking in a word.

It was done: the moves were being made and several sets of players were manoeuvring round the chessboard. The police, Billy Nelson, Belfast Loyalists, Magic McGinty, bent cops and drug dealers were all drawing towards each other, but there was still one more player on the sidelines waiting to enter the game.

22

Bobo McCartney's advocate felt like pulling her hair out. Everyone involved in the failed bank robbery had pled guilty apart from the man himself. He'd decided that he was going to trial come what may, despite the fact that there was enough evidence to convict him in front of ten different juries. Some of the gang had given statements that had stuck Bobo right in it, because they'd realised that the guy was a megalomaniac. They didn't know what megalomaniac meant, but one of the CID team who'd interviewed them kept calling Bobo a fuckin' megalomaniac twat and it had sounded about right, whatever it meant.

Bobo's advocate had defended some hopeless cases in her time but this one took the shortbread biscuit. He kept claiming that it was all a conspiracy – that he'd been 'entrapped' in a plot hatched by the CID and his gang – but Bobo had read far too many books that he didn't really understand. Other people had got off on technicalities, so he'd figured why not him.

They were in the High Court cell area, and the advocate tried again to talk some sense into the fool sitting opposite her. 'Mr McCartney, once again I must say to you that you may well pay a heavy price if you go ahead and are then found guilty. I know your position is that you're innocent' – she tried not to choke on the word – 'and I respect that, but I must tell you that the Crown has a powerful case, and I believe the jury will be convinced by that evidence.' She looked for signs of agreement but Bobo didn't move. 'Your friends, or former friends, will go into the witness box and say that you were the driving force behind the alleged conspiracy.'

Bobo put one finger up in the air to make her pause. 'I just want to make it clear that I was not driving on the day of the alleged bank robbery. I was being driven to Edinburgh to visit the castle by the other men in the car, and they were going to drop me off. If they were then going to rob a bank, I knew hee haw about it by the way.' Bobo was trying to be as polite as possible but couldn't help mixing the street into his newly acquired legal vocabulary.

His advocate wanted to rest her head on the table and cry. She was up to her eyes in work that paid her a decent return and would have liked to have been getting on with it instead of picking up a scrap of legal aid and defending an imbecile who'd read a couple of law books on remand and now thought he was an expert.

'My position is clear, and I believe the jury will see that I am an innocent man.' He tapped the table with his forefinger to give emphasis to his claim, and if anything his confidence was rising. Bobo believed he was far too clever for them all, convinced that he was about to put on a show that would see him punching the air outside the court, celebrating a unanimous and famous 'not guilty' verdict. Night after night in his cell he'd imagined addressing the press and demanding a public enquiry into the 'fit-up' that had seen an innocent man rotting on the remand wing. There would be the press interviews and, best of all, the compensation claim. That would set him up for life.

The advocate sat back in her chair and tried to suppress the urge to scream right in his face. She tried hard, but she was human; she failed.

Macallan paced the cobbles with McGovern outside the High Court, cursing the time they were wasting at McCartney's trial when there was so much on her plate. 'I can't believe this, Jimmy. Bobo's even dafter than I thought when we arrested him.'

McGovern smiled patiently and shrugged. 'Everything's in hand. Lesley's got the team out on Nelson this morning so no worries. To be honest, we might have the old problem that Nelson hands out the orders but doesn't do much that's hands on. Never mind – if nothing else Bobo should be an entertaining distraction.'

Macallan looked round at the man who'd become as much of a friend as a colleague – and a calming influence when the job tested her patience. 'You're right. We'll have a debrief when we get back to the office later. We might need to move the surveillance away from Nelson onto one of the others. There's a lot coming in, and no doubt the analytical team will have some ideas for us.'

They walked back into the court to hear the news that Bobo had sacked his counsel and was going to defend himself. Apparently they'd had some sort of dispute. The trial started and the judge, who looked as pissed off as everyone else in the court, tried to advise Bobo that it was in his own interest to have legal counsel, but the boy would not be swayed. He'd read all about the performance of Tommy Sheridan, and as far as he was concerned, if Tommy Sheridan could do it then so could he.

After the Crown had stuck a couple of his partners in crime in the witness box, it was clear to a blind man that Bobo was a guilty man and a thicko in a class of his own. When that moment came everyone in the court, except Bobo, started to take the proceedings for what they were – a damn good laugh. The judge maintained an appropriate air of solemnity but was secretly pleased that he could recount the amusing antics of the accused to his brothers and sisters in the Faculty of Advocates. It would make a great story for an after-dinner speech.

Bobo tried it all, including accusing his ex-gang members of being police agents, and three of the jury went red in the face trying to suppress their laughter when he repeatedly tried to use the word provocateur but could only get as far as 'provo' before halting in confusion. When he threatened to assault one of his co-accused, who'd pointed to him as the leader of the failed robbery, the judge had intervened, leaving Bobo crestfallen.

McGovern took the stand and had never felt more confident in his life. The witness stand in the High Court could be the loneliest place on God's earth, but for Bobo's trial it had become a place of levity and entertainment.

Bobo felt that things were going badly wrong, and he rightly suspected that no one in the court was taking him seriously. He didn't like the barely suppressed smile on the inspector's face and decided to give McGovern his best shot. He did the preliminary questions and hoped he was leading McGovern into a trap.

'Now, Inspector McGovern, is it the case that there was an undercover agent in this case?'

'I think you might be getting different things mixed up here, Mr McCartney. There was a confidential informant but that's not the same as an undercover agent, who'd normally be a police officer.'

Bobo felt a nervous tic develop near his left eye. He'd

thought he was clued up on court practices but within the space of a couple of hours he'd been made to feel as if he was naked in the centre of some freak show – and that he was the lead freak. 'I put it to you that you're a fuckin' liar, by the way.' Bobo took a step back and waited for McGovern to fold. He'd forgotten that foul language wasn't normally used on witnesses.

The judge struggled to look angry. 'Mr McCartney, you're in serious danger of turning this trial into a farce. Will you please refrain from using swear words in my court.' The judge sat back and thought about the heaviest sentence he could drop on Bobo's head before turning to McGovern, who was waiting patiently for guidance. 'Please continue, Inspector.'

'I am not a liar.' McGovern couldn't have been more relaxed if he downed a bottle of Mogadon with whisky chasers.

'Is that all you have to say?' Bobo's voice had moved a pitch higher as he struggled with his own performance.

'Mr McCartney. You may not be aware but that is all the inspector has to say. You asked him a question and he answered,' the judge said wearily, wishing that, just sometimes, he had the power to hang people.

Bobo stared at the judge and felt like his thought process was being overwhelmed by doubt. 'Fuck off.' He said it as quietly as possible and the judge missed the actual words, but he knew there had been a murmured form of abuse.

'Did you say something, Mr McCartney?'

Bobo blinked rapidly and thought about trying a runner. 'No, Your Worship,' he lied and realised that he was going to prison for a long time.

'Please refer to me as My Lord, not Your Worship!'

Bobo blinked rapidly again and looked back towards McGovern, who was shaking his head. His world was collapsing in front of his eyes and he decided to throw the dice. 'Is it not the case, Inspector, that upon my arrest you did with malice aforethought threaten to kick the shite out of me?'

The court descended into chaos, and although Bobo didn't get the press conference he'd imagined, he did make all the news outlets. When he'd fired his last question at McGovern, several members of the jury plus the clerk of court became helpless with laughter. The judge struggled to control events as Bobo lost the plot and decided to climb into the witness box and punch McGovern in the puss. That was Bobo's last mistake before they carried him off for medical treatment. Only a trained eye would have noticed the short jab McGovern landed on the Glasgow robber's chin, but for someone without any boxing experience, it would have been like being hit by a sledgehammer. The late great 'Smokin' Joe' Frazier was McGovern's boxing hero and had been one of the leading exponents of the six-inch hammer blow.

As far as the judge was concerned though, McGovern had quite properly defended himself when attacked and it had been a proportionate response.

Macallan and McGovern went to a restaurant near Parliament Square and over coffee and tourist-price scones they laughed their way through discussing the already legendary trial of Patrick 'Bobo' McCartney.

'It's a cracker, isn't it, and will definitely keep you going at piss-ups for the next few years. But I suppose we'd better get back to the real world and Billy Nelson, who'll be a bit harder to nail,' Macallan said, and McGovern nodded in agreement as he stuffed the last of the fruit scone into his mouth.

They walked across Parliament Square and saw the

Advocate Depute who'd prosecuted the McCartney case striding towards the Advocates Library. With his wig and gown flowing in the light east wind, he looked like some spectre of retribution ready to slay those who would bring evil to the capital city.

'I think that was a trial I'll remember for some time, Superintendent,' he said with a broad smile, then his face dropped as he realised that Macallan might be interested in something else that had just been passed to him.

He sighed. 'It just occurred to me that you were the officer in charge of the Billy Drew case.'

Macallan nodded and felt her heart sink. The law was an ass so she knew what was coming, and the AD's face confirmed bad news.

'Billy Drew won his appeal today and for all intents and purposes he's a free man.'

Macallan nodded again. The news didn't really shock her as she'd fully recognised the problem with the evidence against Drew, despite him being guilty as sin, and she knew there was a good chance that the other two members of the gang – his brother, Frank Drew, and his mate Colin Jack – would be freed as well.

'Such is life,' she said to the advocate with as much lightness as possible – but it didn't really work.

She turned to head towards the taxi rank. 'Jesus, that's all we need,' she said to McGovern. 'Hopefully he'll keep his head down for a bit, but God knows what'll be going through his mind. I'll need to have a word with Mick just in case. Nobody knows where Jonathon Barclay is so that's just as well.'

'We can get a couple of field officers to start gathering intel on him, but that's about as much as we can spare at the moment. We've a lot on, and of course the Nelson job has tied up what's left,' McGovern said in flat tones, sympathetic to what Macallan was feeling. If anything else happened they would struggle, and the chief super would pile the pressure on them.

They spotted a free taxi and McGovern opened the door to jump in.

'Chief Inspector, how are you?'

Macallan turned and found Billy Drew, smiling broadly. He looked fit and had obviously been hitting the weights when he was inside. He'd always been a fitness junkie, but Macallan wondered if his shape had something to do with a dose of steroids, which were as available inside as out.

'I'd love to say I'm delighted to see you, but I'm not. And it's Superintendent now.' Macallan faced him head-on and kept eye contact.

'No problem, Superintendent. I just want to live the quiet life and be a good citizen now. Say hello to Mick Harkins if you see him. I'd love to have a drink with him some time.'

McGovern took a step towards Drew and Macallan put her hand on his forearm. 'Not now.' A smile spread across her face. 'Some other time, Billy.'

She turned and stepped into the taxi, letting out a long sigh when she was out of sight of Billy Drew. 'What next?' The phone rang just as she finished the sentence and it was the chief super's secretary. McGovern watched her face pale and tense up.

She put the phone back in her bag. 'Great – just great. He wants to see us after the briefing. That's bound to be a pain in the arse.'

She hadn't had a cigarette for months but at that moment she would have killed for a lungful of the poison.

23

When Macallan arrived at the office the early-shift team were back in, buzzing with the high that infects surveillance officers after a good day when they hadn't lost the target and there'd been no major cock-ups. Within half an hour they would fall flat with the reverse drug effect – the adrenalin high diving to an exhausted low.

Thompson had led the team; she looked like she'd aged five years and was already getting what were known as 'detective's lines'. Even Botox wouldn't erase those marks, left by the intense pressure of the job.

Macallan watched the team laughing and stripping off their kit, both men and women getting changed without a thought for modesty. She smiled because they were the best, and the problem with covert squads was that they were what it said on the tin. Joe Public never saw them, only their limp imitations on television. Elsewhere you might find the fuckwits who cut their finger climbing a wall and sued the force for stress, and it was that image of the force that seemed to stick in the public's media-bombarded minds. The women and men Macallan saw in front of her would have run through brick walls for the job and then gone out and got pissed together as just part of a day's work.

'I'm going to a meeting with the chief super, guys; I'll join you for the debrief in about twenty minutes.'

The team murmured in what sounded like understanding and a subliminal message of 'you poor bastard'. They all knew the man for what he was.

Macallan was about five minutes early for the meeting, and when she saw the chief super's secretary was in her office and on her own she smiled and closed the door behind her. The secretary looked up and returned the smile. It was warm, and Macallan knew she hadn't miscalculated.

'I need a favour ... in confidence,' she said. Macallan didn't know any other way to do it, and there wasn't enough time to prevaricate.

'What can I do for you, Superintendent?'

'Straight to the point. When I spoke to you the last time you looked uncomfortable with my colleague. Cards on the table, your chief super has it in for me, but I've no idea what I've done. I need a friend. That's the question.'

Macallan waited while the secretary poured a glass of water and for a moment withdrew inside herself before she answered. 'I'm retiring quite soon, Grace. You don't mind me calling you by your first name?'

'Of course not. I don't even know your name.' Macallan felt embarrassed at the admission.

'It's Shona, a proper Gaelic one because I was born on Lewis. Came to Edinburgh when it seemed like the other end of the world and exotic.'

There was a sad light to her eyes and Macallan wondered what she was carrying after all her years working for the top career men. She'd heard a story that one of them had convinced the secretary that he loved her, which had lasted till the chief constable at the time had told the man that the affair would cost him a chief's job. If the story was true, the secretary never got over the man. Macallan knew exactly what that meant.

'I think you're a very intelligent woman, and I'm sure you've already worked out that my boss is weak and inadequate for the post he holds. His problem is that he thinks he can fly higher, but the chief constable has come to the same conclusion as everybody else and his career has hit the rocks. He's bitter and wants somewhere to lay blame; because that's what weak leaders do, isn't it?' The secretary looked towards her window for a moment, gathering her thoughts, and Macallan wished she'd got to know her earlier.

'I think your problem is that he sees so much in you that he lacks. He's conflicted though, and I've seen the way he sometimes looks at you.'

Then, looking intently at Macallan, she added, 'John O'Connor sees it all.' Macallan knew his name had been coming, but it still made her heart sink. 'He has a different problem with you, and I don't need to explain what you know better than I do. He's a much more talented man and feels his fall from grace, forgive the pun, was undeserved.'

'The thing is, Shona, I agree with him on that. I never wanted what happened,' Macallan said.

'It doesn't matter. He has a huge ego, and he's been wounded by the events. Anyway, he's manipulating the chief super. He wants his career back on track, and he's winding up the man from the back. They're waiting for the slightest problem on your part and won't miss it.'

'You can't avoid "slightest problems" in my position,' Macallan said, almost dejectedly.

'It could backfire though. Remember what that wise old bird Confucius said: before you embark on a journey of revenge, first dig two graves. Don't be too hard on

Lesley Thompson – the girl's naive and over-promoted already. They're using her to get to that slight problem. Poor girl doesn't know that once they've finished with her she'll be left floundering in a rank she can't handle. Just like the chief super – all it's done for him is make him an unhappy man.'

The phone rang and she took the call. 'He's free now and asks that you give him a couple of minutes then go right in.' She smiled encouragingly at Macallan. 'Just do what you do best. You're better than them, and I'm sure you won't let yourself fall to their level. That's how you'll beat them.' Her smile broadened. 'The Force is with you.'

'Thanks. Think I'll need all the help I can get – including the Force if I can get it,' Macallan said as she headed towards the chief super's door.

He was in his seat, rifling through a bundle of documents. He looked up, peered over his glasses and smiled, but it was forced and he looked like he had stomach pains. Smiling meant bad news – it had to.

'Sit down, Superintendent,' he said. 'I just wondered if you could update me on the Billy Nelson surveillance operation?'

Macallan ran through their progress and explained that she was about to go into a briefing to catch up as she'd been at court with Bobo McCartney. He wasn't the least bit interested, and there was no point in describing Bobo's antics, which would have been a must-tell story anywhere else.

'So we don't really seem to be making any progress.' He was still smiling, and she knew that meant he was going to drop something on her.

'I wouldn't say that, and I believe that a full murder squad is about to start on the Fleming case, so the joint effort will make a difference.' She was talking while trying to work out what the bastard was up to.

215

'That's what I wanted to talk to you about.'

Here it comes, she thought.

'This region of the force is struggling with the weight of operations and senior officers to run them. Your surveillance and intelligence unit is well staffed, and the Nelson operation is running along without any great problems that I'm aware of. Correct?'

'That's correct, sir.'

'DCI Thompson is the operational commander. Correct?'

'Yes, sir.' She saw it coming towards her and stifled the urge to ruin her career.

'In that case you're ideally placed to take over the murder squad and will have the advantage of knowing what the intelligence-gathering operation is about.'

His eyes glinted with the energy of triumph as he watched Macallan struggle to form a response she wouldn't regret. She was wearing a dark business suit that she kept for court and formal meetings, and he couldn't help himself – his eyes slid down to the length of her legs. It was only for a moment, and he caught himself, but two bright red spots appeared on his cheeks.

'You start tomorrow, Superintendent.' He saw the look of revulsion in her eyes and suddenly felt less confident. His moment of triumph was wasted by a primal urge that would never be realised – at least not with Grace Macallan.

'I don't understand, sir.' His embarrassment calmed her. She knew this wasn't the time to fight, and the more she struggled the less she would gain. It was a done deal, and she thought he would probably enjoy any hopeless resistance she might offer. 'Who'll run my team?' Macallan asked, but she already knew the answer.

'I would have thought that was obvious. DCI Thompson will get a temporary promotion to super while you're away on the murder squad.' He was tapping the end of a pencil against the desktop in an unconscious attempt to release the tension in his body.

'Sir, it's my opinion that DCI Thompson is far from ready for that role. She lacks confidence, and the wrong call on the current work could cost the force.' She decided that that was enough – anything else would be a waste of breath. She couldn't see him, but O'Connor's fingerprints were all over the moves. The politics were too subtle for the chief super. O'Connor would know that the chances of getting the Nelson gang for murder were slim and the job would be a grind. If it failed it would be a very public failure, and she would be in the right place to take most of the flak.

On the other hand the surveillance operation was covert and very little would be exposed to the public, whatever its successes or failures. Lesley Thompson would be fireproof while Macallan went down in flames. If she ended up having any success with the murder then the chief super would take the plaudits, like a great football manager who'd made the right substitution at the right time.

'Once again I must caution you on your attitude to DCI Thompson. You clearly have a problem with a fellow officer's progress through the force. Try not to worry about the fact that she'll pass you in rank in the not-too-distant future.' The words hung in the air and stank with the venom they contained.

She decided to make one last pitch before she left. 'Can I at least use Felicity Young and her analysts?'

He didn't care; he had no real understanding of what analysts did. 'Of course – I wouldn't want to stand in the way of anything that will help the investigation.'

'Thank you, sir.'

There was nothing more to say, and the chief super

watched the backs of her legs as she walked from his office. He squeezed his hand into a fist and the pencil broke, piercing his skin. He threw the remnants into the bin under his desk and cursed.

The secretary watched her pass the office and mouthed the words 'chin up'. Macallan, stunned and trying to hold it together, nodded but couldn't manage a smile in return.

Think positive, Grace – don't let the bastard get to you, she thought, and repeated it several times as she strode through the dull corridors on a detour to the canteen to get some coffee – she needed time to straighten up and didn't want the team to see her hurting. One thing was certain: she would go and see Harkins when she was finished for the day.

When Macallan arrived back at the office she found Young had joined the debrief, so she decided to wait till it was over to break the news to them.

'What have we got so far then, Lesley?' she asked. She struggled to keep her face neutral, and no one in the room missed it. Macallan wondered how much Thompson knew already and wouldn't have been surprised if she'd been briefed before her.

Thompson looked tired and struggled with describing the technicalities of the day's work.

McGovern, to his credit, stepped in diplomatically when Thompson started to drift. 'Billy Nelson hasn't been doing anything too obvious or that looks like criminality at the moment, which isn't much help. On the upside though, he has been seen to use public phone boxes to make some of his calls, and that's always a good indication that they're business related. We think there might be a pattern developing with the calls, but it's too early to say what it might be just yet.'

Macallan watched Felicity Young scribble furiously;

the analyst loved trying to work out patterns where they weren't obvious.

McGovern continued, 'We've got the exact times the calls were made, and our guys are going in right after and ringing the force number so we can pinpoint what number was called.'

'Good, Jimmy, anything else?' Macallan said, admiring his understated professionalism.

'He's still going walkabout in the university area so I think we'll put footmen up his arse the next time if that's okay? He's up to something there, and we need to find out what it is.'

He looked at Macallan for agreement and she turned to Thompson. 'What do you think, Lesley?'

Thompson, surprised by the question, agreed without figuring out whether it was a good idea or otherwise.

'Felicity, how's the intelligence side coming along?'

'Excellent cooperation from the PSNI and we're building a good profile of Nelson. He's a complicated and interesting man. I should be able to give you a full intelligence picture on him in a day or two. The phone records are coming in, and we're nearly up to date. He seems to have the mobile we know about for non-criminal use, but they all make mistakes. However, the surveillance logs show him as being seen making calls on a mobile at times that don't show on the records of the one we know about.' She pulled the glasses off her nose, which meant she was warming up. 'I believe he has another mobile, and I'm doing some work to try and resolve that. The sightings of him using public phones show that he's smart and capable. All very professional, but these problems can be solved.' She put the glasses back on the end of her nose. 'There's almost nothing coming from his home phone, but I am interested in his walkabouts in the university area and would like any information on what he's doing.' She put her papers back on the desk. 'That's all I have for now.'

'Thanks for that. And Jimmy, Felicity and Lesley – can I see you in my office?' They nodded, following her in without question.

As she told them the news, she noticed how surprised McGovern and Young looked compared to Thompson. Macallan knew then that her earlier suspicion had been correct. She tried to convince them that everything would be fine, determined not to show how she really felt. 'Even though I'm going to be with the murder squad, I'll still be closely involved. It's just the way the job is.'

Macallan went into the main office and told the rest of the team, trying to make it seem like just another day at the office, but they picked up the vibes. The silence that followed the announcement said it all.

'When we put this lot away I'll be back and the drinks will definitely be on me.' She looked straight at Thompson, who dropped her gaze to the floor.

Later in the day, McGovern came into Macallan's office just as she was wrapping a scarf round her neck and held out his hand. 'Make the bastards weep – and I don't mean Nelson.'

She bypassed the hand and pulled her friend close. He was surprised by the warmth. Macallan always seemed to be on her own little island, but he'd known her long enough now to see she was a woman who could be strong and soft in equal measures.

'Christ, I'm still trying to get over Fergie retiring at Man United and now you!' he said, trying to lighten it up.

She left without another word.

Macallan began walking home, and the Christmas trees

she saw starting to sprout in the windows along Stock-bridge just confirmed that she needed a diversion. She tapped Harkins' number into her phone.

'What is it?'

'Jesus, Mick, your diplomatic skills are getting worse. I need a drink and perhaps a weep. Can I come round?'

'Fuck that. I'm now hobbling on my sticks to the bookies so why don't you call me a cab and I'll meet you somewhere.'

'Brilliant. What about memory lane in the Bailie?'

'The Bailie it is and you're on the bell.'

Macallan felt her spirits lift. Harkins had that rare ability to make her take herself less seriously – in other words he was a master piss-taker and knew exactly how to draw the swelling out of the most inflated ego. She knew she had a tendency to see herself as a victim and Harkins would remind her that it was all just shite.

She waited at the bar and resisted the temptation to get one in before Harkins arrived, but with the rate that Harkins consumed alcohol she didn't need a start. She felt her phone tremble, saw Harkins' number and prayed that he hadn't called off or just couldn't make the journey.

'Mick.'

'I'm stuck at the top of these fucking stairs and need a hand.'

Macallan loved Harkins. There was never a dull moment with him. She'd forgotten that the Bailie was a basement bar, and of course he would struggle on the walking sticks.

When she opened the bar door and saw him leaning on the fence at street level she felt a whole mix of emotions for the man. She missed him in her team, but he'd really fucked up on the Barclay case. She wondered if he knew about Billy Drew and how he would react. She could

221

forgive Harkins his faults because the mistakes he'd made weren't mistakes at the time. There had been few or no rules about informants when he'd become involved with Jonathon Barclay, and what he was guilty of was the philosophy of 'noble cause'. He'd paid a heavy price with his injuries, and she just couldn't help liking the mass of contradictions that made up the man – and as he often liked to remind her, 'At least I'm interesting.'

'Jesus, I never thought I'd see the day I'd have to carry Mick Harkins into the pub rather than out.' Macallan got a hold of his arm and helped him slowly navigate the steps down into the half-lit bar where they'd put the world to rights so many times. She felt a twinge of sadness at seeing such a proud and independent man struggle to the point where he needed a helping hand to get into a bar.

The place was quiet and she managed to claim one of the comfier seats for her friend. He settled in and it was like old times, but the journey had obviously tired him, and she realised he had a long way to go.

'What'll it be then?'

'Well it's a bit of a celebration, me still being alive, so I'll have the usual. A double goldie and a half of their finest lager.'

A couple of rounds seemed to put the life back in Harkins, and he demanded that Macallan fill him in with all the latest news from the force. She knew how much he missed the gossip, like all ex-detectives. She gave it all, good and bad, including her problems with the chief super.

'I know the guy of old,' Harkins said before finishing the remains of his beer. 'He's the world's biggest tosser.'

She had to interrupt at that point. 'But you say everyone's the world's biggest tosser!'

She got ignored. 'He started off in the Met, and I've got

a mate down there who worked in the same station as him in their probation days. Apparently he came close to being emptied for groping the cleaners. Can you believe it?'

She nodded. 'You bet I can believe it. Five minutes with him makes me feel like having a shower.'

He pointed at the empty glass. 'You don't expect a man in my condition to go to the bar, do you?'

She shook her head, already feeling the warming effect of the booze, which they were consuming too quickly, but that's how Harkins liked it so that's how it would be.

'I knew there'd be a catch,' she said as she got up to head for the bar. Then she paused. 'Look, before we end up as wreckage, did you hear that Billy Drew got out on appeal today?'

Harkins smiled as if he'd been asked an innocent question by a child. 'I may be retired, but once a detective, always a detective. I knew as soon as you did. Still have my sources, you know. Fuck him; if he comes near me I'll batter him to death with my walking stick.'

'That's the end of that then,' Macallan said and wondered why she'd worried about the man.

The rest of the night reminded Macallan why she had called Harkins. She let her hair down, forgot the problems in the job and just let it all go. He was in an 'I don't give a fuck' mood and ended up being warned by the pub manager for singing a Beatles medley and using one of his sticks as a pretend guitar. By that point her vision was blurred, and she grinned lopsidedly when he threatened the manager with his pretend guitar. Nevertheless, her survival instincts kicked in as she realised that being arrested for a breach of the peace might make the chief super's day so she told Harkins it was time to go. It took an effort and a half to get him to the top of the steps and into a taxi.

She leaned in and grinned at Harkins, who grinned back.

'I certainly told that fucking upstart. Last time I take my custom in there,' he slurred, trying to fumble a cigarette out of the packet.

'I think that'll devastate him. I should take you home, but I'm not so you'll just have to crawl into your flat ... okay?' She closed the door of the taxi and waved like a five-year-old girl. The taxi driver looked sorry that he'd stopped as he moved off.

Macallan felt marginally sharper by the time she'd got back to her flat and fumbled her way inside. It was after 11 p.m. but she was at the stage where time had lost its meaning and all she wanted was to call Jack Fraser. Sober it would have been a bad idea, but Macallan wasn't sober, and she just wanted to speak to someone who cared, because she was lonely.

'Grace? Are you okay?' His voice was thick – he'd obviously been asleep already.

'Just wanted to say hello and that I'm missing you.' She tried hard to concentrate but her head was dive-bombing and it was hard to make sense even to herself.

Fraser smiled and rubbed his head to shake the remnants of sleep from his brain. This was definitely a first for Grace Macallan. 'I thought it was always the guys who did this to the women. You'll be telling me you love me next.'

'I do love you. You know that.' She thought that it seemed like the right thing to say, and she heard a soft laugh on the other end of the phone.

Fraser knew Macallan well enough to know that the call was probably a symptom of a bastard of a day or a bastard of a job. The call warmed him though – it felt like the wounds of the past were healing well and that they might just make it. He hadn't planned it, but after she'd rambled till she'd run out of words or the will to say any more, he told her he was coming over for a short visit.

'I don't suppose you'll remember in the morning so I'll text you with confirmation. Get some sleep, and I'll see you on Friday night.'

But she was already asleep, the phone still in her hand.

He lay back on the pillows, wide awake now, but it didn't bother him. He knew that he'd wasted too much precious time not being with Macallan and promised himself he was going to remedy that. She was a special woman, and he felt he didn't deserve her, but he couldn't afford to lose her a second time.

His mind spun the thought on a loop for an hour before he fell asleep again.

24

During the period between Macallan and Fraser falling asleep, a taxi moved across the city from the Georgian piles of the New Town towards the sprawling Gilmerton housing estate that pressed out to the rolling countryside of Midlothian on the south side of the city. There was little evidence of its ancient mining traditions remaining, and like the other peripheral estates of Edinburgh it had suffered its share of crime and drugs-related violence over the years.

Kristina Orlova had arrived home after leaving her last client, a married businessman. He'd paid her well above the odds, and because of his age and serious lack of fitness she hadn't had to work too hard to please him. Like most of her clients, he was flattered to be in the company of a woman who looked like she could compete in a Miss World competition.

She slipped off her coat and opened a bottle of cold white wine to help her wind down. The phone rang, and she tried to sound enthusiastic when she found it was Andy Clark asking if he could come round. She just wanted to wrap herself up in bed, but that wasn't going to be an option.

When she came off the phone she made the call to Pat Fleming to tell him Clark was on his way. He told her she was a good girl and promised her a nice bonus and dinner.

Andy Clark stared out of the taxi window but took nothing in. He couldn't get his mind off Kristina. She was the most beautiful thing he'd ever seen, and despite what she did for a living, he was convinced that he could take her away from all that and that they could be happy together. He was sick of his life and wished that Billy Nelson had never come back to Belfast. What they'd done to the Fleming woman haunted him, and he struggled to sleep at night. He was swallowing prescription pills in double doses and struggling to keep it together, and now Nelson had noticed that something was wrong with him and was on his case every day. Kristina was the only good thing in his life, and he'd become obsessed with the idea that she was the key to escaping his past and his nightmares.

When Orlova heard the soft knock at the door she breathed deeply and tried to calm her nerves. She'd managed three glasses of wine in the time she'd waited for him – had taken it quickly to get the calming benefit of the alcohol. She didn't dare let him notice anything unusual, but she could have done without his company. He was trying to talk her into becoming an item with him and spent a fortune trying to convince her that it was a good idea. He never pushed her for sex, which was a bonus for a young woman who'd already decided that there was hardly a man on God's earth who deserved her love or affection.

Orlova had arrived in the UK three years earlier, having been conned by a Lithuanian trafficking gang. She'd

227

been raped to show her exactly what she was worth then stuck in a cesspit in Chelsea servicing a string of creeps. The one girl she'd heard complain was never seen again, but her reward for staying quiet was to discover that she would never pay off the interest on the supposed cost of transporting her to her miserable new existence.

Despite her situation she decided not to sink into a pit of mindless obedience but rather watched and waited for her opportunity. She knew one of the minders liked to drink himself unconscious when it was his turn to guard the women working in the brothel, and her chance had come one night when not only was the drunk slumped over his desk but the other guard was with one of the girls. She left her customer dressed in a nappy and managed to get all the week's takings from the open safe behind the comatose bouncer. The bonus in the safe was a half-kilo of good quality cocaine, which would sell wherever she was.

She'd slipped out into the London streets and become anonymous. Her looks were intact and she had enough money to keep well clear of London and anyone looking to make her pay. Knowing that she would be killed if she went anywhere near her old employers again, she'd headed north.

As a promising student in Vilnius, Orlova had loved to read about Scotland and its castles and told herself that she would visit it one day, so Edinburgh immediately became her destination of choice. She had managed to get a job in a Leith café and one morning served Joe Fleming with his daily portion of bacon, eggs and black pudding. He hadn't been able to take his eyes off her and she'd already known he was a bit of a name in the area. In fact he'd been so taken with her that he'd offered her a deal she couldn't refuse: look after him when he was in the mood and she could work for herself but advertise through his escort agency, and he wouldn't take a penny. If she didn't fancy a client then she didn't need to bother. Joe told her he'd only put the loaded business guys her way and he'd been as good as his word. He'd also treated her well compared to previous employers and most of the men she'd known, and she'd taken to the life and the flow of cash. By her calculations, two or three years of the money she was making would set her up well for the future, or perhaps get her back to Vilnius to start again. The other possibility was that some wealthy client would propose and make her an honest woman.

Andy Clark was a good-looking boy, but he bored her and was like a dog frightened to let her out of his sight. He talked too much and hadn't realised that she was indirectly involved with the Flemings. She'd struggled to hide her shock when she'd realised that Clark was one of the Belfast gang, who according to the rumour mill were being tagged for the murder of Joe and Danny. She'd realised that she was caught between her new relationship with Pat Fleming and Andy Clark, and the potential for her to get caught in the cross-fire of the warring factions was real and worrying.

Orlova had wondered what Joe would have made of her relationship with his son, but if it was true that Joe was gone then she could put that aside. In the end she'd decided to put her money on the Flemings, but only because she knew nothing about the men from Northern Ireland, and Pat had seemed pleased when she'd told him, promising her a big bonus if she helped to set up Clark.

When she heard the soft knock at the door, she had already put on a dressing gown and scrubbed the make-up off her face. She didn't need it, but her last client liked her to plaster it on for some reason she left to his own little fantasies.

Clark was wide-eyed and spaced on pills, and she had to work hard on the act that she was suffering from a stomach bug. It took a couple of hours to talk him down, plus a promise of a special night out later in the week. He seemed pleased and just wished he could have stayed to look after her, but when he left the flat in the early hours it was with a familiar feeling of dejection. He wondered when she'd make him feel like he was all that she wanted. That's how it was for him.

He stopped on the stairway, took a bottle from his pocket and dropped three of the small white pills into his hand before throwing them down his neck. He felt exhausted and shivered in the cold air.

As he opened the main door to the flats he pulled out his mobile and tried to focus on the numbers to call a taxi. The cold night air turned his breath to white smoke as he stepped out onto the sparkling pavement, and he screwed up his face as he avoided the remnants of a frozen pavement pizza that some upright citizen had heaved up after a hard night on the happy juice.

Eddie Fleming hit him with the first one. He used a pickaxe handle, taking Clark across the side of the knee to make sure he went down and wasn't going to get up and make a fight of it.

The Belfast man gasped at the searing pain that surged from the shattered bone up through his thigh and buttock.

His two assailants stood back for a moment as he rolled onto his back and looked up at them, his face stretched in agony as he gasped for air. When his eyes cleared he saw the two men were wearing Halloween masks, but they were no more than dark shapes with the harsh light of the street lamps behind them. He knew there wasn't a thing he could do and rolled onto his face again, just hoping he would live.

The assault took no more than a minute. The Flemings

had decided on a beating rather than a killing because they didn't want the police after them as well as Nelson. They knew Clark wouldn't make an official complaint, and the message would get through that if the Belfast boys thought they'd take Edinburgh with no reaction then they'd miscalculated badly.

Orlova had put out the lights and stood to the side of the window that looked out the front of the building. She saw Clark fall and watched the blows rain down on the man who'd said he loved her and wanted to spend his life with her. She gulped back another glass of wine.

When they calmly walked away from the motionless figure of Andy Clark she went into her room and sat on the edge of her bed, wondering what would happen next.

When Pat Fleming called her about half an hour later she still hadn't moved.

'You okay?' He said it lightly, as if nothing had happened.

'I'm okay, Patrick.' She liked to use his full name.

'Is he still outside?'

'I'll go and look.'

When she opened the door to her lounge she saw the trace of a blue light beating a dull arc round the room. She looked outside and saw the paramedics lifting Clark onto a stretcher. There were a few lights on in the flats and two uniformed policemen talking into their radios. As she watched, an unmarked car stopped, and the two men in suits who emerged seemed to take control.

'They're taking him away in an ambulance and the police are there,' she said quietly, trying to keep the tremor from her voice.

'No problem, honey. I'll see you tomorrow. Sleep tight.'

She went into the kitchen and opened another bottle of wine.

Across town, Pat turned to the old barmaid, who pulled the sheets back and gestured for him to join her. He'd put aside for the time being that he was in love with Kristina Orlova, who at the same moment was wondering whether she'd made the wrong call.

25

Billy Nelson bought a paper on his way to get breakfast on Leith Walk. When he wanted a decent fry-up he always went to the same place. He knew it was a mistake in his game (never develop habits – they can kill you), but sometimes there are urges that overcome sound logic. Bacon and eggs with all the extras was one of them.

His stomach had been eating him up over the previous couple of days. He'd finally given in and made an appointment with a GP, who'd referred him for tests, and all he could do now was wait till he heard back from the hospital. He hated all quacks and had made a lifetime habit of avoiding them, aside from a near-death experience in Afghanistan, when a bomb blast had killed one of his mates and ripped a chunk of flesh from his leg. Another couple of inches to the left and the artery would have taken a hit and he wouldn't have had to worry about a bellyache. He had only one more day to wait on the results but the days had dragged with the uncertainty of what they would tell him.

The pain had eased off at last, and suddenly he'd been ravenous so the only thing that was going to do the trick was a full-fat breakfast. One of the things he missed about Belfast was the heart-stopping Ulster fry, but the Scots did a fair impression.

He always felt safe enough in the morning and believed in the old adage that criminals didn't like doing any business before noon. And aside from the food he liked the old-fashioned café for its ambience, and the Turkish waitress whose smile could melt the ice freezing on the windows.

She dazzled Nelson again as he entered, making him feel like he was the only customer she'd ever served, and settled himself down in a four-seater booth, which gave him a degree of privacy but still allowed him to see the door and any unwelcome customers. The last thing he needed was some punter to engage him in a conversation about the weather, or the state of Scottish football, which as far as he could see had about as much life in it as Joe Fleming's corpse.

No more than three hundred metres from the door of the café McGovern directed the surveillance team to take up their positions to cover Nelson when he left. He was the operational commander until Thompson took over with a fresh team later in the evening. A footman deployed to pass the café and check whether Nelson was in on his own reported back within a minute that there was only one other customer apart from Nelson, and he was at a separate table.

'Okay, guys – settle down. It looks like he's getting breakfast, but keep on your toes. Make sure we're ready to shoot some pictures if anyone else turns up.'

McGovern sighed happily and opened the flask of sweet black coffee that kept him going through the long slog of surveillance work. He could relax for a bit – the responsibility for watching the front door of the café had been handed over to the 'eyeball', a two-man team watching the door that would call any movement back onto the street by the target.

Nelson trawled through the sports section of the paper. It was one of the few things in life that gave him a sense of quiet pleasure. He was a man who always did the sport first and then got into the news, which these days tended to be mostly bad.

He lost interest, ignored the paper for a minute and thought about the positives in his life. He had the problem with his gut, but he'd had the tests and if it was an ulcer then at least they could do something about it. He just hated the idea of anyone having to look after him. Apart from that, the money was pouring in from the dope business, and he thought they might branch out soon into property or the escort trade. It was a good way to launder the cash, and there were plenty of immigrant women available who would work for peanuts. The police had recently taken out a heavy dealer in West Lothian, which had created a shortage, so Nelson had bumped his prices and the profits had just kept heading skywards. He'd recruited as many dealers as he needed to move the gear coming in from Belfast and wasn't that concerned about the rest, as they were no threat. With the demise of Joe Fleming the competition was mostly low level and they helped divert attention away from his own business. He threw DC Monk the occasional dealer, including the West Lothian man, but knew that there had to be interest in him at some point if it hadn't started already.

His breakfast arrived just as the phone rang. It was a withheld number and he knew that the call was long overdue.

'How are you?' the voice asked in a polished home-counties accent.

Nelson looked up at the waitress and returned her smile but he couldn't compete with the dazzle factor. He waited till she'd walked back behind the counter before he looked round the café and confirmed it was empty apart from an old regular who was only interested in his racing section.

'I'm okay. Enjoying the life here and think it'll do for a bit. What about you?'

'Need to meet. Things are heating up across the water so we'll need your involvement.'

Nelson wanted his breakfast and there was nothing more to say. 'Okay, I'll meet you as arranged. Text me with the "when" and I'll be there.'

'It'll be tomorrow and I'm on my way.'

The phone went dead and Nelson started on his breakfast. He went back to the sports pages and propped the paper up against the condiment dishes so he could read and eat at the same time.

He wolfed down the food. His stomach was pain free and his mood had lifted like the weather outside, the sun finally out after days of wind and rain. He shoved the plate back when he was finished, wiped his mouth with a napkin and cursed the smoking ban as he sipped his strong black tea and went back to the news section of his paper.

He had done no more than scan the front page – which was filled with the latest attack on the question of independence, outlining why Scotland would sink into the Atlantic if it wasn't joined up to its cousins south of the border – when he heard the door of the café click open and the brief sound of rushing traffic before it fell shut again.

He didn't know the two men who'd walked into the café, but they were there to see him, there was no question about it. There was the quick scan and when their eyes settled on Nelson it was as good as a big fuck-off sign saying 'It's you, pal'. He had to make a quick decision on whether to move before they did. Their hands were clear of their pockets and empty, so they'd no more time to reach for a weapon than he had to pull the hunting knife from the back of his waistband. They were a strange-looking pair – the short one had a face that looked like it had been run over by a steamroller, and the other one was about twice the size and didn't seem to have any eyes. They were cool enough though and looked like they were professionals. In another environment they might have been almost comical, but Nelson knew that they weren't there to try out their latest slapstick routine.

He waited to see what they wanted and then he would decide whether to have a fight to the death inside a small café in Leith Walk.

'From the eyeball, that's two males entered the café. We have descriptions and photographs. To the operational commander, any instructions?'

McGovern felt a tingle of anticipation. Always that feeling that it might be something good, something big. You never knew. 'To the eyeball, get a footman to pass the café again and see if they're there to meet the target.'

The female surveillance officer carrying what looked like a baby and a shopping bag passed the large window and saw the two unidentified men had pulled into the booth with Nelson. 'Confirming that the two UDMs have joined the target.'

McGovern smiled; it always felt good to bring something new back to the intelligence officers and analysts. They had a pretty good idea of Nelson's main associates so these two might be a step forward.

'Make sure to get good photographs of the UDMs

when they depart, and I want to get a footman behind them to see what wheels they've got.'

The big gorilla slid into the booth first and said nothing. The shorter man moved in beside him, facing Nelson, who sipped his tea and decided to let them talk first; after all he hadn't invited them, so he'd wait.

'Do you know who I am?' Short-arse said it to Nelson and fixed him with a hard stare.

Nelson studied him for a minute and didn't like the man's black eyes. They seemed to know what he was thinking. 'I'm sorry but I don't watch the telly much and never go to the cinema. What have you been in?'

Magic McGinty sat back, laughed out loud, and it was genuine. 'Fuckin' magic.' He turned to his minder. 'What did I tell you, Gordon? This one's a bit special.'

Gordon didn't twitch and the reason was simple: he was basically a nice guy, but the only way he could earn a living was by using violence or frightening people, which was usually enough to do the trick. He'd grown up with Magic and had stuck by him through all the gang wars. Although Gordon hardly had two brain cells to think with, Magic had never forgotten him, and when he made the big time, he'd given Gordon the job as his personal minder, though the truth was that he hardly needed one, being a formidable and violent bastard himself. Gordon had been nothing but pleasant when Eddie Fleming had visited Magic, but for Nelson he'd been told just to look mental, which meant saying nothing that would expose his high-pitched voice.

Nelson eyed the big man and had to admit to himself that he looked a handful – if anything kicked off he would have a lot to deal with.

Magic put his elbows on the table and drilled Nelson again with those bullet-hole eyes. He let enough time pass to see the Belfast man start to get uncomfortable and nodded before he spoke.

Nelson had been mesmerised by the eyes, and although he'd never been hypnotised he thought later that it must have felt something like his experience with the Glasgow man. He was so distracted that he never saw the movement of Magic's left hand below the table.

Magic had come dressed in a long, dark bespoke overcoat, which kept out the bitter cold. It also allowed him to conceal a sawn-off in a specially designed internal pocket.

The sensation of something pushing too hard against his balls brought Nelson back to full attention. He sat still and worked out that if they'd come to kill him he would already be dead and they'd have been on their way west again. Whatever their intention they were going to talk first, and he'd have no chance of drawing his knife before the madman opposite blew off his gonads.

'My name's McGinty but everyone calls me Magic.' He said it as if they were discussing the weather. His eyes didn't seem to move and Nelson felt like a snake being eyed up for the kill by a mongoose. 'I'd like you to call me Magic. Is that okay, Billy?'

Nelson nodded and replied as evenly as he could, 'That's fine for me ... Magic.'

'Now I want you to understand that the hard thing you feel against your groin is not an approach from someone in the gay community. Do you understand?'

'Got it, Magic,' Nelson said, keeping his voice and tone as steady as before.

'We have to sort a little problem out, but before we start I just want you to know that I'm a sincere but violent cunt and I will kill you if I'm not happy with the outcome of this meeting.'

He was as cool in a pressure situation as Nelson had ever

seen, even in combat, which meant he was probably mad.

Magic called the waitress over and ordered a peppermint tea each for him and Gordon. When she'd taken the order he looked back at Nelson and fixed him again with those eyes. 'Joe Fleming and the waste of space that he claimed as his son bought their gear from me. I just delivered a load to them and it appears that, prior to paying for said goods, you decided to stick your Prod nose in and send them to Butlins in the sky.'

The herbal teas arrived quickly, delivered by a waitress who looked as if she couldn't wait to take refuge again behind the counter; there was something in Magic's eyes she found fascinating but profoundly scary.

Magic took a sip of the tea and winked over the rim of his cup at Nelson – before jabbing the sawn-off deeper into his groin, making him wince. 'Now, I'm out of pocket by quite a wedge, but I'm more concerned with my image than the money. I just can't have people thinking I'm a fuckin' charity, can I, Gordon?' The big man shook his head once but kept it zipped as instructed. 'What am I going to do?' He sighed as if he was speaking to a child. 'The choices are that you either pay up or you start buying your gear from me. Simple really.'

He sat back and let the man have time to think. It was a big decision.

What Magic didn't know was that Nelson was struggling with a problem and Magic had just offered him the solution. 'Suits me, and I'll take the gear – the same quantities that Joe took from you and maybe an increase once we get going.'

Magic hadn't expected it to be so straightforward and he tried to decide whether the man opposite was taking the piss. It didn't seem likely, particularly when two cartridges were twenty-four inches from ending his sex life.

'What about the man that supplies you at the moment?'

'Fuck him.'

Magic looked into his eyes and believed him. He couldn't quite figure Nelson out, and he'd have to keep a close eye on him, but it was business and he was satisfied with the deal so far. There was something that nagged him about the Belfast man though. It was vague but it was there, and that always meant there was a problem. But Magic liked the occasional problem – it kept him sharp. He knew what had killed Joe and Danny Fleming – going soft, forgetting that they were in the hardest game of all, where your enemies were all around you and your best friend might turn out to be your executioner.

'Okay, one of my representatives will be in touch tomorrow, and can I say it's been a pleasure doing business with you.' He paused and jabbed a finger at Nelson. 'Just remember I'm not Joe Fleming. I'll feed you to the pigs the first time I think you're trying it on. At the end of the day you're a Belfast Prod and my name's McGinty, so it is what it is.'

He stood up and the shotgun was already back in his pocket. 'Take care, Billy. And by the way, you look a little pale. You should try and eat a better diet. Maybe a bit of porridge in the morning.'

He turned, walked into the street and was gone.

The two Glasgow men headed for their car and McGinty felt it had gone rather well. Gordon wasn't so sure. 'What about Eddie Fleming?'

'Fuck him. This is business. I can't help it if old Joe was a twat,' said Magic, with his usual degree of cold-hearted logic.

The eyeball's voice crackled over the air. 'The two UDMs have exited the café and are heading north on Leith Walk. I have them.'

241

McGovern emptied the dregs of his coffee onto the pavement through the car window. He was well away from the café and couldn't see what was happening, but he didn't need to. The foot team were on them, and Nelson was still in his seat. They had to get a car number for the UDMs or something that would give them a name.

The foot team labelled the two men as little and large and they followed them to the BMW parked up in Iona Street.

'Got the car and number.' The eyeball waited for an instruction.

'That'll do. Rejoin the team and we'll wait on the target. Pass the car number to the ranch and let's see who these two are.'

'Will do. Can tell you that they're Glasgow boys alright. Could hear them talking about Celtic's domination of the league and what a bunch of gangsters Rangers are.'

'Takes all types – even Weegies,' McGovern said with a smile.

Nelson let out a long sigh and wondered whether he'd just imagined what had taken place. He ordered more tea. He'd just survived a meeting with a nutter so he decided that he should be thankful, and Magic had given him more than he could know after the call he'd taken earlier.

When the tea and fresh toast arrived Billy relaxed again and got back to the paper. He'd done the first page then flicked open the second and felt his throat constrict when he saw it. A headliner telling the citizenry that there was a gang war in Edinburgh over the drugs business. The report mentioned that two prominent Edinburgh gangsters were missing and 'police sources' had told the reporter that they believed the men had been murdered. Nelson realised that whoever the reporter was they had good sources, both inside the police and on his side of the fence.

He read on and saw that the last two paragraphs were designed to put the frighteners right up the reading public. Other sources had told the reporter that a 'Belfast terror gang' had settled in Edinburgh and were behind the acts of violence that were taking place across the city. The reporter's name was Jacquie Bell.

'Fuckin' bitch.' He slammed the table, but he hadn't noticed the waitress approach to clear his plates.

He looked up to find her smile had disappeared at seeing something in the customer she didn't like. He'd always seemed a quiet man and handsome; in fact she'd hoped he'd ask her out. But in that one moment she witnessed the other side of Billy Nelson and that was enough.

He was startled by her appearance. 'I'm sorry, I never saw you there. Just something upset me.'

She said it was no problem, but the warmth was gone, and he felt ashamed that she'd seen what he really was. He felt the dull throb in his gut and was angry. He'd been fine, but it had only taken a few lines in a paper to crash him back into the real world he inhabited.

He was running the words through his mind, analysing what they meant, and felt pissed off at the reporter. There was a bigger problem, though – she must have had good police sources, which meant they had to have a team interested in him already. It might not be surveillance, but there had to be something on the go.

He ground his teeth at the thought that he was paying Donnie Monk a small fortune and there'd been no warning.

'Fuck.' He said it quietly, but he needed to get it out. He knew that police attention wasn't the end of the world – it was just another problem to be dealt with, but

243

he had a lot coming into play and didn't want them in the way just yet. The time would come, but it had to be on his terms.

Nelson left the paper lying on the table, threw some notes down and promised himself he'd never go back to the café and face that waitress again.

She watched him leave and felt that another one of her many little dreams had been nothing more than an illusion.

He walked out onto the pavement and wondered if there was surveillance on him. Hard to tell, and he knew he had to avoid letting his imagination run wild, seeing police when they weren't there.

Some people became obsessed that the police were all over their lives when it was no more than imagination. Every criminal, even the pettiest felon, thought there was a team on them and that their phones were bugged, but as a Belfast boy he knew that you could still function even with police attention – you just had to be a bit clever. He was keeping his hands off potential evidence as much as possible and, if they were watching, what would they see? He'd decided to keep well away from handling the dope and let the others take the hit if it happened. They could watch all they wanted – he was careful to keep a firewall between him and any problems. If he needed to make sure he wasn't being watched he could lose a tail for as long as he needed. The rest of the time they could do what the fuck they wanted as far as he was concerned.

He wandered slowly up the Walk and stared in a few windows to see if he could see anything behind him, but there was nothing obvious. His phone rang and he took the call.

'It's Dougie. Some fucker gave Andy a right hiding last night and he's in the Infirmary. What do you want me to do?'

Nelson could hear the worry in his voice. He squeezed his eyes shut, felt the throbbing pain in his gut intensify and answered coldly, 'Meet me in Hanover Street – the usual place in about an hour.'

Clark was pissing Nelson off as it was. He could see the doubt and questions in his eyes every time he gave him an order. Now the stupid fuck was in a hospital bed because somehow or other he'd let his guard down. Nelson had already decided that Clark was becoming surplus to requirements and now it was just a case of deciding how he got rid of him.

He put the phone down and looked for a taxi. There were plenty about, including the one with one of the surveillance team driving. He flagged a taxi with a driver who'd definitely eaten too many pies.

'Take me to George Square, driver,' Nelson said, hoping the man wasn't one of the blethering bastard types.

'What you up to today then, chief?' The driver used his favourite opening line; he was interested in his passenger's accent.

'What I'm up to has fuck all to do with you. Just drive.' Nelson was pissed off at the turn of events with Clark and just didn't need to speak to Captain Obesity in the front.

The driver knew he was dealing with someone who wasn't just acting and concentrated on the road. He was used to all types so it was water off a duck's back.

The surveillance-team taxi took the eyeball and followed Nelson up to the university area. They watched him climb out in George Square, pay the driver without a word and head west on foot. Two surveillance officers were a hundred yards behind him on either side of the street. It was busy with students, which gave them all the cover they needed.

'He's away on walkabout again. Instructions?' the eyeball relayed to McGovern.

'See where he goes. Don't take any chances, keep well back and don't risk a burning.' McGovern kept it calm.

The surveillance team were given their instructions as to where each car should cover to make sure that whatever Nelson did they couldn't lose him. When Nelson headed towards Potterrow they decided the street was just too quiet so the footman let him run without a tail; wherever he reappeared one of the teams would pick him up again.

After about half an hour he was spotted by one of the cars in West Nicolson Street, where he jumped a taxi and headed down to Hanover Street. The surveillance team went with him.

They watched Nelson and Dougie Fisher meet up and swallow a couple of drinks too quickly to have enjoyed them. The footman relayed back to the team that Nelson looked severely pissed off and was giving Fisher an earache about something.

After about twenty minutes they left the bar, jumping another taxi and going straight to the Royal Infirmary. McGovern had been told about the assault on Clark and realised where they were headed. That was the opportunity McGovern had been waiting for, and he gave the order for a covert team on standby to enter Nelson's house and place the listening devices.

It took no more than twenty minutes to do the job. When they got further confirmation that Nelson was still safely tucked up inside the hospital they had a fast look round the house to make sure nothing had been disturbed before they left. The team leader noticed the mobile in the hall and remembered the analyst's words at the briefing. The phone was on and there was no security lock engaged. Nelson had slipped up.

'Silly Billy,' he said to himself. He couldn't risk making a call to get the number, but he looked up the phone memory and noted down the last three calls and the times, knowing the intelligence unit would be able to trace the phones and cross-reference them to get the number of the iPhone he was holding. It was possible that it was the phone they'd seen Nelson using already and was worth a try. He shrugged and secured the door then made his way back to the pick-up vehicle.

'All clear, Jimmy, and job done.'

'Good job, boys. Drinks on me later.' McGovern felt the pieces were fitting into place and a noose was tightening round Billy Nelson's neck. He just didn't know it yet.

26

When Nelson and Fisher arrived at the hospital, Rob McLean joined them at the entrance. Fisher and McLean found they could hardly keep up as they speed-walked behind Nelson through the long noisy corridors of the new Royal Infirmary. They glanced at each other and realised they were both questioning their loyalty to the man in front. They didn't like it: Nelson looked like shit, was in a fuck of a mood, and the last thing they needed was a problem with Clark, who seemed to be struggling to keep Nelson off his back as it was. Fisher and McLean liked Clark and couldn't figure out what the problem was, apart from the fact the boy wasn't the brightest star in the sky.

They found the ward, and a staff nurse approached them and asked if they were family.

'Yes, I'm his cousin,' Nelson lied without a second thought. 'How is the boy?'

The staff nurse looked at the three men and felt uncomfortable, especially with the one who said he was a cousin. He looked angry, and she didn't want to spend too much time with him. 'He's suffered a significant number of injuries but luckily nothing too serious to the head. It's mainly his arms and legs that have been affected.'

'It would probably be better if it had been his head, darlin', because he's got fuck all in it.'

The nurse paused, struggling to find an appropriate reaction to this comment, especially as it had been accompanied by a friendly smile. She knew Clark was the victim of an attack and looking at his visitors she didn't want to know any more about them. Having worked as a nurse in Belfast during the Troubles, she knew exactly where they were from. She'd read in the papers about the Belfast gang and guessed it had to be connected. 'I can get a doctor if you want to know a bit more,' she said, hoping they wouldn't want that.

'That won't be necessary,' Nelson replied, almost politely.

'The police have been, but your cousin couldn't remember what happened.' She wasn't sure if Nelson had heard her as he was staring intently through the windows of the side room where Andy Clark looked sound asleep.

The nurse left them and decided she needed a cigarette even though she'd been off them for over a month.

'Andy, it's Billy and the boys.' Nelson shook him roughly and then pulled up a chair beside the bed. 'What the fuck happened, boy?'

Fisher and McLean kept back and knew to keep quiet.

Clark slowly began to wake up, trying to drag his mind clear of the sedatives, and smacked his lips, his mouth bone dry. 'Gimme some water for fuck's sake, Billy. You'll need to do it for me. My arms are fucked.'

Nelson poured the water and held the glass to Clark's lips as if he cared about him.

'I've no idea. They were masked up and said fuck all. Came out of nowhere they did. Never had a fuckin' chance.' Clark avoided eye contact; despite his woozy head, he knew where the conversation was going. He tried frantically to think of a cover story, but Nelson would see through it no matter what he did. There was only one 'least bad' option and that was to just tell him what happened.

'Look, I've been seeing a wee girl up that way and maybe they wanted to rob me or it was a pissed-off ex-boyfriend or something.' It even sounded wrong to Clark as he said it.

'A robbery, Andy? Was anything taken?'

'No,' Clark said weakly.

'Who's this wee girl that you've not told us about then?' Nelson's mouth was twisted into a sneer and his eyes looked as if they were retreating into his face, but they glinted at the mention of the girl.

Clark felt his stomach grind with nerves and any effect the sedatives had had was going with every question Nelson put to him. He'd seen what Nelson could do to women, and he started to panic at the thought of Kristina Orlova coming face to face with him.

'She's a Lithuanian girl. Works as an escort, but only occasional and high-class stuff. Just got a wee thing going with her. She's not involved, I promise you. Just leave her out of this.' He'd started to plead, and Nelson didn't like pleading – he saw it as a sign of weakness.

McLean and Fisher looked at each other and shrugged helplessly, knowing what was going to happen.

Clark suddenly found he was being gripped by the throat; it felt as if pliers had been clamped round his windpipe. Given his shattered arms, he was helpless to protect himself. Nelson's mouth was no more than six inches from his face and he couldn't move to avoid the fetid stench of Nelson's breath.

'Now you listen to me, you little fuck! I'm going to

250

find this whore and ask her some questions. If she was involved and you left yourself exposed and, worse still, us, then you're out. To tell the truth I'm bored with you anyway, and I can't have a fuckin' dummy on the team.'

He let go, leaving Clark gasping for air, his eyes wide in panic, then turned to Fisher. 'Get the tart's address and number.'

As he turned to leave the room, Nelson paused and looked back at Clark. 'You get any warning to her before I give her a visit and you might as well kill yourself.'

'Please, just leave the girl alone. She's nobody.'

Nelson had already left the room. The staff nurse had seen what had happened but was much too frightened to intervene. Her husband, however, was a uniform sergeant in the traffic division, and she would tell him what she'd witnessed when she got home.

Later that evening Thompson had taken over command of the operation from McGovern. She was on the late shift and had the discretion to call it off for the night if she thought they were wasting their time. They were still in the intelligence-gathering stage and keeping a full squad on all night would mean losing troops to cover any activity during the day. They'd followed Nelson home, which might have been it for the day, but then about an hour later they'd watched him leave, dressed in a smart suit and carrying a small case.

Nelson had worked with enough officers during his time in the Army to be able to do a passable impression of a middle-class Englishman. He'd already called up the number for Kristina Orlova, gave her the story that he was a company director in Edinburgh for a couple of nights on business and that she'd been highly recommended. He found it difficult to keep the tone light when all he wanted was to make her tell him the truth – after which he'd do whatever needed to be done – and he felt a trickle of sweat run from the underside of his arm to his waist, even though the temperature was several degrees below freezing.

Orlova liked the sound of his voice and pictured a man of breeding and good manners taken for granted. She liked those types because just for a short while they made her feel special, and a couple of them came back time and again. From what he'd told her, Nelson had already booked into one of the best hotels and taken a suite, so a few hundred pounds obviously made no difference to him, and that type of accommodation clinched the deal for the girl. She thought with a bit of luck he'd do the full tour of duty and buy her dinner. That was Orlova's great advantage: any man would want to be seen with her. She was intelligent, dressed with style and had looks that made every other man in the room wish he could swap places with whomever she was with.

The surveillance team saw him jump in a taxi and take the ten-minute drive to the hotel. They couldn't get too close but they saw him get out and go straight inside.

'Get a footman deployed to have a look and see if he meets anyone.' Thompson called out the instruction but realised they were short of cover because some of the cars were stuck in a jam behind them. As a result, the footman was slow in getting into the hotel and precious minutes were wasted.

'There's no sign of him in the bar or the foyer. Instructions?' The footman was pissed off; like all surveillance officers he hated a loss.

'Is there another entrance?' Thompson asked, her voice full of tension.

'Yes, there is, and he could be well away if it's a bit of counter surveillance.'

Thompson knew that she'd made a mistake – she'd been slow to deploy to cover the possible escape routes from the hotel. Every operational commander makes mistakes but Thompson then made an even more serious one by breaking the golden rule – that you must never presume – and so instead of covering the hotel in case he appeared again she decided that they'd had a complete loss. She took the easy route of running away from the problem.

'Let's call it a night, guys, and stand it down. The early team will pick him up again in the morning.'

Thompson thought that giving the team an early finish would keep them happy, but they all knew that McGovern wouldn't have thrown in the towel so easily.

As they headed back to Fettes, Thompson knew it was the wrong call and just hoped that Nelson was having a quiet drink before going straight home to his bed.

'Fat chance,' she said, without thinking.

'What's that, boss?' her driver asked.

'Nothing, just thinking aloud.'

27

Orlova had decided to put on a bit of a show for the client who'd called her. She'd struggled to get the Flemings and Andy Clark out of her head and was wondering whether it was time to pack up and run again.

She decided to forget about it for the moment, dress up, enjoy the night and put the gangsters out of her thoughts for a while. She was well aware that she was a beautiful woman – still young and educated to a level the thugs that inhabited her life couldn't comprehend – and she thought maybe it was time to find a place in the world where she could have something that would pass for a normal life with a normal man and be able to sleep at night. But her experience had made her question whether there was such a thing as a normal man and, if there was, whether she would spend her life always suspecting the worst of him.

She ached to find a place where people wouldn't know what she'd been and what she'd endured. Before she left her flat she'd soaked in a warm bath and stared longingly at the pages of a travel magazine describing the good life in California. A golden land with pictures of bronzed models beaming with that elixir that could transform her life and take her away from the creatures she relied on to survive.

Before she arrived at the hotel Orlova called the room number the man had given her. That was always the first safety check before meeting a client in a hotel – make sure they were genuine, or at least signed into the room they claimed to be in. If they were checked in then the hotel should know who they were, or at any rate have some way of identifying them. That was the theory anyway. At the very least, if something went wrong there was a chance to make enough of a racket to attract attention. The hotels were normally a safe environment for escorts, particularly those at the higher end of the market. The businessmen just wanted a good time and a woman who they could pay then leave behind.

She walked through the entrance of the hotel and the concierge smiled warmly at the stunning and beautifully dressed woman. Normally they could spot the pros a mile off when they came to entertain the businessmen taking some time off from their wedding vows. Not Kristina Orlova though, who looked for all the world like a very assured woman there to play the power games of the business world. Her smart two-piece business suit, the designer glasses and the expensive handbag all fitted the profile of the clientele the hotel designers thought they should be serving.

The lift had full-length mirrors and she smiled at her reflection, imagining herself in another life taking the elevator to her expensive apartment in New York or to meet her husband for dinner.

'Maybe, Kristina,' she said out loud as the doors hissed open.

The man who answered the door smiled broadly, and she thought he was quite handsome, although maybe just a little weary round the edges. This didn't concern her as most of the businessmen she met were heart-attack cases struggling to keep ahead of their game. At least this one was youngish, and that was a pleasant change for her.

'Do come in and let me take your coat.'

He seemed as polite as he'd been on the phone, and she thought that she might just enjoy the evening as he closed the door behind her.

She walked a few paces forward, looked round the suite and decided it must be one of the best in the hotel. Framed in the window and against the Edinburgh night she could see the outline of the castle towering protectively over the city. It was pleasantly warm and she hoped he would offer her champagne. In this level of room they normally made the gesture to show how important they were.

She didn't hear him close in behind her. His right hand, bunched into a fist with the middle two knuckles pushed out to form a wedge, hit her hard and cleanly in the area of her kidneys. Orlova felt like a fireball had exploded in her back – her breath was blown out and she sank to her knees, unable to inhale or recover from the shock. She felt as if she was drowning and the blow had paralysed her ability to make sense of what had happened. The pain seemed to pulse in sickening waves from the site of the blow, and it was too much to bear.

He'd overdone it. The woman was lightly built, nearly half his weight, and he'd given her the full bhoona, which on another day could have killed her. Her pain didn't concern him, but her ability to answer questions did.

She threw up all over the front of her suit and slumped to the floor, lying on her side.

'For fuck's sake,' Nelson said, annoyed at his miscalculation. He realised that he was making too many mistakes and felt a prickle of fear at something he didn't understand. He'd spent all his life in control, but facing something inside him he couldn't fight made him feel mortal and very ordinary.

He left Orlova gasping on the floor, poured a glass of water and sipped it as he watched the girl fight for breath on the rich pile of the carpet. He bent over her and saw she was struggling to deal with the pain.

He pulled her up by the back of her jacket and screwed up his nose at the stench of her vomit before shoving her onto a seat, taking the tape out of his pocket and wrapping it round her hands and mouth. Her eyes were dull, not fully open or focused, and they didn't look like she was taking in what had happened.

He sat on the bed and watched patiently till she came round. The surface of her cheeks was still pale but her eyes cleared enough to show fear of the man sitting staring at her from across the room.

He lit a cigarette and kept quiet, letting terror soften up any thought of resistance. He wanted her to run through all the worst-case scenarios in her mind before he asked her a question.

'Okay, let's get started.'

He'd dropped the English accent and the sound of the hard tones of Belfast panicked Orlova with the realisation of who the man was. She couldn't control her breathing, and her nostrils flared rhythmically in the search for enough air to feed the heart beating like a hammer in her chest.

'You know who I am and why I'm here,' he said, blowing smoke and the rank odour of his breath into her face.

She looked up at him, her eyes stretched wide in the hunt for a way out of the trap, before she nodded slowly.

'I'm going to take the tape off then ask you some questions, and you're going to answer. If you give me the wrong answers, I'm going to hurt you again.'

Under the excruciating pain in her side and back there was a growing feeling of nausea, which she couldn't know at the time was from the damage inflicted on her left kidney.

As he tore the tape from her mouth, she recoiled at the sensation, but it was nothing to what her body was trying to endure.

'I need to go to the bathroom please,' she gasped, but he wasn't interested because as far as he was concerned the discomfort would help get him the answers he wanted.

Orlova felt sick to her core and knew that something had gone seriously wrong inside her. She knew she might die, but she remembered her dreams from earlier in the evening of escape to a new world, free from men like her tormentor. He was a savage, and she knew that if she admitted anything he would kill her. He'd probably taken and killed Joe and his son. She'd heard the story that Joe's wife had been taken by them and that whatever had happened had broken her mind. What would the man do if he knew that she'd set up Andy Clark? If he did know she would probably be dead already, so there was at least some hope. He couldn't know, or else why would he have gone to all these lengths?

The sensation in her bladder was becoming unbearable. She forced the thought of survival into her mind and refused to accept what this man had come to do to her.

He put his hand on her cold, damp face then his nose wrinkled as he saw the tan-coloured seat turn dark with bloodstained urine. He untied her and decided to carry her to the toilet and try to find a way out of the mess he'd created.

As he removed the tape from her hands Orlova channelled all her anger and all her hopes into one last effort against the man in front of her. She had come too far to die at the hands of a beast.

She didn't move fast, but he'd made the mistake of being distracted at a crucial moment, and she heaved upwards and drove her knee into his testicles with all the strength that she could summon. The strike was perfect. He moaned with shock, caught completely off guard and staggered backwards, helpless for the few moments that she needed. She staggered towards the dressing table and picked up a lamp, dragging its cable from the socket and hit Nelson weakly; that was all she had left. She walked to the door, trying to stay conscious just long enough to get to people.

Out in the corridor, Orlova lost her sense of time as she edged along the wall to stop herself falling over. She made it to the lift and felt for the down button. It could have been minutes or hours later that the lift opened and she staggered into it. The buttons were swimming in front of her, but she couldn't make out the numbers next to them. She thought the lowest one must be ground and stubbed her finger against it with barely the strength to make it work.

When the doors opened again, Orlova crawled out and sat with her back against the wall, gasping the stale air, until her mind slipped into the dark and she felt the pain leave her. Orlova had escaped only to lie unconscious in the basement of the hotel.

Although he wasn't aware of that, it gave Nelson enough time to recover, tidy the room and put on his fedora and plain glasses. It didn't matter if the girl had pressed the panic button, he had no other choice but to try and brass it out of the place – or fight if need be.

But he opened the lift door to the ground floor and found everything was as it should be – no panic and no police. He explained at reception that his business arrangements had been changed at the last minute, paid cash and walked out calmly. He had no idea what had happened to the girl, but his only thought was to get clear of the hotel before she was found.

His groin ached, and the lump on his head pounded, reminding him that he'd completely fucked up.

Orlova was found unconscious about half an hour later by a cleaner. It was presumed that she'd had an accident of some kind, and although the concierge remembered her, he had no idea who she was meeting. The paramedics worked on her all the way to A&E, and she was struggling to hold onto life when she was wheeled into the operating theatre. A couple of uniforms arrived at the hospital in response to the ambulance call, but there was nothing to find and nothing to identify her. Nelson had had the presence of mind to take her bag with him when he left the hotel.

Nelson walked as far away as he could, cursing his aching balls, and then caught a taxi home. Once inside, he tore off his clothes, pressed a cloth full of ice against the pain and gulped down a glass full to the brim with whisky. The surge of warmth stopped his hands shaking, and the pain eased as the alcohol swamped his system. He knew that only months earlier the girl wouldn't have been able to get him the way she had in the hotel. He felt weak and curled up into a ball on his bed.

It was the following morning before a cleaner went into the room and found the stained chair, which had dried in the overnight warmth of the room. She'd come from Brazil three years earlier and found strange and disgusting situations and debris all the time. She didn't get excited about it though, as she had been told not to get too interested in the excesses of the occasional high-paying guest.

At the end of her shift she mentioned it to her line manager, who made sure the seat was dumped in the storeroom with all the other soiled and damaged furniture that was written off as collateral damage in the business of the hotel.

The uniforms who'd attended the incident at the hotel took all the details they could and let the CID know that it seemed to be an accident but would need to be looked at when the girl recovered. They had nothing to identify her till she came round. The fact that she had no money or ID didn't make sense as the concierge remembered her carrying an expensive handbag. The night-shift DI was overrun with two suspicious deaths and a couple of alleged rapes that were stretching his team to the limits, so he decided to leave the hotel incident to the dayshift and allocated it to DC Donnie Monk.

28

Macallan walked into the Leith incident room for the first time and found the dozen officers involved were squeezed into a space designed for half the number. DS Grant Baxter looked up and nearly smiled. He'd met Macallan a couple of times, and despite his reservations about female detectives he knew that she was up to the mark and rated by people he regarded as the real deal.

The force was overstretched and because the case lay somewhere between missing persons and a murder investigation with no bodies, they did what they always did and went for a halfway fudge. Baxter didn't have the rank to head a full-scale murder squad, but because of the circumstances and the fact that he was more than capable, he'd been left in charge until they could dump the investigation on a more senior officer. It was the case that no one wanted, so Baxter had already worked out that Macallan had probably upset someone, and in his book that gave her credibility.

Macallan knew that Baxter was rated as well, and Harkins' appraisal was that he was a boring bastard but a fuck-off detective – so that was alright. Harkins had told her that the neds thought Baxter was a right bastard, but away from the job he was a pussycat, though a bit of a moan about his private life.

'Welcome, Superintendent,' he greeted her. 'Glad you've arrived. I really need someone to take the blame rather than me.'

He stuck out his hand and she shook it warmly, glad he was there. She needed a street detective on the case rather than a systems man who believed that simply following the instruction book would bring home the bacon. The case was about criminals, and she needed people who knew how they worked.

'Good to see you, Grant, and glad you're on the team.' She said it with as much warmth as possible because she needed the team and Grant Baxter onside.

'I'll show you what's laughingly called your office.' He walked her through a corridor where the light bulb had gone out weeks before and no one had thought to replace it. This didn't bother her; years in the service had taught her to expect the worst when it came to office accommodation. When he pushed open the door though she did laugh, because there was nothing else to do.

'My God. This is humble.'

It had been an old storeroom, had no windows and she guessed she would never get so comfortable that she wanted to put her feet up and enjoy the ambience. There was a desk, a lamp and a computer terminal that had definitely seen better days.

'Does that work?' she asked hopefully.

'It does, but you'll find it's a bit slow and will drive you mad. Never mind – it's always this way in Leith.'

He took her round the office and she was reassured by what seemed like a team of doers, but she guessed that Baxter, like Harkins, would have made sure that was the case.

'Let's get some coffee – or what passes for coffee – and you can brief me up on where we are.'

She felt charged despite her reservations about the office; she wanted to get going and had the kick of energy at taking a challenge face on. Her normal intelligence role was always in the shadows, watching people, picking at pieces of information and trying to make sense where there might be none. This was full frontal – and there were only two choices. She knew she could mope and let the chief super see her suffer, or she could do what she'd always done before and give it her all – Grace Macallan was not one for moping.

It was a guiding principle that there should be a firewall between the overt investigation and covert intelligence gathering in order to keep the sources safe from exposure in court. So although she would still be working in cooperation with the intelligence teams, they would be entitled to withhold some of the intelligence from her, but she would just have to live with that and make the relationship work.

Baxter cooked up some coffee, stuffed another chair into her office and told her where they were with the investigation, which didn't take long.

'So far we've been taking statements, but to tell the truth we're not getting far. No one wants to talk and Eddie Fleming is only telling us so much, definitely not all. Lena Fleming is a basket case, and we can't get anything out of her that makes sense. The poor woman has been through something terrible, but who knows what that was?' He poured the coffee and shook his head. 'The docs think she's deteriorating and will never make a full recovery. These are bad guys, and I guess you'll know more about them than I do, but unless we can get someone to talk, we're going to have to go straight for them, and you know that all they have to do is sit tight and we're beat.'

Macallan nodded; she didn't expect anything else and certainly not a miracle. 'Any forensics?' she asked hopefully.

'We don't have bodies or a locus for the murder, if that's what it is, so zilch. However we did get a hold of Lena's clothing from the hospital and that's being looked at by the lab. Strictly speaking it's not our case, but obviously we might as well have it on the assumption that whoever did what they did to her is good for the murders as well.' He paused and smiled. 'If they've been murdered and if she was abducted. Good, isn't it?'

'Let me have the statement files and give me a few hours to read through them, then let's see what we can do.' Macallan said this with more confidence than she actually felt. 'I think the TV detectives would say, "We need a break," at this point, and hey ho it would drop on their desk.' She sighed.

'Aye, but this isn't a TV drama and won't be solved in a half-hour slot. I'll get you the files, such as they are,' Baxter replied, closing the office door behind him as he left.

'No one said it would be easy, Grace,' Macallan said to herself, quoting one of the favourite maxims of the pissed-off detective.

She opened the first file and groaned quietly at the thought of ploughing through the bulging mass of statements inside, most of which would say next to nothing of importance.

At the same time, over in the specialist crime directorate, Thompson sat down with the intelligence officers and her surveillance team for the morning briefing. McGovern and his mob had been back out on the job at 6 a.m., reporting a light on in Nelson's house and that they could see him moving about. It was unusual to see him up and about so early, but Thompson breathed a quiet sigh of relief and thanked her God that he was home.

She ran through the force information bulletins and the relevant events that had been extracted from the mounds of information that had come into the unit over the previous twenty-four hours. Most of it affected the other regions, the eastern federation having had a reasonably quiet night, although Edinburgh city had caught a string of serious crimes. The CID had needed to call out extra bodies during the night to cope.

The DS from the intelligence unit ran through what there was and although it was interesting, it had no bearing on the team's work or other operations.

'Anything else?' Thompson asked, beginning to relax after her sleepless night worrying about the decision she'd made at the hotel.

'Only an unexplained event at the hotel where Nelson was lost.'

'Go on.' She tried not to look too interested, but the whole team's radar had gone live, waiting to see if it was marked fuck-up or unrelated.

'There was a girl found injured in the basement. They think it's some kind of accident, but the strange thing is they can't find any personal effects on her. Robbery seems unlikely as she was wearing an expensive watch. The injury was to one of her kidneys and apparently they had to remove it this morning to save her life.'

Thompson felt a knot forming in her stomach. 'Has she been able to speak?'

'Not so far – she's unconscious and still in post-op sedation. CID has it for enquiry and we'll keep you informed.'

The story didn't really stand out in the stew of unusual events that cropped up every day, and there was probably a simple explanation for the missing bag – the most likely being that some poor, underpaid member of staff had taken their chance, which happened all the time. That's what Thompson tried to make herself believe, but deep down she knew that it was too easy an explanation.

'Who's the CID officer involved?' she asked as her mind spun the possibility that Nelson had a connection to the girl. She wasn't sure there was any need to disclose to the CID that her team had been at the hotel. After all, she was running a covert operation and there was no obligation to declare anything to CID when they hadn't seen any crime committed.

'The DC involved is Donnie Monk so don't expect a result. The man's worse than useless,' the intelligence officer said, eliciting a few nods of agreement round the table.

Thompson's phone went. It was McGovern.

'Just to let you know that our boy has got on the road early and we're heading over the Forth Road Bridge, so it may be something interesting. Keep you informed.' He rang off.

Thompson closed the meeting, went into her office and closed the door. She wished she had someone to give her advice, but McGovern was on the road and she wasn't sure she could look herself in the mirror if she asked Macallan. She felt her first stab of guilt that she was working to undermine the woman who was her boss. She saw how the team reacted to Macallan and asked herself what that meant. Could they really all be so wrong to show such obvious loyalty?

She wondered what sins the woman had committed that seemed to obsess O'Connor and the chief super. She'd blindly accepted what she'd been told because all she wanted was O'Connor, but for the first time Thompson contemplated that she might be on the wrong side. She'd seen something in the team she was with, and that was changing her view of the job. She'd watched the men and women interact, seen comradeship and wanted what they had – to be part of something that mattered – something she could be proud of.

29

Nelson headed north on the M90 towards Perth, trying to listen to the news, but his mind kept wandering to the mess of problems he had to sort out. He kept the car at sixty on cruise control because the last thing he needed was a pull over by some smart-arsed traffic cop. He'd too much on his mind and had to be back in Edinburgh by the afternoon to get the results of his tests.

He looked at his reflection in the rear-view mirror and winced at what he saw. There was no shine in his eyes, like a photograph with a matt finish. He'd never had much colour but his skin seemed stretched and thin and had a waxy dullness about it, and his cheekbones were more obvious. He was sick and he knew it.

The surveillance team were well behind and they didn't need to be close on such a long stretch of road. The tracker they'd fitted to his car let them know exactly where he was, and if they entered a built-up area they could close up using the cover of other traffic.

Nelson lit up a cigarette and the first lungful should have buzzed his senses but the taste was wrong. He threw it out of the window and called Donnie Monk to see if the useless fuck had anything for him. The call was made on his clean phone, which he only used when he was going to discuss business; it was safe and wouldn't come back to him. The other phone he used was registered to him, and if the police intercepted those calls, what they would hear would be no good to them.

Monk answered the call and it was obvious that he was hungover with booze or the after-effects of the cocaine Nelson supplied to him. The detective's voice was ragged and Nelson shook his head, wondering how the man had ever made it into the CID.

'Billy, what can I do for you?' Monk said it without much enthusiasm.

'I've not heard much from you, Donnie, and that worries me. I feed you with your free prescriptions, and you're supposed to tell me things. I take it you read the papers, so is there anyone on my case?' Nelson tried to keep his voice neutral but his dislike of the detective was intense, and he found it hard to contain himself. The minute Monk became surplus he intended to piss on him from a great height.

'Not sure. The murder squad have you as the main suspect but fuck all to back it up so you can deal with that. I'll try and find out if there are any of the surveillance teams involved, but those guys keep it tight.'

'I don't want excuses. I pay you to know, so get on it.' He hit the dashboard with the side of his fist and wished he was alone in a room with the junkie detective.

'Okay, I'm on it, but I'm up to my eyes with this thing at the hotel.' He had Nelson's attention with one sentence.

'What hotel thing?'

'Some girl found in the basement with a ruptured kidney. We think it's an accident but can't find any ID or fuck all on her. Bit of a mystery, but she's a fuckin' honey. I've got the enquiry, but she's still unconscious.'

The line went quiet as Nelson tried to work out whether he'd just had a bit of luck or another problem. 'Keep me informed about that one but don't ask why. I'll call you back later.'

He put the phone down while Monk was still trying to think of something to say in reply, stared at the road ahead and decided that the news fell into the bit-of-luck category. If he was on a roll he decided that it was best to keep it going and move on some of his immediate problems.

He took the turn-off for Perth and decided to park the car clear of the town centre and its frustrating one-way system. The light snowfall from earlier had cleared and the sky was brilliant blue so he decided to walk to the meet in the open park area of the South Inch. He needed to breathe the dry, cold air and settle the problems he had into some kind of order. His head was a mess, and later in the day he would have his test results. He'd tried to put it out of his head, but, no matter what he tried to turn his thoughts to, the diagnosis crept into his mind like a worm. So many possibilities and all he could think of was the worst.

The streets were bustling with Christmas shoppers frantically buying up what they probably couldn't afford and didn't need. His watch told him he was early, and as he walked through the cobbled street in the pedestrian area he decided to brave the cold, grab a coffee and sit outside one of the line of restaurants and bars.

A girl whose name tag told him she was Anna served him a steaming cup, and for the first time in days he ached for the taste of coffee.

He lit up a cigarette and heaved in the smoke. It worked, and he felt the nicotine rush through his blood and heighten his senses. The coffee tasted as it should.

He closed his eyes and just wanted to keep feeling the way he felt in that moment – no pain in his gut and anonymous in this town.

The surveillance officer browsed through some books in a shop about a hundred yards from Nelson, where the windows gave him a perfect view. He could keep the eyeball safely and, even better, stay warm while he did so.

The security-service officer put his paper into a rucksack when the train was about five minutes from Perth station. He sighed. He could have done without the job he was involved in and didn't want to be there given the workload he had piling up and the fact his boss was on his back for results. He was based in the new spook HQ in Belfast that everyone in the province knew about. The other passengers would hardly have noticed him on the journey from Glasgow, and there wasn't much to notice. In his mid-thirties, he bordered on okay-looking and dressed like the droves of outdoor types who headed from the overstressed cities and towns to the soothing hills of Perthshire.

He was Nelson's handler, and he was worried about the way everything was going. Nelson was acting like a cowboy. Despite all the effort he'd put into running him, the service were getting itchy and were close to taking the decision to dump him as a dangerous, out-of-control agent. But the handler was determined to get the job done with him, and then they could do what the fuck they liked as far as he was concerned.

The security service had identified Billy Nelson long before he'd half-murdered the Afghan boy, although that had alerted them that he needed careful handling. He was just too valuable to miss. They knew from old SB intel-

272

ligence that he was UVF and knew why the leadership had pointed him at the Army. The service watched him closely and saw him cross a barrier and become friends with Catholic soldiers. They wanted Jackie Martin's head on a plate, and Nelson was a long-term investment to get to the main man.

They knew that Martin still sat on enough arms to start a small war and had only paid lip service to the decommissioning of weapons during the peace process, and he had an added target on his back because he'd tortured and killed a security-service agent who he'd mistakenly thought worked for Special Branch.

When Nelson had got into trouble they'd made their move and told him he could either do twenty years or come on board with them. He'd resisted but they'd shown him that Martin was no more devoted to the Loyalist cause than Martin McGuinness, and when Nelson had seen the evidence he'd realised how all those boys that had lost their lives had just been used by men like Martin. Now those men were using the peace to fill their pockets and exploiting people in other ways. He'd agreed to help them get to Martin but was smart enough to know that the service was using him as well. If it kept him clear of prison he'd go along with it, but as far as he was concerned, he'd do what was good for Billy Nelson and nothing else.

Nelson's phone rang and he picked it up without looking at the number – he already knew who it was.

'I'm not far away. Where are you?'

Nelson was happy where he was but the spook stuck to the rules of his tradecraft and said he'd meet him at the riverside on the broad parkland of the South Inch. No one could get near them without being noticed, and there were a range of escape routes if they needed

273

to separate quickly. It happened: meetings could be arranged at the other end of the country and you could still bump into your next-door neighbour on a day out.

Nelson walked across the park towards the river. It was too early in the day to be busy; there was just the odd dog walker, and he took one of the seats next to the wide River Tay. He opened his paper, didn't hear his handler approaching from behind.

'How goes it, Billy?' The home-counties accent had been clipped by five years in the Guards. 'This is a beautiful place. Just a pity it's always freezing.' He walked round to sit next to Nelson and noticed the change in his appearance.

'Jesus, are you okay? You look like you've had seven nights on the tiles.' He said it with what sounded like concern, which embarrassed Nelson. He didn't want to talk about it – and certainly not to a spook.

'Just a bug in the gut. I'm on the mend so you don't have to send me a get-well card or anything, Bill.' He paused and lit up a cigarette, which he knew annoyed the fanatical non-smoker beside him.

'By the way, I always mean to ask: is Bill your real name?'

The handler smiled and knew that there was no point in bullshitting a man like Billy Nelson. 'Of course not; it's Mary.'

They both thought that was enough foreplay and the handler got to the point. 'We need to move on the Jackie Martin thing.' He paused to watch for the effect on Nelson but there was nothing, and it was what he'd expected. 'The job's been running long enough, and my masters want him taken out now. What do you think?'

'I'll make the call today, and anyway I'm ahead of the game. There's a guy from Glasgow wants to do business, and I'll move over to him once Jackie's out of the way.'

The spook shook his head. 'You're sure he won't smell something? He's a crafty old bastard is our Jackie.'

'You worry too much. Just you make sure that everything is in place to take him out. I've enough problems without Jackie Martin on my case.' The tension in Nelson's voice was obvious – another problem would be the last straw.

'That's no problem. Once I get the call I'll make sure a police team take him out nice and cleanly with no loose ends. Who's the Glasgow man by the way? I need to know these things. Rules is rules and all that.'

'A guy called Magic McGinty. Fuckin' nutter and haven't met anyone quite like him.'

The spook didn't seem that interested, but that was what spooks were good at. The fact was he was definitely interested.

'By the way,' he told Nelson. 'You're under surveillance, but you might know that already. I wouldn't worry about it – just make sure they don't see you with a bag of happy dust in your hand.' He was completely relaxed and smiled at the pained expression on Nelson's face. 'Look, if there's a move against you I'll let you know. It's only you, and they're not covering the rest of your team apart from checking their phone billing. So just make sure you get them to do any business.' He lied perfectly and his own mother wouldn't have noticed the deception. The agent knew full well that as soon as Jackie Martin was banged up, the service would throw Nelson to the nearest pack of wolves.

'Okay, Bill or Mary or whatever the fuck your name is.' Nelson was reassured by the spook's confidence. They shook hands and he watched the agent head along the riverside away from him. He had no reason to disbelieve the spook, but he wondered why the police hadn't tied him to the girl in the hotel if they were following him.

He would never know that it was just down to luck and a lack of experience on Thompson's part.

'From the eyeball, that's the target and associate parting. What do you want us to do, Jimmy?'

McGovern knew that the meeting had to be important but splitting the surveillance team in two was nearly always a mistake and the rule of thumb was to stay with the target. The riverside walk ran for miles, and there was no guarantee that they wouldn't lose the unknown somewhere along the way.

'Stick with the target,' he replied. 'Nothing else we can do.' He was sure in his gut that the other man was important, but he knew what he had to do. In a city the likelihood was that a car was nearby, but in the sticks surveillance became much more difficult and greater distance had to be left between the watchers and the target.

Nelson walked slowly back to the town centre and thought he would have another coffee before heading back to Edinburgh and whatever lay ahead in the hospital. Now he knew he was under surveillance he'd have to take care, but he knew that the spook was right – he just had to make sure he kept his hands off the gear and said nothing on his registered phone. The news confirmed that Donnie Monk wasn't doing the business though, and once he worked out what to do with the problem at the hotel he'd take care of him.

He sipped his coffee and thought about the girl who'd kneed him in the balls then picked up the phone and called Donnie Monk again, answering the detective's 'Hello?' by telling him to 'Shut the fuck up and listen.'

'I'm going to get one of the boys to meet you and give you a quarter kilo of nose sugar, some tabs and scales. I want you to go to the girl's flat and rig it up like she's a dealer, okay? Don't talk – I'm not finished. I've got a key to her place and know where she lives. Now you can talk, but I only expect you to say, "I've got it, Billy." '

There was a long moment of silence and Monk was sweating from the combination of toxins in his body, self-loathing and the fact that he was in bed with the devil.

'Christ, do you know what you're asking me to do?' he said. 'I've got a feeling the rubber-heel squad are taking an interest in me as it is. The girl nearly died, but then I guess you would know that.' Just for a moment Monk felt like the cop he'd been all those years ago – a cop who would have spat in the eye of a man like Billy Nelson. But the brief flare of anger sputtered then died on the truth that he was a junkie and he was talking to the man who fed him his little moments of oblivion.

'Just do the fuckin' thing and if I find out you've had a sniff of the goods then we have a problem. Do you hear me?' Nelson didn't have to pretend with Monk. It was just so easy to despise the man. 'I need her to be discredited, just in case she makes any wild allegations, if you know what I mean. Think on the positives: you get all the credit for another brilliant detection and the citizens don't like foreigners, especially when they're pros. It's win-win.'

Monk apologised to Nelson; he was beaten and said he'd do the necessary at the girl's flat. He put the phone down and looked in the bathroom mirror of the pigpen that he called home. He was fat, and his face was beginning to look like someone had blown it up with a bicycle pump. His faded blue shirt was covered in dark patches of sweat and he stank. He promised himself, in the way that addicts do, that this was his last day on the crap and that he'd get himself together.

He thought again about what he was about to do for

Billy Nelson and started to shake like a man on the trap-door.

He leaned over, snorted the last line of powder from the toilet cistern, followed it with a shot of cheap whisky and then sat in the semi-darkness of his lounge waiting for the call from Nelson's boys. He was going to take delivery of the gear he would plant at the home of the girl he could safely presume Nelson had nearly killed for whatever reason. He shook his head.

'What the fuck's it got to do with me? I'm only the detective on the case,' he said quietly into the emptiness of the flat.

Monk was the only person who'd been in it for nearly two years, and it had gone well past the point where he would invite another human being in to witness the evidence of his ruin.

He leaned his head back, closed his eyes and worried about his future.

On the road back to Edinburgh Nelson called Jackie Martin after running the script through his mind a few times. Martin was no fool; he'd survived as long as he had because he was born with the instincts of a sewer rat and the legend went that he'd avoided two set-ups in the past through sheer instinct. If the plan messed up and Nelson was exposed then it was all over for him.

He shook his head. It would be worth the risk. As far as he was concerned, Martin was a parasite and no loss to the human race.

He pulled into a lay-by and called Martin's number.

The surveillance car with the eyeball had no choice but to pass him and warned the rest of the following convoy. 'He's making a call and we have to overshoot.'

'Okay, boys, just keep going and head back to

Edinburgh in case you've been compromised. Mark the time and let the intelligence boys know when you get there and we'll see who he called. Might be something to do with the UDM.'

McGovern turned to the female surveillance officer with him in the car. 'I feel it in my bones, Dawn – this boy is going to fall big time. I just know it.'

'How's it going there, Jackie?' Nelson said it in as friendly a tone as he could muster.

'Well now, I'm okay. It's that time of the month so what do you need?' Martin was using a phone registered to a second cousin; it was one of the dozen he kept rotating, and this one was for talking business with Billy Nelson. His eyes narrowed when Nelson asked him for nearly double the normal consignment, and he sat forward when he added a request for another couple of machine pistols and ammo.

'What the fuck, Billy? Are you starting a war over there? From what I hear you're causing enough bother without more artillery.' His voice had an edge, and Nelson wasn't surprised that he knew, given the coverage in the press.

'That's all exaggerated, and I had to take care of the opposition. You'd have done the same.' He tried his best to sound unconcerned.

'Don't tell me what I would have done, boy. Just don't start the Third World War over there. This is business – *my* business and you work for me. Do you hear me?'

'I hear you.' Nelson was imagining his hand round the bastard's throat.

'In fact I'm coming across with the goods. I want to check out the place and might send a few more people over to help out. I might move myself. I'm fuckin' sick of Belfast and need a change of scene.'

Nelson smiled, realising that his luck had changed

– Martin was volunteering to walk into the trap free of charge.

'I'll call you later with the details,' Martin said and put the phone down.

'Cheers, Jackie, you fat fuck.' Nelson put the radio on and felt good. There was no pain in his gut and it looked like he was going to do some business with Magic McGinty after all.

Before continuing his drive back to Edinburgh he called Fisher and McLean and told them to meet him at his house.

A flurry of snow appeared even though the sky was still blue and clear.

Fisher and McLean were waiting for him when he arrived but there were no greetings or smiles, and Nelson realised that the men he'd once called friends now looked at him as if he was wearing a police uniform.

They walked into his house and hardly a word was exchanged while he poured them a drink. He told them what he wanted delivered to Monk but didn't feel the need to say why. He didn't have to – they knew that he was going to visit the girl and had seen the local papers. They'd already worked out that she was Nelson's handiwork but couldn't understand why, when she was half-dead, he needed to plant enough dope to get her six years.

They also knew and had discussed the fact that Clark didn't know about the girl and wondered how he'd react. He'd already fallen out of love with Nelson, and there was no telling what he'd do once he found out. The saving grace for Nelson was that Clark wouldn't be able to go toe to toe with him for a long time – if ever.

'Is this necessary?' Fisher said it in as even a voice as he could muster, not wanting to overheat the situation with the problems that were developing in the team. 'Christ, the girl is lucky to be alive from what I read, so why do this?'

Nelson necked the drink and sat back in his chair, staring at Fisher and trying to read the signs. None of them would have dared question him in the past, and if Fisher was looking for signs of weakness he had to prove that he was making a mistake. He knew that they had to have seen the physical changes that had taken place in him and like rats they could smell carrion a long way off.

'Are you questioning me? If you are then think carefully, my friend, because that's not how it works.' Nelson got up and walked round to the cupboard behind them. 'Let me fill you boys up while you think about it.'

They heard the sound of the whisky being poured but it unnerved Fisher not being able to keep him in sight. Nelson brought a fresh glass for each of them and went back to the cabinet for his own drink.

Fisher put the glass to his lips to try and calm the nerves that were sparking after the challenge he'd made. Then he felt the working end of a gun against the back of his skull and knew that Nelson wouldn't think twice about putting one in his nut. The drink slipped from his hand and his back arched in response to the threat to his life.

'Have you had a think about it, Dougie? I just want to be sure who's with me and who's not. What about you, Rob? Are you with me?'

McLean had told Fisher before the meeting that he wasn't going to make the challenge with him. He was as pissed off as the others, but there were just too many enemies circling to go it alone. 'Whatever you say. We've come this far so let's see where it goes.' He felt ashamed that he'd left Fisher on his own, but he knew that Nelson had turned into a class-A nutter, and if he was going to do a runner he'd make sure he could find a place where Nelson couldn't get to him.

'Well then, Dougie, it looks like you're on your own.' Nelson said it with a smile, enjoying the fear he could see in the two men. He raised the gun about two feet from the side of Fisher's ear and smashed the handle of the weapon into his unprotected flesh. It wasn't hard enough to cause serious injury; just enough to hurt like fuck, and Nelson watched as blood trickled from the open flesh wound.

Fisher came off the sofa and fell to his knees, clutching the side of his head and groaning with the shock of the blow. Nelson walked round in front of him, crouched down and offered him some tissues that had been sitting on the coffee table.

'What's it to be then?' he said softly into Fisher's ear, like a father soothing his injured child.

Fisher had suffered enough and decided that McLean had been right and he'd picked the wrong time for a challenge. There would be another time, but Nelson already knew that. The move had been made, and once that line had been crossed it would come again – and the next time would probably come from behind.

'No more, Billy. I'm sorry – it's the booze. I just shoot off at the mouth with it. We'll take care of the job with Monk.' His teeth were clenched as he tried to deal with the beating pain in the side of his head.

Nelson helped him back up onto the sofa and ordered McLean to pour another round. 'Another drink then I'll need to go, boys. Places to go and people to see.' If they found out that he was on his way to the hospital it would have made him even more vulnerable, so that had to stay under wraps.

They left after the drink, Fisher still holding a bundle of bloodstained tissues to his head. As soon as they were gone Nelson scrubbed his teeth to kill the smell of booze and put on a fresh shirt for his appointment. He'd always been brought up to be clean and tidy for a visit to the doctor.

The surveillance team watched Fisher leaving the house with some kind of head injury. They had no idea what it meant, but it was logged so it would be seen by the analysts and intelligence boys.

Nelson left in a hurry not long after and they watched him jump in a taxi then followed him to the Western General Hospital.

30

'Cancer.' Even saying the word was like a cold hand squeezing his heart, and he felt his chest tighten with the diagnosis that he'd suspected but tried to avoid thinking about.

The doctor had seen the expression on Nelson's face too many times, and it was the part he hated most. Without the bonus of telling some people that they were through it safely, he couldn't have done the job. He'd worked in Scotland for nearly ten years, and although he'd seen the most intolerable suffering from poverty and disease in his homeland of Pakistan, he'd never get used to breaking bad news.

'I'm really sorry, Mr Nelson, but the problem is quite advanced, and I think we'll need to carry out further tests to see what might be possible in the way of treatment or management.'

Nelson looked across the desk and tried to absorb what it all meant. He didn't have a wife or partner and his isolation felt more like physical pain. There was no woman to put her hand in his when the news was broken; no one to absorb part of the shock, worry or fear. For the first time in his life he wanted to whisper to a loved one that he was frightened, but there was only a young Asian doctor called Mohamed.

Nelson stared at the bearer of bad news and forgot why he was there, hate pouring into his mind.

'A fuckin' death sentence from someone like you. Jesus Christ, that has to be the icing on the fuckin' cake.' Nelson said it in no more than a whisper.

The doctor knew that sometimes people would accept it quietly while others would break down and a few would become angry. He'd been trained to know that it was part of the process and it was just a case of getting the patient through the initial shock.

'I realise that you feel upset, Mr Nelson, but let us take care of you and see what might be possible in the way of treatment or care.'

But while he was talking he realised that the expression in his patient's eyes was something he hadn't been trained for at all, and he suddenly felt very nervous about being alone with Nelson. There was only a cheap wooden door between him and his colleagues, yet he felt as if he was a long way from help. Nelson's emotions were raging, and the doctor's instincts told him that he was alone with a man of violence.

'Maybe I should get a nurse to bring you in something to drink. Would you like some tea or coffee?' He hoped the offer would calm the situation but recognised that Nelson was losing any control of the emotions struggling for release.

The doctor tried to stay calm as the Belfast man stood up and walked round the desk, but it was impossible; tremors of fear ran through his body, and he prayed someone would walk through the door unannounced. There was a panic button only inches away, but his fear would not let him move his hand towards it.

Nelson grabbed him by the throat, and the doctor

became fascinated by the saliva oozing from the side of the man's mouth and leaking down his chin. He noticed there was a thin line of blood in the spit.

Nelson's mind was racing and he'd lost all control. The sleepless nights and the pressure of the previous weeks had weakened him. Hurting the doctor would cost him, but he needed somewhere to put his rage. All those years of conflict, the Republican bombs, shootings, Iraq, the horrors of Basra and then watching friends die in Helmand. All those people who hated what he was and where he came from. Then to get the news from a doctor whose accent and skin colour told him all he needed to know?

There was nothing to say to the man so he just went to work and hit him so hard with the first one that the doctor was thrown backwards in his chair, smashing into a glass-fronted cabinet containing some of his most prized books. The doctor was hurt, but the old leather chair had saved him from something worse, and Nelson knew that the noise would bring in the cavalry. He picked up one of the other chairs, threw it through the window and then he couldn't do any more. He threw up all over the carpet.

The door opened and a nurse put her hand over her mouth before screaming her head off. Two beat cops who were in the hospital taking a statement from an accident victim were near enough to hear the racket and respond. A tussle was always better sport than writing a statement, and they managed to overpower and cuff Nelson without much of a struggle. He let them do their best and stayed quiet through the arrest.

By some miracle, the doctor had suffered no more than bruising round his mouth and some cuts, and he knew that he'd been very lucky to come away in one piece.

'From the eyeball, a couple of uniforms are taking the target away in handcuffs. Instructions?'

Thompson had taken over from McGovern and was turning over in her mind why Billy Nelson might have gone into the hospital. The call made her sit up in confusion.

'Say again.' She knew what the eyeball had called but needed to buy herself time to think what to do.

The eyeball repeated the call.

'Okay,' she said, 'we can't declare to the uniforms and not much else we can do at the moment but I'll let Superintendent Macallan know in case it affects what she's doing. Otherwise stand down this surveillance and I'll see you all back at the ranch.'

Thompson was thrown. She'd already admitted to herself that covert work was difficult and that you needed hardened steel balls just to survive. There was never a right and wrong answer – so much of it was a judgement call, and you had to be able to justify decisions then stand by them when the critics took their pot shots.

31

Grant Baxter had always been regarded as a manager's nightmare, but he got the stories about Macallan. She was easy to like and didn't act as if she was anything other than human. No airs, and she didn't try to pretend she was interested in the witness statements. They were a ball-breaker, and if there was one out of a hundred that had any meaning then it was a result.

He knocked on Macallan's door and stuck his head in, his happiness that she'd taken over the role clear on his face. 'How's it going, boss? You ready for a brew?'

She looked pissed off. That was a good sign.

'Wait till you read the files from the psychics and visionaries – that'll really make your day.'

She nodded and put her hands together in the prayer symbol. 'A brew would be great, thanks.'

Two minutes later he reappeared with a tray and some clean cups, which was always a bonus in a police station.

'Anything you want doing straightaway?' Baxter said as he poured the tea.

'There's a couple of things. I saw a statement from a beat cop about this guy Banjo Rodgers mentioning

288

Irish bastards. Just seems worth checking, and he's up in Wester Hailes where they were based originally.' Macallan pulled her fingers through her hair. 'The other one is this attack on Andy Clark – do we know any more about it, and has anyone spoken to him yet? Probably a waste of time and I know he's not making a complaint, but I'd like to see the details of that attack.'

Baxter shrugged. 'It was allocated to divisional CID, and as you'd expect he's not talking to anyone from our side. Nothing more than that at the moment but I'll get you the full SP.'

He watched as her mind started to fire up with ideas and that was what he wanted to see.

'I think we need to make a proposal to get any case connected to this lot under the one roof or we might miss something. Agreed?' She said this as a done deal rather than a question.

'Agreed.' Baxter wasn't about to argue, and for the first time he thought they might have a chance of solving the case. 'The attack has the Flemings all over it but it might be better to leave them alone for the minute,' Baxter said.

Macallan nodded; she had enough on her plate without trying to get an admission from Eddie Fleming. She knew they had to find Nelson's weak spots and tear them open.

Baxter sipped his tea noisily and Macallan was pleased that she already felt relaxed in his company. She'd heard the stories that he could be difficult, but she saw that he wasn't happy leading the investigation. Some people were born deputies; it was no bad thing and an asset where it was recognised by the person themself. The Fleming case was a potential maggot-fest and whoever took the decisions needed to have a mind like a chess player. Grant Baxter was more of a dominoes man.

'Tell me about Eddie Fleming. All of it. I want to get a feel for this family. You've been on this patch for a long time so you must know them pretty well.' Macallan was playing to his ego as well as doing the right thing. She couldn't have Baxter in a stronger position than her, and she knew that his generation loved to keep something back in case they could use it later. It didn't make them bad cops, just a product of their times.

Baxter responded, pleased that she was using his knowledge of Leith, and he took pride in knowing what was what and who was next in line to get locked up.

Harkins had briefed Macallan perfectly on how to play him: 'Don't fuck the man about, Grace; just get him onside and playing the same game as the rest. He's old school and will be running unofficial sources. We can't give them up to the force, it's against our religion – misguided but his heart, or what's left of his heart, is in the right place.'

Baxter spent the next twenty minutes running through the history of the Flemings and his involvement with them over the years. He told a few good war stories on the way and a picture began to form in Macallan's mind. In a way they were familiar, and every detective in the country could have described a similar crime family or families on their patch. Baxter had had his share of run-ins with Joe and his son Danny, but the twins were virtually unknown to him. It was obvious that he hated Danny and saw him as the unpalatable future of crime, or he would have been if he was still breathing – he had no regard for the old rules and would use violence even where it wasn't necessary. Baxter thought it was like a game now – who could be the most heartless bastard on the street.

'I know you dealt with the Barclay case, boss, but I knew Pauline Johansson and what Danny did to her put her where she was the day she ran into that murdering bastard.' He stopped, knowing that he was showing he actually cared, and that wasn't something he did very often.

'I'm with you there, and what happened to Pauline had quite an effect on me too. I still drop in to see her from time to time.

'What about these twins then?' she continued. 'And especially Eddie?'

'To be honest I only know them by sight, and like everyone else who's getting too long in the tooth I was still thinking of them as kids up until this case. Not so. I've heard Pat is a hard bastard but thick as an MP's wallet, but other than that I can't really say.' He paused, waiting for a question from Macallan, but she was still forming the picture in her mind.

'Go on.'

'Eddie is something else. I must confess I was impressed. No doubt that he's yet another horrible product of old Joe's loins, but he's smart, and from what I can gather he got Pat's brain as well as his own when they were spawned.'

Baxter paused as he sank the last of his tea and thought carefully about what he was going to say next.

Macallan was glad that she'd demanded it all. Men like Baxter found it hard to give up any little gem they were holding, but she knew he was smart enough to realise that if Macallan's profile was true then it would end in tears if he held back. The story about Harkins' handling of Jonathon Barclay was already the stuff of canteen legend.

What puzzled Baxter and the others was that she'd forgiven Harkins, and apparently there was no one closer to her than he was. If that was true then Baxter knew that Harkins would have given her all his moves, and he would expect nothing else. He didn't always get on with Harkins, but they respected each other and regarded themselves as part of a small group of detectives that the neds really didn't want on their case.

He decided to be straight with her. 'Eddie has offered himself up as a source if we do the business on Nelson and co,' he said and waited for a response.

Macallan didn't show any surprise. She knew the disclosure must have been hard for him, but his leap of faith probably meant they could work well together.

'Have you handed him over to the source unit?' She already knew the answer.

'Not yet. I was waiting to talk it over with you.'

They both knew that wasn't quite true and he'd only decided to disclose the information to Macallan on the spur of the moment.

'Hand him over, Grant. The force owns the sources now, not the individual. I had enough problems with Mick, and I don't want to see another good man fall for someone like Eddie Fleming.' She said it loud enough and clear enough.

Baxter got the message and nodded. 'Consider it done. I just miss the old days.' He smiled, accepting who was the boss.

'We all miss them at some point in our lives or we haven't lived but let's get back to business.' Macallan sipped a few mouthfuls of the rapidly cooling tea and moved on.

'There isn't a lot to go on and we're going to get pressure on this without a shadow. All we have at the moment is rumours about the Belfast team and not much else. It might be that we have to pull them in cold. I don't need to tell you what the chances are of getting them to cough with no evidence, but it's about the same as this office getting a prize for design. These boys are UVF. They won't talk without an incentive so that's what we need … an incentive.' She swallowed more of the tea and tried to work out a plan that would enthuse the team, if nothing else.

'This is the problem we had all the time during the Troubles. People are terrified of them, and who can blame them? They'll do anyone that gets in their way so we have to box clever.' Macallan stopped and thought she should give Jacquie Bell a call. She'd warned her about the Belfast boys already, but Bell was running the story every chance she got and Macallan was worried she hadn't taken her warning seriously. Besides, calling Bell always cheered her up, and she needed some of that.

The ancient phone on Macallan's desk buzzed almost silently and she realised that it was so knackered the ringer was buggered. She raised her eyebrows at Baxter as she answered it, but truthfully the office was so bad she was starting to like it. No one had an office like hers, and it would make a good story some day.

Baxter watched her smile disappear as she listened; whatever was being said had immediately commanded her complete attention, and he knew she was already making decisions.

She put the phone down and slapped the table. 'Well well. I don't know if this is good or bad but Billy Nelson has been arrested by the uniforms for assaulting a doctor in the Western General. We've nothing else to go on so let's go and see the boy. What's to lose?'

32

Nelson had said nothing to the uniforms who'd been trying to interview him for the assault. That was how he was trained and thought. Say nothing, find a point in the room and concentrate on it till your mind drifts off and let them ramble on. There was nothing harder for an interviewer than a suspect who says nothing.

He didn't have to concentrate too hard to take his mind away from the questions because he was still trying to absorb the news he'd received earlier and all that it meant. It had been there a long time; the gut discomfort in Helmand had probably been the start and not caused, as he'd thought at the time, by field rations or the Afghan bugs that plagued the fighting men and women in the field. The doctor had said that they needed to do more tests, but he'd heard enough to know that he was in a bad place. He could try and fight it, but while the thought of lying helpless in a hospital ward might be okay for most people, for him it was an invitation to the predators to come and get him. The idea of wasting to the bones and emptying into a bag frightened him more than he could have ever imagined, and while he wasn't afraid of dying, he just wanted it to be while he was on his feet and still a man.

His train of thought was broken by the sound of his name. It was a uniformed sergeant who'd come into the room and asked to see his interviewers outside.

'We'll leave you for a bit, Mr Nelson; we need to speak to our colleague outside,' the younger of the two policemen said. He was politeness itself, and Nelson nodded to him in acknowledgement.

He decided that he would have time to think about his problems later. If he was locked up for the night then he might run into a shit storm with Jackie Martin, who was going to be making his run the next day and would hopefully be taken out, all going well. If the cops kept him in, Martin would definitely think he'd made a deal and shopped him.

Nelson shook his head and realised that he'd have to readdress the things that worried him. He had cancer and yet he was worried about a worthless fuck like Jackie Martin?

Outside the interview room the uniformed officers were told that the doctor who'd been assaulted was refusing to make a complaint, which meant their hands were tied. No complaint, no crime and the fiscal wouldn't entertain it. The doctor would not discuss what had taken place or what he'd told Nelson – he did not want to compromise the doctor–patient privilege.

'There's more to do out on the street rather than wasting our time in here when there's no crime,' their sergeant said, shaking his head at the doctor's decision. It didn't surprise him that much, and in a way he admired the man's stand on principle. He didn't see much evidence of that in the modern world, which he tended to despise.

Macallan and Baxter walked into the cell area and met the sergeant, who Baxter had known from their early days on the beat. He introduced Macallan, and although the young cops were impressed, the old sergeant barely stifled a yawn. The suits were just privileged passengers as far as he was concerned, and it was the uniforms that defended Joe Public from day to day while the prima donnas swanned around in their unmarked cars. He followed the old uniform rule that the CID were like bananas – yellow, bent and went about in bunches. He explained what had happened and that without a complaint from the doctor they would have to release Nelson. He ignored Macallan and spoke directly to Baxter. She cut in and decided to try and soft soap him for a bit of leeway.

'We just need to speak to him for a short time, Sergeant, and it's not a formal interview. We're investigating the murder of Joe and Danny Fleming and it would help us enormously if you could hang on to him till we've finished.'

The sergeant wasn't that impressed and he'd been soft soaped by the best, but he wasn't going to stand in the way of a murder investigation even if it was about the Flemings. He chased the young arresting officers back out onto the street and told them he'd do the release.

'You have twenty minutes then he goes. Okay?' He said it like he meant it and Macallan decided there was no point in trying to piss him off.

'Thanks, Sergeant. We'll be out before that.'

Nelson looked up when the door opened, expecting to see the fresh-faced uniforms marching back in to charge him. But the man and woman who came into the interview room were something else, and he spun the possibilities through his head. He decided it must be about the girl and the business in the hotel. All he could do was keep quiet until he found out what they knew. If he was in serious shit then he would try to get in touch with the spook who handled him. They needed him for the Jackie Martin turn and would not want him remanded in custody.

Macallan introduced herself and Baxter and said they only wanted to talk – this wasn't a formal interview. She tried to reconcile the army photos she'd seen with the man sitting at the table. He was definitely a few pounds lighter, the face more gaunt than she'd imagined. He had presence though, no doubt about it, and would be a hard man to break.

'Grace Macallan – I've heard about you, girl.' He said it with a smile; he'd decided that he would talk if it suited him. He needed to find out what they wanted with him. He knew he was under surveillance so he wanted to test the water, and for some reason Macallan impressed him; she was unusual, and it was more to do with personality than classic looks. It had been a long time since he'd been attracted to a woman, but the superintendent made him think about it.

'Quite a woman by all accounts, but you let down those boys in the PSNI a bit turning on your own. Still, you fought the Taigs, same as us.' He tried to put on what he thought was an attractive smile.

'We're not here about my past career, Billy. I'm leading the investigation into the disappearance of Joe and Danny Fleming. We were passing and just wondered if you'd ever come across them since arriving in Edinburgh.' She wanted it to come out as routine, just to get a feel for the man and what made him tick.

'Terrible business that. Can't say I knew those boys though, and to tell the truth I stay away from those criminal types, so it's unlikely we would have met.' He looked at Baxter and noted the expression in his eyes. 'Does that one talk?' He winked at him, but Baxter was too old and too wise to fall for the wind-up.

'Just to let you know that we'll be seeing a lot of people and there's a chance we might want to take a statement from you at some stage. You never know.'

'You do what you do, Superintendent, and I'll do what I do. Funny, we've both been let down. You by the police and me by the Army, but we hang in there. Nothing else for it I suppose.' Nelson studied her eyes, hoping she'd look away, but she never wavered.

'Don't suppose you've ever met Joe Fleming's wife by any chance?' Baxter cut in.

'I never have. The poor woman must be in a terrible state, her husband and son missing like that.' He shook his head in mock bewilderment.

'She's barely coherent. Sometimes she's rational, but most of the time she's in another world. God knows what happened to her, but she'll probably spend the rest of her life in care.' Baxter spat the words at Nelson, knowing he was starting to lose it despite his best efforts.

Macallan read the signs and decided the play-acting had gone far enough. She drew it to a close and told him that the doctor would not be pressing charges.

Nelson sat back in his chair and decided that at least on some things he was clear for the moment. That was all he needed. And there had been no mention of the hotel or the girl. He breathed a little easier, but he also knew why Grace Macallan had talked to him and that she wasn't going away. She was trouble for him and that would need some thought.

Baxter started up the car and headed back to Leith. He glanced at Macallan, who'd hardly spoken since they'd left the cell area. 'What do you think of our boy then?'

'A bad man, Grant, no doubt about it, but we'll be seeing him again.'

When they arrived back at Leith Macallan brewed up

some coffee to show Baxter that she could do it. Then they sat down and went over their priorities for the following day. 'I want to get my hands on this so we'll go and see this Banjo Rodgers. It's somewhere to start, and it'll give me a feel for the job.'

Macallan was clearly desperate to get going and Baxter had the feeling that all social events were off for her till the case was solved.

'Apart from anything else,' she added, 'if I stay too long in this office I'll go off my trolley.'

The knackered phone buzzed on her desk and made her smile. It was Felicity Young, who wanted to go over some of the material she'd obtained from the intelligence gathering and murder investigation. Macallan was relieved. On this investigation she could use all the help she could get – but then what was new? They arranged a meeting for early the following morning, at which McGovern and Thompson would also be present.

She put the phone down and felt the gears were shifting on the investigation. She knew who Billy Nelson was now and wondered what would prompt their next meeting. It was going to happen, but the venue still had to be decided by the gods.

'Come on, Grant,' she said, standing up. 'I'll buy you a nightcap across the road. I think we could both use it.'

As they walked into the bar across from the entrance to Leith police station, a taxi drove past, taking Billy Nelson home. He saw them enter the pub and wondered again what it would be like to know Macallan. He knew it was never going to happen, but it was a thought that gave him a rare moment of pleasure, letting his imagination overpower the reality of what he had been told earlier in the day. The doctor had passed on getting him locked up and he supposed that was some kind of result.

He opened the door to his house and found it felt cold and empty. He'd never noticed it before, but then he'd never been diagnosed with cancer before either.

Nelson put on some blues and although he loved the sound, he decided it was the wrong time and the wrong mood. He found an old Chuck Berry CD instead and tried that as a distraction from his thoughts.

He poured some red wine into a glass and wondered how long he'd be able to enjoy his drink. It had always been part of his life, from a young man getting used to the beer on the Shankill and then in the Army, where the drinking sessions were the stuff of legends. Young men able to take whatever life threw at them and the hangovers hardly noticed.

He peered in the fridge knowing that he rarely kept anything worth eating and had to satisfy himself with a small, dry piece of cheddar before he stood at his window and looked out onto the night: it was clear and a near-full moon hung in the sky like a silver plate.

It occurred to him that somewhere nearby the surveillance team might see him at the window. What would they be thinking, their lives so intertwined with his for the time being? He'd made up his mind that they'd never forget the next few days and Billy Nelson from the Shankill. Loneliness had never bothered him in the past, but now he felt as if it was a dragging weight he had to carry during his days and especially the nights.

He thought about Grace Macallan again for a moment. 'Maybe in another life.' He whispered it towards the night.

In the quiet buzz of an intensive-care unit Kristina Orlova regained consciousness, and as the sedation wore off, her memory of the man in the hotel returned. She'd barely the strength to move but she was angry. Another man who'd tried to use strength and violence to destroy her. She was alive, had survived again, and she promised she'd make him pay.

In another part of the same hospital Andy Clark stared at the walls, unable to concentrate on anything other than the mess that was his life. None of the team had been back to see him, and as far as Billy Nelson was concerned that was okay, but he thought McLean and Fisher would have stuck by him. The police had tried to talk to him about the attack, but he told them he couldn't remember much about what happened and didn't want any action. The thing that troubled him most was that Orlova hadn't been in touch, and he couldn't understand it. In his mind she cared about him and that was all he had in his life that made any sense to him. He wondered whether Billy Nelson had got to her already and tried not to think what that might mean.

As he stared into the darkness, Pat Fleming was getting anxious. He'd phoned Kristina's phone a dozen times, but it was switched off. He'd also driven up to her flat only to find it was in darkness and there was no answer. It was a mistake not to have a key, and he promised himself that he'd get that done as soon as he found her. It was time to discuss a future with Kristina, and maybe he'd suggest getting her off the game just to show how much she meant to him.

He was driving back to Leith when he heard the report on Radio Forth about an unidentified woman being found in a hotel. The description was vague and Fleming just didn't have the nous for it to ring an alarm bell. Instead, he decided Kristina must be with some very wealthy trick and decided to phone the old barmaid.

'Any port in a storm,' Pat said to the dark interior of the car.

The barmaid said she was in the mood and she'd leave the door open for him while she got herself ready.

He put the phone down, slapped the dashboard at the thought of what she was prepared to do for a laugh and forgot again about Kristina Orlova.

Billy Nelson slept and dreamed. He was in a long, dark corridor that seemed endless, and on each side were rows of brightly lit shop windows that were large and symmetrical. They disappeared into the distance and contrasted with the absolute dark of the corridor. The light didn't seem to radiate beyond the glass, and it was an intense, glowing orange that produced no heat.

He moved forward without any effort and it was as if he was flying through the air. In each of the windows he saw the black silhouettes of manikins, male and female in different poses – all naked. He thought they might be alive even though there was no movement, but he was sure they were watching him.

He wanted to get to the end of the corridor and he was frightened to look back because he was sure there was something following him in the dark.

He got to the end and found there was a window facing him. It was empty; he pushed his hand towards it and realised there was no glass.

He stepped through and it was warm like a summer's day. He was safe and whatever was there in the dark behind him couldn't touch him now.

33

Macallan and Baxter walked into the meeting room at Fettes and Macallan was pleased to see Felicity Young rigging up her presentation. Whatever Young did she did it well. She loved these briefings where she could display the results of her endless hours spent poring over and analysing intelligence reports.

McGovern and Thompson were there too, and for a change Thompson gave Macallan a genuine smile before she kicked it off and gave them a run-down on the progress of the surveillance operation. She admitted that it looked like Nelson was being careful and, given the press coverage, must have an idea that they were looking at him, but overall she kept it brief so that Young could bring everything together.

'Before we hand over to Felicity we just need to let you all know that we might have a break,' she added. 'The intelligence unit had a call from Barry Wallace in Belfast last night and it seems like we might be able to wrap up the whole outfit.'

She looked high on the information and Macallan liked what she saw. Maybe Thompson had possibilities after all, if there was a way for her to escape the clutches of O'Connor and the chief super.

'Jackie Martin is shifting a load of cocaine over here, and there's a couple of Uzis to go with the package. It's a deal with Billy Nelson. They're arriving tomorrow morning on the car ferry at Cairnryan, and we're going to put the whole team out to cover it. We've managed to put together two teams. Jimmy will cover Nelson here and hopefully the meet with Jackie Martin. I'll take the job from the ferry and hopefully follow them all the way back here to what we hope will be an arrest situation. We have a firearms team on standby till the job's done.'

Macallan was surprised, but if the intelligence was true then at least they might be able to stick them all in a cell. Getting both Jackie Martin and Nelson would be an absolute bonus, whether they could prove a link to the Flemings' murder or not, and Macallan wondered whether instead of months of round-the-clock stress she might just be able to do some real living with Jack Fraser.

'The plan is that Martin and two associates will bring the gear through here and meet up with Nelson's team,' Thompson carried on. 'That's the only part that bothers me. Nelson's been staying away from a hands-on part with dope.'

'How sure is Barry Wallace about the information?' Macallan asked.

'Solid. Apparently Martin's fed up with Belfast and wants to move over here. Can you believe it? That's all we need.' Thompson said it with a smile. 'We'll probably go through to the port tonight and get everything in place.'

'If you want to come in here in the morning you'll be able to listen in to the progress – or otherwise,' McGovern chipped in, knowing Macallan would hate to miss it – she still felt this was her team.

Young took over and started her briefing. 'I think we've got a pretty good picture of Billy Nelson now. The rest of his team are pretty well known, and the PSNI have given us all we need on them.'

She passed round a paper with all the salient points. 'Obviously Nelson is the target, but we've done a lot of work on all their phone billing. Billy boy's a complex character but I'll stick to what's relevant for us. We know from the Belfast intelligence that as a very young man he was set for the UVF, but Jackie Martin pointed him at the Army. Nothing unusual in that – it happened often enough so they could get the best training possible for the Loyalist paramilitaries.'

The door opened and the chief super walked in. 'Good morning, all. Hope you don't mind me joining you but I'm interested in progress.'

None of them wanted the man there, but they couldn't stop him. He wouldn't understand most of it anyway and wouldn't do much damage. They hoped.

'I think we're all aware that he was drummed out of the Army after a brutal attack on a young Afghan man. Somehow or other he got a surprisingly light sentence, and I don't know how they wangled that one. As soon as he gets back to Belfast there are a number of assaults on young Asians so we can safely presume that his experience in Iraq and Afghanistan damaged him. We're in contact with the Army about any psychological profiling they might have carried out, but they seem to have lost the records.' She stopped and sipped some ice water.

Macallan's alarm system twitched; she didn't like lost records. It did happen occasionally, but too often it was a means of giving someone or something cover. She kept quiet and gave it the benefit of the doubt – what could they do anyway?

'We've managed to build up a good profile of his

associates and the street dealers he employs. The most important material is coming from the phone billing. The covert team were planting a device in his home address, and they managed to get a look at what we think is his safe phone. I have to tell you that this has been very useful. It's early stages, but there's a problem in that one of the numbers he calls on this phone is a detective. There's still a lot of work to be done on that phone but who knows what might turn up.'

The chief super almost came off his seat. 'What detective?'

'DC Donnie Monk. Not someone with the highest reputation, as far as I can gather.'

'What do we do?' the chief super asked, with no idea what the answer was.

'I think we have to wait and carry out a bit more research until we know what we've got,' Macallan said then paused. 'But of course, we have to liaise with the Anti-Corruption Department.'

Everyone in the room realised what that meant. John O'Connor would have to be involved, and he could over-rule them in relation to a corruption allegation. Macallan said that moving too soon against Monk might spook the main targets and the chief super agreed but said that he'd have to inform O'Connor so they could start their own research.

Young continued: 'We have a few unanswered questions. First there was the surveillance-operation sighting of Nelson meeting a Glasgow criminal, Dominic McGinty. He's top tier and a ruthless character by all accounts. There's a full description of him in your paper. The strange thing is that there's no known contact between them before that. This is backed up by our Glasgow colleagues, who've been monitoring McGinty for over a year. The other twist is that it appears that McGinty was

Joe Fleming's main supplier. Unfortunately the Glasgow boys hadn't mentioned that before.'

These latter comments triggered the statutory grumbling about Glasgow holding something back, but it was all part of the game. They just liked complaining about the west.

There were no questions so the analyst carried on. 'There was the meeting in Perth witnessed by the surveillance team and the details are on your briefing note. This seems to be related to a call he took just before McGinty sat down with him. This was on his registered phone and we were listening to that one. The voice was described as home counties and almost clipped. Military. Nothing was said that would expose the caller, but it did seem to be an arrangement to meet in Perth. There is no trace of the number for the caller.'

There was a small movement in Macallan's eyes and she wondered what the meeting meant. She read her notes and thought about the meeting place. The fact that the team got nowhere near it spoke of good tradecraft. Why would Nelson be meeting someone who used good tradecraft? If she had to take a guess, she would have said that whoever it was had received the same training she had.

'On the way back from the Perth meeting Nelson pulled in and made a call. This was to a phone registered to a relative of Jackie Martin, but according to Barry Wallace it was Martin himself using it and they were arranging the shipment coming across in the morning.'

Young put another picture up on her presentation then hesitated as something came to mind. 'Before I carry on I should mention something about the incident you are aware of at the hospital. We don't know why it happened, and the doctor is unlikely to tell us, but I should flag up a couple of points to keep in mind. The doctor was Asian.

Nelson has changed physically and doesn't look his best, and we now know that their meeting took place in the oncology department.'

Macallan interrupted. 'Tell us what you think, Felicity.'

'I think it reasonable to assume that he's had bad news. We already know his feelings towards Asians – or more particularly Muslims.' There was a moment in the room as everyone tried to consider the implications then Young continued. 'He's sick. What we don't know is how bad it is, and I'll leave that there for the time being.

'Last point on this issue.' Young was in her stride. 'The surveillance team have tracked Nelson to the Potterrow area several times when he's gone on walkabout. We've let him run in there but I've had the CCTV checked and it's the mosque he's looking at. Sometimes he smokes a cigarette and just watches. Other times he's gone in, but there's a restaurant there and they serve great curries so there's a chance it's as simple as that.' She waited for a response and Macallan came in.

'God knows. It may be something or nothing, but we've enough to get on with. The fact that he might be very ill doesn't change anything; it just might make him more unpredictable, if that's possible.' She shook her head; there was a lot to consider and a minefield of potential traps if they weren't careful.

'The next two items should be of interest, but we still need to fit a story around the events. It might well be that this is something that Grace and her team can make use of.' Felicity thought for a moment then continued: 'The telephone billing showed that Andy Clark made regular calls to a mobile number and we have just learned that the phone was registered to a Kristina Orlova. Now we only have one snippet of intelligence about her and that is that she worked for Joe Fleming as a top-of-the-range escort. Interestingly, just before he was assaulted, Clark called Orlova, and immediately after that call Orlova called Pat Fleming.'

Macallan was definitely interested and looked across at Baxter. He was a lifelong hater of these briefings but this information looked to have pressed his buttons.

'We know from the time of the ambulance and police responding that Orlova made a further call to Pat Fleming's number during the time the police and ambulance were there. And she lives in the block of flats where the assault took place.'

Young was pleased with their reaction to this piece of news and she could see the questions forming in their minds. She put her hand up. 'There's more, but if you can't hold on then please fire away.'

Macallan was still surprised that this was how it often seemed to happen: one day you had nothing and then, within hours, the pieces drew towards each other as if by their own accord. It was still a muddle, but these events meant opportunities. All they had to do was grab them while they were warm.

'We've also just discovered that Kristina Orlova is the woman who was found unconscious in the hotel. She's come round and been able to give her name but other than that she's too weak for an interview. Apparently the doctors want to give her another day before we speak to her.'

Thompson now knew exactly what it meant that she'd called off the operation at the hotel, and so did everyone apart from the chief super. What she still had to learn was that even experienced surveillance officers sometimes made the wrong call, and it was rare that the team would condemn anyone who'd been in that position.

'One last thing,' Young continued. 'Clark has only had one set of visitors and they were Nelson, Fisher and McLean. A staff nurse who works on the ward is married to a traffic sergeant. She was shaken up by Nelson. It seems that the man was annoyed to say the least at Clark and had him by the throat, even in his condition.'

Macallan knew that it was all relevant but they had yet to make sense of it. Young would at least have one of her famous hypotheses so she asked, 'What does it mean?'

'I think that with the number and frequency of calls Clark made to Orlova it's at least reasonable to assume that he used her services on a regular basis.' She waited for a response but Macallan simply nodded, already forming the lines of investigation. 'The Flemings have good reason to take revenge on one of the Belfast team but they're not easy to get at and careful. I think that Clark unwittingly gave them an open goal. We have a description from a neighbour who saw the attackers walk away and it matches the twins, though their faces were covered. They were young men, no doubt about that, and very similar in build.'

The door opened as the half-time tea and biscuits arrived, but everyone wanted to hear the rest and nobody moved.

'We know that the surveillance team took Billy Nelson to the hotel and there was a loss.'

Thompson shifted uncomfortably in her seat, and Macallan felt for her, but it was part of the learning process.

'Some time later Orlova was found in the basement and what's unusual there is that she'd no personal effects. We can't be sure it was an attack but it's reasonable given Nelson's temper, so it would seem he was involved.' She paused and pushed her glasses up her nose before continuing. 'We have a single call from Nelson's safe phone to Orlova before she was attacked – not enough on its own but could now be crucial circumstantial evidence.'

'Pretty careless in one way,' Macallan mused, 'and he was lucky that night I think. Or let's look on the bright side: maybe we're picking up the luck now.'

'There are other intelligence points in the paper, but that's all I wanted to say for the moment.' She sat down but Macallan knew her well enough to guess from the look on her face that there was something else on her mind.

Then Young stood up again, obviously having decided a final snippet was worth imparting after all. 'Oh, last but not least, the surveillance team saw Fisher exiting Nelson's address with what looked like a burst ear, so there's a good chance there's dissension in the camp.' She sat down again.

'You never know, that might just be the kind of break I'm talking about. Nothing better for us than a falling out among the gangsters.' Macallan said this with a growing sense of confidence. There were lines opening up all over the place and she just had to keep a tight grip of a situation that could run away from them all.

Thompson still looked deflated so Macallan took control. 'With your permission, sir?' She directed it at the chief super, who didn't want to be there any more. He made his feeble excuses and left. He knew when he was out of his depth, and he didn't want anyone to ask him a question about something he should have known but couldn't answer.

'Grant, given what we've been told, we need to get the hotel investigation out of the hands of DC Monk. Please do that now. Fix it up with his boss and tell them we need to tie it in with the murder enquiry. Get one of our boys to make sure no one gets near her flat and we'll have to treat it as a crime scene. Same for the hotel. It's ours.'

Baxter left the room wondering whether to bless the Flemings or make their life a misery. He smiled and had

311

that good feeling he got when the doors started to open up on a case.

When he returned ten minutes later he nodded to Macallan. 'It's done. They're getting a hold of Donnie Monk to take the case off his dirty little hands.'

When Thompson stood up and said she needed to get on the road for the drugs job Macallan asked to speak to her privately for a minute. They found a side office and Thompson closed the door behind her. She looked beaten, and that wasn't the way to lead a team on something like the Jackie Martin job.

'Listen, Lesley, we've maybe not been the best of friends since you started but let me give you a bit of advice. What took place at the hotel could have happened to anyone. We've all done it. Just learn from it. In my opinion you have the makings of someone who can do this and do it well. Just learn. For today, go out there, do the business and no one will remember the hotel. Christ, look what happened to me in Northern Ireland!'

Thompson's face was set and Macallan had no doubt she was learning and asking herself questions.

'Thanks,' she said. 'I won't let you down.'

She left the room, and if Macallan was right she meant every word.

After that, Macallan decided there was no time like the present and told Baxter that they were going to head in and see Andy Clark. He might not talk, but it wouldn't do any harm. They would use the guise that they wanted to look into his assault and then see where it went. It would probably end with the words 'Fuck right off' if he was anything like the Loyalists she'd dealt with in the past, but there was nothing to lose and she wanted to at least try to connect with the man who seemed to have pissed off Billy Nelson.

34

Donnie Monk arrived at his office and though he'd never felt better than shit for longer than he could remember, this was worse. And although feeling crap had become the norm, the combination of his drugs of choice and threats every way he looked had turned his life into a swamp, both physically and mentally. The instruction from Nelson had nearly scrambled his circuits, so he'd taken his usual course when problem solving by snorting the last of his gear and then emptying a bottle of the cheapest vodka he could find.

That's when he'd done it. He'd dipped into the gear he'd got from Nelson's boys for the plant. He'd told himself he'd only taken a couple of lines (or was it more?) from Nelson's packet so who'd notice?

He knew he should have planted the gear as soon as it had been delivered the day before but he'd found any excuse to avoid doing it. It should have been a simple plant. Make it look like a good professional concealment, maybe the back of the cludgie cistern, then go back like a brilliant sleuth and find it.

'Fuckin' simple, Donnie boy,' he said as he pushed open

the door of the corridor leading to the CID general office. Despite the words of encouragement he'd muttered to himself, his heart thumped against his sternum, and he was in a mild panic that he might just fall over. All his energy was gone, and he was running on empty. The priority was to get the plant over and done with; it would be the first job of the day. They'd given him the house keys from the girl's bag so entry wasn't an obstacle. The problem was that he was a walking ruin, and to make it worse he'd slept in the clothes he was wearing.

He knew that in this job it was almost impossible to hide personal crap so he must have been like a firework display on the Eiffel Tower. His investigations were rock bottom, solving nothing unless he could steal a bit from it, and he was making the fatal mistake of claiming piles of overtime. If there was one thing that lifted the rubber heels' noses to the stink of a bent cop it was some lazy bastard filling his or her pockets with no effort. A bent officer who locked up loads of villains was one thing, but a lazy bastard taking the piss and claiming overtime was quite unforgivable.

He arrived ten minutes late for duty, which wasn't bad by his standards, and as soon as he walked through the door the DCI called him into his office. He'd been feeling sick anyway because he hadn't had breakfast or any kind of food since the burger that should have come with a health warning the day before. When you added to that the nervous element caused by carrying a rucksack containing nearly a quarter of a kilo of high-purity gear and scales, the nausea became almost overwhelming. Monk sincerely hoped he wasn't going to throw up all over the DCI's carpet.

The DCI was newly promoted and a good one. Still young, flying through sheer energy, and if he could he would have lived in the office. Monk was a disgrace as

314

far as he was concerned, and when he could spare the time he was going to make it his priority to get rid of him. Unfortunately no one in their right mind would take him off his hands as a swap or transfer. But he was taking the piss with his overtime so he'd make a start with that.

Monk put the rucksack under his desk and went into the DCI's room. He didn't like his boss one little bit – he was too new and didn't understand the old ways. There'd been a day when Donnie Monk had been a name, and this smart fucker had obviously forgotten all that.

'Jesus, Donnie, have you seen the state of yourself? Sit down.' The DCI rifled through some papers and seemed distracted. 'I'm too busy to talk now but we need to make time to have a longer chat when I get some free time.'

Monk wanted a cigarette and noticed that two buttons had popped in the belly region of his shirt.

'The thing is, I've had a call from Grant Baxter on behalf of Superintendent Grace Macallan. They're doing the Fleming murder mystery, and don't ask me why but they're taking over the incident at the hotel because they think there's a connection. That's fine with me; we have enough to do, and as far as I know you've done next to nothing on it anyway.' He waited for Monk to deny it, but it was the truth so he kept his mouth shut.

'They've found the girl's address and are sealing it off as a crime scene, which we should have been able to do … But we are where we are.' He waited for a denial, but it was still the truth and there wasn't a word Monk could say to change it, so he continued: 'We've a new start today, here for a couple of months of assessment to see if she shapes up. I want you to take her to a couple of jobs and see if it does you any good at the same time.'

Monk's breathing turned into a wheeze and his skin took on the colour of recently kneaded putty.

'Are you okay?' the DCI asked, hoping he didn't have

a coronary occlusion taking place in front of him; he was just too busy.

'I've been putting a lot into that job, sir,' Monk said, coming near to pleading as the decaying roof over his head finally gave way. But they both knew that Monk's claim was bollocks and wasn't going to make any difference.

'By the way, go and have a shower before you go out or you'll choke that young woman in the car. That wouldn't be a good start to her career as a detective now, would it?' As the DCI said this he was already looking at the papers on his desk and his mind was wandering elsewhere again. If Monk needed any sign that he was nothing more than an object of contempt, his boss had just given him a full display. The ultimate humiliation.

He left the DCI's office and the new aide smiled enthusiastically at him, waiting for a response, so he ignored her. He looked across the room at the rucksack and realised that he was dead. Maybe not yet, but there was no escape.

He headed for the showers without speaking to anyone – the new start could wait till he was ready.

As the water washed some of the excreted poisons from his skin, he realised that there was nowhere for him to run and all the eyes in the office were watching him like a dead man walking to the last drop into eternity. He'd managed to delude himself for a while, but that was over now. If they started looking into his life and records, he was fucked. He'd been stealing from evidence bags for months to feed his habit, and it was a minor miracle that it had gone undiscovered as long as it had. He couldn't do prison time; he just wasn't equipped. Someone would come for him – it would either be Billy Nelson or the rubber heels, and he wasn't sure which was worse.

He dried himself on an old towel he kept in his locker

and tried to ignore the state it was in. While he worked the cotton on his skin, fresh, toxin-laced sweat bubbled to the surface as his body struggled to clear itself.

Monk sat down naked on the wooden seat in the shower room, letting let the cool air waft over him and trying to see a way ahead that didn't involve him being killed or abused in prison.

There's no way out; just face it, boy, he thought before shaking his head and managing a dry smile. 'What the fuck,' he murmured. It was a done deal, and it was over one way or the other. He had not far off a quarter kilo and it was top gear, so why not just enjoy it?

He stood up, straightened his back and remembered that Donnie Monk had been a man at one time. His head cleared; he'd made a decision and it was better. It was too late to struggle with ways out – there were none.

He pulled on his grubby clothes and made up his mind to buy fresh clobber when he left the office.

All eyes hit the door when Monk came back into the room. A wounded detective was news, and they wanted to savour every moment of someone else's downfall.

Monk picked up his rucksack, ignored his audience and walked into the DCI's office without knocking. His boss was on the phone with one foot up on the desk and looked like he'd just seen Elvis when Monk told him to put the phone down.

'I'll call you back.' He put the phone in its cradle and swung the foot off his desk.

'Are you still here?'

'As a matter of fact I'm not. I'm heading home as I'm ill so you can sign me off.' He felt that at long last he had at least some control, after the terrors of doubt.

'You'd better get a doctor to back you up or you're in worse trouble than you've managed to create already.'

'Fuck you. I'm suffering from stress and all that crap.'

He closed the door and left the DCI gaping in disbelief behind him.

The new suit smiled again at him and he at least returned the compliment this time. 'Hope you have better luck than I had, love.' He meant it; he wanted her to have a good career. He still knew in his bones that it was the best job in the world if you kept your head.

He turned and left the CID office for the last time.

Once he was outside, Monk went to his bank and drew out all that he could get, made his way to Princes Street and bought new trousers, a shirt, underwear and a decent pair of shoes. He felt some energy in his exhausted bones and enjoyed his shopping, something he hadn't done for too long. He hated it by nature, but this time it was different. Work had been the worst kind of struggle and now he was free of it.

He bought some food, some quality wine and some malt. The sun shone, and although it was cold he carried the bags over to the gardens below the castle then sat and stared up at the stronghold that had stood guard over the old city for nearly a thousand years.

Monk had always loved the gardens; when he was just another working detective and about five stone lighter he'd go there in the summer to enjoy the sights and sounds. Especially the sight of the girls who flooded out of the offices and shops at lunchtime then decorated the grass in a celebration of youth and all that it meant.

He breathed deeply and wished it was summer, just for a day, so he could smell the grass.

The phone went off in his pocket and he saw it was Nelson.

'I haven't heard anything. Is it done?' Nelson sounded extremely pissed off.

'No.'

Nelson waited but Monk had nothing more to add.

'What the fuck do you mean "no"?'

'You've got the answer, take it or stop wasting my time.' Monk had regained a semblance of dignity and felt the glow of finding a small part of what he'd lost. It was a gesture and would mean nothing when the knock came on his door, but it made him feel like a man again and he smiled. Whatever else he'd become, he'd just got one over on the man they all feared.

'Grace Macallan has the hotel case now, which means you're fucked. Me, I'm going to have a couple of days in some nice hotel and enjoy your very-high-quality gear. After that you can do what the fuck you like. See you, Billy.' He let it hang for a moment, imagining the man raging on the other end of the line, then added, 'You're on the road to the same shit heap I am. Enjoy.'

He put the phone down and tried to think of the best hotel he could afford for a couple of days. Then he made the call, booked into a suite and felt okay. The fear had gone.

Nelson stared at his phone and ground his teeth, seething with the frustration of having an arsehole like Monk talk to him like he didn't count. *Okay*, he thought, *have your little time off, Donnie, and then I'll come and see you.* He was exposed now for the attack on Kristina Orlova in a way that should have been covered, but it was one of those times when the dice were all rolling the wrong way. It happened, and like Donnie Monk he'd make his own preparations.

The DCI made a note that Monk had gone off sick and filled in the necessary forms. At the time, he couldn't know it would be of interest to anyone other than the personnel department.

35

Macallan, accompanied by Baxter, walked along the corridors of the hospital wondering how all the pieces they'd uncovered would join up at the end of the job. There would be a picture, but it was impossible to predict yet what story it would tell. Along the way, there might be a strong sense that they'd get who they were after, but there was always the unknown factor in between that could mess up lives or ruin a career. The traps were everywhere and only occasionally would you be smart enough to see all of them. It was how you dealt with the situation when the wheels came spinning off on the outside lane of the motorway that mattered.

They spoke to the doctor in charge before trying to talk to Andy Clark.

'Best of luck, Superintendent. He's not been responsive to anyone else and he's definitely a man with a lot on his mind. He's not abusive to the nurses, quite the reverse, but he's preoccupied and clearly under stress.' The doctor was up to his armpits in work yet managed to be patient and polite.

'What about his prognosis?' Macallan asked.

'He'll recover, but he's suffered significant bone injuries that will affect him for the rest of his life. His mobility will be impaired and he'll be lucky to walk without the aid of a stick. He was seriously injured, much like a bad car crash if that makes sense. Having said all that, he's very strong and making remarkable progress so we might get him into a chair soon enough. Anyhow, I'm busy but by all means speak to him. He doesn't get any other visitors.' The doctor smiled warmly and left.

'Okay. There's no plan. Sometimes that's the best way, so we'll just wing it like all the best detectives.'

'Always worked for me,' Baxter said, and meant it. They agreed that he would take the lead with questioning.

Clark had his eyes closed but was wide awake. All he could do was think, and that wasn't something he did easily. What he was doing was spinning the same worries round and round on a carousel without resolving a single thing. Billy was hacked off with him and he'd no idea where Kristina was. It still hadn't occurred to him that she could have been involved in setting him up; he just wanted to know if she was safe.

'Andy Clark.'

The man's voice startled him, and when he opened his eyes he knew exactly who they were. The man was CID and could have had it stamped on his forehead. The woman who was with him had to be the same but was attractive with it.

'Who's asking?'

They ran through a line that they were aware he'd said he couldn't identify his attackers but they were keen to try again to see if he might have remembered anything else. He listened to them, but his instinct as always was to keep quiet. He'd been brought up to be wary of the police, though the truth was that he'd always thought that if he'd been a bit smarter and able to pass the exams

321

he would have loved to have been a Peeler. Baxter impressed Clark; he liked the look of him and his talk. But what could he say? They would know exactly who he was and, more importantly, who his friends were.

'What do you think, Andy – anything else come to mind while you've been lying here?' Baxter said.

The more the two detectives spoke to Clark the more they realised he was a different animal to Billy Nelson. His profile was spot on: much more reserved and not the brightest individual. Macallan thought he was a physically attractive man, and with his looks and quiet attitude, she would have taken him for a gentle soul in another life. It was hard to imagine him as part of a team that had tortured and killed their way to control of the drugs scene in the city, but she knew Clark was capable of terrible violence, though the profile was clear that he never initiated it. However if he was given the order by someone he respected then he followed it without question. What neither she nor the profiler could have known was that Clark questioned what he'd done for Nelson every day now, and for the first time in his life he couldn't work out what to do about it. He wasn't a decision maker.

'I'm sorry – I can't remember anything else. It's all a blur now.' He liked the woman but he just wanted the two detectives to go and let him spin the carousel again, even though it wasn't giving him an answer.

Macallan knew they weren't connecting, although he wasn't being difficult, and she had the inclination to call it a day and leave it till they had a bit more information when she remembered the nurse's report that Nelson had been in his face about something. 'Can you confirm your address for us before we go?' she asked, as if it was completely routine.

He told her; he liked the colour of her clear green eyes.

'One thing I would like to ask is' – she pushed the door just a bit further – 'what were you doing at that address where you were assaulted?' She waited and watched him struggle for an answer.

'I'm very tired and think I'm going to be sick. Could you get the nurse please?' She saw the opening, and he was vulnerable.

'Do you happen to know a woman we're dealing with named Kristina Orlova?' She watched his expression change and knew a line had definitely been opened – they just had to see where it went.

The words 'we're dealing with' meant he needed to know. His heart raced; at the very least he needed to speak to her. The sight and sound of Orlova was what he wanted more than anything – and to warn her to stay clear of Billy Nelson.

'I know her. Where is she now?'

Macallan saw the plea in his eyes and knew they'd found a weak spot they could exploit. She looked at Baxter. They'd both worked out that whatever his relationship with the girl, he still didn't know what had happened to her or that she was in an intensive-care ward not that far from him.

'She was found badly hurt and had to undergo emergency surgery.' Macallan said it softly and watched as Clark's eyes filled and his colour changed. He was angry and frustrated, but he was helpless and all he could do was squirm pointlessly as he tried to cope with his emotions.

'Did some fucker hurt her?' It had gone too far, and Macallan called one of the staff nurses as he managed to dislodge a drip and supports for his arm. The nurse told Macallan and Baxter to leave and they went out into the waiting area to try to work it all out.

'Jesus, the boy didn't know and she's obviously the

323

one as far as he's concerned,' Baxter said, still surprised at his reaction. 'What now?'

'First thing is that we don't tell him yet that she probably set him up. We wait and see what the doc says, and if we can get back in then we grab the chance. If there's going to be a long wait then we can nip up to the other ward and see if they'll let us talk to Orlova.' He nodded in agreement and she added, 'Let's grab a coffee while we're waiting. There's one other thing though, while I remember. In the morning I want to go to the coordination centre to listen in to the surveillance operations, so would you mind going to see Banjo Rodgers and trying to squeeze some evidence out of him?'

'Consider it done, but let's get that coffee. I've a feeling we're going to need it,' he replied and they headed for the café, leaving their numbers with the staff nurse.

It took the medical staff twenty minutes to calm Clark down, although it was as much his own exhaustion as their support that got him there in the end. They tidied him up and on the way out the doctor told the nurses that the police should not be allowed near Clark for the time being.

'No,' Clark said quietly and calmly enough. 'I want to see them – it's important.' The emotion was gone. He knew another struggle would achieve nothing but a heavy dose of sedative, and he didn't want that till he knew exactly what had happened to Kristina. The doctor tried to argue, but he replied that he had something important to tell them. He promised to keep calm and told them it would be worse if he couldn't see them.

Baxter took the call from the staff nurse and winked at Macallan. 'Well well! He wants to see us.'

They quickly drained the last of their coffees and headed back, though they would have enjoyed another one to chew over what was developing.

Clark was sitting up and looked comfortable enough when they arrived. 'Thanks for coming back. I'm sorry I got so upset; it was just a bit of a shock,' he said quietly.

'No worries, son. Just let us help you with this. We'll take our time so there's no misunderstanding.' Baxter said it almost in a growl, which pleased Macallan. He was presenting the older, wiser head to Clark, who was a vulnerable character despite what he was and what he'd done. It seemed like he needed an older figure to follow and Nelson had dropped out of that position in his life. If Baxter could connect even for a moment then they might just get somewhere, so Macallan let him take the lead.

'Tell me exactly what happened to Kristina,' Clark said. His eyes were wide and desperate, so Baxter told him as much as they could, but given Monk had done no investigation, his information was limited. The news that Orlova had lost a kidney made Clark flush in colour though, and Macallan worried that he might throw another one before he pulled it together.

'Have they got a name for who did it?' His face tightened and Baxter recognised the tension and what it meant.

'We have our suspicions, but there are a lot of investigations still to be carried out before we arrest him.'

They had no evidence, but Clark didn't know that. They all went quiet and pondered the words 'arrest him'. Baxter left it dangling perfectly; even without saying the words Clark knew they were talking about Billy Nelson.

'Can you leave me for an hour? I need to think.'

Baxter looked at Macallan, who nodded in agreement. Clark was hanging just over the edge and they had to make it easy for him to jump.

Macallan stood up to leave and decided to take a gamble. 'We're going to speak to Kristina now. If you want to talk to us just get the staff nurse to call our mobile.

If we don't hear anything we'll leave it for the night to let you think it over and then come back in the morning, which might be better. We'll probably be able to tell you a lot more by then.'

As they walked along the corridors Macallan broke the silence. 'What do you think then, Grant?' She slapped him lightly on the back to break his deep train of thought.

He looked round and grinned. 'Fifty-fifty, but if the boy takes the leap then I reckon we're on our way. Let's hope the girl's as pissed off at Nelson as Clark is. She's every reason to be. I just can't understand why he's been so careless, but if the medical stuff is on the money then maybe he doesn't care now.'

Macallan nodded, thinking he was probably right.

The doctor would make no compromise on them speaking to Orlova. The girl was still recovering but very ill and had been lucky to survive. They had ten minutes, and if there were any signs of stress the medical staff would move in and stop the proceedings.

The detectives stepped into the room, which was quiet and cool. Orlova's eyes were open and she watched them enter. She smiled; the nurses had told her that they wanted to see her.

'Please sit down.' Her voice was barely audible but clear.

Macallan introduced them both and told her that they were investigating the attack on her and were linking it to a number of other crimes. Orlova's eyes widened; because of her sedation she hadn't spent long analysing what had happened at the hotel. She'd heard her attacker's accent so there was no doubt it had been Nelson or one of his gang. What she had already decided was that, given what she'd had to endure in her life already, the law of averages meant she wasn't likely to live to old age or do so with her face intact. The next time it might be some psycho with a razor. The doctor had already explained at length that it was her youth and strength that had let her survive a potentially fatal injury, and Orlova had decided that when she was well enough she'd move to somewhere no one knew her and let her looks find her a man. She'd saved hard and put as much money aside as she could afford, and her life as an escort was now over.

Macallan knew that it wasn't the time for a long arduous interview and they still had to work out whether she would help, but she'd decided to be straight up with her. Billy Nelson's world was going to fall no matter what, and Macallan was determined she would be the one to make it happen. More than that, she wanted him to *know* she was there, looking for the evidence that would put him away.

'We believe the man who assaulted you is responsible for a number of terrible crimes. It's my intention to see him charged and in front of a court, but we have a lot to do to get there. We can't do it without help. With you or without you we'll get him, but your evidence would be crucial in showing what he is.' Macallan sat back and looked up at the clock that told her that half her time was already gone and the doctor was hovering outside.

Orlova's lip trembled and she squeezed her eyes shut, wishing she was home and that all of this had been a bad dream. Baxter and Macallan let her be as she shook with emotion, which prompted the doctor to come back into the room and say that the interview was over.

'I can identify the man who hurt me. I want him to go to court,' Orlova said and her expression told them she meant it.

Macallan put her hand on Orlova's forearm and smiled. 'We'll come back whenever you're ready. I'm going to make sure that there's a police officer here at all times to keep you safe.'

The doctor made them leave and they went back for another drink to think about what had happened. Macallan was sitting staring into the distance when Baxter came over to the table with a couple of steaming teas. Coffee or tea – it didn't really matter to her as long as it was drinkable.

'What about that then, Grace?'

'I don't want to get carried away because they could both change their minds. How often does it happen? But this feels promising, no doubt about it. Cheers.' She lifted the plastic cup as if she were toasting him.

'What do we do now?'

'It would be Sod's Law if we take off and Clark decides he's ready to speak, but I think we should take a chance and leave it for the night. Give them both plenty of time to think it over and start fresh in the morning, though I think we should have a couple of officers stay with Orlova.'

'Fine for me. And I think you're right about the uniform protection. I wouldn't put it past that bastard to come back to try and finish the job either.'

Macallan decided on a change of plan and told him they should go for Banjo Rodgers right away.

'He'd not usually answer the door to police, but I can call him first and tell him we're looking into the death of his girlfriend,' Baxter said.

Andy Clark wondered how it had all turned out this way. He'd never wanted to be a big name; all he'd ever thought he'd be was a proud member of the UVF who'd helped fight PIRA to the negotiating table. When peace came he'd been fine with it. The other boys were bored, but for Clark it didn't matter as long as they got by.

When Nelson had returned it had been like the start of a new life and he'd been sure that the man had rated him and what he could do. If Nelson wanted him to dish out violence that was fine – it had been like that all his life. But now it was all just so much shit and he was hurt – badly hurt. The doctor had explained to him that he might always have problems with walking and there'd be pain that the doctor said they could manage. What did manage mean? All he'd ever had was physical strength and an unshakable determination once he was given a job. But Nelson had betrayed him; there was no other way to see it. Taking over the drugs business from the Flemings was fine and that was just how things happened, but Nelson had gone too far where the women were concerned. He was a disgrace and Clark couldn't work for him again, but the final straw was Kristina Orlova. Clark had near begged him to leave her alone but he didn't give a fuck what any of his team felt or wanted. It was all about Billy boy. He had changed from the young man who went off to the Army and he looked sick now, but talking to him was impossible. He hardly spoke to the boys now unless it was to give them an order.

'Fuck Billy Nelson,' he murmured.

The sedation took a grip and he slept.

36

Banjo Rodgers picked up the phone and saw there was no name against the number. He answered the call but didn't speak, a habit from years of being careful, but Baxter knew the drill and spoke first. He explained who he was and that they still had some routine work to wrap up in relation to Maggie Smith's overdose.

Banjo had run into Baxter a couple of times in the past and knew that he had fuck all to do with dope but would be involved in an OD investigation in Leith. He agreed to see them and thought he could watch from his window to make sure they didn't have a posse with them when they arrived. He was almost out of gear and all that was in the flat was a bit of herbal, which shouldn't be of any interest to them. If it did then they had fuck all to do as far as he was concerned. In any case, it would be good just to speak to someone other than the usual line of losers who came to his door for a bit of gear.

He was still struggling with Maggie's death. They'd shared so much – had leaned on each other when they needed to – but now she was gone, and he missed her every day.

He was still dealing for Nelson's team, but they were the worst kind of animals. Worse than the Flemings by a mile. They treated him like shite and whatever he did, it wasn't enough. They increased prices almost weekly and taxed him to the hilt. They'd managed to piss off every dealer in Wester Hailes, but so far no one had had the guts to take them on, although there was a story circulating that the quiet one had had his legs and arms done, but no one was sure who'd made the move. No one thought it was the Fleming twins – they were too young and had a bit to learn yet. But whoever had done it, it made no difference: someone had been able to get to them and it sent out a signal that Nelson was mortal, just like everyone else.

Banjo felt physically sick every time Fisher came into the flat and spoke to him like he was the dog crap on his shoes. He never stopped thinking about the sight of Fisher laughing out loud as he'd pushed the hot iron against Maggie's breast and the smell from her burning flesh. He swore that if he ever had the chance he'd make an exception to his normally non-violent approach to life and knife Fisher in the eye.

He watched Baxter and Macallan arrive and saw there was no suggestion of anyone else hanging around. All the same, when Banjo opened the door to them after they'd climbed the stairs – knowing the usual state of tower-block lifts – he immediately looked behind them for some sneaky bastard, ready to jump in. But it was just the suits so he relaxed.

He took them through to the lounge and sat them down, offering a brew-up. The place was relatively clean so Baxter decided he'd risk it, though Macallan declined.

'How's it going, Banjo? Long time no see,' Baxter said, knowing that Rodgers was no trouble and definitely not one of life's nasties.

'You see it all, Mr Baxter. Just trying to keep my nose clean. Gettin' too old for any nonsense,' he shouted back from the kitchen.

'I was sorry to hear about Maggie. Hellish way to go.'

Banjo came through to the lounge, poured out a couple of mugs and offered the biscuits someone had been flogging cheap in the pub the night before.

Macallan had to admit that Baxter could bullshit with the best –a typical career detective who was able to keep it going for as long as necessary. He chewed the fat, went over some details in the death report but kept away from the real business of the day, inching towards it slowly because he knew that trying to turn Banjo wouldn't work with a full frontal. They had to let him make the first move to get there.

Banjo talked and smoked and Macallan sat back and let Baxter do his thing; he knew how it worked and was getting it right on the money.

'Keep your head down though, Banjo. There's a bit of trouble cooking up, and we'll be coming down hard on some people if you know what I mean.' Baxter said it like it was a racing tip from an old friend.

Banjo wasn't sure what he meant, but he wanted to know. Knowledge for a drug dealer was what kept you out of the pokey.

'What's that then, Mr Baxter?' He lit another cigarette and the room filled with dense blue smoke, much to Macallan's annoyance.

'It's those Belfast boys – bad fucking karma so stay clear of them. One of them, Andy Clark, is in hospital and won't be running the marathon again.' He leaned a bit closer to Banjo. 'We're all over them, and they're about to get a lesson.'

If there was one thing Banjo Rodgers wanted it was to see them dead or inside for a long time. He knew Baxter wasn't bullshitting because it was the talk of the steamie that Clark had been given the message with a couple of pickaxe handles.

He nodded at Baxter and Macallan and asked them if they wanted another cup. They didn't but they knew he was thinking over his options and wanted to give him time.

'I'm not missing this one so go ahead,' Macallan said. She hadn't said a lot but Banjo liked the look of her and she seemed okay.

He went into the small dark kitchen, filled the kettle up and waited on it.

In the lounge Macallan gave Baxter a look and he nodded at her. It was going just about right.

When Banjo returned to the lounge Macallan noticed his hand was shaking as he poured out the brew.

'You okay?' she asked softly, and on instinct put her hand on his. The gesture was small but enough for a man starved of affection. Banjo sat back, put his hands on his face and sobbed loudly and wetly. It was an enormous release of tension and his shoulders shuddered with the effort.

They let it happen, and Baxter poured out a mug for Banjo and put it in front of him. Eventually his sobbing became quieter so Macallan pulled out a packet of tissues and shoved them in his hands. His face was red, blotchy and wet with tears and snot. He took the tissues and wiped his face.

'Fuckin' murderin' bastards – murderin' Irish bastards.' He broke down again. The detectives were used to seeing raw emotion, but it was hard not to be moved by the genuine grief being displayed in front of them.

He managed to calm himself eventually but until then they kept quiet and let him be.

'Who's that, Banjo?' Baxter said. It was time to push the door.

Banjo shook his head at some inner thought and looked up at them with anger sparking in his eyes. 'I'm not a grass but if there's any way I can help you with those fuckers, just tell me.'

The hard bit was trying not to show their own emotion when they made this kind of breakthrough; they just had to sit back and let him dictate the release of information to the point where there was a clear agreement that he was on board.

'Just talk to us. Tell us what happened in your own words,' Baxter said and pushed the mug further towards him.

Banjo was still shaking but he held the mug with both hands and sipped at his strong black tea. He told them everything. Some of it just personal recollections about the life that Maggie Smith had shared with him, such as it was, and much of it was of no use to them, but Macallan was fascinated and wanted to hear it all. He told them about the Flemings and about the years when things had been more or less stable.

When he came to the night that Nelson and his team had come to the door he left nothing out. They didn't have to ask any questions at all, and Macallan found herself visualising the scene in the flat that night and imagining Maggie trying to deal with what had been done to her. She felt a tear wobble out of the corner of her eye and had to stifle the thoughts swimming round her head.

In the end they were there for hours, although no one watched the clock. It was as if the three of them had been locked in a bubble where time had almost stopped.

Eventually Banjo went quiet and looked at them for a response. Macallan didn't really know what to say, but Baxter did.

'They'll pay, son. Don't worry about that, son – they'll fuckin' pay.' It sounded trite, but it worked for Banjo. He smiled weakly and felt exhausted. So did the two detectives who'd watched his grief.

'We need to get a statement,' Macallan said, and Banjo nodded in agreement. They couldn't delay – Banjo was wide open and they had to grab the opportunity with both hands in case he changed his mind later. It often happened. 'Maggie's away and it's doubtful what the fiscal would be able to do with what happened to her, but it would be powerful evidence to support the other crimes.'

Banjo nodded and was thinking ahead of them. 'Just take me out of here as if I'm under arrest, we can go down to the station and I'll do it there.' He thought for a moment and remembered that they were still in the real world. 'What do I tell them if they ask? They'll hear that I was lifted.'

'Tell them that we were investigating the burn marks on Maggie's body and you were suspected of the assault.' Macallan paused to make sure he got it, then continued: 'Look him straight in the eye when you tell him and let them think about that.'

'You've got it.'

About three hours later Baxter came into Macallan's office and put a glass of liquid in front of her, and it was the right colour. They clinked a toast – they'd taken the first steps, and it was a good feeling – but what Banjo Rodgers had told them had hit a nerve and there was no place for backslapping. They were dealing with a disease that had to be cut out and burned.

'In a way what we heard is a mark of our failure,' said Macallan. 'We can't protect people like Banjo and Maggie. We can wipe up after, but they're wide open and whoever replaces Billy Nelson will be able to walk in and do the same and then we'll come in again with the mop and bucket of soapy water. Cheers,' she added glumly and they clinked glasses again. 'What's happening now?'

'Banjo's just having some fish and chips on us then we'll take him half the way home and drop him off. Don't want him to be seen getting a lift to the door.' He threw back the rest of his drink. 'Other than that we have a good statement, so if this goes to court he'll be a powerful witness. And in a way so will Maggie.' He poured another double measure for both of them.

'Here's to Maggie Smith.' They both raised their glasses.

Later on that evening Banjo had settled into his seat and was thinking about the day's events. He sucked in the last of his weed and put his head in his hands, trying to work out what he should do. He'd agreed to help the police but still hadn't told them that he'd made the call to Nelson that had set up the Flemings. He wondered whether that made him an accessory. He slugged back the last of his vodka, lay down on the settee and slept.

37

Jackie Martin turned off the motorway and guided his BMW towards the dock area and the ferry terminal. He handed over his documents to a security man who was wet, frozen through and looked like he wanted to be anywhere else. They'd asked him the usual stupid questions and he felt like making their day by saying, 'Of course there's a fuckin' bomb in the back, guys. Well done.' He kept it buttoned though, knowing that jokes about bombs would get you some time in a cell and negative headlines. Martin liked to present himself to the world as a respectable businessman now and had to avoid the wrong kind of press.

He manoeuvred his car into the line for boarding an hour later and felt that just getting out of Belfast for a while was a bonus. Martin and his wife hardly ever managed a holiday, unless you counted the fortnight away each year to the south of Spain where she roasted to the colour and consistency of dried leather while he watched and wished he was back with his favourite escorts.

He jumped out of the car and headed for the café area in the terminal. It was still dark, and he squinted into the driving sleet that blew across the open car park as he jogged the last few yards to the protection of the terminal building. The wind moaned steadily and he'd been worried that the ferry might be cancelled, but when he'd checked the sailing status, by some miracle it had said it was okay and on time. Short-notice cancellations were common in the winter months though, so part of him wouldn't feel completely confident until he was safely ensconced on the ferry with the steward performing the 'first find your assembly station' routine. There was a steady northwest wind and some swell, but if the ferry was going then that was all that mattered.

It was still the early hours but the place was starting to buzz with cars piling into line for boarding. He ordered some black coffee in the second-floor café and sat at a window looking out onto a thin strip of water on the land side of the quay. The tops of the waves were whipping into spume and he thought how much Belfast had changed over the years of conflict.

His mobile alerted him to a text and he pulled the phone out of his pocket. He smiled – it was confirmation that the boys had arrived with the lorry, and from his vantage point he could see them parking up beside the other HGVs. It meant he could relax and enjoy the trip over. He'd used the same cover for years to bring in his gear from Holland and there had never been a hitch. Those Dutch boys knew exactly what they were doing and had that part of the business down to a fine art.

His supply came into Belfast on refrigerated flower lorries, which on this occasion were being used to shift a load of gear the other way over to Edinburgh. Everything was arranged and would stand up to scrutiny. There was a consignment of flowers to be dropped off on the outskirts of the city and that's when they'd do the handover. It was a perfect concealment, and the compartment built into the lorry could only be discovered by an expert – or where a rat was at work. Rats were always the worry.

He still wasn't sure about Billy Nelson and why he wanted so much – or the shooters. Martin had dealt ruthlessly with suspected informants over the years and he never gave someone a second chance. If there was anything like proof, the suspect was dead, and just to make his or her day Martin would torture them first.

Just in case there was something amiss, he'd stay away from the boys in the lorry till they met Nelson in Edinburgh and he could be sure it was safe.

Sitting four tables away from Martin was a couple who looked married because they were pretty much ignoring each other and stuck to reading the dailies. They were part of the PSNI surveillance team who would see Martin to the other side before they handed over to the Scottish team. Barry Wallace had agreed that he'd run tail-end Charlie till they made the drop. He could listen in but would take no part in the Scottish operation unless they needed advice.

The ferry left on time and Martin decided to get some breakfast while the ship was stable. He saw the two guys who were driving the lorry but he ignored them, sat down and ordered the full Ulster fry. He was starving and looking forward to a good trip, and if Edinburgh lived up to its press he thought he might just make the move he'd mentioned to Nelson.

He dug into his breakfast as the high-speed ferry built up power at the outer limits of Belfast Lough and the ship started to heave steadily on the rolling swell. Feeling good, he grabbed a seat in the lounge and closed his eyes to sleep through the rest of the journey to Cairnryan.

The surveillance team were in place on the Scottish side. Thompson had received the message that Martin would be travelling behind the lorry and keeping his distance till they reached Edinburgh, so she had instructed the team to ignore the lorry and stick with Martin as the target. In any case a tracker had been covertly fitted to the lorry so if there was a serious deviation they would be told.

Thompson was excited about the job and just wanted it to go well. For the first time in years she was getting a kick out of what she was doing and working with people who all wanted the same things. It had made her look at her own values; she needed to think more for herself and make her own judgements of people.

She called McGovern, who was in position in Edinburgh and ready to take on Nelson once he moved from his home address.

'It's fine here. His lights are on and we can see him moving about so no worries. Just bring that man through here safely so we can ruin their day.'

'You've got it. I'll let you know when we're on the way.' She felt the warmth of inclusion. The team were taking to her now she was making the effort, and she felt part of something truly worthwhile.

Nelson sipped a mug of black tea with too much sugar. It reminded him of the army brew and the importance of tea to the fighting man.

He stretched the side of his face and pulled the razor across his skin. Some men hated it but Nelson had always loved to shave, though his skin was slack now and the youthful feel of it had gone. It had passed so quickly and easily.

He sighed, splashed warm water across his face and repeated the motion several times as he watched his reflection in the mirror.

Patting his skin dry he pulled on a fresh shirt and trousers before getting some breakfast, the tension of anticipation having given him quite an appetite. When he was done eating, he stood at the window and looked out onto the frosted road in front of his house, watching as the sun started to spread a grey light over the darkness of the city. The surveillance team would be out there somewhere but it didn't matter – and in fact he wanted them in place.

He called Fisher and McLean and asked them to meet him for a coffee. He'd told them that they'd be picking up a load of gear from Jackie Martin and that the man himself was coming over so they all had to be on their toes. What he couldn't tell them was that Martin was walking into a trap. He had a lot to do but had thought through his plan carefully and knew as an army man that you needed a bit of luck along the way. He put what he needed into a small rucksack and got ready to leave.

Martin woke up with a start and realised that he'd slept through the announcement that they were pulling up to the terminal at Cairnryan. He felt the ship shudder with the power of its reverse thrusters pushing it into a docking position as he headed for the car deck.

Ten minutes later he ran the car down the ramps and onto the picturesque coastal route for Glasgow then Edinburgh.

'That's the target on the move.' Thompson texted McGovern to let him know the operation was running. Coordinating the surveillance teams was a difficult task, but the intelligence officers in Edinburgh and Belfast were at their places and backing up the men and women on the ground.

Macallan and Baxter were in the coordination centre in Fettes and could hear both surveillance teams as they followed their targets. Macallan only wanted to know that it was moving as she'd arranged to go back to the hospital to see Orlova and Clark. A message had come in for Macallan during the night that said Clark wanted to see them, and she was going to let Baxter deal with him while she saw Orlova – then it was in the lap of the gods.

There was nothing she could do to help the surveillance teams and if they could dig up another couple of prime witnesses while everyone else was occupied then they were on the road. She grinned, thinking of the other message she'd received after she'd gone to sleep. Jack Fraser was arriving for a couple of nights. She'd be up to her eyes, but no matter. He would be busy during the day and at least they'd have some time together at night. She needed to put the job out of her mind for a while and Fraser could help her do that at least for a few hours.

Nelson left his front door and caught a taxi into the city, the surveillance team watching him as he headed to the town centre. There was nothing unusual apart from the fact that he was carrying a small rucksack. He headed to the bank in St Andrew Square and became its first customer of the day. He was inside for twenty minutes and the information was relayed back to Fettes so the intelligence teams could get on with finding out what he'd been doing.

When he left the bank he headed down to Stockbridge, a place with a village feel on account of the cafés and posh little niche shops on either side of the street. The area was already bustling with morning shoppers and lines of traffic pushing into the city centre. Nelson chose a popular chain café and settled himself near to a window, which was handy for the surveillance footman, who installed himself into a café opposite to drink his own coffee of choice.

The surveillance team waited well away from the

street itself, relying on the eyeball and the additional footman who'd joined the first one in the café, looking for all the world like any other office worker calling in for his morning roll.

Within ten minutes Nelson was joined by Fisher and McLean, who ordered coffees and sat down next to him with not much more than a nod. The atmosphere between them was still frosty but they were locked into each other for the time being and accepted it.

'Any news?' Fisher asked to break the ice.

'I got a text that everything's sweet and the man's on his way with the gear. Depends on traffic in Glasgow but they'll have a break somewhere and be here in the middle of the day. We've just to wait. They'll give us a call when they're here and then we'll meet up.'

'That's a bit unusual, isn't it, Billy? We're normally waiting for them,' McLean said, biting into a sugar-loaded Danish.

'That's the man's orders and he *is* the fuckin' man.' Nelson made it sound matter of fact, but it was a lie. The arrangement was to meet them on arrival at a car park in Ferry Road, but Fisher and McLean didn't need to know that. They just had to believe what Nelson told them.

'We'll have these coffees and then I need to split for a while to take care of some business. I'll meet you here again at twelve and then we wait for the call. Have you got the van ready for the gear?'

'It's parked round the corner and on a meter,' Fisher said.

After he'd finished his second cup, Nelson left, jumped a taxi back into the centre of town and wandered round the shops in Rose Street.

Jackie Martin drove up the narrow coastal route from Cairnryan and made sure he wasn't being followed.

The road was perfect for anti-surveillance and he went through the whole repertoire but never saw anything that looked a bit smelly. The surveillance team had been briefed by the PSNI that he was good and so they were giving him all the room he needed. They countered his actions by having cars posted well ahead on the route so where they had to hang well back and lose sight he'd always be picked up again by the cars ahead of him.

He stopped in Ayr and bought a meat pie and watery tea that he stuffed down in the car. Then he called Nelson. 'It's all good and the road seems to be clear of any problems.'

'Just heard on the radio that Glasgow's nose to tail so you might be delayed,' Nelson said, wishing he could spit in Martin's face just before they arrested him.

'What's new? Just one of those things, and the beer'll taste even better tonight.'

He put the phone down and fired up the engine before heading back onto the road for Glasgow city.

Thompson was buzzing. The air was filled with high-tension radio traffic as the surveillance convoy tracked Martin towards Glasgow, but her confidence was growing and the rest of the team caught it. They settled down for the long haul back to Edinburgh and prayed there would be no problems along the way.

38

Baxter stood outside the room where they were getting Andy Clark ready for the day. He had a young detective with him as a second witness in case Clark said anything incriminating, and he'd been told to make notes but keep quiet and learn.

The staff nurse who'd spoken to Nelson and watched him grab Clark by the throat came up and introduced herself.

'How was he last night?'

'He's a troubled boy, Mr Baxter. I went in to check him during the night and he was crying like a baby. Wouldn't tell me what was wrong. Anyway, he's ready and when the nurses leave him you can go in.' She walked away and headed home to the comfort of her bed.

Clark looked up as Baxter entered the room and took a seat that was close to the bedside but not too close to get in the boy's space. He asked Clark how he was and noted the red-rimmed eyes as a sign that he'd done a lot of thinking during the night.

'How's Kristina?' Clark asked.

'She was badly hurt but she's conscious, and the

colleague who was with me last night is seeing her this morning.' He let that sink in before continuing. 'She was lucky to survive, but we're worried about her safety and have put an armed guard on her 24/7.'

Clark's eyes widened at the news and the realisation that he was responsible for what had happened to her. She hadn't deserved that. Perhaps she'd only been with him for money but she'd given him something he'd never had but wanted badly. He'd admitted to himself that she'd sold him the illusion that she cared, but it had been a wonderful illusion and he wanted it to be real. She was a beautiful girl, and he knew that she'd suffered some terrible experiences of her own. Clark was as aware as anyone of the kinds of things a girl recruited in the Baltic States and forced to work in London might have endured. She had refused to tell him exactly what had happened there, but whatever it was had been bad, and he knew she would be in danger if she tried to go back – he could sense it.

'What do you want to talk about, Andy?'

Clark stared at the detective, unsure of what to say, but his guilt gripped him and he felt loaded down with the burden of it. His dreams had become recurring nightmares, and he knew he couldn't stay quiet any more. He had to do something. Kristina might not have loved him but she'd made him feel emotions that were new and exhilarating, and he could no longer survive on an existence built on conflict and destroying the lives of people who couldn't defend themselves.

'If I talk, what'll happen to me?' he asked.

Baxter looked into the young man's eyes and wondered what he could tell him that would give him any form of assurance.

'I've no idea, son. I think you've been involved in some bad stuff. In fact none of us can work out what the hell

346

happened to Joe Fleming's wife. Her mind's gone.' He knew that Clark was going to talk – it was just a case of how far he would go – but it would be foolish of him to make promises he couldn't keep. He'd already offered to get a lawyer to come to the hospital but Clark had declined.

'Why don't you go back to the beginning and tell me how you came to Edinburgh and what happened from there?'

Clark closed his eyes and lay quite still for a few moments, and Baxter thought he'd lost it but kept quiet. The next move one way or the other had to be Clark's.

The young man opened his eyes, looked at the detective and nodded. 'Do you want to take notes?'

'If that's okay with you?' Baxter explained that he would have to caution him and Clark nodded again. 'Let's do it then,' said Baxter. He proceeded to run quickly and stiffly through the formalities of the caution process.

The young DC pulled out his notebook and waited. Clark spoke slowly and there were times when he paused for a few moments while he gathered his thoughts, but slowly everything began to spill out. Baxter had been a detective for a long time but he found it hard to control what he was feeling at these disclosures. He wanted to stop Clark, get Macallan in to hear his revelations, but he was frightened the boy would suddenly realise the enormity of what he was describing and close up.

As Clark continued, Baxter became so uncomfortably tense, but he couldn't bring himself to move. Eventually, after about forty minutes, Clark's painkillers had worn off and he said he needed the nurse to help him with the pain in his legs.

Baxter was relieved. 'No problem. I'll get her and grab a coffee and come back after that.'

He walked to the café without speaking to his young

colleague, who felt completely out of his depth. Baxter stared ahead without seeing anything of the hospital around him. The image of how Joe and Danny Fleming had died and what they'd done to Lena Fleming was stuck in his mind.

'Jesus Christ,' he whispered over and over again, and his hand trembled as he gulped back the last of his coffee. He headed back to the ward feeling cold and sick, but there was a job to do, and he needed to stay focused.

He got as much as he could from Clark and told him he'd need a bit of time to think it over. He sent a text to Macallan telling her he was going to have a break and would be in the café. He wanted to talk to her before doing anything else, but he needed to be on his own for a while, and the young detective looked as if he needed a break too, so he was sent back to the office.

After about half an hour Macallan came into the café and looked around for Baxter. She saw him sitting in the corner, looking exhausted, and she wondered whether he was okay.

She walked over to the table and pulled out a chair opposite him. He looked at her blankly but spoke first. 'How did you get on?'

She noticed his eyes were dull and that he was on autopilot. 'Kristina's told me as much as she can and admits setting up Clark for Pat Fleming, just as Felicity thought. That's a problem we'll need to come back to later, but the main thing is that she'll identify the man who attacked her in the hotel. Once we get Nelson we'll stick him in an ID parade and I've no doubt she'll do the rest.' She paused, waiting for a comment, but Baxter hadn't moved.

'Obviously Donnie Monk has done nothing so we'll need to get a team to do a full job at the hotel and try to find out what room they were in. I'll call them to get on to it. That's about as far as she can help us now, but she's vulnerable and we'll have to make sure the guys who're doing the guard job are on their toes.' She studied Baxter again, wondering what he was thinking and what it was that was hurting him.

'Tell me what happened,' she said to him and waited patiently.

It took him a while to articulate the thoughts and images that were crashing into each other in his head, but Baxter told her what Clark had disclosed to him as calmly as if he was discussing the football results.

As the story unfolded Macallan sat back and blinked at what it all meant. None of it should have come as a surprise because they'd known Joe and Danny had to be dead, but it was the horror of what Nelson had been prepared to do for his takeover and the appalling reality of what Lena Fleming had suffered that made Macallan feel physically sick.

She squeezed Baxter's arm and forced him to meet her eyes. 'Listen. We need to get this done right now. No time to dwell, we need to work the evidence up and get it right. There's a shitload to do and I need you focused. Do you hear me?'

He looked at her for a moment and then came back into the room. She saw it and smiled at him.

'I'm on it, Grace. I don't want to leave a single space for that horrible bastard to crawl through.'

'You've done a great job, but we're going to need help. Finish off with Clark and make sure he has the same level of protection as Kristina. I'll meet you back here in half an hour, we'll head over to the coordination centre to see how it's all going, then back to the ranch to brief the troops. Okay?'

Baxter nodded and left her at the table to finish her drink. She shook her head slowly, thinking how quickly

349

everything had changed. They were on top and Billy Nelson was well and truly fucked.

She called Jacquie Bell to tell her she had a story for her.

'I'll meet you later, Jacquie; I want this out to put pressure on the bastard. We've got witnesses but there must be more out there that'll come forward when they realise he's over.'

'Okay, I'll see you then, and thanks – it'll be my pleasure and will cover me in even more glory.'

Macallan smiled. Bell just couldn't do serious.

Baxter told Andy Clark that he'd be back later and that armed officers had already been stationed outside his room. Clark knew that he was going to have to answer for what he'd done, but he couldn't live this way any more. The other truth he'd faced up to was that he was looking at a life of limited mobility. The doctors had been as honest as possible and he was already well aware that he had never been able to rely on brains – that physical ability was all he'd ever had – and he groaned quietly at the thought of his future.

Kristina Orlova was recovering quickly and all she wanted was to face the man who'd hurt her so badly. She was finished with being abused by the worst kind of men and determined that a terrible chapter of her life was going to close, but first she needed the opportunity to look her attacker in the eye.

Macallan arrived at the coordination centre and found the air crackling with the tension of the operations that were running towards a climax. Young was working in an office near to the centre and briefed them on the progress so far. It had been straightforward enough, but the traffic had been solid in Glasgow so the lorry and Martin had only just cleared the city on the M8 heading for Edinburgh. Macallan explained what had happened at the hospital and Young scribbled notes furiously, shaking her head at the revelations.

'My God, this is unbelievable! I'll come down to your briefing if that's okay?'

'Of course – you need to be there, and we have a hell of a lot to do once we figure out where the bodies might be buried and where they were killed. It's going to be another hour or so before Martin hits the city so we'll nip down to Leith and get started. See you there.'

The briefing room at Leith police station was crowded and Macallan filled her team in on the events of the morning. There were a few indrawn breaths as the story unfolded but Macallan knew that nothing had been solved. They had a story from Clark, but unless the rest of the Belfast team were going to sit down and confess they needed a lot more to wrap the case up.

'Our priority is to identify the sites of the murders and the burial. We have a problem in that Clark is still in a lot of pain and we're going back to see if the doctors would allow us to take him out under medical supervision to show us where it happened. Any questions?' There were none and the only sound was Young, scribbling away as always.

'We have a start because Clark has told us that the killing took place in Nelson's old flat in Wester Hailes. I should qualify that because from what he told Grant we're not sure that they were both dead when they were buried.' She paused again, wanting the team to understand exactly what kind of people they were dealing with.

'From what we know, a family of refugees have since moved into that flat so before we do anything we'll liaise with the social-work department and try to get them to

351

arrange them some temporary accommodation. We're going to have to do a full forensic job on the flat.'

'Welcome to Bonny Scotland,' Baxter said without a trace of humour.

'We're going back up to the hospital to see what arrangements we can make. It'll be tomorrow at the earliest before we can start on the sites, but I want you all to get cracking on the tasks you have in hand.'

There was a murmur that told her that they all got it and were ready to move up a gear.

Macallan had been putting off the last thing she needed to do before heading back to the hospital, but once the briefing was over she had no excuses left, so she called the chief super and told him she needed to speak to him urgently about the progress of the investigation. He sounded less than enthusiastic and said that O'Connor would sit in because of the problem with Donnie Monk. She told Baxter, who was heading back to the hospital, and said she'd see him as soon as she was clear of her meeting.

'Best of luck. Don't let him beat you.' Baxter winked, but he was glad it was her rather than him.

When she walked into the chief super's office he was already sitting with O'Connor and sharing some kind of joke. She sat down without being asked and decided she hadn't the time to piss about with them – she just wanted to get him up to speed with the story so far and then get back to her job.

She briefed them as fully as she could and did her best to avoid eye contact with O'Connor, who sat quietly, leaving any questions to the chief super. When she was done with that, she told them that the surveillance operation was on course and going smoothly.

'It sounds like Lesley's doing a good job,' the chief super said with a rat smile.

'She's doing a great job, sir, and I'm so pleased for her.

She's taking to it like the proverbial duck, and the guys like her.'

That reply was not what the two men had expected. *Well done, Grace – you got that one right*, she congratulated herself as she watched the confused expressions spread across their faces.

'What about Donnie Monk?' O'Connor asked her politely.

'There's nothing else I can tell you apart from the fact that he's done nothing on the investigation at the hotel so we're starting it from scratch. He hadn't even got a hold of the CCTV tapes so we're on that now. Our guys have already started viewing and think they've got Nelson, but he's wearing a brimmed hat and glasses. I'd appreciate it if you could leave Monk till we get the surveillance operation resolved so we don't spook them.'

'That's no problem. He's gone off sick and isn't at home as far as we can gather. We're already turning up evidence that's going to get him prison time and the guy's got some serious problems. There are going to be a lot of questions for the people who've supervised him about how they could have missed all this.'

Macallan made her excuses to leave and felt she'd got off lightly, but as she reached the door the chief super had one last order: 'This whole story has to be controlled as tightly as possible with the press so we're going to let as little as we can out till we see how this story develops.'

'Of course, sir,' she said, immediately thinking: *That'll be fucking right.*

When Macallan left his office the chief super turned to O'Connor. 'I thought you told me that Thompson would help us put Macallan in her place? Unless I'm mistaken, that is looking less than likely.'

O'Connor shifted uncomfortably in his seat. 'I'll speak to Lesley when she's finished this operation.'

39

On his way back to meet Fisher and McLean, Nelson stopped at a phone box and called his handler in Belfast, who answered on the second ring. 'Hi, Billy. Everything is on track and they'll be in the city within twenty minutes.'

'Just make sure you call me the minute he's on the approach to the car park,' Nelson replied.

'You'll get it. I'm listening to it as it happens.'

The surveillance team watched Nelson leave the phone box and head back to Stockbridge, where he met up again with Fisher and McLean. He bought a coffee and sat down beside them.

'Any word yet?' Fisher asked.

'Shouldn't be long now,' Nelson said, avoiding eye contact.

Jackie Martin drove past the Ingliston showground under a beautifully clear winter sky. The sun shone, and he was excited about his first trip to the capital city. It had been a long time since he'd felt so energised, and he realised that Belfast was draining the life out of him. The more he thought about it, the more he knew it was time to get out and try something new.

He'd booked into one of the most expensive hotels in the city and the first thing he was going to do when they'd handed over the gear was get a couple of the best hookers his money could buy. And when he was done with them, he would have a good night out on the town.

'It's all fuckin' good, Jackie boy,' he said into the rear-view mirror.

'Okay guys, everything's in place and the arrest units are deployed in the car park, just waiting for us,' Thompson relayed to the rest of her team, who were right up on their toes. They all knew that the danger time was at the end of the surveillance, when they were tired and one mistake could blow the whole operation. But they were focused and knew exactly how important the job was.

Thompson called McGovern to ask what was happening at his end.

'I don't understand it. The three of them are still sitting drinking coffee. It doesn't make sense, and this wasn't in the script from Belfast,' McGovern said.

'Nothing we can do but go with what we've got. Keep you posted.'

In the coordination centre Young scratched her head and chewed the end of her pencil. The news that Nelson wasn't moving didn't surprise her, but she wasn't sure she knew why. Something had troubled her since the beginning of the operation, but it was like an itch she couldn't reach.

The traffic was as slow as every other day on Ferry Road and Martin had closed up behind the lorry as they approached the car park.

At that exact moment Billy Nelson's phone rang and

the call came in from Belfast. 'He's arrived.' Then it clicked off.

Nelson said, 'Jesus Christ!' for effect, and looked like he was near to panic as he punched the number into his phone. Fisher and McLean watched, wondering what the fuck was going on.

Martin was as sure as he could be that they were clear of any attention and manoeuvred into a parking space near the lorry. He thought that if the Peelers were about they would have moved in long before Edinburgh, so he stepped out of the car, walked towards the two boys who'd brought the lorry through and offered them a cigarette.

'Where the fuck is Billy?' he asked without too much concern.

Suddenly his phone rang and he put it to his ear, surprised to hear Nelson's voice.

'I just got a call from the bent Peeler. They're onto you, Jackie – get the fuck out of there.'

The cigarette dropped from Martin's lips as he looked round the car park, but it was already too late. The heavies were coming at them from all directions, and there were enough guns to reduce them to pulp. He screamed with rage and launched himself at the first cop to come within striking distance. There was no doubt about it, Jackie Martin went down fighting and only stopped struggling when he was exhausted. He spat and swore, his rage heated by the knowledge that he'd let a rat get to him – but how?

As the arrest team dragged him into the back of the van he thought again about Billy Nelson. It had never felt right, but for the first time in his life he'd ignored his instincts, and it had cost him.

'You're fuckin' kidding me!' Fisher said in disbelief.

'It was Donnie Monk. Just got the message, but too late

to stop Jackie,' Nelson said as Fisher stared into his eyes and wondered. 'Let's split up and keep our heads down for a couple of days till we see how the land lies. Don't worry if you don't hear from me for a bit.' He got up and left.

'Something stinks here, Rob. I'm telling you, we'll all end up dead with this fuckin' mess,' Fisher spat before they went their separate ways.

Across the street the eyeball had relayed the fact that Nelson had made a call and that the three of them looked panicked. McGovern called Thompson, who confirmed that the arrest had been made, and McGovern told her about the phone call.

'Weird, Jimmy, because Jackie Martin got a call just as they were moving in for the arrest. I don't get it.'

'I'll stick with Nelson, see where he goes next.' There was a flatness in McGovern's voice as he said this, because although Jackie Martin's arrest was a great result, it looked like it was back to the drawing board with Nelson.

Nelson walked slowly and calmly towards Inverleith Park then sat on a bench for a while, letting the winter sun shine on his face. There was warmth even though they were approaching the shortest day of the year.

The surveillance team watched from the edges of the park: it was wide open so there was no need to be close to him.

McGovern was getting even more agitated with Nelson's actions. His supplier had just been taken out and he was acting as if he was on tranquillisers.

Eventually Nelson strolled through the park and even played around with one of the dozens of dogs being walked in the sunshine. He came out of the east entrance, crossed the road and went into the Botanic Garden, over seventy acres of peace less than a mile from the heart of the city.

'Do you want us to go with him, Jimmy?' the eyeball asked.

'Keep with him but stay well back. If you think he's paying any attention to you just back off. We'll cover all the entrances and make sure we can pick him up again when he leaves.'

Nelson knew that the surveillance team would be behind him and that's why he was there. It was time to get on with his payback. He wandered round the ground floor of the entrance building then headed upstairs to the first-floor restaurant to drink some coffee and sit on the veranda looking out over the gardens. He settled in there for over an hour and seemed perfectly at ease.

McGovern called into the coordination centre and spoke to Felicity Young. Thompson still hadn't arrived back in the office. Her team would have nothing to do with interviewing Jackie Martin and the two young men who'd driven the lorry through – a separate team of detectives had been briefed to do the business with them. Martin was still raging but he'd managed to get a hold of his lawyer, who was on his way.

'The financial investigation team have found that Nelson drew out nearly eight thousand in cash this morning, Jimmy. It had been prearranged with the bank, and I've no idea what it means – unless he's preparing to do a runner,' Young said, still writing notes as she spoke.

'I think you should run that past Grace to see if it affects her thinking.'

'I will. The other thing is that the phone call Nelson was seen making just before the arrest was to Jackie

Martin. But he received a phone call immediately before that, from an as-yet-unknown source.'

The footman interrupted with a call that Nelson was leaving the building and on a walkabout in the gardens.

'Got to go, Felicity, but speak to Grace.'

Nelson was wandering aimlessly about the gardens and sitting down on a bench every few minutes, making it almost impossible for the footmen to keep with him without being seen on the long quiet paths. McGovern told them to withdraw to the entrance building and drink something till Nelson appeared again or left by another entrance.

About 3.45 p.m. the sky was darkening and the Botanics staff began to close up shop for the day. The footmen had overstayed and left to be picked up by other surveillance cars.

'Where in the name of fuck is he?' McGovern said to no one in particular. He called round the cars but no one had seen him. A stream of visitors had left during the last hour of business and he was becoming concerned that Nelson had perhaps changed his appearance when he was inside the grounds and then slipped past them.

He called Thompson and gave her the update.

'Can't think what else to do, Lesley. I guess we've missed him. It's a big place and these things happen.'

'Tell me about it,' she said, remembering how she'd felt after the loss at the hotel. 'See you back here then. I think they're going to start interviewing Martin shortly.'

Nelson had settled down in a small copse near a boundary wall of the gardens. He would be invisible to anyone unless they tried to struggle in beside him. With his training it was an easy hide – something he'd done a hundred times in combat situations. His rucksack contained warm clothing plus some food to keep his energy levels up, and he intended to sit tight till he could be sure he was clear of the surveillance team. If he waited till midnight he could then slip unnoticed over the wall. His only problem was that his strength was failing, but he only had to stay there for a few hours.

Slipping into the lightweight sleeping bag made him feel more comfortable, and it would keep the worst of the cold out.

Thompson called Macallan, updated her on what had happened so far and told her they'd lost Nelson.

'What's happening with you, Grace?'

'We had a bit of a struggle with the doctors and they want to wait another day before putting Clark in a wheelchair. That doesn't stop us from doing the flat, but we need him to direct us to where they put Joe and Danny. He says the only way he can find it is by taking us there himself. The social workers have managed to find alternative accommodation for the family so we're just waiting for the call from them before we can go in and get started at the flat. At this rate I think it's going to be an early start tomorrow rather than tonight.' She thought for a moment. 'Think I might go and see Barry Wallace though. I wouldn't mind a word with the man.'

'Okay, I'll see you there myself. Interested to see how they get on with him.'

Macallan had figured out exactly what had happened. She'd played the dark arts long enough in the Troubles, but what she couldn't work out was *why* it had happened, and Barry Wallace was the only one who might be able to answer that question.

40

Jackie Martin had been taken to Drylaw police station, where he was held for interview. No one had said too much to him and he knew the drill – they'd try to make him sweat a bit before the suits came in, hoping to get an easy admission.

'Fat fuckin' chance of that,' he said to the empty room.

It didn't matter what he said to the room though – he was sweating and trying to work out just how bad this might be. On the plus side, the two meatheads who'd driven the lorry through were unlikely to implicate him. It could happen, but it was unlikely given his reputation regarding anyone who'd tried to sell him out to the Peelers in the past. He could make a complete denial about the contents of the lorry, and he had the best lawyers money could buy. If that was all they had then he might just scrape a result, so it wasn't time to panic yet. The main thing was that his businesses in Northern Ireland, both legal and illegal, were not affected by what had happened in Edinburgh. He still hadn't convinced himself about the rat. Nelson had to be the favourite though because he hadn't been at the meet on time – and that stank to the heavens.

Martin had used the same lawyer for over fifteen years and the man had been worth the fees ten times over. Bent as a nine-pound note, but he kept himself the right side of the gates at HMP Maghaberry. He decided that when the lawyer arrived the first instruction he'd receive would be to get the boys going on a full enquiry into what the fuck had happened and to put whoever was responsible in the ground – or, if he was in a good mood, a skip.

In an office no more than thirty feet from Martin's cell DI Barry Wallace sat and waited for his phone to ring. He'd told the locals he was going to contact PSNI HQ in Belfast and asked for some privacy, but that was a lie. The call he was expecting was from a security-service officer in Belfast. Everyone was still waiting for Martin's lawyer to arrive before he could be interviewed, but Wallace wanted to speak to him before the local suits. He didn't like what he was doing; it felt wrong, and he wished the three years he still had to do would pass so he could get out of the business.

Even though he was waiting for it, he was startled when the phone did eventually ring.

'Everything okay there, Barry?'

The smugness in the home-counties accent pissed him off. *How could it be okay?* he thought. 'Well, he's locked up and raging so I suppose that's okay,' Wallace said, his voice flat.

'It's agreed here, so go and get the message to him. Billy Nelson's a liability, and as luck would have it Dominic McGinty's been helping to fund a dissident group in Londonderry for years. We have to protect the source in Belfast for the future, so it's the big picture, Barry. You know that.'

Wallace hadn't time to answer before the line went dead. He sighed and thought about the number of times the 'big picture' line had condemned men to death.

He went through to an adjoining office and cleared it with the interviewing team that he could have time alone with Martin before his lawyer stormed in the door and started accusing the police of another fit-up.

'DI Wallace, didn't expect to see you here, but then maybe I should have,' Martin said as the PSNI detective walked into the room. He felt slightly reassured, because during the height of the Troubles, when Wallace had been a young Special Branch officer in the RUC, he'd helped Martin out of a couple of tight spots. The truth was that Wallace had been trying to turn him as an informant, but he had been only partially successful. Martin had returned the favour with some low-level information on renegade Loyalists who needed a bit of a spell in the Maze, but that was it and he'd refused to become a full-time agent. Jackie Martin only ever did what suited him, and he hadn't been bright enough to see the benefits of a relationship with the force as the peace process took root in Northern Ireland.

Wallace sat down and looked Martin straight in the eye. He had to make the man believe every word he said was true.

'How are you, Jackie? It's been a long time.'

'What brings you here, and how much shit am I in?' Martin asked, realising that it had to be more than a social visit to bring the DI from Belfast.

'It's more than the dope we're talking about here. As we speak the financial-investigation team are taking your world apart in Belfast. They know where you've been laundering the money and are all over it.' He paused for a moment, wanting to let each piece of bad news sink in with full effect. Then he stuck in the next blow a bit further below the belt. 'They're breaking down the doors of the saunas and escort services, and the God-fearing section of the public will thank the chief for that one.' He gave it another moment and watched Martin's face twitch with shock.

'We've been trying for years to find your arms stash. That was opened up about half an hour after you were arrested, and your DNA will be all over it if I'm not mistaken.'

Jackie Martin had no defence against the news that he was fucked. His hands shook – his world was folding inwards only a short time after he'd been imagining his new life in Edinburgh. His throat tightened and he tried to stop himself gagging up his breakfast.

Wallace pushed a cup of water over the table and Martin swallowed it, holding it with both hands to try to control the shakes.

'The thing is, we've been watching you and listening to you for years.' Wallace said this, but it was only part true – the lie was necessary to protect the source in Belfast. If Martin thought the PSNI had done part of it through brilliant detective work then that was a result.

'Jesus, is there anything I can do to help?'

Martin was pleading. Wallace had never thought he'd see the day. Then again, he thought, the truly evil bastards like Jackie Martin tended to fall over the easiest when they were facing twenty-five years in Maghaberry.

'You should have thought about that a while ago, Jackie, when I first made you an offer.' He put on as sympathetic a voice as possible and tried his best to pretend he cared about the murderer sitting opposite him.

Martin looked up and the reality of his position brought back some anger to replace the fear. He tried his best to show a bit of bravado to the detective, who almost felt sorry for him. Martin was like a child being played by men. The ex-UVF brigadier just didn't get it.

'As far as I'm concerned, that bastard Billy Nelson has questions to answer,' Martin said. 'I'm not stupid. He's part of this set-up. Just tell me, and when we're back over the water I'll give you whatever you want about the movement.'

The detective tried not to sigh with disbelief at the paradox of the statement. Martin wanted to find the informant, who he regarded as contemptible, and then become one himself. Wallace did a good impression of someone who was torn over doing the right thing by Martin. He nodded as if he'd crossed the Rubicon, moved his face a few inches nearer to Martin's and dropped the tone of his voice as if he was becoming a co-conspirator.

'There's more to it than just Billy Nelson. He's already set up with a dealer in Glasgow: Dominic "Magic" McGinty. Can you believe it? A fucking Celtic diehard that's pumped money into the dissidents for years. PIRA before that.'

'A fuckin' Taig and Billy Nelson.' Martin almost moaned the words in disbelief. A dribble of saliva ran from his bottom lip, and he slammed the table with his clenched fist.

'I'm going now, Jackie. At some stage you'll be taken back over the water and I'll see you in Belfast. Okay?' Wallace stood at the door and waited.

'I'll see you there, and thanks for that. What I said stands, and I'll do whatever I need to get a deal.'

Wallace had heard that Martin fancied himself as a bit of a Tony Soprano. He thought for a moment and had to admit that Martin looked a bit like the late James Gandolfini from an angle, which on another day would have pleased the man no end.

Wallace just managed to get clear of the room before Martin's lawyer arrived screaming blue murder, which was why only the best criminals could afford his services

– the man just loved to give the police maximum hassle.

Wallace closed the door of the small office he'd been using, which was empty, and sat at the desk for a moment, trying to deal with what he'd done. 'The big fucking picture indeed,' he said as he made the call from his mobile.

'It's done, and he swallowed it without chewing. See you back there.'

No one spoke at the other end and he put the phone down. The message had been delivered and the wheels were turning.

Macallan arrived at the station and caught Wallace as he was ordering a taxi for the airport. She saw the tension in his expression and asked him to hang around for a couple of minutes. He nodded and took her back into the office he'd been using.

'Talk to me, Barry. I want to get the stink out of my nose – and remember what my background is. Is the informant who I think it is? I don't need to say the name, do I?'

His face and shoulders dropped. Conning Jackie Martin was one thing, but he couldn't do it with Macallan. 'You know I can't tell you,' he replied. 'Anyway, the informant works for the security service. That's where we're getting the information from.'

He moved to step past her. 'Look, I have to go.'

She put her hand on his chest. 'Just before you go ... This guy has killed a number of people already, driven one woman to the edge of insanity and another to suicide. I'm going to put him away – and you can tell the service that from me.' She took a step back and saw that Wallace was struggling with what had happened.

'It's the big picture again, Grace. Where have you heard that before? All I can tell you is the scores will be

366

evened up. Let's leave it at that.' He shook her hand and left for the airport.

Macallan felt helpless. All she could do was prove the case against Nelson. And that's exactly what she intended to do.

In the detention room the lawyer was given time to brief his client before the interview started, but Jackie Martin had only one thing on his mind. He was a middle-aged man who should have been allowed to enjoy the rest of his life on the fruits of his labour, but the rats had gotten to him first. That was unforgivable, and if he was going to end up moving to old age inside the walls of a prison then someone would pay.

'I want you to listen to this carefully. Take these instructions back to my boys and they'll know what to do.'

The lawyer nodded; he understood that he had to get this part right and there was no way he was going to argue.

Martin had never met Patrick 'Bobo' McCartney, and it was unlikely that he ever would, but like Bobo, he'd recognised one rat but missed the one that had really got inside his defence. He'd bought the story he'd been told by Wallace and fallen right into the security service's trap. The big picture meant nothing to Martin – he didn't deal in the subtle intrigues of the intelligence community and thought the world was what he saw in front of him – so the traitor's blow that had delivered him to the police had come from someone he'd wrongly thought he knew better than anyone.

It was his wife who had betrayed him, and when she'd taken the call from the security-service officer that he'd been arrested, she'd kissed the giant of a man standing next to her. Martin's minder, his confidant throughout the Troubles, had been involved in an affair with the man's wife for over two years. She'd decided she wanted more and there was only one way to do it, and although the idea that she might be an informant had briefly crossed Martin's mind, the minder had discounted it as impossible in the circumstances.

It was a simple, old story really – he'd just fancied the boss's wife, and she'd felt the same about him. She'd put more than enough safely away and was now rid of her problem, and the minder – who was a practical man – thought he might step into Martin's shoes after a suitable period of time and, with a bit of luck and muscle, build up the business again in his own right.

In the same way he'd never met Bobo, Martin had never met Joe Fleming, and he'd ended up making exactly the same mistakes. He'd gone soft. He was still capable of terrible violence, but he'd lost his edge and had stopped seeing the threats all around him.

The suits interviewed Martin later, and on the instructions of his lawyer he said nothing. The situation was a mess, but when he lay on his cell cot that night he felt confident that it would all work out. He had the best lawyers, a team back home who were right behind him and his wife to back him up.

'No one fucks with Jackie Martin,' he muttered into the cold dark air of the cell, just before he fell asleep.

But in the darkness of Martin's own bedroom his wife stroked her lover's face and reassured him, 'Don't worry – Jackie's fucked.'

The security-service officer stared out of his office window into the darkness of the Belfast night. He felt satisfied that everything was going to plan and that one way or another they would clear up a few problems over the coming days. Martin might talk, but it wouldn't do him much good. His minder would take over, and Martin's wife would be perfectly placed to keep reporting on the new man at the top. They had her over a barrel, although she hadn't worked that out yet. She hadn't realised that one word from them and Jackie would have her gutted and tossed in the river.

Billy Nelson was going down as well; it was just a matter of who got to him first.

The spook lifted his glass of gin and toasted his reflection in the window. He hadn't realised that he was as human as the people he'd sucked into their various traps. He'd miscalculated, and while Nelson had accepted that it was over for him, he still had the ability to dictate events – and the end would come on his terms.

Nelson looked at his watch and saw it was five minutes to midnight. Pulling himself out of his sleeping bag, he worked the stiffness out of his legs and repacked his rucksack. A few minutes later he was over the boundary wall and walking towards Stockbridge, where he caught a taxi. He'd dropped the Belfast accent again, and with his woollen hat and glasses it would have been hard to recognise him. He took the taxi a few miles south of the city to where he'd already rented a holiday flat for the week – though he wouldn't need a week.

41

Macallan chewed her finger near the knuckle of her left forefinger. She realised for the first time that a hard ridge of skin had formed there, which meant she must have been doing it for a while without being aware of the habit. They'd been given access to the flat Nelson had occupied when he'd first come to Edinburgh, and Clark had explained in detail what had happened to the Flemings the night they'd come to hand out a lesson to the Belfast boys. It was only 8 a.m., but Macallan had insisted on an early start and the head SOCO was viewing the flat before they brought the team in.

Macallan and Baxter stood outside the door impatiently but knew that the SOCOs couldn't and shouldn't be rushed. They discussed Clark's statement and the problem they now had: Clark had told them that the Flemings had come from Banjo Rodgers' place and that he'd alerted the Belfast team that they were on their way.

'I'm not so surprised he left that out,' said Baxter. 'He probably thinks he'll end up on a lifer with them. I'll speak to him later and straighten it out.'

'No problem,' Macallan replied. 'And to be honest that's

the least of our worries. Poor bastard was probably terrified to refuse them anything after what happened to Maggie.'

The SOCO came out of the door and removed the mask from her face. 'Pretty much as he described,' she said. 'He says there was just a wooden floor in the room and that they'd lined it with plastic before doing the business. Is that right?' Macallan nodded. 'The council put a cheap carpet down, which isn't a bad thing, and providing they haven't steam cleaned it or something beforehand we have a chance. Even with the plastic lining, the beating he described would leave quite a scattering of debris, so a few bits and pieces might have escaped when they were rolling it up. We'll get on it – see what we can find.'

She called in the rest of her team and they went to work methodically. If there was something there, Macallan knew they'd find it.

'We're going up to the other site now,' she told the SOCO. 'The hospital have got Clark ready and they'll take him over there in an ambulance. He's indicated an area in East Lothian. Are you coming now or waiting till we identify it?'

The SOCO was already making notes. 'There's no way I'm going to miss buried bodies. I'll leave the team here; the second lot are ready to roll. I'll get them to head down that way now.' She seemed genuinely excited by the prospect of digging around decomposing cadavers.

An hour and a half later they were sitting just outside the picture-postcard village of Gifford, at the foot of the gentle Lammermuir hills. The traffic department had closed off most of the roads until the site of the burials had been established. That had annoyed a few important people in the area, and calls were already being taken from people who claimed to be personal friends of the Chief, but it was ever thus where there were people with money and clout.

They popped their heads into the ambulance and said hello to Clark, who looked to be suffering badly in his wheelchair, though the nurse with him was plainly enjoying the break from hospital routine.

'Are you okay to do this, Andy?' Baxter asked. He knew that lawyers could attack their actions if Clark changed his story and alleged undue duress, but he was still refusing to have a brief present, so they were on safe-enough ground for the moment.

In the end it was much easier than Macallan had expected – Clark was able to direct them to a wooded area and a dirt track leading off the main road. Macallan could see why they'd picked it. The area would have been almost deserted during the night hours, and any cars coming along the road could be seen miles away. The ambulance carrying Clark drove into the wood, and he told them to stop after about a hundred yards. He was lowered to the ground then started to shake uncontrollably. The nurse gripped both his hands and talked quietly to him.

'We can stop this now,' Macallan said, knowing that they were still on thin ice and that they couldn't be seen to force him. The nurse would be called as a witness and couldn't be expected to do the police any favours.

'I'm okay. I want this done and those boys lying there to be put in the right place.'

The nurse wiped Clark's nose and dried his face.

'If you look along there on the left just behind that small clump of bushes. Just behind there in the middle of a circle of trees.'

'Everyone wait here please except the SOCO.' Macallan didn't want any distractions.

They walked as slowly as possible, both aware of the danger of contaminating the crime scene. That meant Clark had to stay back too, though she wanted him away as soon as possible if they were in the right place.

They slowed down and circled the bushes Clark had pointed out. That's when they saw it, and Macallan had to suppress the instinct to turn away. It could easily have been missed given its resemblance to a rotting piece of wood among the ground foliage: a hand – or what was left of a hand – standing clear of the ground and pointing to the sky.

'Well well well,' the SOCO said, knowing that this was going to be an interesting day. 'Looks like some of our furry little friends have got here first.'

Macallan walked slowly back to the ambulance and looked at Baxter. 'Get Clark back to the hospital. This is the place.'

Macallan left it to the SOCOs and the scientists to control the scene. The days when a detective could trample all over the evidence were long gone, and her place was to make sure everyone who needed to be there was called and logged in and out properly.

They all got to work while she set up a base on the edge of the road, and within the hour a team had arrived to set up the operation, taking care of everything down to refreshments for the troops. The Fiscal came and did very little but had to be seen to be there, and they had a doctor on standby for when the bodies were removed, so it would take the press no time to hear that something major was happening in this otherwise sleepy corner of East Lothian.

Macallan spent the next few hours making and taking calls because it was headline stuff. A couple of camera crews had already arrived, and the media wanted a line from someone. Her neck hurt and she was tired when the SOCO finally walked back along the path and told her that they'd opened up the site.

'Get suited and masked up, Grace, and hope you've

a strong stomach.' The warning had relevance because she'd felt queasy for a couple of days now, but she was glad to get away from the phone and fielding questions from HQ. Luckily a press officer was en route and would soon take some of the strain.

The SOCO guided her along a path they'd marked out as safe. There was a line of small, raised boards placed so they didn't have to come in contact with the soil until everything had been examined, photographed and samples taken where necessary.

About twenty feet from the circle of birch trees the stench assaulted Macallan's nostrils, and she nearly retched at the stink of rotting flesh. It was nothing new to her and she refused to stick menthol rub up her nose to take the worst of it away. Her friend Bill Kelly had been one of the best detectives in the RUC before he'd reached high office and she remembered his words now: 'Don't hide from it. Even the stink of death is telling you something. You have to get close to it, feel it and then you won't forget when you're tired and have had enough. Those days when you just want to go home, you'll remember what the reality is and what you need to do.'

She walked slowly to the site and avoided the open ground till she was close. She didn't want anyone to see her flinch or show emotion. Although it was her job to lead, she felt nothing but revulsion to the pit of her stomach. If what Clark had told them was true, this was what Lena Fleming had been shown. She couldn't imagine what the poor woman must have felt, and understood why her mind had been torn apart by those events. To make it worse it had happened during the hours of darkness, and Macallan tried to picture what she'd seen in monochrome: nothing but shadows and patches of colourless moonlight illuminating the bodies of her husband and firstborn son. Few people would mourn the passing of Joe and Danny Fleming, but Lena Fleming hadn't deserved this, and Macallan made up her mind that Billy Nelson would pay. What she saw drove out any sympathy for Andy Clark though. He'd been there, and he could take whatever was coming.

She walked back to the road and gave out orders to the police and civilian staff working at the crime scene. She told Baxter to go home and take a rest then return at midnight to relieve her. All she had to do was make sure everyone knew their job and let them get on with it. The scientists and SOCOs knew exactly what they were doing; it was their territory now. Macallan could work from her office in the morning and attend the post-mortem whenever it could be carried out.

She called Jacquie Bell and gave her an update. Bell had been running the story every day and had made sure that the public – and hopefully Nelson – could see that the house of cards was falling in perfect order. The message was clear: Nelson could only hide for so long.

'Thanks, Grace, and no doubt they'll have you in front of a press conference in the next day or two, so see you there,' Bell said. 'By the way, when am I going to meet the new man?'

'He's coming over, but only for the day and one night so not this time, Jacquie. I'll be tied up during the day so we'll just get one night together. Such is the life of a detective.'

She rang off and smiled at the thoughts running through her head, although she also realised she'd probably be so knackered that it would be an early night and not much else.

Well, Jack my boy, this'll test your commitment, she thought, before turning her mind back to the job.

42

It was like a phoney war. In the time after the unearthing of the bodies of Joe and Danny Fleming it was as if there was a temporary truce in the chain of events. All the players knew that nothing was finished and they carried on waiting for the signal that the last part of the game was about to be played out. Macallan knew it was close, but she had to concentrate on gathering the evidence, and all the time she wondered who would actually end up in court.

Her instincts were also trying to tell her something else, but she hadn't figured it out yet.

The post-mortem had been difficult, and the Procurator Fiscal had nearly passed out watching the examination of the Flemings' mortal remains. The bodies gave up part of their story, and it became obvious that both men had suffered terrible injuries from the soles of their feet to the fractures on their faces and skulls. Whatever their sins, the Flemings had suffered a terrible death, and Macallan winced every time the crime scene came back into her thoughts.

Clark had told them that it had been a moonlit night when they'd buried the Leith men, and she wanted to see it at that time of the day – imagine the dark silhouettes of

376

the men dragging Lena Fleming to the graveside, making her stare into the pit. She went with Baxter as near as possible to the time of night Clark had described and ordered the police team still working there to switch off all the lights. They walked slowly towards the circle of trees and stood for a few minutes as she tried to burn the picture into her mind. She wanted to remember it, and Bill Kelly's words came back to her again.

'Jesus, what kind of men are they?' Baxter said almost in a whisper, as if they might disturb something in the shadows.

'God knows. I keep thinking I've seen the worst that men can do then something like this happens. I gave up trying to understand it a long time ago. I just want to lock the bastards up, be normal for a bit then move on to clearing up the next mess. It's not the murders – we've all seen that and worse. But to drag Lena here? Who can explain that?'

They walked back to the car and went home.

The media had gone wild with what had become known as the 'gang wars in the city' and so it was inevitable that a press conference would be arranged. The chief super made up the best excuse he could to avoid the glare of awkward questions and left Macallan to field them for him. She handled it easily though, and the hacks were happy for the time being. She told them in oblique language that they knew who they were looking for but first of all they needed to gather the evidence and wait on the results of the forensic examinations.

After the conference she called Thompson.

'Any news?'

'Nothing on Nelson. He's definitely out of the picture at the moment. We're covering his house 24/7 but he's

377

been a no-show. Even if he managed to sneak in we'd have picked something up on the bug. We've put the surveillance team on Fisher instead and just left the OP covering Billy's place, though if he shows we might struggle to get a team on him quickly.'

'What about his phone?' Macallan asked, already knowing the answer.

'Nothing there either so I wonder if he's ditched it. Would make sense.'

'I'll let you know as soon as we're ready to make arrests, even if it's just Fisher and McLean.'

Macallan pulled her fingers through her hair. She felt uncomfortable. They were going to build a solid case, but there was something wrong. She phoned Young, who was still chewing her pencil and trying to work out what it was that she'd missed.

'There's no doubt he's got a plan, and I think he's been cooking it up for some time. There's too much been happening – the Perth meeting, Jackie Martin, Dominic McGinty and the large withdrawal of cash. Maybe he's tried to get out of the country; that would make some sense I suppose. He has to have seen the publicity and worked out that there's only bad outcomes as far as he's concerned.'

'I don't think he'll try to leave the country, Felicity. He has something else in mind, and I think we'll find out soon enough what that is.' She felt the answer was close, like a dream that she couldn't quite make sense of or explain.

'I agree. I know he's coming back, but what will he do?'

'Just keep that brain working, Felicity. If anyone can come up with an answer it's you.'

The following day had the same sense of time on hold – until about midday when Macallan had a call from the lab. It was the lead SOCO sounding as cheerful and matter of fact as ever.

'Got several minute pieces of tissue, Grace, and a fragment of tooth that was actually lodged in a small crack in the wall. They made a mistake and left small spaces between some of the plastic sheeting. Can you believe it?'

She wanted to shout down the phone but kept her voice level. It was good news and progress – major progress. She gave the thumbs-up to Baxter, who was sitting opposite her. 'Anything else?'

'I would say there was another part of the wall where they'd left a gap. There are definitely indications of fine blood spattering, almost invisible to the naked eye. I think we can safely say we have evidence. Still a lot to do and it'll have to be DNA'd but I'll be astonished if it's not a result.'

'Brilliant.' She put the phone down and told Baxter what had been said. He smiled from ear to ear because he could see the case was building. 'We just need to keep at it and I'll speak to the Fiscal, but I think in the next day or two we should have enough to bring in Fisher and McLean. I just wish Nelson would turn up.' She frowned again, wondering where he was.

'Listen, the man in my life is coming across from Belfast today so I'm going to have an early finish. Can you cover for me? But call if there's anything at all.'

'Of course – no problem. I'll take care of it. Just enjoy the night – and try not to fall asleep while you're eating the first course.'

'Ha! Think it'll be a fish supper and a bottle of plonk.'

'Well, that's five-star dining in Leith so you should think yourself lucky.'

She headed home to shower then attempt to try and look relaxed.

Billy Nelson had read the papers but the stories didn't concern him too much. In another life he might have been angry, but there wasn't much point given the circumstances. It was payback time, and in many ways they couldn't hurt him any more. It was up to him to close his story down, and he'd already decided that he wasn't going to end up feeding through a tube and wearing a nappy. He would end it on his feet. He'd lived a violent life but it was other people and events that had driven him down that road.

He wiped his brow and continued working on the second-hand car he'd bought for cash.

43

Jack Fraser smiled across the table. 'I have to say, the fish and chips were wonderful, and the wine was a great accompaniment. The perfect host.' His eyes sparkled with amusement; he had to admit that knowing Grace Macallan was never predictable and certainly not boring. She laughed easily. It had only taken a couple of glasses of wine for her to relax and get in the mood with Fraser. She was tired, but it was always the same in the middle of an investigation so she hardly thought about it – it was just part of what she was. Fraser had seen the effects of these investigations on so many of the detectives he'd worked with in Northern Ireland, and he'd known her long enough to accept it in the same way she did.

'Mick Harkins says that if you don't like the hours, fuck off and get a job in a tea shop.' She smiled, just glad that Fraser was sitting the other side of her kitchen table. It felt safe. She'd managed to put Billy Nelson and what Lena Fleming had seen in the woods out of her mind for a little while.

'I'd like you to meet Mick the next time you're over,' she added. 'He'd take great pleasure in winding you up, but if you can accept the humiliation you'll like him. He's a class act.'

She stood up, kissed his ear and headed to the kitchen to make some coffee.

'Leave it just now. I have a cunning plan now that you're half-pissed. I think you'll be ready for bed soon, and I want to get this idea passed or rejected before that happens.'

She sat down again and he could see that her eyes were heavy, but she was happy he was there with her, and so was Fraser.

'My old aunt died recently and left me a bit of cash. Not a fortune but it gives me a bit of leeway to follow up on one of my ambitions.' He stopped and finished what was in his glass. 'You know I've always fancied writing a book about the role of the lawyers during the Troubles... well, I've got a publisher interested. Can you believe it?'

'That's brilliant! You should go for it. The courts can live without you for a while, and I quite fancy having an author boyfriend – it has a nice ring to it.'

'Well, the thing is that I don't need to be in Northern Ireland to do it, if you know what I mean. It would take me about a year. The other thing is that I could always pick up a bit of legal work here.' He waited for a response, but Macallan just blinked and poured another glass of red.

'So what do you think?'

'About what?'

'Me living in Edinburgh.'

She put the glass down on the table and leaned back in her chair, considering what had come as a complete surprise. 'But where would you stay?' She tried to keep a straight face, but the alcohol spoiled her act and a slightly drunk half-smile broke out.

'You're pissed and not taking this seriously, Grace.'

382

She stood up and took his hand. 'It's a great idea, and you've pulled, mate, so let's seal the deal.'

He stood up, put his arms round her and held her as close as he could.

'At least I won't have to get that fucking budgie,' she added.

'What?'

'Another time.'

She looked at the clock and put out the lights in the kitchen. It was 11.30 p.m. and she was surprised she'd lasted that long.

Nelson kept the car just under the speed limit. He didn't want any attention from a bored night-shift cop. The news came on at midnight and he passed the sign telling weary motorists that they were entering the city of Edinburgh. His gut had ached all day and he'd hardly eaten, but the pain had eased off now, and the adrenalin pumping round his body had been boosted by a couple of lines of cocaine. He'd never been a heavy user but needed the extra kick for the hours ahead, and, after all, he didn't really have to worry too much about the health implications.

Donnie Monk was back in his flat and trying to watch the news headlines, but his head was swimming from the combination of drugs, alcohol and very little sleep. His time in the hotel had been a distraction and the surroundings had been comfortable, much better than the misery of his place and the accumulated debris from years of neglect. He couldn't remember when it had last been cleaned but he'd stopped noticing a long time ago – right around the time he'd lost his self-respect. His money was nearly gone, but he'd bought enough booze and some dope to see him through the next couple of days, though he guessed he wouldn't have that long. Having seen the headlines, he knew that his sordid little life would be under the microscope of the anti-corruption unit.

He chain-smoked as he watched the door, but at some stage drifted off into a half-sleep, not dreaming and still aware of his surroundings. The poisons in his system kept his body running like a stationary car with the accelerator depressed. Rest wasn't really possible any longer so he shook himself and snorted another line.

He lost track of time as he sat with his eyes closed, remembering the days when he could hold his head up as a rated detective.

After a while he opened his eyes to light another cigarette and noticed that the door of the living room was now open. He hadn't heard anything and sat forward. The only illumination in the semi-darkness was the flickering light from the television.

'You alright there, Donnie? Didn't want to disturb you when you looked so peaceful.' Nelson said it quietly, as if he didn't want to upset the corrupt detective.

'Wondered when you'd come,' Monk said, lighting the cigarette. 'You want one?'

'No. Sorry. Have to be on my way once we finish our business here.' Nelson stood up and walked over to Monk's chair.

'Fuck you. I don't give a shit any more.'

'That's good. I'd hate you to go out full of regrets.'

Twenty minutes later Nelson pulled the door behind him and walked back to his car. He drove to a phone box and made a call to Crimestoppers. He kept the English accent and said what he had rehearsed over and over again. Two Belfast men, named Dougie Fisher and Rob McLean, were going to pick up a 4x4 parked in East Fettes Avenue, Edinburgh. The men were moving several kilos of high-quality cocaine and two firearms concealed in the car.

The girl who took the call had to work hard to contain her excitement. Nine calls out of ten were nutters or trivia, but this was in a different bracket. She'd read the papers and any mention of Belfast men made her pulse race thanks to the headlines screaming about out-of-control terror gangs and the arrest of UVF leader Jackie Martin.

'Is there anything else, caller?' the girl asked, hoping that there was.

'These guys are UVF, dangerous and have said that if the police corner them they'll shoot it out.' He smiled and put the phone down.

Nelson walked back to the car tucked away in a cul-de-sac and settled down till it was time for his next call. He pulled the collar of his jacket up and closed his eyes, although he had no intention of sleeping. He was calm now. Earlier, on his drive back into town, he'd been nervous about being stopped and the script being changed. It was all about timing, but he knew he also needed a bit of luck for everything to fall into place at the right time. The soldier in him knew that something would go wrong. But there was no point in worrying about it so he would take it as it came. All that mattered was that he settled his scores. He'd already taken care of Donnie Monk, and Jackie Martin probably wouldn't drink another pint till he was an old man.

The wheels started to turn. The information from Crimestoppers was passed to the night-shift intelligence section in Fettes and the warning lights started to flash. Once Fisher and McLean were flagged up as high priority, a call was made to Thompson, who was still sound asleep, worn out from the strain of the operation. The intelligence officer briefed her and that weariness was forgotten as her mind fired up a need-to-do list in her head. She had a one-minute cold shower to clear her mind and then called McGovern.

'I'll take the early turn. It might be a long day, so you come in a bit later in case we need to be relieved. Is that okay with you?' She wanted to be sure that McGovern was in agreement.

'Makes sense, and let's hope this gets these two off the street at least. I'll call Grace to let her know, if you want to get on and call the troops out early.'

McGovern put the phone down. 'The girl's learning, no doubt about it,' he said, rubbing the stubble on his chin.

'What's that?' his wife mumbled, only half-awake.

'Nothing, honey, just go back to sleep. Work to do.'

She'd been with him through dozens of night call-outs, and, as always, she didn't go back to sleep but pulled her legs over the edge of the bed and stretched her arms. 'Tea?'

'Definitely. Remind me to buy you dinner after this job.' He pulled her towards him and kissed the top of her head.

McGovern called Macallan, who struggled to wake up but gradually realised it was her phone ringing rather than a dream. He chatted idly to her for a few moments until he was sure she was in a fit state to take in information then briefed her, sticking as closely as he could to what he'd been told by Thompson. Passing inaccurate information could be fatal, and he was too long in the tooth to make that mistake.

'I don't get it, Jimmy. It's too clean. Who would know that much information about those guys? You've seen how tight they keep it. I know we can only go with the information we're given, but I'd really like to know who gave it, wouldn't you? I'm going to call Felicity out to help you. You need all the hands and brains you can get on board. I think we should have enough evidence by the close of play today to arrest them, but if you get them on a dope and firearms deal then so much the better.' She thought for a moment. 'When I get clear at Leith I'll head up to Fettes to see how it's developing. Best of luck, and be careful, Jimmy.' She normally would have said it without worrying, but she meant it this time.

She glanced across the bed at the form under the duvet and smiled as she realised Fraser hadn't moved; call-outs had never been part of his job description.

Next, Macallan called Young, who hadn't slept anyway and was still grappling with all the pieces of information swirling round her mind. She could make some bits fit together but not all of them – there was a piece missing.

'I think this is it, Grace. Nelson might still be keeping his head down, but whatever happens today, he's involved.'

'I know. It's driving me mad as well, but we are where we are. I'll see you at Fettes at some stage. Please just go through it all again in case we can help the team out.'

A full firearms unit was on standby within an hour and East Fettes Avenue was within sight of Fettes, which made it easier to get them ready and in place. Thompson agreed with the uniformed senior officers that when they were certain that they were approaching the right car they would call in the firearms and arrest teams to take Fisher and McLean out of the game. With any luck this would be with minimum force, but they all knew what the Belfast men were capable of and no one was under any illusions.

Thompson got a call from the OP at Fisher's house telling her that his lights were on and they'd seen him at the window. She breathed a sigh of relief that at least they knew where he was.

At the same time that Thompson was briefing the firearms officers, Billy Nelson was parking the 4x4 in East Fettes Avenue with that first bit of luck that he needed. If he'd been even a couple of minutes later he would have run into two of the surveillance team, who'd been sent to see if there was a car matching the description of the one passed to Crimestoppers, but he saw the car lights crawling along the avenue and slipped under a parked van, watching them stop momentarily opposite the 4x4.

'Too close, Billy boy,' he said under his breath, but he realised they'd taken the first bit of the story.

When the car disappeared he got back up, pulled his woollen hat low over his ears and headed for Stockbridge, where the streets were starting to buzz with early workers. He found a phone box and called Fisher.

'Jesus, Billy, I've been climbing the fuckin' walls! Have you seen the papers?'

'It's okay – we'll keep our heads down for a while and it'll blow over, I'm telling you. I need you and Rob to do a job for me. It'll be a good earner and we'll take off for a few weeks in Spain after that. I've got it all arranged, passports sorted and we'll have a good time. We deserve a bit of a break from all this shit anyway.'

He told Fisher to call McLean and pick up the 4x4; the keys had been left under the front offside wheel arch. He gave them an address in Glasgow to take it to and deliver the goods. There was ten kilos of coke concealed in the car, and when it was dropped off the payoff would be put into a safe account and they could be on their way.

'Are you sure? They could be watching us for all I know.'

'Well, just check it and lose them, Dougie. Christ, you know how it's done.'

Fisher agreed, and anyway he wanted to do something rather than sit and worry in his flat. He called McLean, who wanted to get on with it – the prospect of fucking off to Spain appealed to him.

'I want to get the fuck out of Edinburgh, Dougie, and not come back. When we're there maybe we should top Billy and be done with it. We'll end up dead with that fucker leading the way. I'll come round and get you later when I'm ready.'

Nelson found an early-morning café serving breakfast and ordered the full whack but could only eat part of it. What was the point of life if you couldn't enjoy bacon and eggs?

He drank coffee slowly and, when one was finished, ordered another. Nelson had played his hand but still had a bit of time to kill. He would have to wait till he got the call from Fisher that they were on their way and then he would make his move. He had to get back into his house. The guns were stashed under the floorboards, and he would just have to ride his luck that he could get in and out without the police interrupting. By the time he was leaving the house they should be fully distracted by events in East Fettes Avenue.

44

Macallan nodded and scribbled some notes as the scientist spoke to her on the phone. They'd found a couple of hairs on Joe Fleming's clothing, and they were sure they didn't belong to the father or son. She perked up even more at the second bit of information.

'The other thing is that I think we have a partial fingerprint in the sprayed blood mentioned to you before. That almost certainly happened when they were cleaning up. You'll have seen it yourself. Clark says they were wearing latex gloves, but they're prone to tear at the fingertips with any heavy friction. I think we can safely say there was some heavy friction that night. It'll take a few days to run the tests, but we're making progress all the time.'

Macallan immediately called in Baxter. 'I think we're on safe ground now so regardless of what happens today we'll go ahead and arrest them.'

'Sounds good to me, and more will turn up over the next week, that's certain.' He nodded towards the cup in his hand. 'Fancy a brew?'

'Let's do that then head up to Fettes to see how it develops. Don't think I could keep my head focused here when there might be an arrest.' She chewed the edge of her forefinger and worried.

When they arrived at Fettes the call had come in to say that Fisher and McLean were on the move and that the surveillance team were with them. They had hardly settled down with another coffee when another message came in from the CID. Macallan took the call and what little colour there was in her face drained in shock. She put the phone down.

'A neighbour of Donnie Monk noticed his door was open this morning and had heard a disturbance in the early hours. Thought he was drunk again. Her old man went in to check and found him dead with a toilet brush rammed down his throat.'

Macallan shook her head, knowing they were being outplayed. 'Jesus.'

Nelson was heading back towards his house and made a detour to cut through a series of gardens to the rear of the terraced villas where he lived. He slipped the bedroom window that he'd left unlocked and climbed into the house, keeping the lights off as he lifted the floorboards concealing the leather sports bag with the two guns and ammo. He took off his clothes and went into the bathroom to wash before changing into fresh gear. Although he was quiet, the bug picked up the sounds of his movements. The information was relayed back to Fettes, and they called the OP that was monitoring the front of the house.

'We haven't seen any movement and there are no lights on. He definitely didn't go in the front door.'

Both men in the OP studied the image from the high-powered camera trained on Nelson's door. They moved its angle to the windows. After about two minutes they saw it – a shadow moved across one of the bedrooms.

'There's movement in the house, but we can't see who it is. We've no surveillance team here if it's him. Instructions?'

McGovern was in the coordination room with Macallan, Baxter and Young. 'We need to keep the backup here till we see what happens with Fisher and McLean,' he said. 'He had to come in through the back gardens. One of you needs to get there on foot as soon as to watch if he exits. If he does, do not approach him. We don't know if he's armed.'

One of the surveillance officers in the OP dropped everything and ran to cover the back of Nelson's house.

The police weren't the only ones waiting for Billy Nelson. In a van parked in the same street two men sat, watching his place. They saw the policeman run from a house opposite. 'What the fuck is that?' the driver asked in a strong, East Belfast accent.

'Don't know, but let's just wait it out.' His companion spoke calmly and in the same accent.

Nelson was ready. He took the new phone out of his pocket and called Fisher. 'Where are you?'

'We'll be at the car in a couple of minutes. We'll let you know when we're on the road to Glasgow.'

Nelson called a taxi and told the operator where to pick him up. He climbed out of the bedroom window, made his way back across the gardens and waited behind a fence till he heard the sound of the taxi coming to a halt. He then walked out into the street and straight into the cab.

The surveillance officer pulled out his radio and called McGovern. 'That's him into a fast black, Jimmy, and heading towards town.'

The two men in the van saw it and followed the taxi towards town. They had a motorbike in the back; when they were ready they'd dump the van and use that for the job.

'What the fuck is he up to? Is he going to join them?' McGovern said anxiously. He passed the information to Thompson.

'They're only a couple of hundred yards from the car, Jimmy. Will keep you informed. Please keep the air clear now as we need to coordinate with the firearms team.'

'It's Friday,' Young said behind them.

Macallan looked round at her. 'What?'

'I know where he's going. It's Friday – that's it. It's Friday prayers. That's what this is about. He's settling scores. It was there all the time. That's what those visits to Potterrow were about.'

'Are you sure? What about this car?'

'It's a diversion. He's going to the mosque.'

'Come on!' Macallan shouted at McGovern and they ran out of the building towards East Fettes Avenue.

Fisher and McLean saw the car and breathed a little easier. Fisher checked under the wheel arch and found the keys.

'Thank fuck, now let's get out of here,' he said to McLean with more confidence than he felt. As he pushed the keys into the lock they were both startled by the noise.

They hadn't paid enough attention to the vans parked about thirty yards either side of the 4x4. The firearms teams spilled out onto the road and in a few seconds they were covered from all angles. They stood motionless and looked towards each other, realising they'd been set up – just like Jackie Martin.

Thompson got out of her car and walked towards them,

wanting to see the two men up close when the arrest was made. Macallan and McGovern were running round the corner of Carrington Road into East Fettes Avenue when Fisher said, 'Fuck it,' decided to try and break through. He turned the key in the lock.

Nelson had rigged the car using a simple device. There was no need to take the risk of trying to get explosives – the flammable-vapour technique would do the job if he was careful. There had been some problems with it in the past, but they were usually down to lack of care, and as a soldier with explosives training he knew what he was doing. Most of the work had been concealing the gas bottles so nobody would get spooked if they looked through the windows.

After he'd parked up, he'd opened the valves for a slow release, and by the time Fisher and McLean arrived the car would be a bomb just needing a spark. He'd broken the interior light carefully and made sure that it would come on when they opened the car door. It was simplicity – and it worked perfectly.

The car blew. A huge fireball engulfed the two Belfast men and three of the firearms team who'd gone in too close. Luckily, most of the others survived their injuries because of the protective clothing they were wearing for the job. Thompson was blown off her feet and suffered burns to her arms and face.

'Fuck!' Macallan pulled herself up off the ground and checked her reflection in a car window that was somehow still intact after the explosion.

Her chest heaved with a combination of shock and the adrenalin flooding her system. She looked like something from the *Night of the Living Dead*, but what was almost comical was that a concrete lamp post had been between her and the blast, resulting in an unaffected clean line from her face down through her torso. Her legs were undamaged, but the rest of her was torn, filthy and bloody, and she wasn't sure whose blood it was. Some of the people near the centre of the explosion had disappeared, and she was pretty sure she was wearing some of them now.

She lifted her arms in slow motion and found they were working. There were whistles going off in her ears. She knew that was how it was after a blast and hoped there would be no permanent damage. McGovern appeared in front of her and looked worse than she did, but he was a tough bastard and the rumour was the only way to kill him was a stake through the heart. He was shouting at her, but it sounded like they were submerged in water. She raised her hand slowly, palm up. 'Get a car. For fuck's sake get a car.'

He didn't get it. 'What do you mean?'

She read the words on his lips rather than heard them and looked around her – at the carnage, the shock and the dead. She walked clumsily over to one of the wounded firearms officers and took his sidearm. He didn't object; he just wanted the pain to go away.

'Get a car, Jimmy. I'm going to kill that bastard.'

Nelson sat in the taxi and savoured the blue lights and two-tone horns going off everywhere. The booby-trapped car had worked. All the cops would be heading towards Fettes as he went for the mosque.

He pulled out the guns and checked them again. He'd filled the pockets of his jacket with ammo and he was ready.

The driver looked in the mirror and nearly stalled the car.

'Just drive and you won't get hurt.' But he had his

first bit of bad luck then. They were stuck at lights for a minute and a half as a line of emergency vehicles bombed through, so Nelson decided it was time to bail out, and the driver shook uncontrollably as he was given the largest tip of his life.

'Enjoy it, son,' Nelson said with a smile as he turned and headed for the mosque a hundred yards away. He felt fine with it, and he was nearly done. The pain in his gut would soon be gone, and if nothing else they would all remember the name Billy Nelson for a long, long time.

There were quite a few people about, but they hadn't noticed him carrying a weapon in each hand because they were spooked and distracted by the sounds of the emergency vehicles. Like deer on the savannah they knew there was danger, sensed a predator nearby, but didn't know in which direction to bolt.

Nelson hadn't even noticed the car pulling up on the opposite side of the road. Macallan got out slowly, her head still spinning with shock. She hadn't spoken to McGovern on the way to the mosque – he was hardly in any better shape than she was.

'We should wait – we need backup,' he pleaded but knew he was wasting his time. He got out of the car beside her.

Nelson was opposite the mosque when he noticed her. He frowned when he realised how badly hurt she was. 'Jesus, Grace Macallan. I didn't expect to see you here. You're the smart one, right enough.'

She couldn't hear him and struggled with what it was she was going to do. She tried to raise the gun, but her arm couldn't lift it. McGovern tried to take it from her, but it was as if her hand was moulded onto the grip.

Nelson lifted his weapon and pointed it at them. 'Just leave it there.' He took a few steps towards them to close the gap. 'This didn't need to happen, and I'm sorry, but you should have kept out of it.' He intended to kill the policeman first, because although he was hurt, he looked like he could still handle himself.

Macallan couldn't see it through her blurred vision, but McGovern did. Walking behind Nelson, almost at a trot, was a man in leathers and a crash helmet. About fifty yards back another man sat calmly on a motorbike, watching the events unfold.

Just as Nelson was about to pull the trigger, the man behind him put one into the back of his skull. Nelson fell forward and was dead before he hit the ground. The gunman put another two into what was left of his brain for good measure, looked up at Macallan and McGovern and then walked backwards, keeping his eye on the gun still dangling at the end of her arm. He jumped up onto the bike and the two men took off to pick up their van.

Macallan fell to her knees for a minute then keeled over before losing consciousness. McGovern dropped down beside her, turning Macallan on her side in case she threw up and choked. He thought about his wife and promised himself he would buy her that dinner before he called the office, told them what had happened, then piled Macallan back into the car to get them to a hospital.

45

Within ten minutes of killing Billy Nelson, the gunmen had put the bike in the back of the van. Less than an hour later they pulled into a scrapyard on the outskirts of Glasgow where two men were waiting for them. They stripped off all their clothing and it was burnt as they were washed down with a hose. They changed into fresh clothes and then took separate cars for the rest of their journey. One of them was taken to a safe house in Larkhall and the other to Govan, within spitting distance of Ibrox Stadium. They would be kept there till the press coverage of the events in Edinburgh had dropped off the front pages and then they would return quietly to Belfast.

As the unknown assassins were being driven to their safe houses, another team were in a van parked about a hundred yards from the gates of Dominic 'Magic' McGinty's home. He'd just eaten breakfast and clapped the neck of his favourite Rottweiler, who was nuzzling his leg under the table.

'Come on, darlin'; I'll take you into the garden for a wee pee.' He smiled at the dog, who was his favourite creature in the world.

He walked out of the front door of his house and the dog ran to the edge of the bushes where he squatted down happily. Gordon the minder stood at the door and thought once again that working for Magic wasn't a bad life.

Magic was standing only a few yards behind the gates of his home, which were open. He was annoyed when he noticed that. He kept telling his minders to 'keep the fuckers shut at all times', but he knew they had shit for brains and shook his head at the dog.

The two men in the back of the van saw their chance. 'Let's go for it, Frankie.'

The other man nodded and the back doors were opened a few inches, which was all the sniper needed to give him a clear sight of his target. Like Nelson he'd been trained in the British Army, and he was good at what he did. It had been a while since he'd made a hit and wasn't going to pass up the chance. A hundred yards was nothing, but he ran through the drill, making sure he was ready before pulling the trigger.

McGinty felt the chill through his thin shirt; he called to the dog and smiled as it lumbered towards him. The bullet entered his left eye and exited the rear of his head together with half his skull. Gordon froze as Magic twitched on the ground, and he watched the dog yelp in confusion before pushing his master's dead arm with his nose.

Gordon grabbed the dog by the collar and pulled it back inside. The other dogs in the kennels behind the house sensed something terrible and panicked.

The van containing the gunmen was already driving steadily away, taking them towards their own safe houses. The driver shouted to the two men in the back: 'Jackie will be pleased, boys. Good job.'

46

Macallan became aware of light as she regained consciousness. She still had her eyes closed, but she felt warm and safe, and she wanted to stay there for a while. There were voices and sounds but they weren't clear. Eventually she knew she'd have to re-enter the world, but she was afraid of what she would find. Part of the events at Fettes and the mosque had flooded back into her mind, and she wasn't sure what damage she'd suffered. The thought that any of her limbs were gone or that her face might be scarred terrified her, and she moaned involuntarily.

'Grace, can you hear me?'

It was Jack Fraser. She opened her eyes and sobbed. He took her hand gently. It was still wrapped in bandages.

'You're okay. Everything's fine, I promise you.'

She realised there weren't any bandages on her face. 'How do I look?' she said in no more than a croak.

'Terrible, but the doc says you'll make a full recovery.'

'What about Jimmy?'

'He's fine and the same as you. Lesley Thompson is quite badly hurt, but she'll recover – though she'll carry a few scars. Just rest.' He bent over and kissed her gently.

'The other main thing is that the baby is fine, though God knows how.'

'The baby?'

'The baby. You're pregnant.' He smiled, and he wasn't joking.

'I can't be.'

'Well, it beats that fucking budgie, Grace.' Harkins had come up behind Fraser and put a hand on his shoulder.

'Mick told me the budgie story, and you're right – he takes the piss something rotten.'

She smiled weakly at the two men then dropped back into a deep sleep.

47

Mick Harkins still had his sources, and his relationship with Felicity Young looked like it might be back on the cards, so when she'd told him all about the chief super's treatment of his friend, Harkins had known exactly what to do. He'd always kept his sources onside and they'd reported any misconduct they'd come across, particularly among senior officers. His ability to drop people in the shit was legendary and had saved his skin a few times. He hadn't told Macallan the full story about the chief super – there was more; much, much more – but he'd told her enough. He was addicted to renting young men as well as young women, and sometimes both at the same time. He'd done a good job of keeping it quiet, but not from the extended reach of Mick Harkins, who was about to royally fuck him over.

He called Jacquie Bell and told her the news about Macallan.

'Jesus, who's the father, Mick?' she asked.

'Well, it's not me if that's what you're asking.'

They both laughed, knowing that motherhood would

be a shock and a half to the woman who'd always been married to the job.

'Anyway, Jacquie, how would you like to ruin the life and career of the chief super?' he said, getting to the real reason he'd called.

'Bring it on, big boy – I can't stand the bastard.'

EPILOGUE

Pat Fleming tried again to call Kristina Orlova, but she wasn't answering. It was the same for some of her regulars who'd come back to the city with no idea what had happened to her at the hands of Billy Nelson.

Pat turned to his brother, who was pissed off hearing about it. 'Still not answering, Eddie. Just don't get it,' he said mournfully.

'Fuck her. It's over so just deal with it.'

Eddie turned to his team, who were back together and had re-established a grip on the drugs business in Edinburgh. 'I'll never let what happened with those Belfast bastards happen again. Anyone takes us on in future, we go in hard and finish it before there's a problem.'

His team nodded and what they saw was strength. Eddie was young, but he definitely had the balls to do the business. As long as he could keep proving it – he would be safe until the day he forgot that or a younger ambitious beast came along.

His phone warbled the tune of *The Sweeney*. It was Cue Ball Ross.

'Hear you're back in charge, Eddie. Never did like

those Belfast bastards – just too fuckin' macho for me.'

Eddie smiled at Cue Ball accusing someone else of being too macho. 'What can I do for you?' he asked, already knowing the answer.

'Put me back on the list for a regular order. Same as before.'

'The rate's gone up a bit.' Eddie was testing the water, and the phone went quiet for a moment.

'That's fine, but I need it sharpish.'

Fleming put the phone down and nodded to his team. Order had been restored.

Orlova walked through the concourse at the airport and looked at the departures. Only twenty minutes to boarding for the flight to Vilnius and home. A few men had to turn their heads as she passed, and for all the world she looked like a successful businesswoman living the dream.

When she sat down on the plane she leaned back and closed her eyes. She was going home.

Macallan was ordered to take at least a month off by her doctors and there was no point in fighting it, given her injuries and the baby growing inside her. Fraser rented a cottage on the Antrim coast of Northern Ireland, and for a few short weeks they got to know each other again and lived like normal people. That's all they wanted. The only bit of excitement came when she checked the news online one day and saw that the chief super had resigned following revelations in the press about his grubby sex life. The article had been written by Jacquie Bell, and Macallan shook her head.

'I see the long arm of Mick Harkins in this,' she said to the computer screen. But it was the footnote to the article that made her sit back – John O'Connor had been promoted into the vacant post.

'The games people play,' she said, prompting Fraser to turn from reading his paper.

'What's that?'

'Nothing. Nothing at all. Let's go for a walk along the cliffs.'

GRACE MACALLAN RETURNS IN

Shores of Death

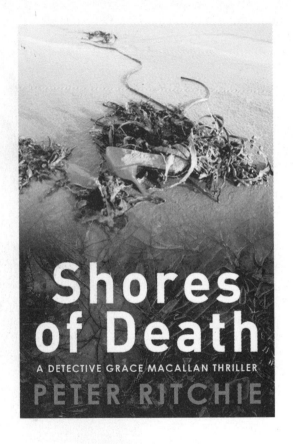

blackandwhitepublishing.com